Olympia Heights

About the Author

Leigh V. Twersky was born in London, where he lives. His stories have appeared in *Chroma*, *A Boxful of Ideas* (Paradise Press) and *A Coup of Owls*. *Olympia Heights* is his debut novel.

Olympia Heights

Leigh V. Twersky

Paradise Press

First published in Great Britain in 2024 by
Paradise Press, BM 5700, London WC1N 3XX.
www.paradisepress.org.uk

A CIP catalogue record for this book
is available from the British Library.

ISBN 978-1-90-458595-4
10 9 8 7 6 5 4 3 2 1

Printed and bound in Great Britain by
Clays Ltd, Elcograf S.p.A.

Cover design by Charlotte Mouncey, www.bookstyle.co.uk

Designed and typeset by Ross Burgess.
Set in Baskerville Old Face, with pop-ups in Calibri
and headings in Clarendon.

For Farilla B

and the memory of Evris Tsakiridis

Part One

Niceboys

ONE

Inside the Recycling Centre, the queue came to a halt.

There were liquid noises and human voices. Distant babbling, cries...

Samina clung onto Irene's arm. They said nothing and waited in the darkness.

They were in a large unlit chamber, which housed the long coiling line of D-classified gynos, and had grown immune to the smell of stale sweat and BestcoeDisinfex®.

The windowless walls, as far as they could see, were bare concrete, like the floor. Neither the opposite end of the room, nor the ceiling was visible.

'I'm sorry,' started Samina, 'I didn't know what you meant when you said you had a son.'

'Drop it.'

Irene had spoken without thinking. *Not like me to lower my guard.* She wasn't ready to talk about him. Her head boiled with confusion. How could she love that thing, that monster? It was easier to accept he was dead, died @ seven, than contemplate having any remotely maternal feelings for an insect.

'Whenever you want to talk, I'm here for you. You know that.'

'I said drop it.'

'I mean it.'

Every two or three deci-minutes they snailpaced forward in silence. A groan from far ahead of them gave Irene second thoughts about progressing any further. *He warned us, didn't he?*

Gynocops in pink dungarettes were patrolling with torches.

'What's gonna happen to us?' asked Irene.

'Reassessment,' said a gynocop.

'Which means what?'

'Which means you don't piss us off with stupid questions.' The gynocop shone her torch full in Irene's face and moved away.

'Bitch. This is all cz I was eighty or so Britz short.'

'Whatever happens, we'll face it together.' Samina put her arm round Irene's shoulder. They moved on again, aware now that there was light in the distance.

In front, someone screamed. The mass of gynos stopped dead.

More shouting followed. From the rapid movement of the torches, gynocops could be seen racing towards the commotion, which quickly died down into sobbing. And then all was quiet again. The gynocops returned to their patrol stations.

Irene gripped Samina's hand. 'What are they doing?' she whispered. 'We gotta get out of here.'

'How? The gynocops are everywhere, and without Eye-Ds... I thought we'd get new ones.'

'We'll think of something.'

Hours passed in the gloom. The D-classifieds had taken to sitting on the floor, although the cold concrete rendered that not much more comfortable than remaining on their exhausted feet.

It had to be night. Irene grew very drowsy, but somehow staying awake and vigilant kept her going. If she surrendered to her natural urge to sleep, it would be like giving up the fight, even though she knew deep down that resistance was futile. But she did succumb, and woke to Samina tugging @ her arm.

'Get up. We're being moved.'

Irene opened her eyes slowly. In the dimness, she saw Samina's bleary face urging her to get to her feet. All around were bewildered gynos stretching and yawning. There'd been a reveille, and gynocops were raising any still slumbering with slaps round the face.

'Thanks. Well timed.'

Irene heard moaning and hushed conversations. A long queue formed for the excretorium. People left items of clothing to reserve their place in the main queue while they waited their turn to relieve themselves.

There was nothing to eat or drink. The morning passed as intolerably as the night, if not worse as the Ds had not been refreshed. Only woken from sleep, their sole escape from their D-classified world.

If Irene didn't have food or water soon, she would pass out. Her mouth was like sticky plasticon and tasted of death.

First came a scream that pierced the stale air and was succeeded by shocked silence, and then shouting and whistles. But these voices were behind them this time. And deeper. *Andro.*

Once more the gynocops rushed about, but Irene sensed the spreading panic. Some went towards the scream, others back to the andro voices.

'Run,' said Irene, as softly as possible. 'This is our chance.'

But the mass of bodies in the chamber worked against her plan. And as the crowd surged first this way and then that, Irene tripped over something, or someone, and found herself on the concrete, scrabbling desperately for Samina, who was borne away by the sheer weight of numbers.

'Samina!' she shrieked, only to hear her name yelled back, but could not move. More and more gynos were falling around and on top of her, and she struggled to avoid being crushed. The din was unbearable. It was difficult to see what was going on. Mustering all her strength, she managed to slide out from under the gynos lying on her, and ran, she knew not where. Samina was nowhere to be seen.

Irene moved back, but the way was blocked and she fell. There seemed to be fighting.

There were more andros now. Androcops, pressing forward. The first andros were pushing them back, preventing them from coming further into the chamber. One of these andros called, 'Irene...'

How does he know my name?

'...get out...run...join us!'

But she couldn't. She was too far inside.

She got to her feet and stumbled away from the dark crowd threatening to engulf her. There was an open door. She went through.

@ first the light dazzled her. A voice spoke, but she understood nothing. Her eyes adjusted. And as she advanced further into the room, closer to the light, she saw.

And what she saw made her scream too, just as all the other D-classified gynos had done when they finally understood what awaited them.

What recycling meant.

TWO

My Eyelid-screen alerts me in the middle of the night.

BESTCOE-MENDOZA INSTITUTE OF ENTOMANTHROPY
UNIVERSITY OF COCKNEYTOWN
Department of Sphecanthropy
Training Manual page 7

A Brief History of Sphecanthropy: Concerning Sphecanthropes[1]

[1] Greek sphex/sphecos wasp, anthropos, human being, vulg. wasp-men/sphecoids.

I start with a fright, banging my head on my kip-cell, spheco-heart a-hammering. Pre-metamorphosis pages should've been archived. For a second I fear someone might suss me. If they find out...but all is slumber-still in the Combs.

I know what I am for fuxache.

Blinking like mad to close the page, I try to catch my breath and get back to sleep. 'It's just gone 14 deci-minutes. Don't need this. Tomorrow's inspection day.'

A grey box appears @ last over the paragraphs growing in my field of vision, line by line.

Read | Save | Close

I left-wink on Close. Nothing happens. Panic casts its net over me. Cold sweat tickles down my chitinex back plates. I right-wink. The text vanishes. I phew and breathe out. But a new box flashes up.

Worry now | Worry later | Cancel

I left-wink on the middle one and drift off. But instead of peaceful spheco-kip, I have another dream.

About the old place.

I wake to syrupy birdsong piping across the dawn sky. The tannoy crackles into life, its sweet gyno voice filling South East Cockneytown District 13.

'Good morning to all on-duty customers! Just coming up to 22 deci-minutes, that's 5.30 am accu-time. Thank you for rising and shining in BestcoeBritain®. Enjoy your day.'

I emerge from my hexagonal kip-cell tube and run my fingers the entire length of my tingling I-brows. No messages. Not quite rested, I yawn and shake my sleep off before gliding down the timberex corridors past the Combs to our excretorium. Other sphecos are already squatting. Worried about the monthly inspection. Like me.

The excretorium is a square room lit by a skylight in its domed ceiling. Slightly raked gutters surround the damp slushy floor, where there is space for up to five sphecos to wait their turn. I wince @ the smell of sewage and BestcoeDisinfex®. When somebody leaves we get into position and lower our arse-slits over the gutters. The acid-hot fluid spurts out, cauterizing me, and flows down to the drain. We don't need to clean up afterwards, unlike humos...I mean humans, even though they call us spheco-freaks.

V157 greets me as he straightens. 'Good luck, V159.'

'Chizz. Likewise.'

I'm too nervous for chit-chat.

We slap I-brows in a sort of vespine high-five, and float out together towards the syngastrion.

The syngastrion is housed in a much larger, similarly vaulted chamber. Daylight squeezing through a ceiling porthole illuminates the grimy black and yellow walls. A huge circular vat, spider-legged by ladders, dominates the space.

To save time, I ignore the steps and fly up to one of the little platforms @ the brim, where I don the black and yellow mask. The suction tube slots between my mouth-part lips, and, ever concerned about spheco viral outbreaks, I'm relieved to smell the BestcoeDisinfex®.

One press of the cheek nozzle and a warm, phlegm-thick fluid floods my mouth. We don't consume solids. Having got used to the oral inundation by now, I am able to control my swallowing mechanism, and get it down in manageable quantities, no longer in danger of choking, like on my first few attempts.

I taste nothing.

Portion control ensures I imbibe exactly 998ml of pre-digested soup. Another press on the nozzle releases the mask and I am more than full. With a light buzz of pleasure, I fly down to V157 to fling my arms round his neck and cover his mouth with mine.

As I snog my regurging partner, I cud 499 ml of broth into his mouth. He gulps it down and hums with satiety, grateful he can trust me not to cheat on the measures like some sphecos do. We slurp up the ribbons of mucus drooling from our mouth-parts, indifferent as to whose spheco-innards they issued from, and link I-brow-antennae for a quick stroke. @ fourteen inches his are the longest in our swarm, and the envy of us all.

Tanked up for the next 50 deci-minutes, we glide through the corridors to the South East Cockneytown Police Station (SECOPS) reception area. As swarm Queen, I take morning roll call.

Vs103, 108, 122, 133, 138, 146, 157, myself and 161 are all present. I remember those no longer with us, and wonder if the others do.

I hope to find out if I am still viable. Not everyone will be observed today, and the agony may be prolonged another 100 deci-minutes.

As each felony comes up on the securicam screen, we are led away in random threes with a couple of humo cops in blue dungarette uniforms.

South East District 13 is a typical C-class area with a high crime rate. As more and more sphecos are taken away, I realize my turn will come. Fear of failure gnaws @ my simplified spheco-guts.

The securicam image shifts to a narrow alleyway shadowed between the high-rise dwelling unit blocks C-class humos call DUBs for short. The lens zooms in on a scantily dressed, nubile gyno scooting backwards on her arse as a scrawny, C-class andro-youth punches her and throws himself @ her.

The nubo slaps his face. He laughs.

Close up of his throbbing reddened cockhead sticking out between his curled thumb and forefinger, as he wanks it harder to readiness and precum milk drips out.

She screams.

He has her backed up against the breezeblock DUB wall next to a BESTCOEBRITAIN® ERADICATING POVERTY slogan defaced with graffiti. He hits her once more. Doesn't want to just force his sex on her. He wants to punish her too.

And I feel the same way about him.

My spheco-loins ignite, and my cock wakes deep inside me. I stare @ the screen, roaring rage and hatred. My nerves vanish.

I kick back with my legs and dive forward, then swim through the still-chill air, gasping @ the shocking temperature drop, my arms eagle-winging me to my destiny, the cold making my furious spheco-eyes water.

V161 trembles with terror.

'Relax,' I telepath.

He lags behind, heavy in the air. V157 keeps up with me as we fly towards the nearby DUB complex. Our Eye-screen nav-systems guide us over cordoned off derelict Victorian terraces, where a few ragged D-classifieds poke about in rubble-strewn streets for edibles. On the ground our humo-cops race us in their van to the felon scene.

In seconds, we see the phalanxes of DUBs loom up towards us, uniform grey tombstone slabs of concrete lined up like dominoes, pockmarked by tiny vitreola windows, one for each unit. Here in DUB city the wind howls between the blocks, and sunshine rarely reaches down to ground level. Each DUB boasts its Bestcoe message muralled halfway up, between the 10th and 12th floors, for all its beloved customers.

BIRTH ALONE IS NO RIGHT TO LIFE
TO LIVE ON EARTH — NEEDS MORE THAN BIRTH

Swooping down from the snot-grey sky, we land, V157 and me graceful as birds, humming our wasp sirens, but V161 struggles to find his balance, his expression sick with fear.

Twenty-four inches of twenty-four-carat chitinex-hard spheco-penis burst forth from my dickslit like a black and yellow candy-striped party blow-out. In my peripheral vision, I see V157's cock quivering in mid air like a spear, and V161 on my other flank, but with no erection.

The felon turns to face us, his eyes widening as he sees what he means to me. He looks around for an escape, but is surrounded and cornered. He raises his hands in surrender, shaking his head.

Too fucking late.

His intended victim whimpers, tears smudging her gold make-up, her pink candyfloss hairdo crumpled onto the wet side of her face.

The humo cops arrive, cow-eyed giant Mike Lagano and his boss, Inspector Tony 'horrid' Horelka, taking notes on their hand-screens.

'ACE him!' my inner voice urges as my spheco-cock pistons. 'ACE the fucker!' shouts V157, and V161 echoes.

The would-be rapist's jaw drops to reveal the void in his andro mouth.

'Looking for a fuck?' I say, spheco-heart disco-bass thudding now. 'Well, here's one you'll never forget.'

My rapier-sharp spheco-dick stabs right through his torso'n-thigh-hugger doublet and squelches into spongy blood-logged tissue, first resting place his slimy warm liver.

His eyes snowball @ me, white goggles in a pale sea of shaven head. He wobbles and attempts a smile to hide his pain and shame, but no smirk can make him look cool with his body burst open. I clap my hand over his rictus mouth to shut out his gurgling rattle.

The gyno's still crouched up against the DUB wall, legs splayed out like open scissors. Poor baby, gyno tears streaking down her face, breaths stalling like an old motor.

'Stop crying, girlie. I won't hurt you. It's him I want.'

I hoist him up off his feet and spin 360 degrees; he dangles a metre off the ground, still impaled on my cock-sting, before I bring him back down to earth.

The humo cops are smiling, approving. 'Goo-ood,' they

sing-song in their patronizing humo way. Mike's clapping, but Horelka's hand is raised.

'Wait for the ACEing, Lagano,' he whispers in his weaselly tenor.

Mike's sweaty palms come to a mid-air halt. Horelka enjoys blocking him. I clock that on my Eye-screen FaceReader before turning my attention back to the felon.

I slide my dick down, left to right, the opposite for him, and slice through various sections of gizzard. The bitterness of bile segues to the sourness of his recently filled stomach.

Semi-digested fried animal product, overcooked vegetable matter and unidentifiable refined carbohydrate coated in hydrochloric acid and enzymes. My cock savours the C-class salt, sugar and fats. They didn't remove my taste buds during metamorphosis, just relocated them.

He's stopped gibbering now.

My loins start the countdown to boiling point. Enraged @ his andro hubris, I lose control. The ACE explodes, and as I let go, shoots out of my spheco-dick like a liquid arrow into his punctured abdomen.

As the viscous toxi-cum flushes his entrails, I scream my sphecogasm out into the gale-wracked world. He gasps as though he needs to suck up all the air in a 50-kilometre radius.

Pop-up text flashes before my eyes.

BESTCOE-MENDOZA INSTITUTE OF ENTOMANTHROPY
Department of Sphecanthropy
Training Manual page 43

Concerning ACE

Metamorphosis Phase 1 involves transforming the scrotal sac and testicles of sphecoids into venom-producing glands.

During sex-e-q-tion (qv) this paralysing venom (aka toxi-cum) is released upon sphecoid orgasm into the body of male (andro) felons.

Bestcoe funds the franchising of this venom under the brand ANTI-CRIMINAL EJACULATE®, commonly referred to as ACE.

The high costs of manufacturing this socially beneficial product demand the stringent penalties incurred for squandering ACE (qv malicious masturbation).

'Something wrong, V159?' squeaks Horelka.

'N-no, sir.' I double blink like mad to close the page while falling forward to conceal my dysfunction, thereby toppling the rapist onto his skinny arse. We lie face to face, me on top. Missionary, they call it. He goes limp as the ACE paralyses him. His eyes uncouple their stare, dead globes racing each other to the back of their sockets, and he self-sculpts into a foetal pose, hands bent down @ the wrists like all saturated with toxi-jism, but he hears my every word.

'I love you,' I buzz, stroking his sweaty forehead with my I-brow-antennae, running my jaundiced spheco-fingers down his slack sunken cheek. 'Now you're no longer a threat and...you're the same as me, as I was, when you...your type made me feel different, inferior, pushed me away, cz I was *nice*.

'Why did I ever fear you?' I whisper into his bleeding ear as the last blobs of poison exit my body to do their work on his. 'Now I've got your respect.'

Physical respect. That's what it's all about.

'You're being discontinued,' I inform him audibly, not that he can do anything about it. I don't even know his name, but I never stop loving this drug-high moment, every time. 'Thank you for being ACEd with Bestcoe Anti-Criminal Ejaculate®. Enjoy your day.'

I withdraw my cock with a plop and wipe it clean on my shiny yellow spheco-hands. It coils back into me, traces of muck and gore from the youth's insides soiling my dickslit rim.

'Neat work,' says Mike Lagano, slapping my chitinex-buff spheco-back, then shaking and blowing on his puny humo fingers. 'Fuxache, man, I always forget how hard your exo-skeleton is.'

'Chizz, Mike.' I chuckle the sweat-drenched laugh of adrenaline-powered relief.

'Not bad, V159,' adds Horelka with a faint smile.

'Thank you, sir,' I pant, still breathless from enjoying my job. 'We need gynocop backup to sort out the victim and a clean-up team for the felon.'

'And I require a Felon Discontinuation Fact Document by the end of the afternoon.'

'Downloading, sir. FD2 for 75 deci-minutes.'

Horelka's face winters over. 'Surely while on duty you mean 6 pm accu-time?' he snaps.

'Sorry, sir.' My charcoal and custard face conceals my embarrassment, but I bristle with resentment.

Mike's surreptitious sympathy wink cheers me up until I clock the upright, silver-haired figure of Professor O. B. Knox marching round the DUB corner.

'Results, Inspector?' he barks.

Horelka clears his throat with a delicate cough. His frizzy, almost white, halo-cut hair teased out in a six-inch horseshoe round the sides of his bald pate, follows the slight incline of his head in our direction. 'Passes for V159 and V157. V161 non-starter.'

Fuxache, Horelka. Loosen up, man. Give V161 a break.

Knox goes up to V161, who takes a step back and looks around nervously. Mike and Horelka flank him, and hold him steady while Knox puts his latex-gloved hand over V161's dickslit and starts rubbing like he's wanking him off. V161's black saucer spheco-eyes dart from side to side, and his mustard and coal spheco-hands try to push his masturbator away.

After a few seconds Knox complies, and withdraws a couple of paces. Without looking @ V161 he says, 'Symptomatic impotence. What would this sphecoid have done if V157 and V159 hadn't been present? Non-viable. Metamorphosis and programming failed. Wrong sort of homo.'

V161 sinks to his knees. 'Please,' he implores. 'It's just a blip. I'll be all right next time.'

Knox ignores him. 'All this investment in these homoniceboys wasted,' he tells Horelka. 'So many years of research and training to make them useful, and they still fuck up on us.'

I register the insult, but it's buried deep under other concerns. @ least today I'm viable.

Knox snaps his fingers. 'Discontinue the sphecoid,' he says loud enough to make V161 howl with despair.

Two gynocops appear and grab V161, who screams before being frogmarched away.

I want to rescue V161, comfort him, but there's no reprieve.

Knox's real-leather soles tap on the pavement as he departs for other felon scene inspections, and then back to his A-list goldeye home with the stars on Olympia Heights. After a few steps, he spins round and adds, 'Make sure the successful sphecoids get to observe the discontinuation process, Horelka. It'll be a useful exercise. Don't forget, they're only niceboys.' He finally shuts his oral sphincter, and turns the corner.

And so do I. I'm still a *niceboy*. I remember. I blackboxed everything.

Illegally.

Reddardable.

Discontinuable.

THREE

Sacking notices always came first thing on rest-day via Face-Chirp® chirrup-text.

—Fialka, Irene
dashtagFialkacommaIrene has been approved for disem-ployment from BestcoeDisinfex®, as of today.

Disemployment will no longer oblige you to use the C-class amenities hitherto enjoyed, however some withdrawals will take immediate effect.

An appointment has been made for you @ your nearest D-class Reception Centre for 47 deci-minutes 11.16 am accu-time today when the full D-class benefits package will be presented and your FaceChirp® dashtag deleted.

Lateness will incur benefit deductions.

Thank you for being disemployed from BestcoeDisinfex®.

Enjoy your day.

BESTCOE PAY-AS-U-LIVE (P.A.U.L.) TEAM

Irene fell back onto her worn sofa. This was what had happened to George twelve years before when he got ill. People said terrible things about the Reception Centres, called them scrounge-lounges, but Irene was in no mood to scare herself.

'I'm still young enough,' she shouted @ the wall-screen and dulled the image. 'Fucking...fucking Bestcoe.' She put her slippers back on and trudged to the bedroom.

The dressing table mirror revealed her lank, greying hair, smoker's wrinkles on gaunt cheeks and scrawny turkey neck. Her hazel eyes had no spark, just a glimmer of doggedness.

She combed her hair and applied what little make-up she had left. A bit of lippy, a hint of blusher, the rest of the mascara. She held her best dress against her body. It was clear she'd worn it before, but the black slimline cut gave her an elegance her dungarettes couldn't.

She'd show them. She'd succeed where so many failed, even without a FaceChirp® dashtag. The DUB wasn't flooded — a good omen. She'd be able to get out in the dry weather and jobseek. Anything to avoid being D-classified.

On her way out, she chucked her monthly rubbish down the disused lift shaft. The uncollected bags had already reached the fifth floor. Then she rushed down the stairs, as carefully as possible in her high heels, her only decent pair of shoes, and out into the blustery grey daylight. If she hurried, she'd get the next autobus, but didn't want to be dishevelled and sweaty, and spoil all her hard work. So she took an easy strolling pace to the pick-up point and was pleased to discover there was still time. She looked @ her watch — damn, 38 deci-minutes — she hadn't even converted to accu-time. She flicked the switch. 9.09am. 21 accu-minutes to go.

Without warning, a feeling of panic overtook her. What else had she forgotten? Looking for work while still on relax-deci-time made a bad impression. Breathing a sigh of relief, she found her blue plasticon Eye-D hiding under her smokes.

People did get re-employed. The Carlinis @ No.1425 had been lucky. He'd lost his job and got reinstated three weeks later. Miracles did happen. Like folk suddenly recovering from cancer, or even...withertongue.

Fierce gusts of wind deconstructed her home-made hairdo. She could see @ the bottom of the hill the stationary vehicle, a rusty, windowless steelex cylinder attached to a truck, and a plump gyno she assumed was the driver laughing with her colleagues and sipping from a steaming plasticon cup.

The pick-up point was between two DUBs, Soxbury and Mollinsea Towers, which stood on the artificial, wind-trapped plateau. This stop was the only one for the last seven blocks, and a large crowd had gathered for the ride @ 40 deci. Irene hoped the wait wouldn't be too long. The new deci-schedules allowed autobuses to be up to quarter of an hour late, yet still be on time.

People were jostling for the best position by the roadside, but nobody could predict where the driver would stop. Irene chided herself for not getting up earlier, although the bus was always full.

A cry spread through the crowd like fire, as the coughing of the engine starting reached their ears. They watched the bus chug its way up the steep rise to the DUBs and winced and moaned in disgust as the smell of the faeco-fuel exhaust fumes hit their nostrils.

Irene had been right. The gyno with the cup was the driver. The bus came to a halt a little way ahead of the crowd, so everyone had to run to the door to get on. @ least it was empty, with more chance of embarking. The next one, @ 44 deci, started from a nearby resettlement DUB complex and was always packed.

The fittest members of the queue hurled themselves up the entrance stairs as soon as the doors opened, ready to touch their Eye-Ds. Irene fought her way to board early, so that she wouldn't have to hang onto the roof-rail straps and risk injury or accidental discontinuation. And if she was extra quick, she might even get a seat, something she hadn't done for years, although as she strained her eyes into the dark interior, she saw it filling up fast.

She could hear beep-beep as people pressed their Eye-Ds onto the reader pad, and as soon as she saw an opening, she reached out and slammed hers down. But the reader didn't go beep. It croaked. And then an alarm bell started ringing. She tried again, but got the same result.

A steelex barrier whizzed across the aisle, blocking her progress, and a mechanized voice yelled, 'Halt, Fialka, Irene.'

Fear and embarrassment drained the blood from her face. She turned round, hope rapidly evaporating. 'What's the problem?' she asked in a timid voice.

The driver pointed @ the Eye-D reader. 'Says you're unclassified.'

'But that's impossible,' protested Irene, fighting back tears of frustration. 'They can't be that quick, surely.'

'Well, that's what it says.'

People in the queue were still clambering up into the confined entrance area of the bus and demanding to know what was going on. The driver shouted @ them to wait. When they started swearing and throwing stones @ her transplasticon protection pane, she swung the doors shut, trapping a screaming gyno in them and forcing another two to fall out onto the waste ground with heavy thuds, and moved the bus off.

The mob followed, incensed now @ being held up, and started banging on the doors and windscreen, trying to smash whatever they could.

The driver smiled @ Irene. 'Sorry. Can't let you on. Account frozen...no Britz available for the fare... Just been sacked?'

'Disemployed,' Irene managed to correct between sobs. 'Please...I gotta get to the scrounge-lounge...'

The driver shrugged and opened the door. 'Thank you for being ejected from BestcoeBus®. Enjoy your day.'

'Selfish wankress,' shrieked a sharp-featured bottle blonde

from behind. 'Hope you end up in one of them Recycling Centres.' She dragged Irene back to the steps and together with the other passengers kicked her off.

As Irene fell, banging her head on the stony walkway, her face a black well of screaming mouth, the rest of the queue trampled over her in their hurry to board, cussing her for spoiling their journey even more.

Irene was crying so loud, she didn't hear the bus drive off, or notice the stink it left in its wake. She just lay on the ground, dreading to think what she looked like, and felt the tear in her dress with her bruised hand. Her dismay deepened, like a gong going off in her brain as she struggled to her feet, and realized one of her shoes was still on the bus.

Every swear-word she had ever known she bellowed up @ the granite sky. She yelled herself hoarse as she reached her DUB, and climbed, defeated, back to her unit.

She closed the front door, out of breath after twelve flights of stairs, and went to the tiny window near the ceiling in her living room, and stood on a chair to look out over the city.

She liked to think she'd be able one day to spot George somewhere in that concrete desert clawing his way back to her. Hope kept her going. She wondered whether the Freebies really existed or were merely an urban myth. So many rumours about raids and escapes. Perhaps he'd joined them.

She could see under the grey canopy the panorama of Dagtown, and further in the distance Cockneytown East, and the wide road leading back down from the artificial hill, built to re-house all the small-town and village folk. It was about to rain. The clouds were getting blacker. And then the joke would be on the budget architects who dreamed up these blocks. The concrete base and paved-over expanses simply collected the water, inundating the entrances and releasing raw sewage, which then flowed down in a mud and shit slide onto Dagtown itself. Happened constantly.

And as the first huge drops spattered on the dusty pane, Irene knickertwisted over being late for her appointment, the fine and her lost shoe, and opened a can of Beerola®.

FOUR

I'm a-rushing to complete Horelka's FD2, when the alert comes @ 63 deci. Bestcoesecurity® have apprehended a felon.

Remembering the Inspector's reprimand, I convert to 3.12 pm accu and grab V157 and my deputy, V146. As we take off, the whoosh of cool air thrills our streaming eyes.

Pink-uniformed gynocops patrol South East 13 Plaza, a C-class PAULie thoroughfare dominated by a BestcoeBlue Superstore® and slogan-boards proclaiming that Pay-As-U-Live works. Behind the breezeblock shop spreads a network of walkways leading to the dense grey DUB complex. Hard to tell where the blocks end and the clouds begin.

Pedestrians cower beneath us, the tinnitus of personalized music throbbing and humming from their audi-pods.

We arrive in seconds, zooming into the entrance. Two bad-tempered crows caw 'Faak Faak' @ us for rivalling their airborne ascendancy. Satan's Garage music blasts through the aisles.

In the bare interior, a gynoguard sits on a trembling, supine andro, her hands gagging his cries. A bar of Chocolette® lies nearby. 'All yours, sphecoids,' she says.

I tut @ her offensive remark, and jab my spheco-foot into the prisoner's groin. The guard gets up.

'Nicking a bar of Chocolette®?'

'I...I'm sorry,' he stutters.

I laugh, and savour the burning tickle pleasuring my lower

abs, as my felon-busting organs crank up. The guard passes me the red Eye-D.

'D-classified, eh?' I raise an I-brow-antenna, which brushes the low corrugated steelex ceiling. 'Flouting class law and stealing a bar of godshit.'

'Please...' The thief doesn't finish, but I know what he'll say. What they always do. Snivel, beg, apologize and give back what they've taken.

Short, black, greasy hair matted with sweat frames his plain face. Scruffy green dungarettes haven't been washed for ages, and he stinks, of stale perspiration and fear. He's quaking now, crying and screaming 'No,' as he sees my erection catch the fluorescent light on its gleaming chitinex edge.

A voice from deep inside me, one I've long known I would hear one day, whispers.

Don't.

I try to ignore it and swallow hard, but it roars up from my buried blackbox.

DON'T...THIS...IS...WRONG

'ACE him,' I say to myself, desperate to work up killer anger, wondering why V146 and V157 are silent. *Taking what wasn't his. Irredeemably destitute. Setting humos back in their quest for perfection. Who needs his ilk in the gene pool?*

His Eye-D reveals he's 20 and only recently D-classified. I search his wide-open eyes. FaceReader locates hunger and terror.

Waste of ACE.

I gotta do something, so I stab my spheco-dick an inch into his thigh. He yelps like a smacked puppy.

The significance of my decision not to discontinue him dawns on me like a cold shower. My vespine moral code struggles against something I didn't realize was within me. This mustn't get back to Horelka, except as a false alarm. I withdraw my cock-sting from the felon's leg, and spear the godshit instead.

'Forensics'll want this,' I lie, and toss the bar to V157, who catches it on his penis. Should keep him happy. Like me, he rubs the shaft enough to get it well smeared before passing it to a grim-faced V146. Tiny pulses of sweetness ignite our taste-buds like twinkling stars, and make our I-brow-antennae curl over @ the ends. Our way of going 'Mm-mm.'

They say the genuine article is indeed the food of the gods; hence, access is restricted to A-listers, but imitations are still worthwhile. Every spheco's dream sex-e-q-tion is to ACE a celebrity, who's digesting the real stuff. For non-As, though, chocolate is just a colour.

'BestcoeDisinfex® his wound and release him,' I command the shocked guard as my dick folds back inside me, my sac heavy with unspent ACE.

'Th-thank you.' The felon can't believe his luck, but shrinks back from me as if he fears I might yet change my mind, and allows the guard to whisk him away to be washed and treated.

V146 discards the godshit bar as we take off through the endless DUB blocks, which I imagine is how an oldtime graveyard appears to a fly. We say nothing during our brief flight home. I retire to our spheco-timberyard for peace and quiet to finish my paperwork.

'Funny we still call it that,' I say to myself, chewing a splinter of timberex, 'when you have to visit the BestcoeRetro® Museum to see real paper.'

It's a few deci-minutes before nightshift when I catch V157 treading air around me.

'Can't you see I'm busy, for fuxache?'

'Us two,' he says, hovering, 'we got a special bond.'

I roll my spheco-eyes skywards and shrug. 'Sure, we got

through metamorphosis together. So?'

'But we have something extra.'

I begin to get afraid. He mustn't suss me. But if only he would!

'It's like there's more humo in us than there should be, V159.'

'Meaning what?'

'That was a humo thing you did, not ACEing that villain, but it's okay.'

'Chizz, V157. I report to you now, do I?' He doesn't answer, so I carry on. 'FaceReader downrated his felony. Besides, he was D-classified. Why discontinue him?'

'I...' he starts, and then blurts it out. 'I need your advice.'

I frown. Regular sphecos don't have dilemmas. I cast V157 an oblique squint as he continues.

'And I reckon you'll want mine.'

'Don't be impertinent, V157. Remember I'm your Queen.'

Oh, how Knox and his team of labrats must enjoy their little joke!

'You know what I mean.' He gogs @ me like he's accusing me of something.

I think of my pop-up dysfunction. A bell-peal of terror rings through me. I spread my spheco-cheeks and fart a purple cloud of soli-pherum as a precaution. His eyes close in ecstasy. As the solidarity pheromone wafts up his nostrils, he buzzes with pleasure, and his I-brow-antennae quiver in mid-air, taut as shitting dogs' tails. When he comes down, however, his expression holds the same challenge.

'I know what's been going on with you, V159. Don't deny it.'

I square up to him. Special bond we might have, but no way am I putting up with this. 'What exactly are you after, V157? Quit bushbeating around, and spit it out.'

His answer takes me by surprise. 'Cz it's happening to me too.'

I swallow hard, and my chitinex-hairs bristle, but I still have to make sure. 'What is?'

He hesitates a bit before speaking. 'The pop-ups from the Black and Yellow Training Book? They come to me, all the time. I can't close them down. There's something wrong with me.'

'And what makes you so sure I've got any idea what you're talking about?'

'You kept double-blinking while you were ACEing that rapist. It's happened to me too. I was sex-e-q-ting a mugger when the sphecanthropy page flashed. I figured you must have the same problem.'

'Recite this page.'

V157 takes a deep breath and clears his graceful sphecothroat. 'Sphecanthropy, aka vespulism, phenomenon discovered in the 19th century by Dr Isaac Mendoza, born 1837, died 1868, and recently studied and harnessed to benefit BestcoeBritain®...

'Male homos, Not Into Conventional Eroticism, commonly referred to as NICEBOYS, qv, displaying early signs of alienation and social rejection, see also bullying, are separated from their families and peers @ seven for their burgeoning aberrant sexuality and infantile resentment to be channelled into crime-fighting...'

He gogs @ me.

'Go on,' I say.

He continues. 'After rigorous physical and psychological training, adolescent homos metamorphose into adult wasp men, i.e. sphecanthropes, a human-vespine genetic hybrid, are grouped into swarms serving their Queen, qv, and assigned to police forces, to genetically cleanse BestcoeBritain® of male felons...'

He pauses, and then remembers. 'Ah! The former, socially useless, homosexual urge is transformed into arousal triggered by anger and hate, and the old penis fashioned into a lethal sting, used for summary sex-e-q-tion, qv vivisexion.' He phews.

'Orgsome, V157, verbatim, but shouldn't be in your conscious memory.'

V157 lowers his voice to a whisper. 'Why is this happening to us?'

'I don't know. You haven't told anyone else, have you?'

He shakes his head.

'This has to remain strictly between ourselves.'

He nods, I-brows drooping like a scolded dog's tail.

'Retroception's redcardable.'

His sunglass-lens eyes widen, and he turns to leave, but after a couple of steps, he pauses and faces me again. 'There's something else.'

My spheco-innards churn over. I sort of know what he's going to say, but don't want to hear it. Not yet. But he says it anyway.

'I've been having...dreams.'

'Ssh.' I look away and rest my forehead on one of the timberex trees. I shut my eyes, hoping that when I re-open them, he'll be gone, but he's still there, behind me, waiting for guidance, maybe just one little word of comfort, but how can I give him that, in my position? 'This isn't appropriate, V157,' I start, in a feeble attempt to assert my Queen's authority, but he interrupts, his tear-thick voice shaking.

'They're always the same. That shouldn't happen, should it, V159?'

'Don't do this to me,' I telepath, biting my knuckles to keep myself from crying out, spheco-heart banging away. 'The recall is bad enough. Don't make me say it.' I shake my head, close to crying myself. And then it slips out, barely audible.

'So have I.'

I don't look round. Just stay propped against the fake trunk, aware my confession is a terrible mistake, but relieved to share the burden of secrecy. Footsteps crunch on the timberex chips. His I-brows stroke mine.

'Soxbury.' I turn and face him. 'Always Soxbury. And you?'

'Mollinsea.'

I clear my tight spheco-throat. 'Little pre-fab huts @ the bottom of a gentle hill, and big, grown-up hands in blue sleeves squeezing my tiny arms, dragging me screaming out of that classroom. And the other kids jeering, and me crying for my mum from the darkness inside the black and yellow van. Then blank.'

'Me too,' he says, his face filling with wonder. 'It's all coming back.'

'And I had a name, for fuxache. A real humo name.'

'So did I, V159. But not any more.' He shakes his cute spheco-head as if shrugging off the past.

'This conversation ends now.'

'I can see in your beautiful eyes you don't mean that, V159.'

'It could be our discontinuation warrant.'

V157's face clouds over. 'What now?'

'We go to the syngastrion, V157. That's what. Earplay it. I'm starving, and I bet you are too. In a couple of deci-minutes we'll have to switch over to accu-time for nightshift. Don't look so alarmed. Not enough has returned yet, but it will. Then we'll know. For the time being, though, let's have a quick cud. Your turn to tank-up first. I didn't sleep much last night.' I whack his I-brow-antennae with my own.

He flinches. 'Fuxache, V159, that hurt.'

The sight of his mouthparts slowly widening into a grin as he retaliates warms my spheco-blood, and I laugh my husky spheco-cackle. We fly out of the yard, past the Combs, and head for the syngastrion, where other on-shift sphecos are gathering. As I watch him leave after regurgitating, I gog @ the black and yellow bands on his sleek hourglass torso, and a twinge in my crotch disturbs me. That isn't right, surely. I feel no anger, outrage or hatred. Only...but I dare not admit it. Impossible. And yet it's happening.

The day is over. I am transformed.

Memories flood back. Soxbury Ness Primary. Timberex desks worn smooth by generations of kids. And the bullying. And the teachers who blindeyed it.

Playing on the sandy beach in summer, watching the tides, wishing the grey-brown water was clean enough to paddle in. Believing my Dad's yarn that the Thames Estuary was really the sea, and the opposite shore I could just make out in the haze was BestcoeFrance®. As this flashes before me, I remember my dreams, and my thorax constricts. I'm not supposed to be able to retroceive. It should all have been wiped.

It's been thirteen years now. The urge to find out who I was flares up within me. I blink in Soxbury on my Eyelid-screen, but there's nothing. Proscribed info that can only be in one place. The Institute Database. On Olympia Heights.

In the Vespiary Combs it's dark. The only sounds are birds tweeting and my thoughts, till the tannoy comes on.

'Hi, folks. Just coming up to midnight, zero-deci. Thank you to all our customers for buying another 100 deci-minutes in BestcoeBritain®. Enjoy your kip.'

A switch clicks, and the birdsong shuts down. All is silent, apart from the pounding of my spheco-heart, and the voices reawakened in my troubled little spheco-head.

FIVE

A week passed before the flood sludge dried up enough for Irene to be able to get out. She'd managed to subsist on dry bread and Beerola®. Brightsiding her outlook, she realized the 6am start was no longer necessary. She'd just turn up and wait, but they'd hardtime her for being so late.

She squeezed into her scruffy trainers and started walking the seven kilometres down the slopes to the scrounge-lounge. When the hill levelled out, the DUBs came to an end. There was a busy intersection, and Irene continued in the same direction to central Dagtown. On the left was a flat-roofed concrete block, the old C-class superstore, where she used to be registered for provisions.

She thought of all the chicken legs, potatoes, cabbage, apples and ice-cream-based desserts they called gonoffi pie that had sustained her for the past 39 years. Her insides groaned with hunger, but her expired Eye-D wouldn't open the turnstile, and the guards didn't help. On the windy street, as grit flew into her eyes, Irene sighed in despair, and carried on walking.

The road veered to the left past some small shops, many boarded up. Gynocop pairs in squeaky pink leatherex dunga-rettes patrolled the street, while swarms of sphecocops hovered in the distant skyscape. A packed autobus with people hanging from the straps attached to the exterior roof-rails ploughed its smelly way through the pot-holed road on its route back to the resettlement DUB complexes.

Not far now. Irene was nauseous from starvation and sore-eyed from fatigue. If only Nelson had turned out different, George might've remained the rock she'd always believed he was, and she wouldn't be trudging through these stinking streets. *But you can't undo the past.*

Another intersection, and she could see the building. A breeze-block mass at least five storeys high with no windows. Just a street door in a wall.

How can anyone bear to work there? She rested to ease the pain from her blistered feet, and thought again of what people said about the scrounge-lounge, but put that out of her mind. She had to sort out her Eye-D.

The door was locked. Irene pressed a buzzer and waited. She called 'Hello' into the entryphone, but nothing happened. 53 deci-minutes.

She buzzed again. Another interminable pause. She decided to return @ 25 deci the following day.

After she'd only gone a few steps, the buzzer fizzled into life. Anger and relief mingled inside her as she ran back.

A mechanized androgynous voice demanded, 'FaceChirp-dashtag?'

Irene cleared her throat, recited *dashtagFialkacommaIrene* and swiped her Eye-D through a slot. Once again she heard the croak and bell, @ a volume so intense it startled her, and she stepped back, cradling her ears.

'Your appointment was seven days ago.'

'There was a flood. I tried to contact you.'

'Wait.'

The word made Irene's blood boil. 'But I've been waiting for the last two hours just to get in the door, for fuxache.'

After a few moments of silence, during which Irene kicked herself for cussing and probably alienating the one person or thing that could help her, the Voice spoke again. 'Do not swear, Fialka, Irene. We have been waiting one week.'

'I know. I'm sorry,' she whined in an attempt to sound contrite. She was shivering now from the cold.

'Open the door when you hear the buzzer, and join the end of the queue on the third floor.'

'Oh, thank...' The buzzer sounded, and she was inside.

The gloom within was relieved by faint, horizontal slices of daylight that filtered through ceiling-high vitreola slats @ the far end of the bare uncarpeted room. Irene walked across this grey, concrete space, which led to a stairwell. Gagging @ the smell of unwashed human bodies, she climbed to the first floor, where a heat sensitive ticket dispenser beeped @ her. She took a plasticon chip with her queue number 1539 and carried on up.

As she reached the landing between the first and second floors, she heard a murmur. Looking up, she saw an unkempt, fat bearded andro standing on the stairs with some other people above him.

'Excuse me, is this the queue for the third floor?'

He nodded, his vacant eyes looking right through her.

Irene took up her place.

The Voice announced 1231.

When the queue moved, the line went through swing doors into a grimy grey and cream painted corridor on the second floor, stretched past four doors and snaked through another opening. On one side of the wall hung a couple of faded, dusty posters.

The first showed a smiling, early middle-aged couple with a laughing boy and girl holding up silver B-class Eye-D cards. The caption read:

EARN YOUR RIGHT TO LIFE — BIRTH ISN'T
ENOUGH!
THE P.A.U.L. TEAM.

The second poster just said:

NO POVERTY WITHOUT POOR PEOPLE!
NO POOR PEOPLE — NO POVERTY!

C-class PAULies like Irene'd been strolled from office to office, holding piles of red and a few blue Eye-D tokens and data discs, the odd twitch of the nose or slight wince of the lips being the sole acknowledgement of the human dregs in their midst. As the hours passed, the day shift went home. Irene tried to leave with them.

'You. Here,' a blue uniformed C-class gyno grunted @ her, as though Irene didn't speak Brit.

'Can't I come back tomorrow?' pleaded Irene.

The gyno moved her head back sharply, as if grossly affronted. 'You. Stay. Here,' she barked twice into Irene's face. 'Forbidden. Exits. Locked. Wait. OK?'

She trotted off, looking back once to make sure Irene wasn't following her, but Irene was too stunned to react. All she could do was listen to the clatter of the gyno's leatherex heels as she descended the stairs.

The next shift arrived.

The lights stayed on all night. Irene could hear drizzle spitting against the tiny panes under the ceiling. While most queuers huddled up for warmth, she and some other gynos stretched out on the stairs, wary of the andros.

She didn't sleep long. It was cold, and impossible to relax with the sharp, concrete edges of the stairs digging into her back. And the excretorium wasn't for the fastidious.

The rain continued the next day, when the queue inched forward after long intervals of inertia. The Voice had only reached 1353.

Like the others, Irene alternated between standing up to stretch her legs and sitting on the concrete floor, back to the wall, listless eyes focusing on nothing in particular.

There was a water fountain and a pile of plasticon cups. In the morning a tray bearing food was left on the floor. In the ensuing stampede, Irene got pushed out of the way and returned to her place dejected and starving. @ midday, when the tray reappeared, she raced over and before the fights started, managed to get a square of stale bread, a dry cracker and a cube of sour, bruised apple.

In the early afternoon she reached the identical third floor, where the queue stopped @ a steelex door. A C-class gyno gave the Ds a watery, lukewarm beverage that could have been either Caffeinola® or Tanninola®.

The bitter taste wasn't a problem. Irene's priorities were quenching her raging thirst now the water tap had dried up, and convincing herself she felt underweathery just from the lack of fresh air, and not... *withertongue.*

In a silent panic, she checked her lips weren't swollen and phewed she could still move her feet.

'Soon be over,' she said to herself in an attempt to brightside, and closed her eyes. She woke, groggy and disoriented, to the sound of someone screaming and sobbing behind the door, not from pain, but despair, reminding her of her anguished shrieks when she'd been ejected from the autobus, but the noise was too muffled to make out any words.

The queuers exchanged nervous glances and shook their heads, but no one spoke. The Voice called out 1538.

The fat andro hauled himself to his feet, brushed himself down and waddled over to the steelex door, which he pulled open with effort and disappeared behind.

Me next. Irene heard the rumble of andro voices and looked round @ the dispirited, defeated faces, lowered eyes and sagging shoulders. The people stank, like her.

Laughter from behind the steelex door interrupted her thoughts. A sound she hadn't heard for some time. It cheered her, allaying her fears and renewing her hope. Perhaps, the rumours were false, and one shouldn't believe everything one heard.

But suddenly, there was shouting. Startled cries. Someone banged a fist down. On a desk? Irene's optimism faltered.

An unseen door slammed. Once again all was quiet.

Then the Voice said 1539.

SIX

The crystal pyramid roofs of Olympia Heights skyscrapers are visible from all over Cockneytown, and their glitter shines as an example of celebrity success and superiority for all to emulate, from silvereye Bs down to the lowest sphecanthrope.

It's 9 deci. I can't sleep, and break out of the Combs. The insult of pre-dawn air slaps my face and makes me cry. As I soar away from familiar ranks of DUBs standing to attention like soldiers @ reveille, my eyes overflow and I breaststroke through the aether over the Thames towards North East District 14.

There's a small patch of green, where I land, electrified in the knowledge I'll be crossing a line the most laid-back Inspector couldn't blindeye. Leaning against a tree I chew on the bark. All sphecos come out @ night to do this. My I-brows curl over @ the texture of real wood. Can't help that. Like boozing, it's a spheco thing.

Satisfied, I fly above palaces on the man-made slopes of the Heights.

The Bestcoe-Mendoza Institute of Entomanthropy is tucked away behind twin groves of poplars, planted to commemorate the area, which once bore their name.

But how can I forget my alma mater? Dwarfing the neighbouring villas and mansions, she nestles between the ninth and tenth poplars on the right flying north from the Thames, a massive marble cube, like a temple: ornate sculpted façade, crystal domed roof and pediments over her closed floor-to-ceiling windows.

A terrace of squat guards obscures the entrance, but I don't need the front door.

There's a frosted genuine glass pane on the side. I tread air a metre away and hear a tinkling noise as I smash it open with my foot and fly in.

It's a humo excretorium, the thing they sit on. I vaguely recall learning to use one, but there's no time to dwell on that now. Gotta find the database.

The place teems with guards, sphecos and humos. I prepare sacs of soli-pherum in my anal glands and spray the whitewashed corridors.

Countless doors. Endless rooms. I hesitate for a second. Sphecos approach, cock-stings cuckoo-clocking their warning. Mine stays hidden.

'Database?' I ask, releasing another arseful of soli-pherum. It blows them. Their eyes narrow like a cat's when tickled under the ears, and they buzz with pleasure. My I-brows stroke theirs. 'It's okay,' I telepath in spheco-lingo. 'I'm of the ilk. Trust me.'

They let me pass, but divulge nothing. The soli-pherum droplets won't last and they'll return, hostile and un-ilky. I can't waste all my strength on manufacturing pheromone.

The ceiling resonates with footsteps. My Eye-plan of the building reveals stairs. Up I fly. On the next level throng humos. I use their prejudice to my advantage. We all look the same to them. Naked black and yellow men with pretty wasp mugs. FaceReader pinpoints a sympathetic gyno.

'Urgent requirement to access individual computer database.'

She smiles up @ me, nervously. 'You must be new. I'll show you to one if you like.'

'Chizz. Directions adequate.'

I'm in. Easy. Struggling to stay awake now, I click the door shut, and fly over to the monitor.

After never-ending accu-minutes, my file finally downloads. I read, anxious to scroll down ever faster.

V159
Symmetamorphs: Other sphecoids in metamorphosis grouping — V157 & V158 (discontinued).

I stare @ the next line, not believing my bleary spheco-eyes.

Metamorphosis incomplete due to power failure. Future dysfunction probability: high.

They've known all along.

I shudder as I recall the screen not bluelining, labrats panicking and Professor O. B. Knox fuxaching and then phewing, 'That was close,' palpating us and smiling into my face, but @ himself, his success. And V158 not making it. I continue, breathless.

Human name: Fialka, Nelson. Place of Birth: Soxbury Ness.

Orgsome! All the sphecos in my swarm — their humo names, places and dates of birth, and the schools they'd been plucked from to be sphecanthropized. All there. Details I'd never remember. Blocked on my system. Transfer prohibited.

Everything is coming back to me, but then the V159 page shuts down. I try to reopen it, but the Black and Yellow Training Manual's Brief History of Sphecanthropy pops up instead. Exhausted now, I almost doze off scrolling down with my Eye-mouse mechanism, but manage to stay awake through the familiar info.

Sphecanthropes do not participate in Pay.As.U.Live P.A.U.L. schemes or FaceChirp® and are not subject to disemployment concerns.

A few niceboys escape detection @ seven. Unsuitable for training, they are treated equally with other BestcoeBritain® customers, who often refer to them as decaffs, she-men or flutterboys.

Oh, our dear little Black and Yellow Book. How fondly I recall every word now. And then my heart stops, and my sphecoinnards fizz with fear. There's another paragraph, which didn't appear in my nocturnal pop-up.

Following successful metamorphosis, sphecanthropes, and especially queens, can currently expect to enjoy an enhanced vespine life-span of up to two years, although many will discontinue after nine to ten months, which creates a shortage in the winter.

My heart pounds. Sweat pours down my face. My respiration is shallow, rapid panting. I've already been @ SECOPS for eight weeks. I try taking slow, deep breaths to help me relax and focus, but stagger back from the screen, sending the swivel chair spinning wildly to the door.

Humo footsteps in the corridor. Heavy boots on plasticon tiles. Androguard.

Too easy.

I've come this far. Giving up now's unthinkable.

He's stopped outside. There's a slight click as the handle gives and turns downward. I sense it in the blackness. If he's armed, chitinex won't stand a chance against bullets @ close range.

'I'm *chitin* myself.' I remember the terrible jokes we made while training. Besides, it's pronounced kite-in. I keep dead still.

The spheco-crime of retroceptive blackboxing carries a maximum penalty of discontinuation. And while I shudder @ the prospect of Knox experimenting upon me, I realize the full significance of what I've discovered, and can't tear myself away from the screen. I blink in V157, and read until I feel the barrel of a gun pressing into the small of my chitinex spheco-back.

SEVEN

Irene got up, handcombed her hair, and despite the throbbing behind her eyes and the sick feeling gnawing @ her insides, managed to get herself through the steelex door without tottering.

The room she entered was painted the same as the corridors. Seated @ the opposite end @ a metallic fold-up desk, watching a mini-screen were an andro and a gyno, both with black dyed hair cut halo-style.

The gyno looked up. 'Fialka, Irene?'

Irene approached.

'Stop right there.'

'Sorry.'

'Don't speak till you're addressed.'

Irene nodded and shook her head, uncertain which was the best response. She felt faint now, and wanted to sit. They'd surely let her rest on the floor until they were ready. Her legs decided for her; before she knew it she was in a heap on the concrete.

'Stand up,' barked the gyno.

Irene struggled back to her feet, and carried on waiting, almost amused that now she had finally arrived, all she wanted was to lie down and sleep.

After several more accu-minutes, the andro raised his head. 'Fialka, Irene. Come here.'

Irene went up to the desk and looked around for a chair,

but there wasn't one. She stood, leaning her weight against the edge of the desk.

The gyno tutted. 'Back,' she yelled, not looking @ Irene, a hysterical tone in her voice. 'Move away...now.'

Irene obeyed. She noticed the andro was bald on top, making him look like an electrocuted monk. The thought tickled her, but her smile was cut off by the gyno staring @ her.

'What's funny, Fialka, Irene?'

'Noth...' Irene started, but simply shook her head.

'Eye-D?' Without looking up, the andro held out his hand, and Irene gave him her blue plasticon eye-shaped token, which he swiped on the side of the screen.

'Oh yes,' he drawled. 'You're late.'

Irene wanted to say the thirty-hour wait should've covered it, and mumbled about the flood, but the andro held up his hand to stop her, and her voice petered out.

He examined the screen closely with the gyno, and their halos got entwined as if they were mating. The woman's tiny blue eyes studied Irene's face. Then she spoke.

'You've been disemployed and D-classified...'

'I'm...'

'Silence! This is because @ your last birthday review you had 9806 Britz 38 centz in your Eye-D account, a sum insufficient to cover your next in-advance annual P.A.U.L. life-fee of 9887 Britz 66 centz. Stand still! As a burden on Bestcoe-Britain®, you have been removed from your Pay-As-U-Live scheme, and we are pleased to confirm your D-classification...'

Irene gasped. 'I'll pay the shortfall next month,' she cried, clutching the desk and nodding her desperate promise.

'Back,' screamed the gyno. 'Don't interrupt.' She cleared her throat. 'You'll be entitled to receive D-class benefits for three months from receipt of the notification, minus a seven-day dispunctuality deduction, and no longer obliged to use accu-time.'

'But...'

'Shut up! You're strongly advised to seek other employ-ment. An allowance of ten percent of your previous salary will be credited to your Eye-D every month. The D-class shop in the basement caters for all your needs as long as your Eye-D's in credit. Failure to secure re-employment results in re-assess-ment. You leave through the rear exit.' She indicated with her head, her sharp, beaky nose doubling as a pointer. When she looked back @ Irene, she drew her thin, pink-glossed lips into a smile. 'The stairs lead to the shop...and the street.'

'What about the money we lost on Nelson?' Tears were soaking Irene's cheeks. 'We paid for him, but you took him away. Why can't you use that?' Snot bubbled from her nose as she sank to her knees.

Then the andro spoke. 'Don't waste our time, Fialka, Irene. Finding work's difficult @ your age.'

'But what if I don't get another job?' she wailed from the floor.

'I told you,' the gyno butted in with impatience, her smile lingering. 'Your situation will be re-appraised.'

In her panic, Irene's mind shut down, and she said the first thing that came into her head. 'Can I use my Eye-D on the autobus?'

'Public transport isn't one of the D-classified benefits you'll be enjoying.'

'Which are?'

'The D-class shop and a weekly list of vacancies and new goods @ the shop.'

'Is that all?' cried Irene, understanding better her pre-decessors' reactions. 'What about my C-class shop?'

'Access withdrawn,' explained the gyno. 'You must manage your limited funds carefully. We can't afford to support you indefinitely. That's why you're not permitted to make C-class purchases or use FaceChirp®. Poverty leads to social irresponsibility and criminality. It may indicate the presence of undesirable genetic material. BestcoeBritain® cannot assist those who perpetuate the vicious circle of social decline. Thank you for being D-classified from BestcoeDisinfex®, Fialka, Irene. Enjoy your day.'

'Is that it?' asked Irene, but the gyno was nosing @ the door, and Irene, relieved it was over, and bursting with anger and despair, stood up, snatched her new red Eye-D from the man and pulled the door open.

It was heavy, and she felt most undignified as she struggled to open it, and then it slammed into her back as she was leaving. Embarrassment flooded her cheeks with weary blood as she heard them mutter something she knew was about her, and then titter. How she wanted to march back and smash that beaky nose into the bitch's face and pull that stupid halo hair off the wanker's head!

But the door had shut, and couldn't be opened from Irene's side.

There was a concrete staircase, which she followed down to the basement, where a long corridor led to another steelex door. She pulled it towards her and went through into the shop.

The first thing she noticed was the smell.

EIGHT

I sense his breathing, sweat and body presence as my back arches away from his gun. I'd see him too if my eyes weren't focussed 100% on the screen where info about V157 is revealed.

The guard'll be arresting me any moment now.

The anger mounts. Tiny horses gallop up my spheco-thighs and across my groin and crotch. I reach erection mode in a split second. My cock darts out, but I lower its aim to avoid it pinging against the screen. And then I execute the manoeuvre that got me the distinction award.

BESTCOE-MENDOZA INSTITUTE OF ENTOMANTHROPY
Department of *Sphecanthropy*
Training Manual page 209

Manoeuvre 87 — the Undercrotch Uppercut (aka the undercrotch upperjab):

The penis folds back between the legs and then shoots up at 45 degrees backwards into the body of an unsuspecting felon lurking behind. Manoeuvre 87 usually results in Manoeuvre 87a — the Reverse Surprise Navelfuck (aka Reverse Surprise Naveljab).

Very few sphecos manage this. It's how I queened, and why V146 failed. I didn't mind then. The honour and prestige were what counted. Plus the perks. And respect. My own spheco-swarm, loyal and obedient. Ready to die for me. Apart from V157, but he was special. And all cz I was endowed with the ability to fart roomloads of soli-pherum.

The guard makes a plaintive cry. His gun clatters on the floor.

Lucky for me my chitinex-armoured cock is hydrochloric acid resistant. My victims can't digest me.

I pop my cock out of him and then utter 'Uh!' as I forget where I am and it hits the workbench. 'Fuxache, that hurts!' It half-coils up inside me. I wipe my slit clean with the back of my yellow spheco-hand and smear it on the still protruding part of my dick. A strong, meaty, bloody savour with an aftertaste of shit.

The syngastria will have him now. The best bits'll be sent nationwide. The muck'll go to the Recycling Centres.

While I was dealing with him, the screen told me what I needed to know. My antennae can't load these redcardable files, however much I try.

I slide round the guard, who is still standing and begins to sway, so I hold him in an embrace to right his balance. I think 'If only...' but I don't finish the thought. I can't bear to. I kiss his cheek. 'Not long now...' I whisper. He's still paralysed. The puncture wound will finish him as well.

The fruit of my dysfunction kicks in and humo thoughts start a-nagging @ me. It's not just him; what I've done will probably condemn his entire family to D-classification if they rely on his income. My insides become a sack of boulders. Is this what they call conscience? My spheco-self quickly steps in to the rescue. Circumprehension's a deadly weakness.

How long before more guards come? I return to the screen. Finish V157's profile and touch in another name. Residence: Soxbury Tower DUB, Dagtown. Ex-C-class/P.A.U.L scheme.

D-classification completed.

My gaze freezes, spheco-brain hammering away. No mention of Dad. Very little time left.

More forbidden yearnings flower inside me. To see her again, talk to her, kiss her...

But what I've learnt I can't unknow. Not now. The last thirteen years of my life have been based on my ability to unknow things...a skill I wish to unlearn.

I switch the database off. The room is pitch black now.

'Soon be over.' I caress his sweat-drenched brow and snog his lips, then close the door as quietly as possible and fly down the corridor, looking for a room with a window. To leave without having to explain myself to androguards saves so much time.

I was so hoping my visit would go unnoticed, but now I've stupidly committed redcardable vivisexion on an androguard, one of the worst spheco-crimes. Better start working on my alibi.

Oh, V157. Wait till I tell you what I've discovered. You'll be so proud. Just like you were the day we became fully-formed sphecos.

And Professor O. B. Knox was there @ the Institute too. What was it he said to us?

'Congratulations. Now get out there and do your job well. Don't wanna see any of you here ever again.'

But you will, Professor. You will indeed.

NINE

An odour of dirty laundry and rotting cabbage permeated the entire shop, a room about ten by ten feet. Piped muzak was barely audible.

Satan's Garage...can't they play anything else?

In the centre were two oblong plasticon tables, around which a number of people Irene recognized from the queue were examining piles of old clothes and scraps of food. @ first, Irene stayed by the door, taking in the scene.

The fat andro was holding up a grease-stained yellow shirt with a tear up the side, and shaking his head. In the corner, a short, wiry gyno-assistant having a smoke with her sleeves rolled up was watching them all with a mixture of pity and disdain. She appeared poised to jump up @ any minute.

Standing back from the group was a black-haired gyno, her brown eyes wide open with horror, and her lips apart as if she was going to cry out.

Tentatively @ first, then more boldly, Irene wandered over to the tables.

The clothes were in a jumbled heap, and all second hand, dirty or badly worn. There was nothing that interested her, and she made for the food.

If she'd been unimpressed by the range of garments on offer, she was horrified by the victuals.

There was one hard loaf of white bread, a patch of green mould spreading up its side. Next to that were a few wrinkled apples and small pieces of stale yellow cheese cut close to the rind, which resembled the hard skin on the soles of her feet and stank like it. A pile of potato peelings was soaking in a chipped enamel bowl, and a number of coarse, outer cabbage leaves were arranged next to that. Cooked bones from chicken drumsticks that had had most of the meat chewed off them were standing in a cracked plasticon dish.

The assistant stubbed out her smoke on the concrete and kicked the butt into the corner, where it found plentiful company. She cleared her phlegmy throat and said, 'That's all there is. Take it or leave it.'

Irene's heart sank. From basic, but decent provisions to scraps in one week. Yet she knew she had to eat something if she was going to survive, and steeled herself. She picked up a wormy apple, some cheese, potato and cabbage, added a chicken wing and approached the assistant.

'How much?'

The assistant shook her head, and asked for Irene's Eye-D. 'It gets deducted. Don't you want bread?'

Irene nodded. The assistant sliced off a thick wedge, which included a generous helping of mould.

'Do I have to have that slice?' asked Irene.

The assistant threw her a look, which said, 'Fuck off. You're D-classified now. You've got no choice. I'm the one holding this knife.'

Irene understood, and handed her Eye-D over. The assistant swiped it.

'When are you open?'

'Hours are on the door as you leave. More tomorrow, depending on what donations we receive.'

Irene took her food, which she cradled in her arm, using one of the cabbage leaves as a makeshift bag. She then went over to the black-haired gyno.

'You really ought to get something; otherwise, you'll starve.'

The gyno looked @ her and burst out crying. Irene managed to transfer her cabbage leaf to one arm and put the other round the gyno's shoulder to comfort her.

'You can share mine if you like. It's not so bad.'

'It's terrible,' the gyno said between sobs.

'Come. We'll find somewhere to eat. I'm Irene.'

'Samina.'

As they went out into another corridor, Irene remembered to check the opening times. 59-79 deci-minutes every day. Obviously, she realized, they received slops and leftovers from local well-wishers during the morning and @ lunch time, and that was how they were restocked. So she would have to save a bit for breakfast, although now she had Samina, breakfast might have to wait for another day.

The corridor came to an end. A staircase led up to turnstiles and barriers for entry and exit. They had to swipe their brand-new red D-class Eye-Ds to leave, and went through another steelex door into the street, opposite the Recycling Centre.

It was early evening. The sun had already set and the street-lights were on. Irene led Samina to a boarded-up shop doorway a few yards from the exit and gave her half the bread.

'Thanks, Irene.'

'You'll help me one day. What happened to you?'

Samina took a bite of the bread, but her grimace said it all.

Irene also started eating. The taste was of plasticon. While she was gouging pockets of gristle, sinew and meat off the bone, and dividing up the raw vegetables and cheese, Samina was struggling to swallow her bread.

'Better get used to it, Samina.'

'I never thought things would come to this.'

'Nor me.'

'This time last year, can you believe this, my partner and I were Silvereye-Bs.' Samina swallowed her mouthful and tore off a piece of cabbage leaf. Brushing her hair off her face, she bit into the leaf, which was tougher than she expected as she had to tug @ it with her teeth. 'He died. Murdered. Robbed in the street. We were thinking of starting a family...have you...?'

'I had a son...he... Did they get the killer?'

'Spiked by sphecoids, but it didn't bring him back and I only had my income. I was a scientist.'

Irene raised her eyebrows.

'We were trying to find an antiviral treatment, or @ least a vaccine for viral aphthodic disease...'

'You what?'

'Oh, I mean withertongue. Human foot-and-mouth. But they closed our unit down...'

'You're not...' Irene moved away.

'Don't worry. I'm not contagious. I...' Her delicate features crumpled up and she started crying again.

'Oh, you'll find something, pretty girl like you.'

Samina shook her head. 'Because I only had the one salary, I was reclassified as a C. That wasn't too bad. I got used to it. The move. The downgrade. Restrictions. It was all bearable.

'I got work in a C-class Supastore. Even tried looking for another partner, but...' She breathed heavily, and put her uneaten cabbage down. 'Two weeks ago, I received my Disemployment Notification. No warning. No reason. Upstairs in that place,' — she cast a look of hate @ the Reception Centre still visible above the smaller shops — 'I begged those vile people to find me @ least other retail work, but they told me to shut up.

'I kept shouting, "Who do you think you are? I was once B-class. You're probably no better than C-class PAULies." And that wankress just turned round and said, "Well, you're D-class shit now, so get over yourself, stuck-up bitch"...then they dismissed me.

'Couldn't bring myself to...is this all I've got to look forward to for the next three months? And what happens then?'

Irene shrugged and gave her some potato peelings and a few shreds of chicken she'd managed to salvage. 'This is as good as it gets. You've gotta eat it. It's trash — we both know that — but from now on it's the only food there is, unless you wanna be caught stealing, and arrested by the gyno-cops, or starve to death. So, do yourself a favour, and eat.' She put her hand on Samina's arm.

For the first time since they'd met, Samina smiled.

They finished their meal in silence, and when Irene told her about the flood, Samina offered to put her up in a nearby DUB, where she'd been recently rehoused.

Irene hugged Samina and said, 'We need friends @ times like this, and we've both found one.'

TEN

The Institute's Sphecanthropy Department Head, Professor O. B. Knox, addressed us.

We sat in two rows, listening to his voice echo through the Dominic Knox Lecture Theatre, named in the memory of his son.

I looked @ V157 on my right. Things were changing so rapidly, and I hoped our friendship would survive. I didn't know why we'd remained so close, but I felt a special bond between us.

'Make the most of your time here,' boomed Knox, pointing to the large, curved windows, with their views of the Thames River and Cockneytown, cz once you graduate, it's goodbye.'

We laughed. It was a privilege to be in Olympia Heights — not that we ever got to explore — and to know we were in the same area as A-listers and celebrities.

When I tuned back into Knox's drone, he was talking about emotions. 'I know you brim with hatred, fury, jealousy, all sexualized, but dislocated from the emotional complex we loosely label as love. That door is firmly closed.

'Not your fault. It was beaten out of you @ too early an age for me to do anything about, and manoeuvred out psycho-logically and too subtly for you to have been able to prevent it. Your feelings were perverted, and we all know how and why, and what we feel about that.'

Murmurs of assent, mine included, rumbled round the

room.

'But I'm gonna unlock another door, one that will channel your confused desires, which help no one. And yes, we know what you are @ that tender age of seven. We recognize the signs, handpick and train. And now you've come this far, we're gonna do something worthwhile with that sex drive of yours, make it serve BestcoeBritain®, but it takes time. You're almost spheco-cops, and we're gonna mould you into an elite force, chosen for BestcoeLaw&Order®, to repay your social debt.'

Most of Knox's talk went over our heads. None of us understood what was in store for us. We just knew we were physically altered, having come through a painful process he called metamorphosis.

On bittersweet days much later, V157 and I used to reminisce about the early period when we still looked normal. We could remember, whereas I doubted that any of the other sphecos could, articulately.

We used to talk about the school classes we eagerly attended, learning to convert both time systems: one new deci-minute equals 14.4 accu-minutes, 100 new deci-minutes equal one new day, and calculating how many seconds is 0.4 accu-minutes. Good things that stay with you for life to balance out the slights.

@ first we were shy, but gradually found out we were there cz of bullying. Bit by bit we unlocked our hearts and spilled out our stories. That's how I got in with V157, although we had other names then, names they removed.

We grew in confidence, learned to trust. And that's when they organized the physical games. Sports, like the ones we'd known, but less rough. We were still delicate, sensitive souls.

The way they disinhibited us made us all happy. The games became gradually more competitive. We used a very soft ball that couldn't hurt even if it was kicked directly @ us. We practised throwing it @ each other before playing. In the beginning, we had one goal, and took our turn to defend it, later progressing to teams, with a goal each. As we became more relaxed, an urge to win took over.

Next we graduated to fights. Just friendly ones @ first, group activities, where one individual would get used to receiving punches, soft blows gradually getting harder @ Knox's instigation. Everyone had to stand in the middle and take hits, and also deliver the blows.

I recalled, as V157 did, the elation as we felt our physical inhibitions evaporate. We were ready to go back to the schools we'd been taken from and face those bullies. But that wasn't to be.

We had to practise fist-fighting in pairs. A different androlad each time. Every afternoon was devoted to physical training. In the beginning, we took it in turns to deliver single punches, learning how to throw straight lefts and rights, hooks and jabs. There were no winners or losers. Just the growing ease with which we held our bodies, and lack of self-consciousness.

Soon we were able to perform these fights in front of the others, to rapturous applause. Knox took notes and encouraged us to win. These were the happiest days of my life.

Then the knockout competition started.

I had victories I was proud Knox observed, until I was in the final. Knox blew a whistle and we squared up: two skinny barefoot twelve-year-olds in shorts. But my opponent, V121, was bigger than me. If he was as scared, he didn't show it.

V121 was coming @ me. The audience's jeers and shouts echoed in the hall. My eyes flashed round to take in a sea of scornful, laughing faces witnessing my downfall. Shame @

Knox seeing me defeated boiled the blood up to my temples, and it flooded my cheeks. I couldn't go on.

Someone yelled, 'Kill him.'

My elbows were just over my body to ward off his blows. I was crouched into myself, fists covering my face. Eyes closed, I couldn't bear to look. I hadn't even got near to hitting V121, who'd already wrapped his arms round my neck in a sort of headlock and was butting my scalp with his forehead.

I yelled, begged him to stop, prayed Knox would break it up, but he just let him batter away, crashing his fists down, making me dizzy. I could take no more. I peered through my fingers and realized if I was to salvage any self-respect and the respect of my peers, I had only one option.

A bad one.

I jerked my knee up, and only stopped when it hit the soft flesh of V121's bollocks.

I felt them wobble inside him.

He stopped bashing me, and let go.

I stood back, suddenly desperate to masturbate.

He was standing still, staring past me, opening his mouth as if to cry out, but without sound. The hall was deadly silent.

V121 gasped, his knees buckled together, and he crashed down, cracking his elbows on the timberex laminate floor.

Someone said, 'Illegal.' Someone else said, 'So's head-locking.'

I advanced on V121, but felt a strong grip restrain my fist as Knox whispered, 'That's enough, V159.'

On the count of ten Knox raised my right arm to whoops of delight and loud boos. Another flush of pleasure caressed my groin.

'You may sit down.' Knox eyed my erection with approval. He kicked @ V121 and said, 'Get up.'

V121 struggled to his feet, nursing his testicles.

'You,' Knox said to me, 'used your brain and found an opening, a chink in the stronger boy's armour, and defeated your opponent. Congratulations. You are the champion, V159.'

There was more applause. I thought that was going to be it, but Knox threw a sharp punch into the demoralized V121's stomach, making him grunt.

'Whereas you,' he said, the contempt in his voice almost palpable, 'disgraced yourself. You didn't think things through. You underestimated your opponent and exposed yourself. You let the weaker boy go that bit further and beat you.' He smacked him hard round the face.

V121 was crying now, ugly sobs, rubbing his belly while tears streamed down his cheeks.

Knox addressed the other androlads. 'In ancient times,' he said, 'the crowd used to decide whether the loser lived or died.' He explained about northbound and southbound thumbs. 'On the count of three. One...two...three...'

We raised our hands in silence.

Knox chuckled. 'The crowd has spoken,' he said. 'Due to the enormous disgrace of your shock defeat, V121, you will be discontinued.'

We didn't know what that meant then.

Knox snapped his fingers.

We gasped as a guard appeared, human, yet insect-like, all green. Wingless. It stood, backside sticking out and forearms raised close to its torso.

We looked to Knox for answers, but he simply clicked his fingers again.

The creature's triangular head swivelled round on its long neck, huge wide-set eyes homing in on a trembling V121, who whimpered as it pushed him out of the hall.

Knox laughed, and we copied him. @ the time we thought

it was a joke.

We never saw V121 again.

Knox looked me up and down. 'What you did was nasty, dirty and illegal, but necessary. Your first victim.'

He pointed to me and the other boys and said to the trainers gathered in the centre of the hall something I did not understand until years later. 'Even little niceboys can be turned into savages.' He walked out, leather soles tapping, followed by the trainers, who dismissed us.

V157 yessed me, but I just said, 'You've no idea.'

We never mentioned V121 again. I got over him because I had to. Otherwise, I'd have gone mad. Besides, everything was happening so fast, our bodies were developing and changing, and we were learning so many new things about the world, and becoming so much stronger, there wasn't time to dwell on him.

When we started fencing bouts, Knox said, 'Think of your sword as an extension of your body.'

We didn't realize then how relevant those words were.

ELEVEN

Samina's place was in the basement of a low-rise DUB two deci-minutes on foot from the Reception Centre, where a new law stipulated they were to report daily to monitor their welfare.

'Isn't there a more convenient way into your home?' asked Irene.

'This *is* my home,' Samina said bitterly.

'Oh.'

'I think it used to be a storage space.'

'@ least it's got a roof,' Irene said, looking with dismay @ the dark rooms. Near the ceiling little horizontal slits acted as windows. The toilet and washroom were shared with other D-classifieds.

'This is where they re-located me,' said Samina. 'I've tried to make it cosy, but it'll never match up to our little house.'

She showed Irene a communal room lit by a wall-screen. A few andros were snoring on the floor, stinking the place out. But there was some light, and a bit more warmth. Outside, the North wind whistled its warning to stay indoors.

They returned to Samina's space and nibbled on the scraps they'd brought back.

When it got dark, they huddled up together with the light off cz of the cost. Being enclosed within concrete walls was preferable to standing around outside them, exposed to the nocturnal chill.

The next morning, Irene could barely see her way around in the gloom. She was stiff and frozen from sleeping on the hard floor, and struggled to get warm, breathing on her hands until blood began to flow back into her fingers.

Shivering uncontrollably, she hugged Samina. 'Let's go to mine,' she said. 'I'm on the twelfth floor and it's comfortable. I don't think I can take another night here. I'm sorry. There'll be plenty of room for you, and the walk should warm us up.'

'Are you sure it'll be all right?' To Irene's irritation Samina seemed to lack enthusiasm.

'Why shouldn't it be?'

Samina took a deep breath as if she was going to speak, but just shrugged and said, 'I dunno.'

The trek took eight deci-minutes, and they held hands, saying very little. Irene kept mumbling, 'Not too far now,' and glared @ the C-class Supastore she was no longer welcome @ and @ the autobus when it chugged past them, farting its stinking exhaust.

The thought of lying on a bed, having a warm bath and some tea filled Irene with renewed energy for the final part of the walk. The climb up to the artificial dwelling plateau was arduous and muddy and their shoes were soaked. The flood waters had largely subsided, however, and by a hopscotch-style dodge round the pools and puddles, they managed to arrive @ Soxbury Tower fairly dry from the knees up, but spattered with mud. After a night @ Samina's, her old C-class DUB was how Irene imagined a de-luxe Olympia Heights mansion block looked.

Irene swiped her new D-classified Eye-D card through the entrance slot.

Nothing happened.

'It does that sometimes,' she said, trying to reassure herself as well as Samina, and tried again.

Still nothing.

The third attempt started a high-volume alarm and a red light on the reader flashed.

'What's going on?' screamed Irene. A feeling of fear and helplessness rose up through her body.

A huge crowd of people fighting to board an autobus looked over. Blood flushed Irene's cheeks. She knew some of those gynos. But however much she waved @ them and called out, they ignored her, and all the time the alarm was doo-doo-dooing its contribution to the soundscape.

Then a neighbour turned up. A short, squat middle-aged woman with a wheelie-basket.

'Tara,' panted Irene, relieved to see a familiar face. 'Can you let us in? My Eye-D's not working.'

Tara frowned. 'What's up with it?'

'It won't unlock the door,' Irene said, trying not to snap, and brandishing the piece of dysfunctional plasticon.

Tara's eyes widened. 'But that's never gonna work. It's the wrong class.'

Tears of frustration welled up behind Irene's eyes. 'Tara, please, I lost my job. I'm begging you. Let us in. You know me.'

'Well, I...' Tara hesitated. 'I suppose...just this once. But don't say it was me, please. And don't talk to me once we're in. Infringing class regulations is yellowcardable. There's Eye-cams everywhere.'

'No, of course not. Thanks.' Irene was almost laughing with relief. Tara swiped her blue Eye-D and the alarm stopped. Tara went in and let the door close after her, but before it clicked shut Irene got her foot in, and waited a few seconds and then kicked it open again and entered with Samina. They climbed to the twelfth floor, making sure they were way behind

Tara.

'I'll have to sort this out @ the Reception Centre next time I report,' mumbled Irene.

Samina cleared her throat. 'Irene,' she started. 'Are you sure we'll be able to get into your unit with that?'

Irene didn't answer. She held her breath and swiped her Eye-D outside her apartment, but once again nothing happened. @ the third attempt the same alarm went off. Irene banged on the steelex door in desperation and frustration. Finally she slid down the closed door and sat on the floor, sobbing and smashing her fists on the linolicon tiles. Samina knelt down beside her and put her arm round her shoulder.

'It's what happened to me when I got relegated from B-class to C, and again...'

Irene shot her a fierce look. 'Why didn't you say, for fuxache?'

'I wanted to. Was going to. But somehow, you'd never have believed me. Just like I never believed the person who tried to warn me...besides, I'd rather be out than stuck in that cellar.'

Irene didn't move Samina's arm and they both remained on the floor, but started when they heard the draught excluders peel away and felt the door open behind them.

They leapt to their feet and found themselves facing a youngish andro in a blue torso-hugger and shorts.

'What the fuck's going on?' he asked. 'Why are you snogging on my front door?'

Irene felt her life collapse inside her. 'First of all, we ain't snogging, you shit. And second, this is my home.'

The force with which she answered made him step back and blink. 'Er, I think you'll find it's mine,' he said with a little laugh and added, '...now.' He flashed his blue Eye-D and swiped it on the locking device, silencing the alarm. And Irene.

'Come on,' said Samina, taking Irene's arm. 'Let's go.'

'No,' bawled Irene, struggling to free herself from her grip, but not succeeding, her red Eye-D still in her hand. 'This is where I live...what about my things?'

The andro shrugged his shoulders and frowned. 'Sorry,' he said, trying to soften his voice. 'I don't understand how you got in. But I was relocated here yesterday. I'll show you the verification on the wall-screen if you like. Your stuff'll've been recycled. It's all on FaceChirp®. Sorry. Now...if you'll excuse me...'

'Wait,' cried Samina. 'Her dashtag's been dissolved. Can't you see she's distraught? This was her home. Those were her possessions. Haven't you got a heart?'

'Of course I have,' he said, waving his arms to prove he did. 'And I'm really sorry for her distress, but this is really not a good time right now. There's a DUB supervisor on the ground floor. She might be able to help.' And he slammed the door shut in their faces.

Irene took some deep, jerky breaths, as her crying fit passed, and, arm in arm with Samina, walked back down in silence.

The supervisor, a sweaty fat gyno with her black hair pulled back so tight off her face her eyes were almost on the sides of her head, was busy. She clicked her tongue and made Irene and Samina wait outside for 2 deci-minutes, before checking Irene's red Eye-D.

'Your unit was disappropriated,' she said, without any emotion in her voice, apart from annoyance @ having her day disturbed.

'Nobody...'

'They should've told you.'

'But they didn't...'

The supervisor breathed out rapidly and grimaced, barely concealing her irritation and impatience. 'I'm not saying they did. They should have.' She fiddled with her screen, which was out of view. 'You'll have been re-located.'

'But I haven't.'

'Look,' snapped the supervisor, turning the screen round. 'I'll show you cz you're obviously not understanding.'

Irene read 'Re-located' and said, 'But I've not been given an address.'

The supervisor sighed in exasperation. 'Re-location means that unit's been assigned to another PAULie. It's done while you're @ the Reception Centre. You have to find your own D-classified accommodation. The Reception Centre is not a housing agency. Who let you in?'

Irene blinked back tears. This was too much to take in @ once. 'No one,' she said defiantly. 'Somebody — I don't know who — opened the door for themselves and I got my foot in before it closed. No one let me in.'

The supervisor nodded. 'Don't worry. I'll check the Eye-cam later when I've got a minute. Anything else, ladies?'

Irene and Samina exchanged a tense glance, and the supervisor waddled before them to the door, her arse and thighs billowing with each step like two wind-blown sails, and saw them out.

It was bitterly cold on the gale-swept plateau, and once more they hugged each other for comfort and warmth.

'Thank the powers-that-be I've got you, Samina.'

Samina nodded. 'Likewise.'

'I hope Tara'll be okay.'

'Will that bitch check the Eye-cam?'

Irene nodded. '@ least they won't be able to prove collusion, but they'll do her for lack of vigilance. She'll either be fined or sent on compulsory class-consciousness training. Unpleasant, but not the end of the world.'

'Isn't there anything we can do?'

Irene shook her head. 'Apart from warning her, no. We can't afford to contact her, plus I don't know how to, so it'd be a waste of time. And even that wouldn't help much. Our only hope is that the lardy cow'll be too lazy to check. Just talking to us made her feel she was being run off her feet, so she'll probably resent having to wind back an Eye-cam film upload.'

Samina smiled. 'If we jog, we'll get warm. There are still a few pieces of potato peel for lunch back @ mine...I mean, ours.'

Back in their cellar, Irene and Samina did what they could to protect their food from the rats and cockroaches scurrying over their faces and bodies @ night, and eventually accepted the inevitability of sharing their meagre provisions with other species.

With no job prospects in those first few days, which became weeks, Irene lost track of time.

TWELVE

Metamorphosis Phase One, done under coma-inducing anaesthetic, took several days. I came round to a new body and still emerging mind.

I was in a high-domed circular cell with three beds, but standing, attached to a rail above the bed. My symmetamorphs V157 and V158 were with me, both still unconscious. We were chained, hooked up and leaning forward.

As I examined my fellow-sphecos, the realization of what we'd become hit me.

Bald, shiny black and yellow heads, eyes set much wider, sculpted I-brows @ least a foot long, taut, quivering, crackling with current and static in the sterile atmosphere.

And *wings*...

Waist like an hour-glass, V157's thinner than V158's, bands of yellow on black.

Chitinex-plated torso. Metal-hard, but tender. Nerves still raw.

Twenty-pak abs.

A slit where once protruded a cock.

A wave of something beyond revulsion engulfed me. Nausea. Then fear. I trembled till my chains rattled. But I understood. And was overcome with pride, tempered slightly by shameful remorse.

I was strong. What I saw was power. Strength. Might.
And everyone knows what might means.

I was now V159. Full name Vespulist159.

Thanks to Knox's harnessing and channelling of Vespulism, aka Sphecanthropy.

DNA from past sphecanthropes gave him and his teams of labrats the answers. Long live the Mendoza Institute of Entomanthropy's Department of Sphecanthropy! And praise the powers-that-be for Latin and Greek, without which we would be unable to classify our discoveries with clarity and euphonics. And last, but not least, bless us niceboy misfits, without whom there would be no raw material to experiment on, and fashion wasp-men from.

In the days that followed we learned to walk again, to breathe and to feed @ the syngastrion, imbibing liquid nutrition through a tube attached to a mask. Food was pre-digested in the syngastrion tank — the communal stomach — breaking down the nutrients for our simplified, vespulized innards.

A lot was just blank. We touched I-brows and saw a white expanse we knew one day would be loaded with meaning. We learned to take off from the ground and kick backwards with our feet. We stayed airborne by swimming with our powerful webbed-arm wing membranes, creating robust currents beneath us that held us aloft.

The eye-watering, spine-tingling sensation of those first flights, the fear of falling and the exhilaration of realizing we wouldn't even when we trod air. All a distant memory now.

Phase Two followed. Everyone took great pleasure in telling us survival rates were still low. And even if you lived, there were more tests afterwards. Always a minor chord to darken the bright, cheery soundtrack of those first few days.

We called them 'hairdryers' even though we were all bald by then. There was a row of hollow, inverted, three-quarter steelex egg shapes, painted with glossy yellow and black stripes, above each seat. We'd take our assigned places and the 'hairdryer' would be lowered till it covered our heads.

Labrats fitted things to our temples. Professor O. B. Knox said, 'Open your blackbox.'

@ first I didn't understand.

Images of handsome young andros graced my Eyelid-screen. My new spheco-cock shot out from my dickslit.

Knox added, 'What do you feel about these guys, who are everything you ain't and have everything you don't?'

I realized I had to get turned on. Much as I fancied them, I hated them. It was they who were responsible for me sitting under the 'hairdryer', having elbowed me out of the early mating rituals so they could breed. I wanted revenge on their andro beauty for fucking me up.

My spheco-cock extended to its 24-inch limit. Unseen hands sheathed the tip inside what felt like plasticon tubing.

Jism stewed in my loin glands. Those masculine good looks filled me with rage, and that fury with desire. I knew what I wanted — own that savage handsomeness, make it love me, remove its threat that I so feared and loathed. And there was only one way to do that — turn their hated guts into the 'cunts' they thought I'd never want.

Without knowing how loudly, I screamed as cum gushed out into the tubing, which was removed, probably for analysis.

Admiring those tight, lean bodies and pretty-boy features, I was consumed by paralysing shame @ baring my soul. I saw how wrong it all was and hoped none of the trainers could read what I dreamt up in the 'hairdryer' cz there was no love in me, just hate, anger and bitterness, but as the 'hairdryer' was lifted and my eyes adjusted to the artificial light in the training room, my embarrassment faded and I accepted it all — my fate, my nature, and they unstrapped me and muttered great to each other, excluding me even though I was the subject of their monosyllabic discussion.

And then V130 panicked and broke out of his hairdryer, racing to find an exit, but as he yelled and banged on the locked door, a pair of green entomoid arms suddenly clasped him in their embrace.

I hadn't noticed this creature lurking, the same type that had taken V121, but now saw the spikes those raised forearms had concealed then.

V130 shrieked as the spikes crosshatched his thorax.

'Behold the farewell kiss,' said Knox, clapping his hands.

The entomoid tilted its head down, opened its huge mouthparts and sank fang-shaped jaws into V130's neck.

Knox addressed us all. 'Meet my elite guards. *Obknoxians*...named in my honour. Andro felonspawn spliced with mantis DNA, serving the BestcoeSecurity® sector. So, my advice to you is stay put and enjoy your time here.'

The obknoxian bit V130's head clean off his neck and dragged the impaled corpse away, chewing noisily.

Remembering V121, I wanted to scream, but that was when the technical problem occurred. Labrats scurried about, shouting unintelligible things to each other. I didn't know @ the time what was going on, but Knox was flushed, his eyes wide open. He was screaming @ the labrats, 'Sort the fucking power out before it's too late.'

Then the pain started. Just a burn @ first, but it grew till it was like a white-hot effigy of me had been forced into my skin. I stayed still to withstand it, and blackboxed my life, my memories, as the fire threatened to engulf them.

I concentrated, screwing my eyes more shut than they'd ever been, aware I was making a keening noise.

I shifted my blackbox somewhere, and something told me that was the solution even though it was forbidden.

I could see V158 writhing and hear him moaning. His pain

seared my eardrums. I kept thinking, 'Fuxache. Shut up!' He did. His head slumped forward onto his chest.

Labrats ran around, knickertwisting in panic.

Knox phewed, 'That was close.'

The alarm stopped. The pain amplified.

*Is this what death is like? Having a tooth pulled without anaesthetic, a rough twist, a yank and a crunch as the bone is split asunder...but...*you're *the tooth?*

They fingered me. Put their filthy machines on who I was, sullied my inner self, and erased my pride. So I could only embrace the future.

The machines whined to a halt. The pain throbbed into a memory. Knox came over, fiddled with V157, and tut-tutted when he palpated V158's face.

He stroked my cheeks, chest, waist. It was all new. He nodded and muttered to the labrat behind him, who typed something onto his hand-held screen.

The ordeal wasn't over yet. I had to be tested more. Knox kept looking @ me and whispering, nodding and smiling into my face, not @ me, but @ himself, his work. I wasn't included in that smile.

'Ready for Phase Three,' he said.

THIRTEEN

The shop was closed. No food till further notice.

Panic enveloped Irene and Samina.

What's going on? Why haven't we been warned?

As their initial shock gave way to resignation, they began to make out the cacophony of D-classified gynos shouting in the distance. Then silence. An authoritative gyno voice said something, followed by moaning.

Irene and Samina ran to the end of the concrete wall and, crouching down, peered round the corner. A group of Ds was draining through an entrance into a squat domed cube of a building, murmuring and wailing. They waited and watched, hearts beating like drums, each breath held as long as possible.

After a couple of deci-minutes, a few Ds came out and wandered away from the grimy walkway, probably back to whatever DUB cellar they'd been assigned to.

Irene looked @ Samina. 'They keep coming,' she whispered. 'They're not killing them.'

Samina shook her head, but her now-matted hair didn't fall in layers like it used to. 'I don't like it,' she mumbled back. 'Could be a trap.'

'They're all coming out. Maybe they're feeding them cz the shop's closed. Look, that one's wiping her mouth on her sleeve.'

'Yeah, but she doesn't look too happy.'

'@ least she's eaten. C'mon.'

Samina couldn't resist the enthusiasm animating Irene's face. 'Okay.'

The building wasn't as dirty grey as the surrounding edifices, and had obviously been assembled in the previous couple of days. It stood ten metres high in the centre of the broad precinct, and above the tunnel-shaped entrance were written the words:

D-CLASSIFIED SYNGASTRION
SPONSORED BY BESTCOE

Irene entered the dark interior. Samina followed.

'Eye-D!' barked a gyno voice.

They got out their red eye-shaped Eye-Ds for checking. It was difficult to see the gynocop in the murk, but she seemed plump with wispy black hair and a stubby nose.

'This is where you will report for feeding in future @ 27 and 77 deci-minutes daily. Understood?'

The gynocop waved them through into a dark chamber with a vaulted ceiling. Dominating most of the space was a huge, three-metre high metal vat, with step-ladders @ various intervals leading to platforms. Irene and Samina climbed up, quickly @ first, and then more gingerly when they saw the distance between them and the concrete floor, which would not spare their malnourished bones should they lose their footing on the slippery rungs and fall.

Reaching the top, Samina and Irene needed almost a whole deci-minute just to pluck up the courage to overcome their vertigo and stand upright on the narrow, unprotected platform.

They took deep breaths and tried not to look down. Steam bubbled out of the vat, which was filled with a viscous brown liquid. On the rim of the vat by each platform was a kind of mask with a tube extending from the mouthpart into the bubbling goo.

The gynocop stood below them. 'As it's your first time, I'll talk you through it. Don the mask and insert the tube into your mouth. Next to the nose is a button. Press that and food'll come into your mouth via the tube. A cooling device ensures you won't burn yourselves. Repeat the process until the portion control mechanism prevents you from overeating. The mask self-disinfects after each feed. Don't forget to chew each mouthful thoroughly. A water fountain's on the way out. Thank you for feeding @ your local Bestcoe D-classified Syngastrion®. Enjoy your day.'

Irene braced herself to bend over and grab hold of the mask. Straightening up took all her courage and concentration on keeping her balance. She fingered the mask. It was an uncomfortable fit and the eye rims scratched her face.

The tube tasted of BestcoeDisinfex® cleaning fluid and was also quite large, so her first reaction to inserting it into her mouth was to gag. She heard Samina having the same difficulties. Then she found the button, just over her right cheek and pressed hard.

A slurping noise followed, and a splattering of hot stuff like lumpy soup spurted into her mouth, surprising her so much that she almost choked. Irene wanted to spit out the tube, but it seemed that once it was inside and in operation, that was impossible. As was chewing. She wanted to scream, and run from that strange torture chamber and eat grass in a field, anything, but she managed to prevent the food from shooting down into her throat.

It had a cheap, meaty taste, and a spongy, gristly texture. She felt her gorge rising @ the sensation, but forced herself to swallow the lump of fatty tissue whole. It burned its way down, despite the cooling device, and the accompanying 'gravy' dribbled from her lips and tickled down her chin.

Too hungry to surrender to fastidiousness, Irene pressed the button once more, remembering to close her throat as the fodder shot out of the tube, scorching her tongue and gums. The volume of food in her mouth made it very difficult to swallow in small quantities. The overriding fear of choking rendered any enjoyment of this breakfast an unattainable dream.

The second mouthful had a stale, fishy savour and odour, although the scalding had deadened her tastebuds, but Irene was also aware of some limp vegetable matter in the mulch. She knew she had to keep this meal down. Otherwise, she'd starve.

Samina was groaning, like those other D-class gynos they'd seen earlier.

With fifty deci-minutes to supper, Irene pressed the button for a third mouthful, but nothing happened. That was her morning ration. She had eaten her fill, according to the syngastrion rules, and now was able to detach the feeding mask from her face.

Samina had already done so. From her foetal position on the platform, she eased one leg over the edge and felt for a foothold on the rungs.

Irene followed her, telling herself she'd get used to it and soon be able to shoot up and down the ladder and shut her mind off to the taste and just fill up to survive.

The descent got easier once she felt both her hands and feet secure, even with the distance between the rungs greater than comfort allowed.

On the floor @ last, she sighed with relief. The gynocop marched over and showed them the water fountain, which to Samina's greater dismay had a single tap, the top of which they had to put their mouth completely over to drink from. The water was rationed too, and the flow dried up after five gulps.

'The old foodstores were unhygienic,' said the gynocop as

if reading from notes. 'All D-classified citz will henceforth be sustained in these clean syngastria. They're being implemented nationwide by BestcoeBritain®.'

'What does syngastrion mean?' asked Irene.

The gynocop shrugged. 'All I know is, this is where you come now. A twice daily deduction is made on your Eye-D even if you turn up only once. You will find that due to the cost of creating these foodhalls, the amount debited is slightly higher than what you would have paid @ the old shop. But you'll agree two hot meals a day is more healthy.

'Thank you for breakfasting @ Bestcoe East Cockneytown D-classified Syngastrion®. Enjoy your day.'

With that she disappeared into the gloom, probably to process more newcomers, and left Irene and Samina to find their own way out.

As they emerged into dismal grey light, Irene realized that they too were moaning in disgust and wiping their mouths on their grubby sleeves.

The look of horror in Samina's eyes said everything. She buried her head on Irene's shoulder. 'Could only bear one gulp. Think I'm gonna be sick.' She walked a few steps away and threw up.

Irene shut her eyes tight, as the vomit splattered onto concrete.

'Sorry,' Samina gasped between coughing and spitting. 'I'll have to get used to it. I know. Or else...'

Irene put her arm round her. *How long will she last?*

FOURTEEN

Phase Three was a field trip to see if what happened in the 'hairdryer' could be replicated on the streets.

I knew from gossip that some sphecos had never responded to this part of the training. Rumours abounded of how difficult it was to get aroused when under intense nervous pressure. If the sight of androfelons didn't excite me with sexual hatred, I'd be discontinued.

My test was a youth mugging an older andro.

South East District 6, known locally as Cat Town, near a decaying infirmary and a complex of plasticon and vitreola buildings.

'Cash to pay for his next Deadly Sin,' Knox explained.

@ the sound of the name, FaceReader flashed up on my Eyelid-screen.

Sexually Intensified Narcotix, aka Sin. Illegal drug pushed by 'tempters', taken by 'committers', for whom it creates the illusion of fulfilling one's deepest desires.

Everything I'd been trained to feel I felt.

My hum crescendoed. Rage fizzed up @ this swaggering felon, and it all came clear in a blinding flash with an erection that risked unbalancing me as I flew towards him.

I landed, my spheco-cock spearing him between the shoulderblades and stabbing down deep into his burning entrails.

I held him still. 'I'm discontinuing you,' I gasped, thrilled to be his judge, jury and sexecutioner. 'Thanks to genetic cleansing,' I add, 'sphecanthropes are defelonizing BestcoeBritain® by sending scum like you straight to the Recycling Centres.'

He made a coughing, choking sound as I reclaimed from him the physical respect he and all his type owed me. My juice flowed and filled his cavities, the toxi-cum taking immediate effect.

He slumped, paralysed and still impaled on my sphecosting.

I buzzed and retrieved my spent cock. It bowelled back inside me, gore-stained, the blood remaining round my slit to be wiped up afterwards.

The older andro fled.

'Clean-up's arrived,' said Knox. 'Blattoids.'

Small chestnut-brown creatures, whose I-brows reached down to their knees, paid no heed to us, but set about their tasks.

Pop-up text filled my Eyelid-screen.

BESTCOE-MENDOZA INSTITUTE OF ENTOMANTHROPY
Training Manual Glossary Page 8

BLATTOIDS:

human-cockroach hybrids, highly efficient waste disposers. All clean-up teams are composed mainly of blattoids. Their life-spans stretch over several years.

Voracious, non-aggressive omnivores, they live in Recycling Centres, sewers and dumps.

I was shortbreathed from my orgasm. Applause filled my happy spheco-ears as the training inspectors gathered round to congratulate me.

'Superb, V159,' said Knox. 'You've passed your final basic test with full marks. Instinct was spot-on perfect. Mike Lagano'll be your ASLO — Androcop-Sphecoid Liaison Officer. We're recommending you be referred for the Spheco-Queenhood Aptitude Test.'

My mouth-parts broadened to a huge proud grin. Taking the SQUAT was an honour not given to every spheco. I breathed out heavily, exhausted by passion and physical effort.

I said nothing. Part of that runt Nelson still cowered in my blackbox. Somehow I knew that should remain my secret.

'Congratulations, V159.' Knox smiled. 'Your first felonburst-sex-e-q-tion.'

'Let's hope the first of many,' I panted.

The addiction was strong. It was a hunger that was only satisfied temporarily, a thirst slaked just for the moment.

But the irony of our new purgatory didn't escape me. We didn't want to fight when we were boys, but were condemned to spend the rest of our lives doing just that. And getting turned on by it.

'You see,' said Knox. 'Andros feel pain too, and are just as vulnerable as you were. That will be the hardest lesson you'll ever have to learn, given your erotic makeup.'

FIFTEEN

Irene heard their words loud and clear. They didn't realize she was outside the chamber. She'd got lost. The D-classified syngastrion was a confusing place.

In the crush of bodies queueing and fighting to leave she'd called out Samina's name, heard the reply, but the surge of Ds took her in a powerful current, and she got wedged up against a door.

In order to breathe, she opened it and slipped through into a dark corridor. She'd wait, panting, digesting her syngastrion lumps in peace, till the rush was over. So she sat on the cold, concrete floor, trying not to cry, until boredom replaced panic. She'd find Samina on the outside.

She got up and explored the blackness. There seemed to be doors... Voices. Andro voices. She groped her way towards them. They might help, tell her where the exit was, although deep down she doubted it.

Treading carefully so as not to make any noise, she came to a halt when she reached the room where the andros were talking.

She put her ear to the timberex-laminated door. From their words, she'd know whether they'd be friendly...or hostile.

'...streamlining plans underway for the foreseeable future,' went one voice. 'The D-classified syngastria trials have been a massive success. Not a whimper of protest.'

'So, will the extension plans be expedited?' asked another,

higher voice.

'Total C-class conversion is expected within the coming year.'

'What...the entire PAULie class?' asked a third andro.

'Mm, well, yes. Blue-collar syngastria — naturally we'll do trial runs in Geordietown, Scousetown and Brumtown before introducing them in Cockneytown, but the initial experiment in Jocktowns 1 and 2 went very well — exceeding all our expectations.'

There were sounds of approval, and a little applause. He continued. 'Bestcoe maintains that conversion to syngastria will allow it to close the C-class Supastores and concentrate on streamlining A-list and white-collar B-class food emporia.'

'But won't blanket Supastore closures mean mass disemployment?'

'Exactly,' laughed the first andro. 'Isn't that the desired outcome: constantly cleansing the gene-pool, refining our folkstock and reducing the population surplus? We can't have too much recycling...besides, we'll have to keep stoking up all the new syngastria, won't we?'

More clapping.

Cold sweat trickled down the back of Irene's neck and almost made her cry out. She was going to tiptoe back to the syngastrion chamber, when something caught her attention.

'And what will the Freebies make of this?'

There was silence followed by murmuring. 'Who cares about the Freebies? By the time they find out, we'll have implemented the syngastria conversions and presented them with a *fait accompli.*'

Freebies.

So they are *real.*

Like most C-class PAULies, Irene'd thought they were just a legend, something to dream about or be afraid of. Now she longed to know what else these unseen andros would reveal about them, but the voices were getting louder. They were approaching the door.

Holding her breath, she backed away on tiptoe, heart drumming a Satan's Garage bass line. The door clicked open and she flattened herself against the wall. Without moving her head, her eyes strained to the left.

In the wedge of light invading the corridor a line of young andros in black torso-huggers filed out. As they turned away from her, she exhaled with relief, controlling the flow of breath to keep it silent. She caught their excited chatter as they disappeared into the darkness to the door that would take them back to their white-collar silver-Eye-D world, away from the syngastria and scrounge-lounges.

When she was certain they were all far away, she walked to the end of the corridor, and snuck back into the syngastrion chamber.

'Where did you come from?' demanded a shrill gynocop.

Irene pointed to the door.

'Eye-D.'

She handed over the red eye. The gynocop checked it on her machine.

'Feed time?'

'77 deci-minutes.'

'It's 81 deci-minutes now. Account for the 4 deci-minutes.'

'I...I...'

'Well?'

'I was afraid I was gonna be killed in the crush. The door was open. I sat in the dark. Must have dozed off.'

The gynocop handed back the red Eye-D. 'Access to that door is prohibited. I'll have to report this infringement. It'll come up @ your next review. You might have four days removed from your three-month allowance. Understand?'

Irene nodded.

'Thank you for suppering @ the D-class syngastrion sponsored by BestcoeDisinfex®. Enjoy your day.'

Irene left, hiding her tears from the gynocop. Four days was a terribly high price to pay for straying into a corridor of power. The white-collars and silvereyes didn't want their plans getting out.

Samina hugged her when she told her what had happened. 'Sounds like the end of the world,' she said.

'No,' said Irene. 'Don't you see? Freebies — they're our only hope now. It's not the end. It's the beginning.'

SIXTEEN

Satan's Garage gig @ disco-duelling dances and flight-fights. Jaxxon Gobbs and Don Sauternes sing. Maxx Smacker deejays.

Tickets are a week's wage sold on FaceChirp®. The authorities welcome the bouts cz they keep the population entertained and weed out inferior males, thereby cleansing the gene pool of substandard DNA.

The only penalties are financial – to recover the cost of the smashed flight-fight cabs. The losers' families pay.

I'm in the SECOPS staffroom, still recovering from V161's discontinuation yesterday, which has made me worry more about my vivisexion and retroception. I'm also wondering where the fuck V157 is – he scrimshanked morning roll – when in strides Horelka and targets Mike, whose assignment was to inform the loser's next-of-kin in full by showing a video-record of how he died.

We watch day-old footage from Mike's headcam.

The video shows a DUB like any other: Maidstone Tower, South East District 9. People relocated from a place called Maidstone. Like my Soxbury.

The camera zooms in on a middle-aged gyno giving Mike a quizzical look as she opens the door and glances @ his Eye-D.

We listen to the audio.

'Ms Kamara?'

She nods. 'What is it? Something wrong?'

Mike pauses.

Horelka stops the film. 'Next time, Lagano, come straight out with it. Don't make an innocent Bestcoe customer — even a PAULie — stew. Play on.'

Mike clears his throat, on and off screen. 'It's about your son, Milo.'

Another pause.

'She'll have guessed the worst by now. You're torturing her needlessly. Continue.'

'I'm afraid there's been an accident.'

'Stop!' screeches Horelka. 'How many times, Lagano? It wasn't an accident. Don't you remember what I drilled you?'

Poor Mike swallows. His eyes dart round in embarrassment. We're all staring @ him. He shakes his head. 'Sorry, Sir. It all went when I was faced with the about-to-be grieving Mum.'

'Ms Kamara...' Horelka looks round the room, '...once you've verified her Eye-D, Lagano, which you didn't, I regret to inform you your son Milo has been discontinued in a flight-fight, and I am required by law to show you evidence of his death and retrieve certain costs for the loss of his flight cab.'

The film continues. Ms Kamara reels backwards and screams 'no' so loud the distorted sound hurts my delicate spheco-eardrums. She collapses sobbing onto the floor. Mike helps her to her feet and leads her into her cheaply furnished living space, where the truth about her son's demise is relayed on her wall-screen.

We see what she sees: the lens panning across the amphitheatre cut into the hills of South East District 18 to the Thames and beyond that, towering above the distant metropolis, Olympia Heights, home of Satan's Garage.

Instrumental dance music swells the twilight. The clear pink and blue sky is a-fading. Smacker's beat provokes clapping.

Close-up of Gobbs announcing the duel contestants: Milo

vs Ethan, both eighteen.

@ the sound of each name, wild cheers rise from the audience.

'People, Milo Kamara.'

A good looking young man in a black flight suit boards his flight cab, and, waving his sword, rises steadily, then executes figures of eight in the air above the crowd to hearty applause from one side, and deafening jeers and boos from the other. Gobbs laughs, and introduces his opponent, who manages a series of backflips and somersaults in the air, landing perfectly on his flight cab floor each time. Whoops and whistles of support from his faction are met with silence from the other.

Ethan is thin and sinewy. Something delicate and pretty in his fine features vies with deadly determination in his black eyes. His dark brown hair is tied in a ponytail.

Equipped with a steering gearstick and overhead propeller, the flight-cab is a plasticon disc, large enough for the fighter to stand on.

'And now, people, the nubo prize.' Gobbs's voice silences the crowd.

A young gyno, still a pubo, flies up alongside Gobbs and hovers in her cab. Screens around the amphitheatre show her silver-streaked dark hair, lightly made up face and blue tunic.

'Who do you want as your champion, Milo or Ethan?'

'I will have,' she husks, 'the victor as my champ. May the best andro win!' And as her voice rises, she tosses a flimsy turquoise scarf into the space. It floats down.

Milo grabs it and winds it round his neck.

That's the signal for the fight to commence.

They fence about ten metres in the air. Rhythmic clapping and name-chanting wells up from the crowd. I marvel @ the skill displayed by these boys — wielding a sword in their right hand while piloting the flight cab with their left.

'To the death.'

Gobbs cries those words, and starts the eponymous song. The lyrics are audible despite the extra amplification and the noise from below.

> *I'll ensure survival, by runnin' thru' my rival*
> *That's what my sword'll do*
> *You will be my luvver, I don't want no other*
> *With sweet kisses I will smother you*

On the screen, the number 72,106 flashes the number of spectators.

While the song's playing and the youths are jousting in the air, Ms Kamara's covered her eyes with her hand and is shaking her head, wailing 'No, no.'

Milo manages to slash part of Ethan's white flight-suit wide open, to gasps from down below, but the other swordsman flies past him and, grabbing hold of the nubo's scarf, pulls it from his neck, prompting cheers.

Milo cries out in despair. Bad omen. The movement almost throttles him and sends him into a five-metre spin-dive. He ascends again, full of rage, and strikes out with his sword @ Ethan, who dodges the blow, drops a few metres and suddenly rockets up, his sword vertical.

The song's coming to its end.

> *To the death! His last breath!*
> *I prevailed, my opponent's impaled*
> *'Twas heated, he cheated but he got defeated*
> *To the death! His last breath! To the death!*

And so's the duel.

Ear-splitting gasps burst from everyone as Ethan's sword

enters Milo's lower abdomen, and erupts bloodied from the centre of his back.

Milo lets out a scream of pain and drops his own weapon, which partly buries itself in the soft sand. Ethan keeps his hand on the hilt and begins to descend, ripping the steelex blade out of Milo as he swoops down.

Unarmed, demoralized and mortally wounded, he desperately tries to fly himself back to the ground. Gripping his wheel with both hands, head slumping forward, grimacing in agony, he's unable to prevent Ethan slicing through the propeller stem with one deft stroke. For a split second, Milo hangs in the air, and then plummets ten metres.

As Milo falls, Ethan soars up to the music platform and disco-station and scoops up the squealing nubo into his strong arms.

Raucous applause bursts forth from the auditorium as Ethan flies a lap of honour, holding her up with one arm round her tiny waist, his other hand brandishing the blood-stained sword he's wrenched from Milo's spent humo-guts.

His flight-cab on auto-circuit, Ethan then clasps her tighter towards him, and when they're so close their lips are touching, he starts pumping his hips in and out.

She screams with delight. Their microphones relay the heavy breaths, groans and cumshrieks of their mid-air shag.

The crowd goes wild as they descend like large snowflakes, one hand out to acknowledge the adoration they have won. As they land on the ground, someone's voice gets picked up on the loudspeaker system.

'Clear that mess up now.' A cleaner points @ Milo's corpse, disgust and contempt etched onto his twisted mouth

Ms Kamara swears @ the wall-screen and looks away. Mike goes to pat her arm in sympathy, but is in a lose-lose situation. She shrugs away from him.

'Fuxache, man,' she screams into his face. 'Turn that shit off this minute, you hear?'

He does what she asks. I feel for both her and Mike, and the kid Milo.

But my sympathies don't last. If you wanna survive, you gotta switch off your sensitivity fast. No place for circumprehension here. Empathy's a lethal vice.

I don't hear the victory speeches, cz I'm watching Ms Kamara lying face down, banging her hands on the floor till they bleed, and Mike trying to calm her. After a while, he gets her to sit up, and fixes her a drink.

She's crying.

He writes out a form, which he makes her look @.

'Ms Kamara, this is a demand for 1,408 Britz for the non-accidental destruction of a BestcoeSportz® flight-suit and cab. You do not have to pay now, but each day you delay will add one Brit to the bill. I'm sorry for your loss. Enjoy your day.'

Horelka stops the film playback.

The screen pauses on an image of Jaxxon Gobbs, whose rainbow-glo halo-cut coiffure has been teased out from his head like the rings of Saturn.

When will these celebrities ever learn? I wonder if anyone has ever counted the layers of dye in his fucked-about hair.

Lights shine through his sparse halo, and the lumino make-up he's sporting accentuates his excellent bone structure and sucked-in-cheek look. He's so skinny one exhalation from a spheco-cop would blow him over.

Horelka's voice jolts me back to reality. 'Neat finish, Lagano.'

Mike looks sick. 'Really? I hated doing that. I...I'll never be able to get that image of her outta my mind, and then me being so insensitive.'

Horelka puts his face real close to Mike and looks him in the eye. 'But that's the recommended behavioural code, Lagano. It promotes social cohesion. Sure, it's a bad day for Ms Kamara, but she knows exactly where she stands.'

'Her partner was D-classified last year, sir,' says Mike. 'She was relying on Milo for support. Her younger son's delinquent. She could go D herself. It's a lot of money for someone like her.'

'That's just the way it is. It's Milo's recklessness that's @ fault here. We can only afford to support those who can support themselves, I'm afraid, tough though that is. We're all starting to see the benefits in BestcoeBritain®.'

Mike nods, unconvinced. Poor bastard. That'll gnaw @ his conscience for the rest of his sorry humo life. However, Horelka hasn't finished highhorsing him.

'You redeemed yourself, Lagano, but I'm gonna award you a borderline on that one, cz of your initial knickertwisting. Good, firm finishing though. Work on those nerves, and curb those qualms. Hope this has been useful, everyone. Lagano, I'm afraid you'll have to repeat the exercise before I can approve your completion of this Training Module. You're on probation.'

Mike stares @ the floor.

I sympathize, but what's really bugging me is V157. I know he attended V161's discontinuation cz we left together, and Mike's headcam footage showed him, V103 and V146 assisting the androcops @ the flight-fight, but I ain't seen him since. And now Horelka's mentioning ongoing inquiries into a SECOPS Sin-theft...

I search the timberyard, syngastrion, excretorium and Combs. I check the rota. Not on duty. Means only one thing. And I'll take the rap.

SEVENTEEN

They were moved further west, to special fenced-off quarters, where D-classifieds could eke out their Brit-free lives in condemned Victorian terraces.

It was in a dingy basement in East Cockneytown District 6 that Irene and Samina found shelter.

A few houses still remained in the nameless terrace, easily accessed from the front and back entrances. Littering the ground were shards of real glass and fallen masonry, spears of broken furniture further lethalized with large rusting nails protruding @ various angles, and rotting beams of timber with deadly splinters all vying to impale human flesh.

They were pushed through a cellar door, down the steps and groaned @ the bumps and bruises. This was home now. Worse than Samina's place.

Their new syngastrion was a two deci-minute walk away. The gynocop made Irene and Samina wait hours before allocating their feeding times.

'@ 25 and 75 deci,' she said. @ 79 deci. 'Come back tomorrow.'

They went hungry.

Irene no longer bothered to check how many Britz she still had in her account. She was sure she'd lost those four days, but the gynocop revealed nothing.

There was an andro in their D-classified compound she caught gogging @ her, and who looked away whenever their eyes met.

Samina noticed him too. 'You've pulled.'

They both burst out laughing.

The next day, he stepped down into their cellar, startling them.

'Don't be afraid.' He was about Irene's age. Grime had encrusted the lines in his scarred and once handsome face. 'I'm Garcia.' Barbs of light lasered through a tiny grille in the wall, dappling his muscly chest as he stood in their trajectory. He held out his hand.

Irene shook it, and so did Samina.

'Thing is,' he said, 'we need gynos to pick apples.'

'Why gynos?'

'Raids can come any time. Andros climb up there, the sphecoids'll get 'em, know what I mean? We all hate them spheco-freaks, don't we?'

Samina nodded, and Irene copied her, unsure where this was heading.

'But they don't menace gynos,' he said. 'So, you'll be safe. We got an old ladder lying around somewhere. One of you holds it, the other goes up. Easy.'

Garcia had a mate called Heathcote, who took Irene and Samina out @ night. The tree was the other side of the fence.

The tannoy crackled into life. 'It's zero deci-minutes 12 am accu-time for those...'

Overhead flew sphecoids and on the ground, cop sirens whined. In distant DUBs, someone screamed and muzak boomed. Around the compound loomed searchlights emitting a greenish luminescence.

'I've almost forgotten what it was like being part of that out there,' said Samina, pointing into the distance.

Heathcote was wiry like Garcia, and carried his end of the

rusty ladder with one hand and a bucket with the other.

He can't be more than twenty. Irene and Samina took the other end of the ladder and crunched through the rubble.

Progress was slow. Irene's hands burnt under the weight. Samina kept complaining and losing her grip. Eventually they got to some branches overhanging their side of the fence, against which they leant the ladder.

'They're Bramleys,' said Irene. 'Where do you cook them?'

Heathcote looked nonplussed. 'We don't.'

'Aren't they sour?'

'You get used to it. Better than that syngastrion shit.'

Samina held the ladder steady for Irene. 'Not great with heights.'

As Irene began climbing, Heathcote said, 'Not so fast. The tree's outta our D-zone. We could be arrested for class-crime. Look!'

When Irene examined the adjacent searchlight, she started. 'It's *alive*,' she said. 'It's got...eyes...under its...*mouth*. What the fuck...?'

'Arselights,' whispered Heathcote. 'Upside-down entomoids...hasn't spied us...*yet*...but if it sees us redcarding, it...*alerts* the cops.'

'So, how do we get the apples?' asked Samina.

Heathcote scooped a handful of earth and gave it to Irene. 'Stuff this in its gob to silence it.'

'Does it speak?'

'Don't let it see you.'

Struggling to control her breathing, Irene reached the top of the ladder, between the tree and the arselight, above the eyes. Not daring to look directly @ it, she groped for the mouth, cringing @ the touch of living flesh.

Something twitched and opened. Without hesitating, she

crammed the clod of soil in.

The creature writhed and hummed in discomfort, trying to eject the dirt.

'How long before it...?' asked Irene.

'Dunno. Gotta work fast.'

Irene stretched towards the tree and grabbed the nearest apple. Her fingers sank into a squelchy bit, but the fruit came away easily.

She couldn't help taking a bite. The tartness speared her neck glands, but the sensation of eating real food made her giggle. She threw the apple down to Samina.

It was when she reached for another apple that the arselight's three legs nearest her seized her round her waist. She screamed.

With great effort, she managed to prise them off forcefully enough to hurt the thing.

Suddenly, Samina yelled, 'Quick! It's spitting out the...'

As soon as Irene was free, she descended the ladder, two rungs @ a time, jumping the last three and bruising her foot.

Then they heard the hiss.

As all the compound arselights took up the alarm, cop sirens sounded. Brakes screeched. Boots pounded on concrete. Androcops everywhere.

'Run!' Heathcote dropped the bucket and ladder.

Irene's heart was drumming as they reached a house.

Garcia stood @ the door, holding a knife. He looked left and right and pulled Irene and Samina inside. 'Find somewhere to hide,' he whispered, and grabbing Heathcote, raced out into the street.

Irene led Samina to the upper storey, their plasticon footwraps crunching over shards of vitreola and rubble in what remained of the hall. Irene winced @ the stink of sewage and ash. They took the stairs, two @ a time and marched into what was once the front box bedroom, but was now roofless.

The floorboards creaked, and Irene feared @ any time they could give way, and they'd plummet fifteen feet to broken legs and their end. So they tiptoed gingerly to the side of the window and peeped out.

Androcops in black torso-hugger uniforms were dragging a group of a dozen or so men into a cylinder van about twenty yards away. In fours, the cops hurled these guys into the windowless back of the vehicle.

No sign of Garcia and Heathcote.

Irene flinched @ each scream as flesh bruised and bones cracked on impact, and winced as the van's motor revved up and the stench of faeco-fuel wafted up. The stink penetrated the already fetid air, and they moved back from the window, and retraced their steps across the wonky floor to the stairs.

Our day will come too.

EIGHTEEN

Cleaners found Jaxxon Gobbs, foetal, in the bloodstained arena.

'Throat slit,' says Mike Lagano, draining the dregs of something in a plasticon cup. Caffeinola®, knowing him. Keep telling him to cut down but he won't listen.

The felony occurred on our patch, so investigating his murder's our job, but sphecos mainly do the dirty work. Not allowed to be involved in inquiries.

@ first, Mike noways my participation. 'You know the regulations, V159.'

'But I can contribute. I got a hunch.'

'Which is?'

'Can't say till I'm sure,' I improvise, and start humming the dumb tune of *Disco Disco Discontinuation*.

'Hey, I never knew you sphecos liked muzak.' He smiles his wistful humo-smile.

'Love it. So, your first call?'

'Remember the flight-fight loser, Milo Kamara? His brother's wanted for petty theft, minor felonies. May have a grudge against Gobbs for singing @ Milo's death. I oughtta stop by, ask him a couple of questions, gauge his reaction. Check up on the mother and ask to see her other son.'

I tail Mike's car in the air right up to Ms Kamara's DUB.

He turns and sees me swooping towards him, his face an

icon of shock and anger. 'Thought I vetoed this, V159?'

I land. 'But...I got an idea.'

'An *idea* is it now? What happened to your hunch?'

'Oh, c'mon, Mike. Wanna help, cz we're mates. You're my ASLO.'

Footsteps from inside. A door-chain rattles.

'Fuxaches,' hisses Mike. 'Too late. We gotta present a united front. Earplay it. Keep your spheco-gob shut and let's pray she don't complain.'

'If she does, I'll fess up. Promise.'

He winks. I reciprocate with a northbound thumb.

Ms Kamara nearly faints when she sees me.

'What's the sphecoid doing here?' She backs away.

'It's all right, Ms Kamara. Just routine. He's not...'

'I paid that money yesterday,' she shouts. '1409 Britz. It'll be on the system. You can check if you like. What more do you want from me?'

'It's okay.' He's hushing her, reassuring her in his firm but gentle way, calming her down without telling her to. 'We know. I haven't come about that. I just wanted to see how you were getting on. You were very upset the other day. Understandably so.'

She shakes her miserable humo-head. 'What do you care about how I'm coping? All you want is my money.'

'No. I want to make sure you're managing.'

She clicks her tongue and doesn't invite us in.

'So, how *are* you coping?'

Obviously, not very well, judging from her jumpiness and puffed up eyes. Mike does all the talking. I just observe.

'I'm sure your other son'll be looking out for you.'

She closes her eyes and bangs her fist on the doorframe. 'You talking about Olivier? I'll be discontinued before that good-for-nothing lifts a finger to help his poor old mother.'

She's crying now, tears of rage and grief.

'I'm sorry to hear that. You want me to have a quiet word with him?'

'If you can find him.'

'Isn't he @ home?'

'He's gone again, officer. Left.'

'He's done this before?'

'Always coming and going.'

'No forwarding address...or dashtag?'

Her face a sky of storm clouds now. 'Don't you have that on your database? You seem to know everything else about us. How come you can't find Olivier?'

'I'm afraid we don't have that info.'

'That's a first.'

He ignores the barb. 'When did he leave?'

'Not sure. Could be three, four days ago. Or more. Ain't seen him since.'

'No idea where he could've gone? Any friends he'd contact?'

She shakes her head. If she knows, she ain't telling us.

I fly back to SECOPS. Mike drives.

I go to the Combs to prepare for night-shift, pondering the fate of Jaxxon Gobbs, 20, muzak-star darling of Olympia Heights.

V157 scrimshanks roll again.

The pop-up flashes on my Eyelid screen.

Data Tracker communication
21 deci/ 5.02.24-5.16.47 a.m. accu-time.
V157 officially missing, possibly in South East District 18.
As Queen, V159 is responsible for V157's arrest and the discontinuation process initiation.

I need to find him before they do, but fresh news on my Eyelid-screen freezes my spheco-blood. V157'll have to keep.

NINETEEN

Like a grimy orange nuke, dawn mushroomed over Cockney-town's horizon. Irene was already in the street savouring the silence. The autumn air was cold. She shivered in her torn torso 'n' thigh huggers. Samina would soon be out looking for her, but Irene wanted to cherish every last second of solitude.

She squatted on the stone ground and enjoyed the now yellowing sunrise transforming even the bare concrete DUBs outside the D-class compound into gold bars. She'd always loved this time of day, when George was around and Nelson was a little boy, before he...she quickly put that thought out of her mind. The past was over. Nothing she could do about it. Nelson was what he was. George got D-classified. Never came back for her.

George. He must've wanted to forget, to start afresh. The bastards set you up somewhere else, didn't they? New name, new Eye-D. Perhaps it was a felony to make contact with the old life. Had to be why he'd never got in touch all these years. That was what they said, anyway, the brightsiders. The others, well, there'd always been rumours and scaremongering. Didn't do to think the worst.

BestcoeBritain® cares.

BestcoeBritain®'s eradicating poverty, isn't it?

Sirens der-derred. The crunch of boots. Irene spun round.

Three gynocops in pink plasticon uniforms.

'Fialka, Irene?' asked the oldest gynocop, aiming a headcam @ her. 'BestcoeDisinfex® Medisquad.'

Irene's eyes opened wide as she took in the unsmiling faces of the younger gynocops. 'It's not my time. My three months aren't up yet.'

The gynocop smiled. 'Don't worry, Fialka, Irene. It's just a routine check in the wake of a new outbreak.'

'What outbreak?'

'Human foot-and-mouth. Withertongue.'

Weighing up what she should say, Irene stared @ the gynocop.

'Fourteen cases in this district yesterday. It's a precautionary measure. Been feeling underweathery?'

Irene shook her head.

'Eye-D?'

Irene handed her red plasticon eye over for inspection. One of the sullen gynocops scanned it with a device and whispered something to the other surly one. The cheerful gyno returned the Eye-D.

'Wait here.'

'Is everything alright? Is this a new strain?'

'This won't take long.' Leaving Irene, who was trembling uncontrollably now, under the supervision of the other gynocops, she headed towards the shell of their house and her chunky body disappeared inside.

'What's she gonna do?' Irene asked, looking @ both the gynocops in turn, but there wasn't so much as a twitch on those faces.

A few moments later, the older gynocop emerged from the paneless bay window with Samina. 'East District 6,' she said on her Eye-phone. 'Two full-term D-classifieds.'

Irene opened her mouth wide with outrage. 'We're not...we've still got a couple of weeks.'

The gynocop nodded, sympathy oozing from her smile-lined eyes. 'Sure. But this...' she pointed to her Eye-cam, '...says you are.'

Still sleep-dazed, Samina shook her long, matted hair. 'The dates are on our Eye-Ds.'

'You will come with us.'

Irene and Samina exchanged a nervous glance.

'But we've got a review @ the Reception Centre tomorrow,' protested Samina.

'All taken care of. This is your review.'

'No,' screamed Irene.

'This way, please.'

Irene and Samina's backs were up against the crumbling Victorian walls. They were outnumbered, cornered. *Nowhere to run.* With a shrug they allowed the gynos to lead them to a black metalex box on wheels.

The two young gynocops sat next to them in the windowless back. Samina and Irene soon felt sick from the turning motion, but had little inside them to chuck up. In the darkness, the only sound was retching and gagging.

The D-classified Recycling Centre, a filthy, five-storey, grey-brick building with no windows, stood opposite the identical D-classified Reception Centre they knew so well.

After a single deci-minute, they were pushed out onto the road, grateful the ride was over. Their eyes readjusted to the pink daylight, so beautiful now, and their bodies got re-accustomed to the lack of motion.

There was a long queue of about two hundred gynos tailing out of the Recycling Centre, some just waking up. Andros were taken round the other side, stewarded by androcops.

The young gynocops took their places in the patrol. The older one lit a smoke-stick and drove off.

'This is wrong,' Irene whispered to Samina. 'We've still got a fortnight.'

Samina nodded. 'We'll just have to explain there's been a mistake. They've got to let us go. Besides, that smirking bitch wouldn't let me bring any food with me. I'm starving.'

'Here.' Irene halved the last bit of apple peel she'd been fondling in her pocket.

'Queue's not moving,' grumbled Samina, as she nibbled.

A few moments later a collective gasp made them crane their necks to look up @ the sky, where a figure was hovering.

'Fuxaches, Irene, what's a sphecoid doing here?' Samina swallowed the last morsel of peel. 'This is gyno-only.'

Irene shook her head. Ragged, dishevelled gynos in front were pointing and murmuring.

The sphecoid landed in a graceful crouch about thirty yards from the back of the queue and stood up straight to his full height, searching with his saucer-sized black eyes, long-lashed domes of precious stone encrusted into the sides of his bald jaundiced head.

A sphecocop. Sphecanthrope. Everyone knew who they were and what they did, but harassing gynos was not one of their misdeeds.

What's he looking for, probing with those twitching I-brows?

The queue backed away as he stepped closer, the shadow of his naked, hour-glassed powerhouse body falling on a couple of cowering gynos.

There was no escape, even though gynocops were still patrolling in pairs. The sphecoid's I-brows resonated with a faint hum and pointed in the same direction, towards Irene, whose face screwed up as if she was going to cry.

She staggered back.

Samina stood protecting her from the sphecoid's slow advance. 'We haven't done anything. We're D-classified.

We've nothing to give you. Leave us alone.'

Her voice trembled with fear, but she never took her eyes off the sphecoid, who considered her for a moment before speaking.

'Don't be afraid,' he said. 'Ain't gonna harm you.'

Two gynocops rushed over, pointing their buzzing Eye-cams @ the sphecoid.

Irene heard them exchange words and caught something about a felon. The sphecoid rotated his head 180 degrees and the gynocops moved away. He turned his attention back to the queue.

Samina was still shielding Irene, who was shaking her head and gibbering, 'Please, no. It can't be.'

He took a step forward. 'I don't have much time,' he whispered to Irene, who was staring @ him in horror. 'There ain't no felon.'

'What do you want of me?' Her voice quivered.

He only managed to mumble the one word.

It was enough.

'Mum?'

TWENTY

I see her and my heart dies.

She's joined the queue trailing round the dirty brown-bricked corner, dwarfed by the Recycling Centre walls.

The gyno entrance. Some'll've been waiting all night, their freezing breaths like harbingers of mini-souls leaving the moribund. There's no movement, just endurance, expectancy, hope.

A couple of gynocops keep these colour-drained, defeated people in order. Do they know what D-class expiry means?

The breeze ruffles her greying hair. She's staring straight ahead.

Been monitoring her movements on Mike's system. *Do they suspect I know my true Eye-D now, and are tracking me in turn?*

The gynocops haven't clocked me lurking over the road, or if they have, aren't too bothered by the presence of a spheco, and are some distance from her. I have to take my chance.

But two intervene, pointing headcams @ me. 'Sphecoids do not deal with gynos,' says the taller one. 'Go now, or I contact your ASLO.'

I clear my articulated spheco-throat. 'Chasing a dangerous andro felon,' I improvise, 'Sin tempter and killer I believe is hiding nearby.'

A murmur of alarm spreads through the queue. The gynocop, however, registers no emotion.

'Wait for veracity check,' she barks.

'And lose the felon?' I lean down close and stroke her peaked cap with my I-brows. 'My Eye-pods,' I say, indicating my I-brows with a casual flick of my black and yellow fingers, 'sense he's here. Do you wish to obstruct a criminal investigation, gynocop?'

She backs off, frowning when I spit out the last word.

'Permission to search granted under Rule 253,' she mutters, deep resentment in her voice, and turns her back on me. The gynocops tune into their Eye-cams and waddle off like pink leatherette ducks as the pop-up flashes.

BESTCOE-MENDOZA INSTITUTE OF ENTOMANTHROPY
Department of Sphecanthropy
Training Manual and Rule Book Page 556

Rule 253: Concerning interaction with female humans (gynos):

Sphecoids are not allowed any form of intercourse with gynos, except where this assists the interception of an andro (male human) felon, or in the course of procedural and investigative discussions with colleagues in the female police force (gynocops).

All gyno-sphecoid communications must be logged to check for possible sphecoid dysfunction.

Infractions of Rule 253 are considered yellowcardable and can be disciplined by the spheco-queen or the swarm's androcop sphecoid liaison officer (qv ASLO).

Out of the corner of my spheco-eyes I see another gynocop-pair approaching.

Mum.

My voice is just breath. Perhaps she hears me. Recognizes

me even. Her friend's shielding her from me, but I see the bitterness in her hazel eyes tightening her lined face. I think she's gonna yell @ me, but she shakes her head and pulls her worn, beige jacket tighter round her skinny shoulders. I notice two of the buttons are missing.

'Go back to your friends,' she says wearily, and looks away, as if I'm not there, searching for the front of the queue. Her quiet words are like a knife.

I stand there like an idiot, speechless. My spheco-eyes burn and my spheco-throat constricts. I want to pour my heart out, tell her I'll help her escape, that it isn't my fault and I can't help what I am. But the words won't come, and each time I make them up in my head they dissolve. I cup my hands over my face as the tears flow and my I-brows droop.

She turns to face me again, the hatred and resentment in her eyes a shotgun blast, and pushes me away. Not a forceful shove, just a gesture. Enough to reject me, to say everything. As she does this, the queue starts to edge forward a little. The phlegmy sky is as bright as it can be on such an autumn day. I retreat, and fresh tears sear my eyes.

The gynocops are coming back. I gotta do something. Think on my spheco-feet. I grab her arm. 'Come with me.'

She shrugs herself free, just as the two new gynocops run up.

'What's going on?' asks one while her colleague Eyephones through.

'Episode @ Recycling Centre. Sphecoid interfering with queue.'

'No!' I yell in desperation. 'I'm just...'

I want to assert myself, but gynos don't arouse sphecos. I'm one big, clunking, useless entomoid in their hands. Oh, they're smart. They got it all sussed, and know exactly how to overpower a spheco. We never succumb to a gynocop's charms. Other gynocops materialize, dunno how many, and hold my arms behind my back. I struggle to free myself, but am totally immobilized.

Mum flashes me a look of contempt and chizzes the gyno-cops, who are now marching me away from the queue.

I keep howling. 'Let me go.'

But they aren't listening.

'Don't go in there, Mum. It'll be the end.'

I remember V161.

She just shakes her head again and turns her back on me as though she's died in front of me, deliberately, with nothing resolved between us.

With a cry of despair, I watch as the queue disappears through the doors into the grey-black hole @ the foot of the breeze-block monster and the gynocops frogmarch me away.

Convulsed with sobbing now, I have no idea where the gynocops are taking me, and I don't care. I can no longer see Mum, or the Recycling Centre.

We're in a narrow street with tall buildings on either side, and I'm still being led backwards. The gynocops say nothing. After a deci-minute, they release me.

Spheco-knees a-trembling with guilt, grief and fear, I sneak back to SECOPS, expecting arrest, interrogation, incarceration and worse, but instead am confronted with the sight of Mike Lagano eating a sandwich @ the reception desk. A sweet wave of relief sweeps over me like a gentle breeze on a sweltering day.

'Had a report on you, V159,' he says without looking up.

'Mm.' My entomoid half takes over and earplays.

'Says here...' He swallows his mouthful and points to his screen. '...you've been interacting with gynos.' His large brown eyes make me wanna tell the truth. Well, some of it.

'I thought I saw a Sin Tempter near the Recycling Centre.'

He shakes his head and takes another bite of his sandwich. Animal product. I can see it. And smell it. But I wouldn't be able to taste it. Not the way he can. Not any more.

'You do realise what will happen *if* Horelka finds out?'

I smile.

'Chizz, Mike.' I really want to confess, but stop myself. Don't wanna burden him with all that shit. He's got enough family problems of his own from what I've read between the lines on his face. 'I tried to explain, but you know what gyno-cops are like.'

He rolls his eyes up to the ceiling and finishes his sandwich. 'One of Fraser's mob?'

I nod, hating myself for deceiving him. He doesn't deserve that.

He whistles. 'I should let Tony know...'

The sound of a plan backfiring. Last thing I want is Horelka involved. But coldfooting it looks suspicious. 'Sure,' I say, voice neutral. 'What do you think he'll do?'

Mike shrugs his shoulders and starts munching an apple. 'Dunno. Send in some androcops, or get you to take the swarm.'

My heart belly-flops onto the freezing surface of a deep, dark stormy sea.

'Suppose you'd better track Fraser down first,' he says, his mouth now full of chewed-up light green fruit pulp. 'I'll tell Horelka thanks to you we may have a lead on Fraser's gang. Who knows, V159, you might make the old bastard smile yet.'

As I leave, he's Eye-phoning Horelka and wiping crumbs off his desk.

Alone in the Combs, I check my pop-up-bombed Eyelid screen. My heart sinks into that tempestuous sea.

V157 tracked to South East District 2. Linked to stolen Sin. Scrimshanking is discontinuable.

Why are they blindeyeing this?

The answer comes immediately. But from whom...Horelka? Knox?

V159 — apprehending V157 may mitigate your own redcardable spheco-crimes: non-ACEing of proven felon, retroceptive blackboxing and offside androguard vivisexion.

TWENTY-ONE

They'd chosen him on the coldest day of the year. Irene had gone for him. That afternoon she'd never forget.

They should've told me sooner. Eye-phoned or chirruped.

She wrapped herself up and walked briskly down the road to the school. Soxbury Ness C-class Primary.

He'd never been the first out; he was usually one of the last kids to leave those cast iron gates. The wind howled through the playground, escaping from its trap behind the new blocks.

'It's too cold to snow.'

One of the other mums.

Irene nodded. She didn't know her name. And it was too cold for casual talk.

A few flakes and flurries had floated down earlier, but the clouds were constipated.

'Hurry up, Nelson,' she moaned, stamping her feet to keep warm. Years five and six were coming out now. She recognized some of them as they ran shouting past her into the street, or greeted mums like her, who took them by the hand and led them over the road to the small terraced cottages opposite, identical to Irene's further up.

Year three appeared at last. Irene's heart quickened in anticipation. It always did just before he walked over to her and she'd hope to hear all about his day, although he usually just shrugged and said nothing.

She knew these children. They didn't return her smiles or

waves. *Too excited, no doubt.*

'Oh, where is he?' she muttered, rubbing her hands furiously to bring some blood back into them. The last trickle of year threes had long stopped and years one and two had begun to emerge together with some of the teachers.

Perhaps he'd been naughty and was being detained. *They'll be out to tell me. Better still, I'll go in to enquire. I'd rather wait inside. It'll be warmer.*

'Fialka, Irene?'

She looked round. Nelson's teacher was addressing her.

'This way, please.' He led her into the main building.

Irene breathed a sigh of relief. *Detention. Heating.*

'What's he been up to?' She tried to make out it was just a bit of a joke, that naughtiness was adorable really, but deep down was a well of doubt — not like Nelson to misbehave.

'This won't take long.'

In the office Irene entered stood the teacher, an androcop and a gynocop.

@ the sight of police, Irene panicked. 'Oh, Nelson! What's happened?'

They calmed her down and made her sit on a child's chair. The grey walls seemed to press in on her, crush the air out of her lungs.

'What have you done with my boy?'

The gynocop cleared her throat and spoke, putting her hand firmly on Irene's shoulder as a way of keeping her in place. 'Nelson's gonna be alright. Don't worry.'

'Has there been an accident?' She wanted to scream, but the gynocop was looking sternly @ her.

'Not an accident. Nelson's not hurt.'

'So where is he? What's going on? Why can't I see him?'

@ this point the androcop intervened. 'Fialka, Irene,' he said, 'can you confirm Nelson's age for me?'

'Seven.'

Ignoring Irene now, he addressed the others. 'So we were right to act when we did after all.' He looked @ the teacher. 'BestcoeBritain® thanks you for your cooperation... Mister...er...'

'Mallister,' the teacher said quietly to help him out.

The androcop repeated the name and opened the door for Mister Mallister, who left after apologizing to Irene.

'Why's he saying sorry?' she asked, wide-eyed now.

'Keep calm,' said the gynocop.

'How can you expect me to keep calm when you won't tell me what's happened to my son?'

The cops exchanged glances. 'Congratulations!' said the gynocop with a big smile. 'Nelson's been selected. Ain't that wonderful?'

'Selected? What do you mean?'

'Their seventh birthday,' said the gynocop. 'That's when they're chosen. Nelson'll be continuing his education else-where.'

'Where? Who decided this?'

'His teacher.'

'*His teacher?*' Irene rose to her feet, her heart racing. 'Why hasn't anyone consulted me or George?'

'Don't raise your voice. This isn't up to parents.'

Irene staggered back and tripped, so she ended up on the floor.

'No,' she yelled. 'You can't take him.'

'You should feel...'

Irene didn't know how she should feel according to the gynocop because she'd passed out. They brought her round with a slap on the cheek. When she opened her eyes, she screamed and screamed. And only shut up when the androcop produced a syringe from his pocket.

'What are you gonna do?'

'Are you gonna stay calm?'

Spheco-freaks. That's what they churned out on those programmes. Irene knew. She'd heard the rumours. He'd've been bullied. Her heart exploded. 'It must be a mistake,' she yelled, tears streaming down her cheeks.

'That's what they all say,' said the gynocop with another smile. 'There's no mistake. They took him this afternoon, erm, about two deci-minutes before you arrived. I don't think there was any trouble, was there?' She looked @ the androcop, who shook his head. 'You see,' she continued, 'it all went smoothly. He'll be well taken care of. Nothing to worry about.'

'I want to see him. When can I see him?' Irene got up, but they pushed her back down into the chair.

'It's forbidden.'

'What about his present? Where can we send it?'

'He won't be needing any presents now, Fialka, Irene. We can't divulge his new address. You aren't allowed to send him anything, or contact him.'

'Why are you doing this?'

The gynocop beamed @ Irene and helped her out of the chair. 'Thank you for having a son selected for the programme sponsored by BestcoeGenetix®. Enjoy your day.'

She was ushered through the cast iron gates for the last time, reassured this was all a good thing.

Outside in the street, she sank to her knees and lay on the freezing pavement. There was no thought in her head, just sobs coming like heartbeats and screams punctuating the tears. She stopped feeling the cold.

Back home, George kept shouting 'What happened? Where is he?' @ her, desperate to get some sense from her. Eventually her circulation started up again and she screamed.

He stepped back in terror. 'Have you gone mad?'

Her eyes looked right through him.

'Where's Nelson?' He had to ask three times.

'Oh, George,' she said, bursting into tears. 'They've taken him.'

'What?'

'They've selected him. That's what the cops told me. They've chosen him for the sphecoids.'

Blood drained from his face as he sank into the worn armchair. He looked as if he was going to vomit but he just stared @ the bare walls of their little living room and said, 'No.'

'Our little Nelson.' Her face crumpled. 'We've lost him.'

'...lost everything.'

'How can you think of that @ a time like this?'

'Well, it's true, isn't it?' He shot her an indignant look. 'Everything. All wasted. We'll never get a cent back.'

'Don't reduce him to that,' she shrieked.

He couldn't meet her stare. 'But that's exactly what they've done. And we're the mugs who paid up.'

She left him sitting in the armchair and went up to their little bedroom to grieve in private. But that was denied her.

FaceChirp®'d chirruped confirmation on the wall screen.

We are pleased...

Irene scrolled down.

...the 49,999 Britz 95 centz you paid for the Ten years of life for the price of seven special offer for Fialka, Nelson will be used for his future training and accommodation.

Thank you for your contribution to BestcoeBritain®.
Enjoy your day.
dashtagThePayAsULiveTeam.

'Fifty grand,' George said. 'Wasted on a *niceboy.*'

She hadn't noticed him come upstairs and looked up in horror. He took a step back, afraid she might hit him.

'You heard me, Irene. *Niceboy.* Fifty grand's a lot of money to throw away. That could've been our future. He could've been our...' He collapsed face down on the bed, shaking with grief.

All down the drain. After everything Mum did. She'll be... She put her hand in his hair to calm him. *I'll have to be strong.*

Niceboy. The shame of being a spheco-mum stung her to the quick. They'd have to say he'd died, like everyone else did. Suddenly. In the night. Taken to the infirmary. They'd think of something. But folk would still know. From FaceChirp®. She looked @ George lying there and felt a sudden revulsion. She stopped massaging his scalp. 'Where did we go wrong, George?' She considered the little plasticon androcop doll they both thought he'd be so excited about. They'd had no idea.

'Guess he won't want that now.'

'He can't have it.' She told him what the gynocop had said. 'Is it my fault?'

He didn't reply.

She lay on her back, looking for answers on the ceiling.

TWENTY-TWO

Leaves rustle as I land on acid topsoil dotted with anthills. Cool moonbeams spotlight the grassy scrubland clearing. Squirrels seek shelter in the whispering, swaying trees.

V157's not far. My night-track facility scans its 100 metre radius.

8 deci.

Should be beautykipping, not sphecohunting.

A bramble patch on the right yields the strongest signals. I turn, and with each approaching step my I-brows hum louder. Thorns no sharper than hairs tickle my exoskeleton thanks to chitinex.

Will I be able to go through with this? My humo sense of right and wrong struggles to prevail over my spheco-urge to survive @ any cost.

'Time's up, V157.'

A sad spheco-head pops up from the brambles like a sprung toy, ten metres away, doleful eyes glinting black domes on the sides of that triangular spheco-face, I-brows plastered to his scalp with spheco-spit.

'Why have you...?' I want us to talk as equals, so don't fart out soli-pherum. 'And what did the Sin do for you?'

'Had to experience it for myself,' he gabbles. 'I was normal again. One of them. None of this spheco-shit. I highheaded among them, equal. *They* think they're sex-gods. Well, I was humo for a few accu-hours. Is that so bad? I connected with the muzak. My arms and legs had suspension, man. Was floating to the beat and harmon—'

'Shut it! You're an idiot. They must've sussed you.'

'I'm *atoning*.' He shivers from withdrawal-freeze and shakes his head, teeth chattering, I-brows unsticking and erect now.

'You're under arrest.' I hate saying that. 'For scrimshanking and Sinning.'

'Whatever.' He reflects a moment. 'Can't you understand how much I loathe this?' He runs his hands down his smooth black and yellow striped torso. 'I *wanna* be discontinued. Just get it over with. That's what you're here for, innit?'

Brain's a misery-mush. Losing V157 heavyhearts me. I should come clean, confess I'll survive by betraying him, but keep stalling. 'I've come alone. To talk.'

'And say what? To tell me what a wonderful existence I'm turning my lousy spheco-back on? That I should be relishing the prospect of spheco-life as my payback for being nice? And grateful? Cz I ain't. So come on, V159, lance me now. I can't bear another accu-minute of serving BestcoeBritain®. There's gotta be more to life than chewing wood, skewering andro-felons and cudding up @ the syngastrion.'

'Listen,' I say in as calm a voice as I can manage, consider-ing I want to yell his spheco-ears off his head. 'I'm putting my weary, but pert, spheco-buttocks on the line for you.'

A gust of wind covers the silence while he ponders my words.

'That's right. While your tragic spheco-soul's been knicker-twisting, I've been struggling to save your self-righteous spheco-arse before the androcops get you.'

'But...'

'Don't look so shocked. We've always had a special bond, ever since that first day @ the Mendoza Institute. I don't wanna have you discontinued. But right now I'm thinking this ungrateful wretch is costing me a night's kip.'

'I'm sorry, 'he mumbles 'Thought you'd come to get me. For real.'

'Don't make me want to. Let's go.'

'Ain't going back.' He scoops up dew on the back of his shiny yellow hands to slake his Sin-induced thirst.

'I'll explain, shall I? You can stay out here and rot, but they'll find you, cz their tracking's pretty hot. And discontinuation you'll recall from V161's is way below pleasant. And I'll suffer the same...'

Shouting interrupts me. I notice a few androlads walking purposefully into the undergrowth, some of them darker, some paler, all various shades of humo. Like Mike. And *her*. But none black and yellow like us.

'Hey...!' V157 looks @ me. 'Met them last night...'

'Spheco-freaks!'

Five hate-eros surround us.

You hate-eros are right. We are spheco-freaks.

The names kindle my fire. V157 just looks straight ahead, ignoring them. I take off, poised to swoop.

The clanging of stones smashing on chitinex sickens me. They're throwing rocks @ him, but he doesn't react, even when they hit his cute face. Just staggers back and recovers his pose.

'You're gonna die, sphecoid.' When the gang leader realizes V157 isn't retaliating, he cackles @ his mates. 'You know why this freakoid ain't fighting back, don't you...? Cz he's yellow. Geddit?'

Hate-ero voices guffaw. The pebble rain intensifies.

'Bullseye.' Right between the eyes.

Moaning, V157 totters back and falls to the ground.

I dive, spheco-cock flaming out.

'There's another one of those cunts.'

Stones start hitting me now as they turn their attention to

their new enemy.

'Hold on in there.' My voice jerks on each syllable as they pelt me with rocks. I'm beyond pain. Just want to soar skyward and slash them open, but the missile storm grounds me.

A falsetto scream displaces several flocks of birds.

Four hate-eros scatter.

V157 retrieves his soaking penis, which glistens in the moonlight, from the adjacent gangleader's paralysed supine body.

It's the first time I've seen V157's cock in action.

He clocks my amazement-gog and giggles. 'Been practising,' he says between great sighs of relief. Cupping his hands over his shaft as it re-sheaths sideways, he wipes the andro-gore on the grass and paces a bit before speaking. 'How's your head?'

'I'll live. Yours?'

'Fabbo.' Then he stops still and yells, 'I...I...'

The sun rises inside me @ his joy, periscopic flexidick and perfect ilkiness. 'Chizz, V157.'

He embraces me. 'No, V159. Something snapped in my stupid spheco-head. I guess it took something like this to make me see what's important. I was quite prepared to allow them to kill me. But you...I couldn't let them do that.'

'I'm so proud of you, and your...superdick, V157.'

He forces my mandibles open with his and snogs me.

I'm shocked @ first, and grunt. We all do this when we cud and regurge the broth. But what throws me is how pleased I am. I let him. I want him to do it. Something weird shuffles in my insides. My spheco-cock heats up once more, but not like with hate-eros and other thugs. This is different. It's warm. It's happened before, but I thought we weren't supposed to experience anything like that.

'Do you feel it too?' I whisper in his ear after our drooling mouths part company.

From his smile I know that he does. I smile too. It's a moment I don't want to end, an image I wish I'd captured on my Eye-cam, something I never dreamed I'd live to enjoy. I feel the birth of a secret life fizz into existence in my spheco-guts and kiss him back.

The words spill out of me. I know they're heresy, that they mean serious trouble, but I can't hold them in any longer.

'I love you, V157.'

He grins so widely I fear the top half of his happy sphecohead will topple off.

'Downloading, V159. And likewise.'

We lie entwined together in the bramble bushes, oblivious to the thorns, just staring up @ the sky as the sun rises, not knowing how to continue.

My Eye-pod resonates and a sleepy, but seriously irked voice snaps, 'V159?'

Horelka. My luck's out. 'You've found him.'

19 deci. Just after 4.30 am.

I reluctantly leave our dream world.

Horelka drones on. 'So why the fuck haven't you apprehended him and got yourself yellowcarded?'

'Sir, I...' I glance @ V157. I could still shop him to save myself. Course, they'll force me to attend his discontinuation and scan my spheco-brain for joy @ his fate.

I avert my gaze. *Shame on me for even thinking of turning him in after turning him on.*

Horelka's saying something else, but I'm not listening. The humo and spheco in me dovetail @ last. I'd rather decease than betray V157 to redeem myself. I look @ him again and my spheco-heart melts, but he doesn't have the answer.

He *is* the answer.

I cut Horelka off.

V157 dogshakes himself free of burrs and bits of dead

vegetation. 'I vivisexed that andro for you. I enjoyed it, I won't deny it, but it was only physical. That's all. I want you to know that.'

I don't reply. I've fallen in love with a liability...

V157 and I have both committed redcardable vivisexion now. Self defence is inadmissible as we were both offside, and I'm shielding a scrimshanker and Sinner as well.

My Eyelid screen buzzes into life.

DISTURBANCE
@ EAST COCKNEYTOWN RECYCLING CENTRE

No details. My spheco-innards lurch.

'I'll help you...' I say, '...but you gotta do one thing for me.' I telepath everything.

We fly low over the Thames.

I pray we arrive before it's too late.

TWENTY-THREE

The line of placid, worn out Ds waited in the brightly lit room for redemption and re-entry into BestcoeBritain®, away from the commotion.

@ first, Irene saw gynocops injecting the Ds, jabbing syringes indiscriminately, desperate to sedate as many as possible. Whatever the drug was, it made them slump to the floor senseless.

Then Irene saw the conveyor belt. And the gynos now being hauled onto it. It moved the gynos slowly towards purple velvet curtains, and through them to Irene knew not where.

Irene turned and ran back to where she'd entered, but gynocops blocked her, exchanging glances as they made to seize her.

Screaming, she dodged them, flying past a gynocop stabbing a syringe into a fellow D's arm. The D sighed and crumpled floorwards, and another gynocop caught her under the armpits and hauled her up onto the belt.

Only now did Irene notice next to the curtains swallowing the conveyor belt and its human cargo...a door.

Escape! Irene made a dash for this exit.

She clutched the handle, but a gynocop pressed her back hard against the door, so in her weakened state, Irene couldn't pull it open. The gynocop with the syringe approached.

Irene heard andro voices. She kicked the gynocop blocking her escape out of the way, marvelling @ where she'd found the strength.

The gynocop cussed and fell down.

Irene turned the knob.

She found herself in an enormous chamber. The stench hit her like a physical force. She uttered a cry and reeled.

Blood. Gore. Burning flesh. Death.

Sphecoid-like creatures lined one side of the conveyor belt. Quite different from Nelson, they were smaller, dark brown, like large wingless ants. Their antennae were shorter, and they chirped @ each other constantly.

The nearest 'ant' stripped the rags off the first D-classified gyno, and the next 'ant' thrust its pelvis @ her naked body. From a slit between its legs, it sprayed a substance. Smoke rose from her joints, and the bug, twittering away, pulled her limbs and head off with ease.

The third one sprayed her torso. Dark, spindly hands removed the inner organs and dumped them into a vast tub.

Irene was struck dumb. The 'ants' didn't appear bothered by her presence and continued sorting the severed members into piles.

So this is recycling.

Irene sensed the gynocops before they seized her from behind.

A hand gripped Irene's arm like a vice, and marched her over to a colleague with a syringe. 'Another one. Trying to abscond.'

'Hold her tight.'

Praying they'd not injected or recycled Samina, Irene struggled, but the gynocop was too strong for her.

'You have trespassed.'

Irene took nothing more in.

And this is my destiny.

The gynocop with the syringe came right up to her. 'Keep

her still.'

Mustering every atom of strength she still possessed, Irene managed to wrench one of her arms free and stay this gynocop's hand, not realizing that in the process she'd been twisted round and pushed onto the converyor belt.

She lay on her back, trembling from the effort. As the belt moved, a massive bald entomoid head loomed over her, all vibrating antennae and huge black eye domes scrutinizing her. Scratchy foreleg claws tugged and ripped @ her clothes. Pincer-jaws opened and snapped shut.

Clackety-clackety-clack.

Distracted, Irene forgot the gynocops.

Until she felt the prick by her elbow.

Her vision blurred. She no longer cared.

TWENTY-FOUR

As far as I can tell no one follows us. Circling in the death-yellow sky, we land @ the entrance. My spheco-heart beats out a funeral march. I fear we're too late.

We vault over the turnstile. Our spheco-eyes gradually adjust to the gloom.

Everywhere is chaos.

This is not the orderly recycling of expendables I have witnessed elsewhere. Bodies are lying in heaps. I clock the presence of androcops among the corpses.

A gynocop approaches. 'This is most irregular...' she starts.

'What's happened?' I ask.

'And your business is?'

I squeeze V157's hand. 'Searching for andro felon, suspected of hiding in here. Need to question gyno cit believed to know his whereabouts and able to provide us with valuable information.'

'Name of gyno?'

'Fialka, Irene.'

'Wait here.'

Typical tight-lipped gynocop.

She trots off, to check data.

I notice two immobile andros on the floor, and grip V157's hand. 'There must've been a riot here and they called the androcops.'

He shrugs. 'But...that don't make sense. How could D-classified gynos kill armed androcops?'

A throat clears. 'Fialka, Irene definitely passed through the turnstiles,' the fussy gynocop says. 'We have her Eye-D.'

'So, will it still be possible to interrogate her?'

The gynocop looks flustered. 'I dunno.'

'Does that mean she's been processed?' I try to hide my desperation. 'Is that what you're saying? Am I...are we too late?'

She shakes her head. 'No. I can't say.'

I'm dumbfounded. 'Whaddaya mean? Don't you keep any records here?'

She swallows and gestures round the chamber. 'As you can see, we've had an incident.'

'Yes, that's pretty obvious. What happened?'

She looks round and leans in closer. 'Not s'posed to broadcast this, but there was a bit of a...disturbance cz of the new withertongue quarantine law and some Freebie opportunists took advantage of the situation.'

I'm confused now. 'What are you saying?'

'I'm saying some D-classifieds failed to recycle.'

I was right — the dead androcops, the chaos. 'So did Fialka, Irene fail to recycle as well?'

'That's what we don't know. We're trying to identify these bodies by Eye-D matching, but it's gonna take days. Can you do a visual Eye-D?'

I nod.

'Okay then, as you're on a criminal investigation, feel free to have a look. If you can't find her, it means she either left with the Freebies or recycled before the incursion. In the meantime, I'll cease the recycling until you leave.'

'Thank you.'

We walk into the huge antechamber.

Gynocops are milling about and dragging the bodies

towards the recycling room.

I telepath her image to V157, so he knows who to look for. My spheco-heart does a flip and a somersault. We turn over the bodies in the chamber with our spheco-feet, but none are hers. These gynos appear to have been trampled and suffocated.

We leave the andros. Entering the recycling room, we hear the myrmecoid-formicans giggling and squeaking in their high-pitched lingo before we see their brown-black forms.

So like ourselves, but utterly alien.

Recalling how they processed V161, I shudder @ these ant-gyno hybrids.

The myrmecoids are working by a long trestle table. We do not interest them.

Gynocops stand between us and the myrmecoids as we rummage in the basket bins.

My spheco-guts rebel @ the task, but I control my urge to vomit by concentrating on the job in hand.

Each basket's a game of Russian Roulette. I fear sooner or later we'll see her head and it'll all be over. I check we've not missed any bins. After about five or six deciminutes, with no sign of the end in sight our gynocop marches over.

'Well, any luck?'

I shake my weary spheco-head @ her.

'It's possible the Freebies took her,' she says.

'OK.' I deadpan. Have to hide my hope. 'And where might they have gone?'

'East.' She points vaguely. 'They couldn't've crossed the Thames, so they'd've gone into the Eastlands.'

'Chizz. You've been very helpful.'

She smiles. Actually looks proud of herself. 'I do hope you find her.'

'Yes. I have a lot of questions for her.' I resume my search.

Distant voices unsettle me.

Androcops. Obknoxians.

I look @ V157 and telepath my concern, which he transceives and buzzes his alarm.

They've found us. No time to complete my search.

'Is there another exit?' I ask but the gynocop's gone. The voices are getting louder. Running footsteps.

We're surrounded.

'App-re-hend-the-sphe-coids,' demands an obknoxian.

V157 gogs @ me in terror. 'You said you'd help.'

'Follow me,' I telepath.

Taking off, we soar close to the high ceiling, way over the heads and raised armspikes of our hunters.

@ the swish-swish of each tranquilizer dart as it leaves their guns, we employ our lightning-fast spheco-reflexes to swerve and dodge their missiles.

Hotly pursued, we whizz over the turnstile entrance. The smoky East Cockneytown air currents bear us aloft as we soar ever higher towards the clouds and out of range.

'She has to be alive,' I cry to V157 over the urban din once we are out of that place, clinging onto hope, but knowing deep down in my spheco-soul I didn't finish the search.

Just as he asks, 'Where to?' I transceive a message on my Eyelid-screen.

No confidence alert.

I read aloud with increasing dismay.

The SECOPS spheco-swarm has issued a vote of no confidence in the Queendom of V159 following a series of spheco-dysfunctions, and now shielding a scrimshanking Sin-thief.

The swarm demands that V157 and V159 be brought to justice to answer for their crimes against BestcoeBritain®.

In addition, that V159 be unqueened by deputy V146, who will receive immediate solipherum implant.

'V146?' I scream. 'How...?' My voice trails off.

You have failed. You cannot be our Queen.

The buzz of vespine sedition. No humo words.

Discontinuation awaits you.

V157 pings my I-brow with his. 'What'll happen to us?'

I clear my tight spheco-throat. 'Don't fret. We ain't going back.' I laugh out loud @ the nonplussed look on his pretty spheco-face. 'We're heading east and you're a-coming with me.'

'Why east?'

'Aw, c'mon. Even you should be able to work that out.'

He puts a finger on his mouthparts and frowns as his spheco-eyes windscreen-wipe his search for the answer. Presently, they stop. 'Give up.'

I click my bristly spheco-tongue. 'I'll let you know nearer the time.' I've always assumed his superlong I-brows make him extra-transceptive. And to think he's one of the brighter ones. I kiss his polished forehead.

'B-but won't they send out a search party?'

I shrug. 'They ain't got the andro-mandro. There's enough felony in the SECOPS zone to keep them busy. Hopefully, they'll write us off as two dysfunctioning bridgeburnt sphecos and let us rot in the wilds.'

We fly ever higher, the sudden whoosh of air bracing and

thrilling.

'Hey, won't the Freebies get us?'

'They're no match,' I call back, adding, 'Some folks are a-saying they're just a bogey to frighten Cockneytowners off from leaving the city.'

He's drawn level with me now, to hear better. 'Do you believe the Freebies exist?'

I nod. 'Yeah, they're real all right. The question is, will they be friend or foe?'

And you, my new spheco-mate, are you gonna be a true friend? I know in my exoskeleton I'm gonna find out and both long for and dread the transpiry.

The sea of DUBs and official buildings transforms into lakes of low-rise and then just wasteland and fields with pockets of disused villages dotted here and there. Our nav-systems guide us ever eastwards until we deem it safe to alight in a meadow near a stagnant stream.

The Eastlands.

Part Two

Freebies

ONE

The Eastlands are mostly flat.

We soar over fields and meadows and hover above the fenced off agrocomplexes dotted around, our enhanced spheco-vision revealing newgro shoots and gynos in brightly coloured nylon dungarettes, bent double, picking stuff and filling baskets. Feeding Cockneytown. Nothing for us. If they see us, they'll think we're birds of prey after rodent meat.

'We're gonna have to check out every place we find,' I say. 'She could be anywhere. It'll be a long search.'

We twist to high-five I-brows, happy to have got this far, and glide under the dull BestcoeBritain clouds. V157 points downwards. A small forest.

We swoop down and relish the sensation of foliage tickling our chitinex as we enter the canopy and find a hefty bough to perch on.

'There's no turning back,' I say.

He doesn't speak. Just holds my spheco-hand. I've never mentioned our life expectancy. *Bad enough* I *know.*

After gazing @ the leaves around us and listening to real birdsong, he says, 'We'll need somewhere to sleep.'

We set to work straightaway, pulping wood from bark. A hundred deci-minutes later, we have one hexagonal double kip-cell. Exhausted from kip-lack and exertion, we clamber inside.

It is cold @ first, but the proximity of our bodies swiftly

warms us. There's sufficient room for manoeuvre in the smooth papery enclosure.

We rub noses like we've seen humos do, and giggle. It's so silly. We lie on our fronts, worm ourselves a bit out of the opening and peer up @ the gradually darkening sky.

'You've always been special to me,' I start. 'You know, I used to think of you as the "boy without a face" cz you had such an amazing face. It was my secret name for you although you were still called Tariq then.'

He squeezes my hand.

I continue. 'Every day I couldn't wait to see you, play with you. I so wanted to be your best friend. Once, you said, "If you were a gynokid, you'd be beautiful." I felt heat rise all through my body and keep me warm the rest of that day. I thought they'd destroyed all that, but here we are, reliving it.'

He pecks my mouthparts.

The sun blasts furnace-red in the west. I spend a long time contemplating our new world, wondering how we'll feed and whether we'll ever reach our destination.

We have one night's logsleep before heading towards the sea.

Flying over woodland would provide better camouflage, but the terrain is mostly deforested, so we mount higher to appear smaller, more bird-like.

My spheco-pulse quickens as I catch my first glimpse of the water, like a vast, flat sun-lit strobe. I point it out to V157, who just stares @ it.

The outlines of urban buildings come into relief, a long concrete and breeze-block strip by the sea.

Some distant memory has guided me here. Strange I've managed to find my way home when I saw nothing from that van. It's been thirteen years.

And then doubts assail me. What am I doing here? Why

come back...and subject myself and V157 to this?

But...my — our — destiny is spread before us. I banish my fears and scan for the best route to take.

A straight road leads downhill from cordoned-off fields. We follow it in the air, dodging the overgrown branches of trees reclaiming the land. Cracks in the pavement and tarmac yield outgrowths of weeds. Thistles, nettles, brambles. Sturdy plants with prickles, thorns or stinging hairs. Ivy smothers the few buildings still standing; houses are in a state of advanced decay: roofs collapsed, window-panes missing.

As we get lower, my breathing becomes more constricted. The main street with the clock tower is still recognizable under the verdure. I give a little sigh and alight. I no longer understand the clock face — the position of the hands means nothing to me now. The sculptured dragon on the top of the little tower is crumbling away. Shoots sprout from cracks in the marble.

The old shop fronts are boarded up, but in some cases the interior of the buildings themselves have rotted away or fallen through so all that remains is the façade, as if the road has been bombed. I suspect it has, for where once stood outhouses and flats extending behind, is now a huge crater supporting colonies of rosebay willow herb and ragwort.

I fly up to the eaves of the former grand parade of shops and survey the ruins and abrupt stop where the sea breaks on the beach, and the rolling hills leading inland.

My next call is the gentle slopes where my school was. I dart down and make for the bottom of Deaconscastle Road where those tiny huts once held me captive for that day when I so trusted Mr Mallister, whose soft voice led me to those strange grown-up arms yanking me away from everything familiar.

Should I be grateful? They saved me. Plucked me from a free-fall to doom.

Heart a-thudding, I land awkwardly, thankful we're alone

and no other sphecos can see that disgraceful move. V157 is mercifully quiet.

The school.

The last place in Soxbury I was @ before now. Tears sting my eyes and tickle my cheeks; my in-breaths jerk their way down into my sorry spheco-lungs. Then I laugh.

Why am I so upset? It's not as if I was happy here. My experience was wretched.

The foundations of the huts are still there, although the flimsy temporary building material has all rotted away. Vast stone rectangles speckled with tiny green weeds waving in the breeze are all that remains of that taught-ure chamber. And what of the other kids and teachers? Are they just traces in the ground too, or do they still exist somewhere?

Nothing more for us here.

We take off and go back towards the seaside. In one of the little side streets stands the terrace of cottages. Double-storeyed, flat-fronted grimy ruddy-bricked slums. 'Two-up two-downs' they used to call them. I called it home. Once again my chest heaves and, without warning apart from a sigh of recognition, the sobs come like an April downpour. The secrets of my first seven years hidden in piles of masonry and rubble adorning the shell of our house. Bare window and door-frames. Mum and Dad and guilt.

We make for the beach. I knew this wouldn't be easy. The water's grey and brown now, waves rolling and breaking on the rocky shore with relentless force. I learned happiness here, where the estuary becomes the sea; it was my sanctuary.

Time to go. Just like it always was time to leave the refuge of the beach back then. There are no permanent havens; one's constantly being moved back into danger. We're probably under surveillance: easy to work out where we'd be.

TWO

But I have to care... Samina.

Irene fought with all her strength to push the needle away and slide off the conveyor belt, taking the surprised gynocop with her to the floor.

Getting to her feet, Irene did not know what to feel or dare hope for. Someone grabbed the gynocop from behind before she could jab Irene again and made her drop the syringe. The vitreola tinkled on the concrete and the needle reflected a glint of light in the dimness. The spilt drug pooled round the shards.

But did any get into my bloodstream?

An andro voice boomed in her ear. There were protests, rebukes, gyno cries and the custody of her arms changed hands. The 'ants' had stopped twittering and started hissing. They approached her, thrusting out their pelvises, aiming their sprayslits @ her.

A force carried her away even as they closed in on her, and a boot kicked the door shut in their faces.

She lost her footing and was dragged backwards through the well-lit injecting room into the dark chamber where she'd last seen Samina.

She called out her name, but the andro hushed her and pushed the gynocops away.

Irene could only think of one thing. *Samina.* Had she lost the lot — partner, son, job and now her best and only friend? 'But you don't understand,' she cried.

The andro led her away in a nightmare of loss. The gyno-cops were shouting for backup, but they were receding into the distance. Irene heard one mention Freebies.

'Are you really a...?'

'Be quiet.' He carried on pulling her back towards the turnstiles.

'Let me go,' she shouted, struggling.

'Don't you get it, you stupid gyno?' he snapped with his gruff voice. 'I'm setting you free.' He vaulted over the turnstile and held out his arm.

Irene stalled.

'Move!' he shouted.

'I ain't leaving without Samina. She's still in here. Gimme two accu-minutes.'

He tutted. 'Not an accu-second more.'

She smiled at him, her first smile for as long as she could remember and bellowed for Samina.

Through the racket of fighting and confusion, Irene heard a tiny voice call her name.

Samina was wedged under a couple of unconscious andro-cops.

Irene heaved and rolled the androcops off her friend, helping her to her feet. They embraced.

'We gotta go.'

She didn't need to explain.

They raced to the turnstile. Her time was up. She could see the andro beckoning to them and coming towards them, but it was a blur now. He hauled them clear over the barrier into the cool, airy street and the glare of daylight.

There were a couple of bodies on the pavement. Sirens whined.

He grabbed both of them by the hand and ran to a waiting van. 'There's water,' he panted, and shoved them into the back.

The door slammed. The van screeched off.

Inside it was dark, but light from the windscreen was sufficient to reveal a gyno driving, and perched over a rear wheel, an andro. *Garcia?* He passed a water bottle to her. She took a sip.

After a few deci-minutes, the van stopped and the driver turned to look @ them with piercing black eyes. 'Listen up everybody. We'll tell you more when we get home.' Irene imagined she also said, 'You'll be fed and clothed and looked after. Welcome to the Freebies.'

But then she finally gave in to the injection and lost consciousness.

THREE

Mollinsea is the next town on. The town centre is better preserved and less overgrown than Soxbury's, leading me to believe that relocation was more recent.

V157 gogs @ the battered 'Welcome to Mollinsea' sign creaking as it sways in the breeze, but backs away. Maybe he had it tougher than me.

'You're not afraid, are you?'

He shakes his head. 'They're all dead. Look @ Soxbury. Everything destroyed. What good has it done you?'

I splutter, not knowing what indeed, but I give a stab @ a reply. 'I've done something I had to. That's good enough.'

He nods, a grim expression on his chitinex-buff lips.

I hold him firm and press my mouth to his. 'Don't give up now.'

'But I don't wanna rake it all up again,' he snarls with sudden rage, making me step back and my cheeks twitch with embarrassment. 'Can't you understand that?'

'If you don't revisit now you've got the chance,' I say, mustering as much authority in my voice as possible, 'you'll regret it for the rest of your sorry spheco-life.'

He spits @ me. In my eye. I smack his face. Chitinex clatters against chitinex. His eyes open wide in surprise and he nurses his cheek with the back of his hand.

'You struck me, V159.'

'You gobbed me, V157.'

He walks away, but in an accu-second I've flown by his side.

'I'm with you. It'll hurt, but you'll be glad you did it. And then it'll be over.'

I put my arm round his shoulder and he buries his face in my chest. Warm tears flow down my armoured front.

V157's school is an ugly concrete block with small windows. @ the sight of it I feel his whole body stiffen and shake. That's where he was selected for sphecanthropy, wrenched from the bosom of his family.

'Tariq...'

'Don't call me that,' he snaps with a vehemence that startles me. 'Tariq died thirteen years ago. Just like Nelson.'

'We're still part human.'

'But we're not all human, are we?'

'I'm sorry.' A mistake to try and resurrect his humo past. Not a good time to call him touchy. I shut up.

He just stares @ the building as we skirt the perimeter.

'Do you know what they used to do to Tariq?' he asks me, not expecting an answer because he just carries straight on before I can open my spheco-gob to say no. 'See that window up there?' He points to a square hole three floors up. 'They used to dangle him out of that, holding him by the ankles...imagine what it's like...to feel your flesh burn as their grip weakens...the ground starts to come a bit closer to your face...the yelling and cackling as they grab you @ the last minute and yank you back inside and beat you up...and...you don't even mind cz you're grateful to them in a stupid kinda way for rescuing you, and the contempt, and no one talking to you or wanting to be your friend, and hiding that from your parents cz you're so ashamed...that's what they did to Tariq...

'So I'm glad Tariq's no more...and he's not a part of me now...and I'm V157 just like you should be proud you're V159.'

I can't speak. Whatever I say will sound banal, so I just button my chitinex lips.

'Then they took Tariq, those grown-ups with the fixed smiles and the firm grip, pulled him out of this hellhole. And you know the worst? Tariq's Mum happened to be walking past the school @ the very minute they were spiriting him into that van — you remember the black and yellow van with no windows — and she called out, "Tariq, what's happening?" and Tariq screamed, "Mum, help me!" and she ran to him, but they beat her back, those grown-ups, so she cried and howled and so did Tariq, but they were too strong, just like the child bullies, and they threw Tariq into the back of that van, slammed the door shut and drove off, and all Tariq could think about was his mother's wailing getting fainter and fainter. And now it's all over, V159, and Tariq's in another place, where I want him to be, far, far away from me and you and that's how I want it.'

I take a deep breath and put my hand on his arm, expecting to be shrugged off.

He just stands still.

'Do you want to see your home?' I ask in a quiet voice.

He nods, fighting back tears, more successfully than me, I have to admit. His unit isn't far. He walks purposefully down a path that leads to a multi-dwelling complex. A few windows still have transplasticon panes. Weeds sway in the breeze.

He points to a section on two floors.

The front door's fallen in. We enter, treading carefully over rubble strewn in the hall. Fungal growths and mould cover the walls.

V157 examines a cup before setting it down with care.

'Dad's.' His eyes betray a mixture of tenderness and anger, and a touch-me-not warning. My Face-Reader understands why.

We wade through more bits of smashed up furniture and

he comes to a halt and says 'No.' He bends down and I strain to see what he picks up.

A fading real-paper photograph, torn @ the edge, but the three faces are still visible. A young man and woman, and in front of them a boy, all beaming.

I'm standing behind him, peering over his shoulder and I don't want to ask him to stop shaking as I can't see the detail in the picture clearly, but I don't think he'd have heard me @ that moment.

He sinks to his knees and lets the photo drop. His arm cradles his eyes.

'I'm so sorry,' I whisper.

He nods slowly and gets to his feet, indicating the door with a movement of his hand. 'Time to go,' he manages to croak over his tears.

'Don't you want that?' I ask.

He takes one last look @ the photograph and smiles @ me, molten diamonds glistening in his long I-lashes. 'They're still just as I remember them,' he says brightly and marches out into the sunshine empty-handed.

We wander arm in arm along the beach. Mollinsea did not boast as grand an esplanade as Soxbury, but the chilly sea air dries our tears, and the shrieks of the gulls punctuate our thoughts. We say little and sit on the sand.

'This is all we have, Tariq.'

'V157. Tariq belongs to the past.'

'But it's the best we can do. What else is there?'

'The past. Make this the past too, like Tariq. And Nelson.'

'What are you so ashamed of, V157? That we can't love like normal people? But we aren't "normal people", so why should we copy what they do?'

He sits up. Turns his back on me. I stroke it, softly, with my fingertips. He doesn't flinch, just enjoys the sensual pleasure of being tickled and says nothing.

I continue running my fingers over his chitin back. 'You're the most important thing that's happened to me.'

He writhes out of reach and turns round. 'So, I'm a thing now, am I?'

I click my tongue in frustration. 'Don't make an argument for the sake of it. *Knowing* you's the thing, silly.'

He rolls over onto his front and picks @ grass sprouting in the sand. 'I feel such a fraud. Like I don't have the right. After everything I've done...'

I massage his hairless scalp. 'You...we...have every right.'

We kiss and get aroused once more, but do nothing. I lie down next to him. I also need a tickle.

'We oughtta head off...' I don't finish cz what happens next is as unexpected as it is wonderful. V157 turns and plants a huge spheco-kiss on my mouth-parts. 'Thank you for insisting.'

The tingling in my groin comes instantly. I reciprocate the kiss. V157's lips part and my bristly spheco-tongue slides in and twirls round his, like two flaps of velcro-lux. We both arch our backs so our shafts can spring out harmlessly. Gripping each other in this position, we tumble onto the sand and roll over, taking care not to spike each other. Grains of sand getting between our chitinex plates don't bother us.

'I never dreamed I could love like this,' I say between panting breaths.

We use one hand for hugging and the other for cock stroking. Our mouths open as the jism cooks and then we spring apart with a shriek, just in time for our spurts of sallow toxi-jism to spatter the sand.

'That's Rule 19 down the sewer,' I joke.

'Yeah. To the blattoids.'

BESTCOE-MENDOZA INSTITUTE OF ENTOMANTHROPY
Department of Sphecanthropy
Training Manual Rule Book page 53

Rule 19: Concerning Masturbation

The sphecoid sexual urge has been developed to a state of communal beneficence. The creation of ACE-producing glandular implants involves a high-cost investment from BestcoeBritain®. Accidental wastage is a disciplinary matter to be resolved with sanctions against the individual in question.

Deliberate squandering of ACE (aka malicious masturbation) is a felonious act and must be treated accordingly.

Onanism, although unusual, can occur in sphecoids with abnormally high sex-drives, who experience frustration @ a low felon count. Mutual masturbation is a phenomenon, which should not happen if all programming precautions have been correctly observed, but in extremely rare cases would necessitate instant referral to the Institute for special measures, which may include discontinuation.

We dogshake, sand grains raining on seaweed, and take off, flying close together. Holding hands and I-brows, we somersault in the air, zigzagging and buzzing with delight until a sobering Eye-pod message smacks me round the sphecochops.

Mike?

Probably worried about me.

FOUR

The house brought back primal memories to Irene, still shaky, but breathless and light-headed with relief and exhilaration @ having found Samina.

She sat down on the grass in a yard, shivering after a cold bath, and listened to the andro who'd freed them strumming an old guitar. She held Samina's hand.

The andro stopped playing and squatted beside them. He had short, curly black hair and a waxy sheen on his face. Delicate, chiselled features and a broad smile. He was older than Nelson would've been and needed a shave. But he had saved her from the horrors of recycling.

Irene introduced herself and Samina. 'Thank you.' She wanted to say so much more, but just smiled.

'It's okay,' he said. 'I'll come back.' He got up, surveyed the surroundings and swaggered his andro-walk away.

They were on a small lawn bordered with olive trees. Straight ahead of them was a three-storeyed house, a very old building with shattered windowpanes. Victorian — red bricks and complicated details round the windows, so unlike the simple square DUBS. It reminded Irene of her first home...before Nelson was taken.

Suddenly, it hit her and she sobbed. What she had witnessed in the Recycling Centre, but did not fully comprehend, had surely been George's fate.

The house came back into focus as Irene's tears dried. It

was taller than their old home in Soxbury, that brief period of happiness when they still believed life was good and Nelson would grow up strong and bring them joy. The events of his seventh birthday were still far off in the distance. Then, they'd been relocated. And now she was returning to something familiar.

She could not see what lay beyond the yard and the walls. The house was detached and they were somewhere in the countryside, ten deci-minutes from Cockneytown. In the panic and confusion of the rescue, she hadn't noticed in which direction they were travelling.

The air was clean and fresh, but clouds were gathering in the sky.

Is it gonna rain? Can't afford to get ill. Neither can Samina.

She wiped her eyes with the back of her hand, remembering when she had a handkerchief for that, and taking Samina's arm, led her towards the house. As they got to the door, the andro reappeared.

'Come in,' he said with a smile, his rough voice @ odds with his pretty, sensitive face. He stood to one side to allow them to pass.

They walked through a dark corridor into a spacious lounge. The first thing Irene noticed was the high ceiling. It was years since she'd been in a room that wasn't low and claustrophobic and made her feel like stooping.

The second was Garcia. She'd been right earlier. They acknowledged each other.

@ least it wasn't so cold. The walls were covered in patches with some old faded brown wallpaper, but vast areas were bare masonry or brick. Light came through a large bay window fitted with a sash, although the panes were plasticon and needed washing. The floor, where Irene and Samina had sat down, was bare wooden boards, splintering and rotten in places. In the centre of the opposite wall was an empty fireplace.

Irene wanted to ask Garcia about Heathcote, but the andro came in, closed the door and cleared his throat.

'My name's Olivier Kamara. I'm gonna explain what we do. You're free to leave @ any time...if you wish to return to BestcoeBritain®.

'We're giving you a chance to take back the lives you had before BestcoeBritain® stole them, or prevented you from ever having. You'll be clothed, fed and put to work. It's not easy. As you can see, we have very little. No FaceChirp® cheerup-chirrups. Bestcoe's against us the whole time. But it's still a genuine life you don't have to pay for.'

'Why did you save us?' Garcia introduced himself, and then stared @ the cracked floorboards.

'Well...it's a mutually beneficial transaction. We needed new members, so who better than those with nothing to lose in the cities?' He looked @ them. 'We get hunted by the andro-cops. BestcoeBritain® has declared war on us, just as it has on all you former D-classifieds. They were about to recycle one of us, and we tried to get him back, but were too late. We lost three more in that raid.' He smiled.

'Soon it'll be dark. There's no power here. We live a simple, frugal life. But @ least it's honest. We eat early, sleep @ nightfall and rise with the sun.'

He pointed @ the gyno with piercing eyes, who'd appeared in the doorway. Irene remembered her from the van. 'Phoebe will show the gynos where they'll sleep. I'll take you, Garcia. Once again, welcome to Phoebe's Freebies.'

FIVE

I call Mike back on my Eye-pod, anticipating his joy @ hearing my husky spheco-tones.

But I don't expect his response.

'Where the fuck you been?'

My voice shrinks to a whimper. 'Hey, what's...?'

'Get your skinny spheco-arse back here @ once. I need you on the Gobbs case.'

'How? Me and V157 are redcarded and...'

'Knox's problem. This is urgent.'

'But...'

'Just make sure you ain't spotted, or we both cop it.' There's a click. His image disappears.

My legs buckle. I turn from V157, torn between him and Mike.

We find a forest clearing to nest in. The sun's just past its midday point in a hazy sky. The trees are shedding the last of their foliage. Flocks of birds speckle the heavens and flies buzz. I should be rejoicing in this freedom, but I'm withering away.

Vespine instinct's made V157 forage for nectar to suck and share. We need a lot of flowers to be sated and are constantly hungry. Once the ivy's over, there'll be nothing.

He lands gracefully as always, and folds back his armwings with a flourish. The smile on his mouthparts means he's jackpotted. But I have no appetite, not one that food alone can satisfy.

My refusal baffles him. He flings his sinewy spheco-arm round me and asks what the matter is.

@ first I just sulk and mumble minimal replies to his questions. Eventually, it comes out, piecemeal. I neither expect nor want sympathy. I don't get any.

'So,' starts V157, 'you're doing this for...him?'

'Why? You jealous of a humo?'

He looks away.

'Really don't wanna leave you,' I continue, 'but he needs my help.'

'And that's more important than... I thought...'

'I'll be back. Don't worry. Well, perhaps I'll stay with you tonight...'

A smile lights up his face and then goes out. 'And go through all this dithering again tomorrow? For fuxache, stop knickertwisting and go.'

V157 can certainly be dimmer than a humo arsecrack, but for once he's right.

'Fuxaches, V157, this is why I love you, and if I help nail the killer...'

He slaps my spheco-shoulder. 'You mean *we*. You ain't doing no spheco-sleuthing without my assistance. How am I gonna fill my exile days? Only so much real wood I can chew.'

We high-five I-brows and snog.

'Now, where's that nectar you guzzled?' I demand. 'I'm a-starving.'

I receive the regurgitated nectar, some of which dribbles from our interlocking mouthparts onto the grass.

I smile and start feeling one of my new arousals stiffening my spheco-cock, which flies out of my slit. I stroke it, and then V157's does the same. Without speaking or orgasm, we masturbate. I scoop up some of the spilt nectar on the shaft, savouring the sweetness and registering the sourness from V157's digestive tract. He copies me. Then we stand apart and wank ourselves till we cum, our jism spurting harmlessly onto the ground.

It isn't the erotic rush of impaling an androfelon, but it still feels good, if puzzling. Is this what humo sex is like — pallid, lukewarm? I dunno and right now don't care either.

Then he asks, 'What if it's a trap?'

Haven't thought of that. I mull it over. 'I'll take that risk. But don't come a-looking for me if I don't return.'

He shrugs.

I peck his spheco-cheek and buzz off before he can reply. The cool breeze bolsters me.

The way back to Cockneytown is hard, the distance great for one designed for short urban flights. I rest frequently, remembering the best places from our outward journey. Only the miracle of spheco-wings keeps me airborne when missing V157 would drag me earthward.

Mike's @ his desk, chewing some humo-snack. Only one light's on. I've guessed right — he's alone.

'Mike..?'

He doubletakes when he sees me glide into his office.

'V159.' His eyes dart this way and that, to ensure we're not seen. 'What kept you? I need this case solved. Horelka's test-ing me. Can't afford to fail and get demoted.'

'But I thought sphecos weren't supposed to...'

'You ain't, but we might be able to exploit your...gifts. It's a big gamble, but we're lucky — Ms Kamara hasn't complained. Only you and I know you're here. Gotta try and keep it that way.'

'Okay, so who's our first suspect?'

'Don Sauternes,' he says. 'He knew Jaxxon Gobbs very

well.'

A grin reshapes my cute spheco-chops. 'Where do I...?'

'On the Heights.' He mumbles an address.

'Chizz. I oughtta check Satan's Garage out on your database.'

'Eye-screen dysfunctioning?'

'Proscribed info. Really grateful, Mike.'

He waves this away.

I phew, sit @ his desk and key in names and dates. I try transferring to my personal database, but it's blocked.

'You glad to see me?'

He doesn't speak. Just coughs. Perhaps his food's stuck in his throat.

I ask, 'How long you here for?'

'Till morning.'

'Grim.'

'Yeah.'

'When you next on nights?'

He kind of croaks like it's difficult for him to talk. 'Day after tomorrow.'

His terse replies are fuxaching me off. 'Hey, you want my help, or not?'

After a bit, he shakes his head and says sorry. His shoulders heave and he hides his face.

'What's up?'

'I'm okay. It's nothing.' His hands cup his gentle humo features.

'No, something's the matter. Tell me.'

'Don't worry, V159. Ain't nothing to do with you.'

'But you're upset.'

'I'm fine.' He wipes his face. His cheeks glisten in the light.

'You've been crying.'

'Just something in my eye.' He then blubs.

I touch his shoulder with my comforting spheco-palms. 'I might be able to help.'

'You can't, V159. Not with this.'

'Try me.'

'Don't wanna burden you. It's a long, complex story.'

'So tell me.'

'Shouldn't really be saying this, but...it's my mother.'

I nod, waiting for him to continue.

'Chirruped me she's booked a voluntary pre-mortem.'

I raise my I-brow-antennae. 'Sorry, Mike. I had no idea. If I'd known...'

He puts his hand up to stop me interrupting. 'Wait. It gets worse. That was two days ago. I didn't tell anyone. I was too shocked. And proud. But now...' It's getting harder for him to speak. I have a horrible feeling I know what's coming.

'Trouble is,' he struggles to say, 'We still gotta pay for Smantha. She's just turned eight. We wanna buy her another five years. There's a special deal @ the moment — buy your kid five years' life and get one free. Lin and me think that's a great idea.

'We been saving up. That's why I need this promotion. Then Mum steps in like this. She's had over seventy years. That's what she keeps telling me. The money'll ensure Smantha teenages.'

I keep my hand on Mike's shoulder and feel the seismic rise and fall of his frame as the emotion rocks him. I remain silent for a few moments, mulling over his words and allowing them to dissolve in the air.

After a few moments, I speak. 'Your mother knows what's going on, Mike. You'll have told her about your plans for Smantha, I'm sure, before she made her decision. It's tough, but she accepts Smantha's your priority now. That's why she's doing this for you.'

'Chizz.' He smiles @ me. 'I'm downloading that, but it's still gonna be hard. For all of us.'

'This heavyhearts me, Mike. You know if I could help, I would.'

'Of course. Ain't your fault.'

I shake my head. Sphecos don't receive a wage. Well, not in Britz. Being allowed to live our little spheco-lives is our payment. I am choked @ being unable to do anything for him, the last humo I would wish this on. I squeeze his hand as gently as I can and leave.

SIX

The following afternoon, Phoebe took Irene, Samina and Garcia out into the yard.

The sun had hidden behind clouds, but it was mild. All around the house was wasteland. The fields had gone to nothing and were littered with rusting metal panels, oil drums and broken plasticon computer parts. Walking over the uneven surface was a hazard.

'Securicops are constantly searching for us,' rasped Phoebe, a homemade cigarette constantly balanced on her lower lip. She was petite, with waist-length curly black hair, a complexion like Olivier's and face lines reminding Irene of isobars on a weather-map.

'We daren't grow anything,' she continued. 'If the andro-cops saw signs of cultivation, they'd know...we'd have to move.'

'So how do we get food?'

'Raiding.' Phoebe gogged @ them and waited for the reaction.

Irene exchanged a glance with the others. 'But we're not trained for that sort of work. Isn't there other stuff we could do?'

'You'll be doing that anyway.' Phoebe dismissed her objection with a sweep of her veined hand. 'The raiding's what's important. But don't worry. We'll show you everything. We try our best to avoid any confrontation or violence. It's not in our interest for *them*...' she spat, '...to capture our dead and injured, or to be missing any of their workers or androcops.'

'Like the raid on the Recycling Centre?'

Phoebe clicked her tongue and tossed her head. 'Different kind of raid. That was a rescue mission and became a recruitment drive. And why not? We saved you from being recycled. I'm talking about foraging. I'll show you what's edible.'

Later, Olivier appeared and lit a fire with sticks. There was an old pot and an oil drum full of rainwater. They ate boiled nettle leaves, wild chestnuts and crab apples for dinner. For breakfast too. And drank weak black Tanninola®, one infusion bag between five people. But it was preferable to the syngastria.

'Powers-that-be,' cooed Irene. 'Real food and birds. No Eye-Ds. Or withertongue.'

Phoebe and Olivier exchanged glances.

'There's also cobnuts, if we can beat the squirrels to them, and sometimes, we'll even manage to get the odd pigeon or rabbit, or...' Phoebe paused. '...but then, there's the acridians — the reason we keep the kitchen door shut.'

Irene looked puzzled.

'Oh, sooner or later you'll meet them. Everyone does.'

Irene and Samina shared the cellar. Damp and cold, and not much better than Samina's place, but there was no threat of reassessment, only a remote worry of what would happen if they were caught.

Nightmare images of the ant things in the Recycling Centre flashed through Irene's mind and lingered after she woke in a sweat.

The next day, she told Phoebe, who gasped and lit a new roll-up. 'Don't worry. There's no sphecoids here, but we hate them just as much as anything else that comes out of BestcoeBritain®, and we treat them all as our mortal enemies.'

Irene's heart somersaulted. *Nelson*. How could she say that her son, however much she herself despised him and loathed what he'd become, was a sphecoid, and that, in spite of everything, he was still her child, her flesh and blood, even though she hated the insect part?

'I...I thought you avoided confronting the forces of BestcoeBritain® head on.'

'We do. They have much better technology. But sometimes it's unavoidable.'

Phoebe walked them to a nearby overgrown field, where she instructed them to gather blackberries and dandelion leaves to be steamed for lunch. 'Subsistence food,' she said. There was more watery Tanninola®.

Olivier joined them. He smiled @ Irene and Samina when he offered to show them a new Bestcoe agrocomplex. 'I'll take you two now. Phoebe will accompany Garcia. Ready?'

They nodded and followed him. It was a grey afternoon, with sunlight providing a whiteness that hinted @ an underlying chill in the air. They'd been given a coat each, threadbare and tent-like, but effective @ keeping them warm.

'What about your van?' asked Irene.

'Had to dump it. No faeco-fuel. Better camouflage on foot.'

'And no guitar?' added Samina, smiling.

He looked @ her. 'Not on a raid.'

He kept stopping and listening for motor sounds and scanning for movement on the horizon. The land was uneven with rolling hills to the south and east and woods to the west.

'Are you the only Freebies?' asked Samina.

Olivier shook his head and grinned @ her. 'No. We're dotted all over the country. But we have no communication.'

'Shouldn't that be a priority?' wondered Irene.

Olivier's smile disappeared. 'Survival is,' he snapped.

'But think how much stronger you'd — I mean we'd be if we

could act in coordination with other groups.'

Olivier turned to Samina. 'Your friend talks a lot, don't she?'

Samina gasped and looked @ Irene. 'My friend talks a lot of sense.'

'I appreciate your enthusiasm,' said Olivier. 'But you're inexperienced, and have no idea of the practical difficulties we face. That's why Phoebe and I'll train you. You'll soon see what Freebie life really means.'

They were walking through the trees now.

'But don't you think...' started Irene.

'Ssh! Keep your voice down,' he hissed.

'But you've just been banging on...' said Irene.

'You've no idea who might be hiding or listening. Outside, we keep conversation to a bare minimum, and when we speak, it's because we have something important to say, and we say it quietly like I'm doing now.'

Irene squeezed Samina's hand.

'Tread softly.'

'Of course,' they answered, no louder than the breeze hushing the branches and forged on, trying not to crunch twigs underfoot.

There was an autumnal smell of rotting vegetation, and the fallen leaves had become mulch. It was hard keeping up in the ill-fitting shoes they'd been given. Every so often Olivier stopped and waited.

The trees came to a sudden end and there was a steep ascent, leading up to a grassy plateau. They climbed or rather Olivier did, in leaps and bounds, and then stretched out his hand to pull Irene up the last few yards.

'There,' he said, not even out of breath. 'We can talk normally now.'

'You're fit,' panted Samina.

He smiled @ her, and Irene thought, held onto her for longer than necessary as he hauled her up.

They had been walking for @ least four deci-minutes, but Olivier gave no indication that they were to have any kind of rest. He threw Irene a look, which she interpreted as a sign of resentment @ her presence. Not wishing to gooseberry out the rest of the trip, she stayed close to Samina.

'Down there, on the left, you can just make out the green-houses.'

Irene scanned the horizon. The agrocomplex stretched out beneath them. She whistled. 'That's one fuxaching fortress of a farm.'

@ the far end, behind endless cornfields, gleamed rows of plasticon greenhouses.

'That's what the A-listers get. And some of the luckier Bs,' he said.

'I was a B,' said Samina. 'Once,'

Olivier nodded. He didn't look @ her, but his hand reached for hers.

How can she be so easy? Irene felt the chill of being left out of something. 'How did you become a Freebie?' she asked him.

'Oh, that's a long story,' he said. 'Another time. Today we're just gonna lie low, here, watch all comings and goings and work out when's the best time to pounce.'

They made beds out of piles of leaves and twigs and used their coats as blankets. They ate rotting blackberries that tasted of the earth they were one day to return to and become part of, and sour crab apples and wrinkled tiny plums Olivier insisted were edible, and drank water from a brook.

'If we light a fire, we're dead.'

'So we don't light a fire,' said Samina.

'We'll have to keep each other warm.' He searched

Samina's face for reaction. Irene couldn't believe he could be so forward in her presence.

They watched the agrocomplex for hours. As the sun began to set, an autobus drove up and people, mostly gynos, boarded.

The vehicle set off, chugging away across the valley towards whatever Bestcoetown those gynos called home. Darkness descended and it was silent.

Green-glowing floodlights revealed two uniformed andros patrolling the perimeter fence with alsatians.

'Arselights,' said Irene. 'Even here.'

'Fuxaches!' Olivier stamped his foot. 'And forgot the wire-cutters.'

The guards reappeared after a deci-minute.

'That's how long we'll have,' he said.

In the middle of the night, Irene woke to a noise. She started, and then remembered where she was. She'd been dreaming about Nelson coming to rescue her from the Recycling Centre and from the Freebies. Nelson as a young man, not the monster she'd seen, Nelson as Olivier.

Olivier's face. Staring @ her. No, not Olivier. Like *Olivier.*

She stared back, too terrified to react. The face disappeared into the gloom.

Her heart pounded. Androcops. Searching. She listened hard.

Olivier and Samina were asleep.

Should I wake them?

A twig snapped.

SEVEN

I'm halfway up a hill, with a view of the glittering lower slopes of Olympia Heights leading down to the Thames.

I circle Don Sauternes's villa, which still has lights on. I see Sauternes andro-hugging another guy. The muggy weather's on my side; a French window's open. I glide in and make my way to their room.

Hovering like a humming bird, I wait by the door and listen. No eavesdroppings of interest.

@ last I hear footsteps. Out totters Sauternes.

I fly behind him. He slips inside another room. A dog barks and is silent. I turn the handle and go in. He gasps.

'Sauternes Don.' My silkiest spheco-whisper. 'Coupla questions.'

He thinks for a beat, recovering from his initial shock @ my appearance and @ the presence of my spheco-cock on his trim waist.

'What do you want?'

'Didn't know you were nice.'

'What the fuck...?'

'C'mon. Who's the andro you been shagging next door?'

'You been spying on me? Fuxaches, that's Reza Sharpe, our new vocalist. I was welcoming him into the band.'

'Wow, some welcome...and Gobbs's ashes have only just been urned.'

'That's showbiz. We need a new member.'

'I'm sure he'll confirm this, but that ain't why I've come. I'm more interested in your past.'

'I never done nothing wrong.'

'I mean your distant past. Remember any of that?'

He frowns.

My spheco-dick helps him out a little. 'Like your schooldays?'

'Sure. Happiest days of your life, aren't they?'

'Specially if you got friends. You had friends @ school, didn't you?'

'Yeah. Like everyone. So what?'

Not everyone has friends @ school. That's why... I don't continue that thought. Too painful.

'It's curious you went to the same school, Blueburymead Juniors, as Jaxxon Gobbs and Maxx Smacker.'

Something about that name on Mike's database is familiar, but I can't define exactly how. It'll come back. I let it fester in my spheco-brain and concentrate on Satan's Garage.

Sauternes shrugs. 'Yeah, we been mates all this time. Jaxxon...' He breaks off.

'You're very lucky. A niceboy who dodged the radar. How'd you do it?'

'What the fuck you talking about, sphecoid? I ain't nice. You must've seen me making out with all them nubile gynos.'

So many beautiful nubos in your life...but you prefer andros.' I tickle my cock up and down his taut torso and shave off some of his chest hair. He inhales sharp. 'Your parents bribe anyone so you could stay humo?'

'No!'

'You know what a fuck with this would do? You'd like that?'

It's evil of me, but he's getting me more and more aroused by the accu-minute. His face is a paragon of andro-beauty. Body too. Perfect chest-waist ratio, the latter being very narrow for an andro-mandro like him. Gorgeous muscle-tone. Probably nice as fuck too, despite his protestations.

'Look, I really don't care about your private life, but if you and Gobbs were such good friends, going back @ least 13 years, then wouldn't you be a bit more upset?'

Silence.

'How many Deadly Sins did Gobbs commit?'

He bristles, that humo-bristling thing they do when you irk them. I rub an internal pair of spheco-mitts with spheco-glee.

'You reckon that's got anything to do with it?'

'So, he was on them, then?'

'Yeah. I guess he committed five or six.'

'Who was the tempter? Fraser?'

He shrugs. 'How should I know?'

'You a sinner?'

'I'm clean.'

'Sure. Tell me how you formed Satan's Garage.'

He takes a deep breath. 'Me and Jaxxon both played guitar and Maxx deejayed. So we had a lot in common. When we wrote Disco Duelling, it all took off.'

I retract my cock and swagger my best spheco-swagger to the window. Then I turn to him. 'Oh, and one other thing.'

He rolls his eyes skywards.

'Did Jaxxon know you're nice and was blackmailing you?'

His entire face explodes with outrage and he splutters. Eventually he manages to say, 'I'm telling you I ain't no fucking niceboy.'

'I'll check your Eye-D account. And now I'm gonna interview your "new member."'

'He'll be asleep.'

'So I'll wake him.'

I close the door and leave Sauternes to stew. I skirt the wide landing, admiring the sweeping staircase that plunges to the front door. Androscent guides me to Sharpe.

I don't bother to knock.

It's dark, so I pass my hand around the doorframe. Eventually the light switch mechanism senses my movement and a dim glimmer suffuses the space.

He's on his back in a large double bed. I sniff for cumscent, but draw a blank. The room suddenly gets brighter and this makes him stir. He moans a bit and starts when he sees me.

'Reza Sharpe?'

'What the...?'

My cock's on his lips before he can say more. 'Shut the fuck up till I tell you to speak, okay?'

He nods very carefully.

'On your feet. Face me. Understand?'

Another nod. I back off a nanometre and allow him leeway to get into a standing position. His navy-blue torso-hugger's unbuttoned to the waist, revealing his six-pack. He shouldn't've let me see that.

'Care to give me a blow job?'

His eyes widen in terror @ my proposition.

'Or would you prefer me to suck you?'

The disgust never leaves his eyes, and he shakes his head slowly.

'So, who fucked who just now? You do Sauternes, or the other way round?'

He looks @ me as if I'm mad. I feel his revulsion @ what I'm saying is genuine. Maybe Sauternes was telling the truth after all. I tease my cock down to below his chin. 'You don't want to arouse me more, which you will if you irk me. So you'd better give me some straight answers.'

He mumbles something. Sounds like okay.

'What were you doing with Sauternes before?'

'Celebrating being the new vocalist.'

'Yeah? You a niceboy?'

'Is that what you're looking for?'

I cockslap his face. 'I'm looking for Jaxxon Gobbs's killer. You know anything about his murder you wanna share with me, Mister Prettyboy?'

He gasps.

I dig my cock under his chin and push his head up. 'Well, I'm waiting.'

He shakes his scared andro-head.

I lower my dick till it's over his heart, still threatening. He coughs.

'I hope for your sake you're not lying.'

'I ain't.' He swallows.

'We'll see.'

As I withdraw, he flops back onto his bed and sighs with relief.

I make my way to his open window and launch my tired spheco-self into the cold night air.

EIGHT

Almost unable to breathe, Irene stretched out her hand and rocked Samina gently. 'Ssh!' she said as quietly as possible. She could hardly hear the sound of her own voice herself.

Samina moaned 'Mm' and rolled over. She did not wake. Irene reached over and tapped Olivier's shoulder, repeating her hushing.

'What is it?' he whispered after an interminable silence.

'Someone's...I heard...'

'Probably a dream, for fuxache.' mumbled Olivier. 'Or a fox. Go back to sleep.'

Then it was light. And freezing cold. Irene groaned and tried to gather herself into a ball to stay warm, but it was impossible. Her hands and feet felt as if they were made of ice and dripping frozen water. She forced herself out of her 'bed' and jumped up and down, rubbing her hands together, trying to thaw them in the steam of her breath.

Olivier appeared from the trees. Irene wished to relieve herself too. He pointed back down the slope and said, 'Find somewhere comfortable.'

When she'd finished, she dragged herself up to their look-out post. And then she knew, from their faces. Samina was different. Not in a bad way. But everything had changed during the night. And Irene had woken them up. 'It's cold.' she said.

'Keep moving,' said Olivier. 'It'll warm you up.'

'What do we do today?'

'We go in @ nightfall. That's the best time. After the workers have left.'

Irene nodded. Samina was gazing @ him, enthralled.

'I'm gonna look for some more berries. You coming?' Olivier addressed these words to Samina.

Samina smiled. 'No, you're alright,' she said, looking @ Irene. 'I'll stay here if that's okay with you.'

Olivier said nothing. Just glared @ Irene and set off.

'Go after him,' said Irene.' You can tell me all about it later.' She smiled @ Samina, whose face blossomed with joy @ these words for a few seconds and then clouded over.

'But I can't leave you here alone. We must stick together.'

'I'll be alright. Don't worry about me.'

'Sure?'

Before Irene could answer, two andro Freebies came towards her and Samina, one holding Olivier in a stranglehold.

The agrocomplex seemed further away now, as though the next meal was beyond their grasp.

Samina grabbed Irene's hand and shouted Olivier's name, but he could barely grunt back. 'Let him go,' she called.

They were in ill-fitting coats too. Andros with beards, breath spiralling from their mouths like steam engines.

Olivier struggled, but the andro choking him was bigger and stronger. When they were a few yards from Irene and Samina, they stopped. No one spoke. The andro yanked him up, and the other andro, who was wearing binoculars, punched him hard in the stomach.

Winded, Olivier gasped and groaned, his knees buckling. Embarrassment clouded his cheeks.

'I said let him go.'

Binoculars looked Samina up and down and said, 'How many are you?'

'Just us three.' Irene spoke this time.

He shook his head. 'No, I mean in your group.'

'We're new. We don't know.'

He punched Olivier in the solar plexus again, making him grunt.

'Stop that,' screamed Samina.

He laughed. 'If you want your boyfriend back, you'd better answer our questions.'

'I told you, we don't know.'

'Oh dear.' This time he whacked Olivier's mouth, splitting his lip.

Olivier spat blood. 'They're telling the truth. They joined us two days ago. We're five strong.'

Binoculars smiled @ Irene and Samina. 'Thank you. That's what we wanted to know.' He nodded @ his mate, who released Olivier, kicking his arse and sending him sprawling forwards, half staggering, half falling towards Samina.

Olivier wiped the blood from his mouth.

Samina touched his arm.

The andros stood before them like oaks. Oaks with knives. 'Where's your base?'

Olivier cleared his throat and pointed to the hill, but Irene smacked his arm down.

'Are you insane?' she whispered. 'We don't tell them nothing.'

Olivier looked down @ the ground.

Irene squared up to the andros. 'Where are you?' she asked.

Binoculars raised his head and once-overed her. 'This is our land. You come from some godforsaken shithole and think you can muscle in on our territory? You're fucking wrong, lady. We're the ones who raid the farms round here, not you. I dunno how you strayed so far east, but you can fuck off before we boot your stinking arses back to whatever hell you crawled out of.'

'Look, we're new @ this. We dunno nothing about your rules. Up till yesterday me and my friend here were ordinary D-classified gynos awaiting recycling. Our colleague,' she pointed to Olivier, 'rescued us. So tell me how, without any means of communication, we're supposed to know you claim ownership here?'

He narrowed his eyes. 'You know now, lady.'

'Aren't you interested in what we have to offer?'

He raised an eyebrow to signal curiosity. 'And what might that be?'

'We can help you raid. Share the spoils.'

He burst out laughing and looked @ his mate. 'You hear that? She thinks we're gonna let her and her mangy cronies muscle in on our kill.' Then he looked @ Irene. 'Tell ya what. If you wanna help, join us. You don't go back to your old friends. And you do as we say.'

Irene nodded. 'Okay, we'll go elsewhere.'

A glint flashed like lightning in the andro's eyes. 'Ain't that simple, though. We've seen you. We know you're here. Can't have that. Wanna make sure you fuck off for good. Watch you fuck off, not take your lousy word for it. So here's the deal. We take you back to ours and then we exchange addresses. Understood?'

'And if we refuse?'

'Then I use this.' He produced a gun. Irene didn't know if it was loaded, but it was hard to argue with a pistol.

'So start walking. Hands up. That's right, high above your heads. Remember, we're right behind. One false move and we got you, so don't try nothing stupid cz the shot might disturb the local androcops and we'd have to butcher all of you. Flint, you get behind loverboy and his tart. I got the mouthy bitch.'

In silence, they walked through a waterlogged field,

bordered by silver birches and forested with dying thistles, nettles and brambles. They crossed over a stile into an almost identical field overlooking the agrocomplex and came to a halt.

Irene turned and said, 'We can help,' but Binoculars slapped her round the face. She screamed.

'Oy,' cried Olivier, spinning round. 'Touch her again and I'll...'

'You'll what?' Binoculars laughed in Olivier's face and walloped him. Olivier staggered back, clutching his nose. Blood trickled between his fingers.

'Shut it.'

Flint sniggered and slapped Binoculars on the back. 'Nice one.'

The look Olivier shot the one called Flint was a bolt of pure hatred.

In the grey-green daylight, they huddled on the grass, Binoculars's gun trained on them.

'The others have been ages already,' said Flint, surveying the agrocomplex. 'Shouldn't they be back by now?'

Binoculars shrugged. 'Could take anything up to twenty-five deci if they hit trouble.'

'What are we gonna do with these three...you know, after-wards?'

'Dunno. Whatever they tell us.'

The first of the Freebies returned @ twilight. Everything was deep blue. He ran straight up to Binoculars, totally out of breath, and pointed to the agrocomplex.

'Cops,' he panted. 'We gotta be on our way back. Jake said.'

Binoculars screwed up his face, incredulous. 'What you talking about?'

He never got an answer. A shot rang out. The Freebie screamed as the bullet tore into his back. He fell forward into

Binoculars's embrace and coughed his last.

Binoculars let him fall to the ground. 'Looks like we better get going.' He motioned with his gun to the prisoners to get to their feet.

They set off along paths by fields and brooks. All requests for water were denied. The captors never addressed their prisoners, except to give directions.

After eight deci-minutes when it was now dark except for moonbeams illuminating foliage, they came to the derelict outskirts of an urban area.

The pavements and roads were strewn with rubbish — real-glass shards from smashed panes, crumbling bricks, rotting timber, old furniture, plasticon bags flapping in the breeze — impeding their progress. The prisoners were made to keep close to the walls, lest they were being watched, and were the first to turn corners, to take any bullets a sniper — rogue Freebie or androcop — could fire.

'Halt!'

Hearts in their mouths, they stood outside a small terraced house, with no roof or window panes.

Flint knocked twice on the front door and called his name into the letterbox. Bolts and chains sounded and the door opened.

A grizzled andro looked @ the prisoners. 'Who the fuck are these?'

'Trespassers,' explained Binoculars. 'The cellar?'

'Yep.'

Binoculars pushed them down a creaking staircase into a dark windowless space.

'What are you gonna do to us?' asked Olivier. 'Can't you let us go?'

Binoculars laughed. 'No way. You know where we live.'

'But...maybe we could...'

'Shut up. It's late.' He left. The bolt scraped across.

Irene knew there had to be rats, mice and cockroaches. As she lay on the stone floor, she heard things scuttling about on the floor and felt them sniffing her, filthy whiskers and antennae tickling her face, probing her to see if she was edible. But she was no less rank than they were. And she remembered what Nelson had become.

She must've slept because suddenly it was morning. A strip of light filtered through the crack under the cellar entrance. The bolt moved. Someone looked in and secured the door again.

Irene heard him say, 'Sure they're asleep, but couldn't see much.' She was wondering how many people were in the house when her thoughts were interrupted by andros and gynos shouting.

'Securicops!'

NINE

Maxx Smacker's complexion has that glossy, unlived-in sheen the wealthy acquire. Tall and thin, but not what one would call pretty, and his black, frizzy halo-hair is gagging for a wash.

He hasn't spotted me hiding behind his outrageously massive loft cocktail bar; that's a pleasure to come. All mine, I guess.

Androguards downstairs had told me to wait in his spacious loft; I fancied having a bit of spheco-mischief.

I observe how he makes his drink with jerky, angular movements, and how his dainty, mincing gait — all feet and eyes — gets him to the chaise longue he then reclines on.

He takes a sip and I clear my throat, suppressing a spheco-giggle as he chokes and splutters, ice cubes tinkling in the glass.

'Who's there?' He doesn't get up off his skinny, massaged arse. I only speak when he reaches under the table, probably for a panic button.

'I'll've run your guards through before they can even think about...'

I make myself visible. He stifles his cry of surprise with a hand over his mouth. Perhaps deep down he's pleased to see me.

'A sphecoid.'

I correct him.

He tuts with irritation. 'Don't you need a warrant?'

I shake my head. Folk are dumb enough to accept whatever

an authority figure says, even if he's just a lowly, despised spheco-cop.

'What do you want? Why are you here?'

I hush him. 'Maxx Smacker?'

'The very.'

'I'm here to ask you a few questions about the murder of Jaxxon Gobbs.'

He draws breath. 'Dreadful business. Awful.'

'Did you have any disagreement with Gobbs prior to his death?'

Smacker's eyes search his soul. 'Not that I can think of. No.'

'Did he have any enemies?'

He shrugs. 'Who can say? What he did outside of the Garage was his own business.'

'Is there anyone who might know of any contacts he had?'

'You could ask Don Sauternes.'

I nod.

'Er...shouldn't you be accompanied by a proper androcop, sphecoid?' He gets to his feet, but realizes he shouldn't have said that when my cock darts out in anger and hovers in mid-air. Without taking his bulging eyes off it, he adds, 'Oh, sorry.'

'This inquiry's top secret. And had better stay that way. Kapeesh?' My dick-tip rests on his Adam's apple.

He goes boss-eyed gogging @ the shaft and swallows hard. 'Y-yes.'

I retract my penis. 'Splendid. Now we've cleared that up, we can continue. Sit.'

He obeys. I continue.

'Just speak in response to my questions. Okay?'

He nods. I grin.

'Besides Sauternes and Gobbs, who else do you see from your schooldays?'

He shakes his head. 'No one.'

'You sure?'

'Yes.'

'If I find out you're lying...'

His face stretches in terror. 'I swear it's the truth.'

'Who's Reza Sharpe?'

'The new band member.'

'What can you tell me about him?'

He looks down @ the genuine wooden floor, which I could chew up, and then @ his barely-touched drink. 'I don't know. Don chose him. I concentrate on the deejaying.'

'I know, Smacker. Everyone loves your deejaying.'

He attempts a smile.

'Is Sauternes a niceboy?'

Maxx Smacker tuts and opens his mouth in a mixture of surprise and outrage @ the directness and personal nature of the question. 'I can't speak for Don,' he says.

'No, but you can speak about him. Remember, this is a murder investigation.'

'I don't see what Don's sexuality's got...'

I cut him off mid-cliché with another dick-poke in the throat. He squeaks like a mouse and shuts up.

'You've known him since you were boys. You must be able to tell me.'

He hesitates and then blurts it out. 'He's one hundred percent normal.'

'Like Gobbs?'

'Oh, you had to peel the gynos off Jaxxon.'

'Which brings me to you.'

His ears twitch in alarm. 'What about me?'

'I've heard rumours you're a niceboy too. Is that so?'

He screws up his face in indignation, looking for all the world like he's going to deny the accusation, but resigns himself to a single nod and turns his timberex varnish hued face away.

I laugh a high-pitched, husky spheco-laugh. 'Nothing to be ashamed of. And you escaped detection @ seven.'

'Yes, I did. I was lucky.' He looks me straight in the eye and his face twists with scorn. 'Otherwise, I'd've ended up like you.'

'No, you'd've ended up under me.'

He tosses his head. 'Whatever.'

'Do you recall anyone who was selected @ that age from your school?'

He frowns. 'No, I don't think so.'

'Think hard, Smacker.'

After a few moments, he looks @ me again. 'No. Can't remember.'

I exhale a laugh through my spheco-nostrils. 'Where were you between 1 and 2 am accu-time, on the night of the murder?'

He sits up straight. 'You don't suspect me? Why would I kill one of my own band members?'

'Your movements between those times?'

'Er...I was in the DJ booth, sorting my equipment out.'

'Did you see Gobbs after the fight?'

He looks up, trying to remember. 'No.'

'So, you don't know where he went after his song?'

'I saw him put his arm round Don, and then they split up. Jaxxon made for backstage and Don came to see me. He commented on the show, said goodbye and left.'

'Was Fraser in?'

His eyes pinball around in their sockets. 'Er...don't think so.'

My cock's back on his neck in a trice. 'Oh, c'mon, Smacker,' I whisper. 'You can do better than that.'

'I'm not sure...he may have been.'

I push a bit more. 'How much did you pay him?'

'Take your cock off me,' he manages to croak. 'I don't deal

with that side of things.'

I ease back a bit so he can speak more comfortably.

'He made a delivery. He's got a special account number. He just deducts his...er...fee and...'

'What'd he bring you — a Deadly Sin?'

'You can't touch A-listers for drugs. I've got celebrity-immunity for Sinning.'

'Not for murder you haven't.'

'I didn't kill Jaxxon.'

'But you might know who did.'

'Well, I don't, sphecoid. All right?' He smiles a sly humo-smile, which my cock's reappearance swiftly swipes from his chops.

'How many you committed so far? Three? Four?'

'It was my third.'

'Was Gobbs on Sins?'

'I think so.'

'Tempted by Fraser? It makes sense, two clients in one place. Did Gobbs have the same payment arrangements as you?'

'Dunno. I never asked.'

'How did you escape @ seven, Smacker?'

'I wasn't bullied. Wasn't a victim.' He spits his words out @ me.

His contempt for what I am, the fate he dodged, stings me. And I remind him of what he is.

'I didn't know I was nice till I was older. Much older.'

'You done pretty well for yourself.'

'I have, and I'm proud of what I've achieved.'

I nod. *Yeah, I'm a bit jealous. If only I'd been stronger back then.* Our resentment's mutual.

'I know where to find you if I need to quiz you again.' I walk to the window, open it and look round, to see him put his longed-for drink back down on the table the minute his eyes meet mine.

'Oh, did you bet on the duel?'

'Everyone does.'

'I take that as a yes. Did you win?'

He shakes his head. 'I bet on the favourite.'

'Lose much?'

'Only 10 Britz. It's more the fun of it. It's not as if I need the money. I don't gamble on anything else. Only the flight fights we gig @.'

'Did Gobbs bet?'

He raises his eyebrows. 'Probably. We usually do, me, Jaxxon and Don.'

'Do you know if he won?'

Smacker shakes his head.

'Enjoy your drink. It'll need more ice now.'

I take off from the window ledge and wing my way out of East Cockneytown. Past Dagtown DUBs, over flat, marshy fields by the Thames and north to where V157's logkipping.

TEN

It was hard to make out what was happening in the house, apart from gunshots, yelling and people running about.

Irene grabbed Samina. Olivier groaned. They shushed him and listened, their hearts pounding.

'That cunt betrayed us.' Flint's voice. 'Told them everything. He's been working for securicops all this time. We been set up.'

They heard sirens and cries of despair. Then rapid footsteps and more gunfire. And screams.

The bolt moved. Light from above made them screw up their eyes.

Binoculars came down a few steps followed by the old andro.

'This true?'

Binoculars had his hands up. He shook his head. 'Course not. I'd never squeal. C'mon, you know me.'

The prisoners were pressing their backs into the wall in the corner of the cellar, praying they'd been forgotten. Irene hardly dared breathe. She clutched both Olivier's and Samina's clammy hands.

'Traitor!'

Binoculars hesitated too long before answering.

'No, you got this wrong. We...'

'You lying...'

A shot rang out. Blood sprayed out of Binoculars's back.

He said, 'What...?' and fell backwards, landing with his legs bent under him @ the foot of the stairs. He writhed, his arms scissoring as he groaned in agony.

'Shut it.' The andro fired again. Binoculars shut up for good. But another shot flung the andro off the stairs and onto the cellar floor next to his victim.

The cries and screams were dying away now.

Irene held her breath, her heart a hammer on an anvil as a voice called out, 'Round the survivors up for recycling.'

She exhaled as quietly as she could and breathed again, listening hard. An engine started outside.

A ray of light flashed down the stairs.

Just once, but that was enough.

'Hey...' The androcop had seen their startled faces. 'Who the...?' he started, but a hand clamped over his mouth interrupted him. A glint of steel scored his throat and a kick from behind catapulted him off his feet. As he somersaulted down the stairs, the torchbeam pinballed across the ceiling.

Flint raced down, two steps @ a time. Wiping the blade on the cop's uniform, he turned to the prisoners. 'If you wanna live, shift your arses and follow me.'

'They'll come for him,' whispered Irene.

'There's a way out the back.' Flint fumbled in Binoculars's coat pockets. 'Move!'

They sprang to their feet and hurried up the stairs into the kitchen. Bodies lay on the floor and it stank of rotting food.

@ the front, andro voices shouted and heavy boots clumped on the creaking floorboards. More and more cops piled into the house.

Irene froze, staring @ Olivier and Samina.

The cops investigated the cellar.

'Go,' mouthed Flint. He carefully opened a door to a passage. They tiptoed through this and out into a dirty back yard, @ the end of which were some pine trees. They hid behind the trunks for a few accu-minutes.

No cops emerged from the house.

Between the terraces was a network of narrow alleys, over-grown with dying weeds. Flint led the way. 'It's a maze,' he whispered, turning round. 'They'll never find us here.'

Through a gap in a fence, they managed to squeeze into an old shed.

'Now we wait,' said Flint softly.

Heavy footsteps could be heard in the vicinity, sometimes running, sometimes walking. Several deci-minutes passed. It was afternoon when they finally heard the androcop van drive away.

Once again, the town was dead.

'I thought you were an established group,' said Irene as they trudged through undergrowth, every so often stopping to push back bushes and shrubs blocking their way.

Flint smirked. He was tall and broad like Olivier, but his head was shaven and he looked much stronger. 'We were,' he started, 'when I joined not so long ago. We even had a secret place to grow stuff — you know, vegetables and all, but got set up by that...snake.'

'How do you know he betrayed you?' asked Irene.

Flint flashed a green Eye-D. 'Found this in his pocket. Fucking undercover greeneye. Freebie traitor working with securicops.'

Nobody answered.

Olivier broke the silence. 'Phoebs'll cut my bollocks off.' He was walking hand in hand with Samina.

'Do you know the way back?' Irene asked him sharply.

'Erm...not sure.'

'Great. I might chop them off myself first.'

'Look, I'm trying to retrace my steps. I think we're going in the right direction. The main thing is no androcops.'

The nocturnal cold descended upon them abruptly, as if the day's warmth had evaporated. It was dark, except for the moonlight and a fire burning in the distance.

'Your old home?' asked Irene.

Flint shook his head. 'Withertonguesters. Cremating the local victims.'

'Even here?' said Samina.

Flint nodded.

'We'll still get lost if we can't see our way around properly,' said Irene. 'So we should get some sleep now until it's light again, and then find our way home.'

Flint slept with his back to Irene. Samina was next to Olivier. They'd put their coats together in one enormous blanket and snuggled up under it. It was one of the most uncomfortable nights Irene had ever spent, worse even than queuing in the scrounge lounge all those months ago. She didn't manage to sleep much. Just a few fitful bouts grabbed here and there when she wasn't going over in her mind the events of the day.

She was relieved when she woke to daylight. It was even colder than it had been the previous morning, yet she'd survived another hundred deci-minutes. But she dreaded the reception they'd get from Phoebe.

ELEVEN

I startle Mike. Even though he's expecting me, he still jumps when he sees me.

'I'm beginning to think you got some guilty secrets.'

He closes his eyes. 'Yes. Letting you in here. Talking to you, for fuxache. Allowing you to access my database. Red-cardable...want me to go on? I got my birthday Brit-account review tomorrow.'

I pat his arm, as gently as I can. 'Many happy returns. Your livelihood's on the line as it is if you don't clear up this case.'

'Should be okay, but chizz for reminding me. Is that what you've come for?'

I shake my head with a knowing smile. 'Nope, but I wanna check Gobbs's Brit-account. You find out anything?'

He nods. 'Gobbs bet on Kamara to win, but not a small sum. We're talking fifty thousand-odd Britz. That's a helluva lot even for a guy who earns that much in a single gig.'

I hendonhaw like humos do when they ain't convinced about something. 'It possibly meant nothing to him as he was so rich. Losing 50K wouldn't be...'

Mike suddenly gogs @ me in horror, frantically waving @ the floor.

Someone's approaching. I smell spheco.

Suppressing my breathing, I crouch behind his desk, shielded from view by a reception panel.

V103, V122 and new spheco-queen V146 on night duty.

Wherever they're going, they'll be back. Gotta be quick.

V146 farts soli-pherum.

Does he know I'm here?

I'm going under its spell...must resist...not panic...

I manage to retaliate with a burst from my spheco-arse and pray it'll still work.

Mike greets them. Their scent fades in my spheco-nostrils as they recede down the corridor.

He phews to me. 'That was close.'

'Where were they going?'

'No idea. Why?'

'No reason. Old mates. Kinda miss that camaraderie.'

'Course you do. Look, what I wanted to say before was I thought the same as you about Gobbs betting large sums,' says Mike. 'But he wasn't rich. He must've gambled it all away.'

I tap my spheco-fingers on my nose, as I often do when I'm busy a-thinking. 'So, Gobbs's lost most of his seven-figure fortune, why risk the last 50k?'

'Unless he was desperate for cash.'

'And why would he be? He can earn it back in a single night.'

'To pay someone off, V159. Someone very demanding.'

'Okay. Can't see your screen from down here, but how much did he have left?'

Keys click, then Mike whistles. 'Nothing.'

'So, he was broke. And the bet was his last chance. But didn't he get paid for gigging @ the duel?'

'That's what I'd've thought.'

'And Sauternes?'

Mike taps a few keys. 'No big receipts. Some payment. Five grand.'

'Hm. Probably a Sin. Gonna make another couple of visits. So I hope you appreciate my efforts.'

A gentle kick.

'Ow! Sphecos hurt as well, you know.'

'Go before your ex-colleagues return.'

I get to my feet, hoping that none of my fellow sphecos scented me on their way out. I try to convince myself that as there were three of them, my fourth smell wouldn't have intruded too obviously. But I know it could have, with our heightened contrapuntal olfactory sense. They didn't react, but might be storing that info.

I take off and make for the Heights.

Don Sauternes's mansion is quiet and dark. No easy entrance this time, so I shatter a window, and having invited myself in, graciously accept the invitation.

No lights are on, but footsteps alert me to danger. Body-guards? All the Olympians employ them. Lucky C-class tough guys plucked from the shit-heap.

I hide ninja-like on the high ceiling of a reception room, the sucker-pads on my spheco-digits holding me in place, black and yellow on the mock-classical painted vault providing camouflage. My 180-degree vision captures all movement below.

I wait a long time. Then the door opens. I hold my breath.

Sharpe enters. The light comes on. He looks around and leaves. He doesn't check the broken window. I resume respiration.

I swoop down and land silently on the deep carpet. My I-brow antennae lead me to the first floor landing round the great sweeping staircase, where I cling to the ceiling and observe.

Sharpe appears with a guard in the entrance hall.

'Checked upstairs, sir. No one's there.'

'All the rooms?'

'The lot.'

'Okay. Must've imagined it.'

I phew in my dizzy spheco-head. Let them puzzle their soppy humo-brains over it when they discover the broken glass.

Sharpe chuckles. 'Lucky bastard, Don. Slept right through it.'

'Yeah.' The guard laughs. They say goodnight.

I fly down and stand outside Sauternes's room. I grip the knob, spheco-heart a-beating away like a downpour on a sky-light, and turn it.

I sneak in.

Sauternes is lying on his side, naked, with a single cover over his midsection. The light doesn't wake him.

I mount the bed and lie beside him, leaning forward to watch his torso rise and fall with his regular breathing. *What would it be like to be able to have a normal, love-based relationship with a humo? Would it be better than what I have with V157?* I suddenly forget why I'm there. I just want to fling my spheco-arms round him and hug him close to me and kiss his cheek, his face and fuck that cute, tight arse and cling to him till dawn, not feeling like an outlaw, a freak. But there's no time for daydreams. I stroke his shoulder. He mumbles and twitches. I put my hand over his mouth.

He wakes, and panics.

'Ssh. Just gonna ask you some more questions.'

He can't talk, but flails when he realizes I'm right behind him.

'Don't make me fuck you. Neither of us wants that. I want you alive. You want you alive. So shut up and listen. I'll tell you when to speak.' I remove my hand.

He grabs it and tries to pull it towards the edge of the bed, probably to a panic button.

Gotta act fast. My cock shoots out a bit and scratches @ his buttocks. 'One more move and I impale you.'

He stops still.

'Good boy. You're learning. Now listen. Nod if the answer is yes. Shake your head if it's no. Understand?'

A nod.

'Super. Now, on the night of the Kamara flight-fight, did Smacker pay you and Gobbs for gigging?'

Another nod.

'Before the gig?'

A third affirmative.

'Okay. I'm gonna remove my hand from your mouth now. If you scream, or try and get the others' attention, I'll skewer you. Arse to throat. Answer me in whispers. Remember my cock is ready to spear you right through.' I take my hand away. A satisfying silence.

'Seems like me and you got a great little understanding here. Now, tell me, who tempted Gobbs with his Deadly Sins?'

He shakes his head.

'C'mon, you can do better than that.'

'I don't know.'

'I don't believe you and you don't wanna know how I feel about liars.' My cock probes his crack, without penetration. 'Keep very still. Wouldn't want to bloody yourself now. Think again.'

He clicks his tongue. The parting of his lips is accompanied by an inhalation of breath that tells me he's finally going to speak. 'He never said.'

'You disappoint me. You take me for a fool, with my dick about to run you through? Plus you lied about being clean. Not very clever. Especially as you both shared the same tempter.'

'Please,' he whispers. 'You know what'll happen to me if I squeal.'

'And you know what'll happen if you don't.'

'Fraser.'

'Thank you. That wasn't so difficult, was it? How much you pay for a single Sin?'

'Five K. A-list tariff.'

I whistle. 'That's a lotta Britz for one pill.'

'It's okay. I can afford it.'

'What about Gobbs? He was broke. How'd he pay Fraser?'

'He...he...'

'Spit it out. I'm waiting.' My cock tickles his buttock flesh.

'He owed him.'

'How much?'

He almost shouts his reply. 'I don't know.'

I cockwhip his face. 'Fuxaches, keep it down. So Gobbs was in debt to Fraser?'

His breathing has changed and his whisper sounds choked. 'Jaxxon wanted to go for the whole seven and get the prize.'

'Prize?'

'If you survive the seventh Sin, you get as many as you want free. For the rest of your life. It's on FaceChirp®. Course...so far...no one's managed it.'

I chuckle. 'Neat.'

He whispers on. 'He told me he was in trouble with Fraser, but didn't go into detail. I think he owed him big time for the Sins he'd already committed. He used to come crying to me, begging for a loan. I lent him once, but later, when I realized I'd never see that money again, I said no.'

'He asked you more than once?'

'He was always trying it on, but I put my foot down.'

'I'll check with Fraser.'

I let him turn in my embrace to face me.

Panic stretches his eyes. 'You won't tell him I've spoken to you?'

'You forget I'm a spheco-cop. I only ask questions.'

'Fraser's a dangerous man.'

'And I'm a dangerous cop.'

He nods. He's staring straight ahead @ the wall.

I dismount and stand up, having got what I came for.

It's early morning now. Too late to return to Mike. That'll have to keep.

'Night night.'

No answer.

I close the door of his room, and fly back to the living room, squeeze through the still standing glass shards and am off.

But a nagging thought bugs me during my dawn flight. Was Gobbs blackmailing Sauternes about his over-denied niceness for desperately needed cash? It looks like I'll need to make another visit.

I arrive @ our spheco-nest some time after sunrise, joyjumping @ seeing V157. He's watching out for me. I kiss him. We lie in each other's arms for two whole deci-minutes.

'Time to get up.' I murmur.

On the way to the stream for a drink, I tell him everything I've discovered. V157 flies over the brambles and I walk, being too exhausted to fly. I need water.

There are still some tiny plums, red and yellow, which we suck for the sugar, and overripe berries, but they're manky and my thirst wants a-quenching. Dewdrops go but a tiny distance towards slaking it.

The sky's cloudless, and outside the wood the open country is exposed, but the tree canopy affords us shade and some camouflage. A sunlight-dappled brook flows by a glade.

The cool liquid on our lips is enough to set our spheco I-brows a-waving with pleasure.

We sit on the bank and throw pebbles into the diamond-clear babbling water.

'Gobbs was desperate for cash. Sauternes is a niceboy

decaff, but hides it. Doesn't want to spoil his image. Gynos gag for him. Gobbs finds out the sordid secret and before you can say closet case, blackmail.'

'And you reckon Sauternes would kill to save his reputation?'

'Fuxaches, V157, who wouldn't? And save his Britz @ the same time.'

'And...was Kamara's brother @ their school...?'

'Nope.'

V157 thinks. 'From what you've seen, is Sauternes capable of murder?'

'Everyone is. Don't underestimate anybody. But he might've got someone else to do the job.'

'Fraser?'

I weigh this up. 'Possibly.'

'Sooner or later you'll have to interview him too.

I swallow. 'Yep. Felonland's Numero Uno himself.'

TWELVE

Phoebe did have Olivier's balls.

She gave Olivier one glance, a glimpse of what thunder would look like if one could see it, and then ignored him.

They'd gathered in the living room. The house seemed colder and less hospitable now there was tension in the air.

Irene introduced Flint and explained what had happened.

Flint raised his hand in acknowledgement. Everyone mumbled hello.

Phoebe and Garcia had been looking for any food they could find. There were apples and berries and rat. Boiled and barbecued chunks of sinewy, gristly meat, more like life-saving medicine than food. Irene chewed and chewed and tried to shut the flavour out of her mind, telling herself it was stale chicken. Eventually, she managed to swallow, and encouraged Samina to copy her.

'We're hungry,' began Phoebe, 'and securicops are patrolling again. Flint's group was disbanded yesterday, so we may be the only Freebies locally, which means less competition for food, callous though that sounds.'

'Also,' interrupted Irene, 'the androcops might think they've eradicated us. Policing of the area could slacken.'

'Good point,' said Phoebe.

'We should go back,' continued Irene. 'Do it by night, after the day staff are bussed home. Not go in @ the wrong time like Flint's lot.'

Flint sat up on his haunches and cleared his throat. 'They weren't my lot,' he protested. 'I only joined recently, having escaped from the Recycling Centres, like you. We was gonna do it under cover of dark, but that Bestcoe double agent tricked us.'

Phoebe looked over @ Olivier, who was staring @ the floorboards. 'By all accounts, it didn't go well for you,' she said with a slight smile.

Olivier shook his head in agreement, but didn't look up.

Samina was sitting next to Irene and seemed to be pretending he didn't exist.

The wind whistled and the trees swayed. A few drops of rain fell. Irene drew her coat tighter round her shoulders. Garcia stared out of the window.

'Let's do a recce first,' said Irene. 'Plan properly.'

'Excellent,' said Phoebe. 'Flint can accompany you. Olivier'll stay here.'

Blood rushed to Olivier's cheeks. He spluttered, and left without a word.

Samina followed him out with her eyes and shot a guilty look @ Phoebe and then @ Irene. She shifted as if she wanted to get up and run after him, but thought better of it.

They heard what sounded like a fist banging on a wall and exchanged glances.

Phoebe ignored the fallout from her decree. 'You'll start tomorrow. Don't do anything rash.' She made her way through the bodies on the floor and swept out.

@ first everyone listened for the inevitable row between her and Olivier. A door slammed, but that was all.

Garcia said, 'I'm starving,' and they each munched an apple.

Somewhere, a guitar started playing. Samina rose, and followed her ears.

THIRTEEN

Satan's Garage are gigging a disco duel tonight.

The venue, the Aesthetica Ballroom, is a converted warehouse in South East District 10, where wealthy Bs — and As who can't afford Olympia Heights — live alongside better off C-class PAULies.

Energy restored, I kiss V157 and take off without looking round. I fly high, skirting the boundary of Cockneytown to cross the Thames and approach my destination from the southeast. My nav-system tells me when and where to swoop.

But my plans to re-interview Sauternes and get access to Fraser don't have the expected transpiry.

Androguards on the door wave me in. I phew. For them a spheco is just another cop.

Once inside, I float around, checking for alcoves and crevasses in the black-painted walls.

The main auditorium consists of a large rectangular disco-arena covered in sand to ease the clean-up afterwards.

Personnel are too busy with their preparations to take much notice of me. Entrance to the arena is from a tunnel I dart into. It leads underground to a corridor of dressing rooms, equipment stores and various cupboards for the competitors and artistes.

I fly out of the tunnel, and scan the arena. On three sides are several rows of raked seats. The fourth side, one of the shorter ones, is a stage cluttered with DJ paraphernalia where

Garage will perform, opposite the VIP seating.

I soar up to the ceiling to hide as I'll be well camouflaged.

Gynos are taking their seats amid a buzz of excited antici-pation reverberating throughout the arena.

A rich baritone addresses the fighters. 'Positions, lads.' Maxx Smacker's professional voice. Not the whine that con-versed with me the day before. 'You've been training months for this. Now's your chance to prove yourselves and win the nubo of your dreams.'

The young andro combatants are getting ready for the dance. Flick-knives out, swords drawn, practising moves. Black tailored suits, late 20th early 21st century style. Costs a lotta Britz, that antique gear. Where do these C-class kids find that kinda money? There must be a lot of unreported felony.

The gynos compare Eye-pix of their rival suitors, choosing who they fancy and hoping the one they like wins. There's a betting stall in the corner with a long queue.

Smacker's halo-frizz has been tinted gold, and he's wearing a silver all-in-one doublet. His lipstick and eye make-up match his hair and pointed shoes.

A medium fast beat starts up. The audience screams. The noise hurts my spheco-ears.

The combatants do their strut thing when the umpires shout 'En garde.' The andros cheer to the rhythm and aim their weapons.

I glance @ the stage. Next to Smacker are Sauternes and Sharpe, both androclad like the fighters in black with red carnation buttonholes.

Sauternes's juicy voice shrills over the speakers. 'Evening, nubo gynolasses and androlads. Welcome to this disco duel sponsored by BestcoePops® in conjunction with Bestcoe-Genetix®.'

The cheer deafens me.

'We are Satan's Garage...I'm Don Sauternes...but cz I *lurve* wine, women and song, you can call me Sauternes Don.' He has to scream over the racket to be heard.

I chuckle to myself. Most of the audience have never tasted wine. Only Vinola® if they can afford it.

'You all know the rules,' continues Sauternes. 'You've applied for the nubo of your choice and been paired off to fight to the death. Up to the third verse you show off your skill and expertise and only in the second chorus do you get real. The winning thrust has to come on the top note @ song's climax. That's what you've practised alone, but now you have to vanquish the unknown talent of your adversaries. May the best androlads win and may all the nubo gynolasses get shagged happy.'

More applause. The muzak changes and Sauternes starts to sing. His ghostly countertenor freezes the ballroom to temporary silence. But not for long.

> *Ain't gonna die tonite, winnin' my lurve in the fight,*
> *gotta make her feel alright, ooh ooh ooh.*

The slow verse.

The duellists dance and play-fight throughout most of the song. Umpires shadow the fencers, ensuring each thrust and parry is executed only on the music beat.

Now the moves get harder.

The second chorus has a faster tempo.

> *Cz I ain't foolin' when I'm disco duellin'*
> *and I'll be rulin' your heart, your heart.*

The gynos shriek and pull their hair, crying, hugging each other. No blood has been drawn yet.

Everything happens @ the same time. The music dies down, accompanied by raucous applause, wailing and yelling.

I see the carnage.

Some have slain their opponents with a mortal blow. Others have merely wounded them. A few pairs have failed to strike and are still alive, shaking hands or embracing with obvious relief. And in some cases both androlads are dead.

But then my heart stops. The familiar weaselly voice snarls, 'What the fuck kept you?'

Horelka, bursting in on the auditorium, brandishing his white androcop Eye-D, closely followed by Mike, more cops, V103, V122 and V146 shuffling in.

V146 clears his spheco-throat. 'Sorry, sir. Androguard trouble. Bouncers obstructed our entry. Called us sphecofreaks. We had to deal with them. Clean-up required outside as well now.'

Horelka tuts. Androcops herd the survivors into the centre of the arena. Not a shred of remorse taints any of those baby-adult faces. Just self-satisfied smirks @ each other.

Horelka holds up a little golden cube, which he crushes in his hand. 'Chryso-choc. The latest illegal drug craze. AKA a Deadly Sin...'

The victors stir. Most of them'll be Sinning, the only way they can find the courage to risk their lives. Fraser's andros — if Fraser's the tempter — will have scarpered long before Horelka's arrival.

The forces of law and order search the androlads, who'll be interrogated about the tempters and reveal nothing. Fraser'll carry on undercutting BestcoeNarx®'s monopoly. Sex, drugs, music and violence. *What's not to like?*

Gradually, the ballroom empties. Satan's Garage pack up their set and exit into their individual dressing rooms. Androcops take the duellists away for further questioning and cautioning, with the sphecos employed as a threatening presence to deal with any trouble and prevent the winners from grabbing their nubo prizes. A blattoid clean-up team arrives to remove the dead and wounded.

Disappointed gynos wander back out into their unromantic C-class lives.

I crawl over the ceiling and position myself above the now bare stage before creeping upside down along the wall and through the plush-curtained exit.

Smacker has gone; so has Sharpe. Their doors are open and their changing booths deserted. Sauternes's door's shut.

I try the handle. It turns and I dart in. He's in his chair and doesn't react to my presence. I can see his reflection in the mirror.

He seems to have two carnations now, the new one on his white-shirted stomach.

But it isn't a flower. It's blood. I leap over and without touching anything, look @ his neck. No pulse twitch. Nothing. Eyes dead. Fuxaches! They got to him first.

I punch the dressing table surface under the mirror, making his wine glass and bits of make-up rattle. *Did Fraser find out Sauternes squealed?*

I fuxache again. Mike'll be busy all night.

As I breathe deep to calm my nerves, I detect a faint, fleeting whiff of...something, which trackstops me dead. *Is the killer...?*

But approaching voices and footsteps interrupt my thoughts and force me up to the ceiling.

Humos come a-running. Presently I hear them scream.

I scramble out upside down till I'm able to fly away unseen.

FOURTEEN

They left @ dawn. Irene and Flint led Garcia to the agro-complex. The ground was damper now, and rain had added to the bogginess. In places, they had to jump over pools of mud and sludge to avoid ruining their leaky footwear and soiling their already frozen feet. The wood came to an end and they climbed the slope to emerge onto the plateau. Exposure had dried the ground here somewhat and the tall, brown grass afforded them a little camouflage.

It was late morning. Clouds of birds, many hundred strong, whizzed around the grey sky, reminding Irene of sphecoids patrolling. From their vantage point they could see the agrocomplex. Fields of ripe wheat tantalized them as did the rows of fruit trees in the orchard. There were tomatoes, beans and maize.

Hidden by the deep undergrowth, they crawled down the gently inclining field to get a better view, Irene wishing she'd had the presence of mind the day before to get those binoculars.

They'd remembered the cutters, but the barbed-wire fence was probably electrified.

Yet, they were determined. They'd get in and take what they needed. Even plant some, somewhere, and pray the signs of cultivation would elude the securicops.

They waited in silence all afternoon. So many stories to tell each other, but this was not the time for speaking.

The sun was beginning to set, like an orange bacillus dissolving in a larger, more powerful organism. The sound of the engine and stink of faeco-fuel heralded the arrival of the autobus, which stopped by the entrance. The driver honked the horn thrice. Andros and gynos appeared among the rows of maize and filed towards the vehicle.

The bus chugged off.

'Shit,' said Flint, pointing to two androguards with Alsatians patrolling the perimeter. 'Course they're gonna leave security all night.'

As he spoke, the arselights came on. He gave a little laugh of resignation. 'Terrific. We give 'em a floorshow.'

'Fuxache, don't be so negative,' snapped Garcia. 'We've come this far. The light'll help us find chinks in their armour.'

Flint shrugged and spat.

When the guards reappeared, Irene said, 'We'll have one deci-minute.'

Having retreated further up the hill, they took in the surrounding countryside. Apart from where they lay, the landscape was completely flat. There were fields for miles around.

They waited till the sun set in the bloodshot sky and when it was dark, they slithered back down towards the perimeter fence, moving carefully to avoid snapping twigs. The wind added more disguise as they swished through the long grass.

They had no torch, but the arselights illuminated the area round the agrocomplex.

It was Flint who discovered the fence was electrified. He backed into it, and then was suddenly several metres up the field on his back and unconscious.

The others scurried over.

'Flint! Flint!' Garcia slapped his face three, four times.

Eventually he opened his eyes.

'You okay?' asked Irene.

'Bit of a shock. Think I've wet myself.'

'Can you move?' She lifted his hand.

He nodded and pulled his knees up to his chest. 'I'll live. Obviously for keeping livestock in rather than us out.'

'Just lie still and take it easy,' said Irene. 'We'll come back for you.'

They waited for the guards to return and crept up to the perimeter, looking for ways to get in. They were some distance from the arselights and the main entrance.

'It's doable,' said Garcia. 'The wires are far enough apart. I can dodge the current. I'm skinny enough to get through those gaps. Look.'

Eyes wide in amazement, Irene watched him bend over ninety degrees @ the hip and sidestep over the bottom wire, his perfectly straight back clearing the top wire. He then brought his other leg over and was inside.

She clapped quietly. Garcia took a bow and picked six cobs of maize, which he threw to her. Once more he performed his manoeuvre and stood with her, beaming @ his success and her admiration.

'Tomorrow's dinner,' he said. 'Dad always used to say whatever you learn'll be useful one day.'

As they crouched down to get back to Flint, they saw the guards again.

'And how did you learn all that body bending?' asked Irene.

Garcia looked around. 'It's how I managed for so long as a D-classified,' he began. 'We could always escape. They never caught us. We'd get in anywhere, me and my bro.'

'Heathcote...' Irene said. 'Been meaning to ask you.'

His smile disappeared. In the stark floodlit glare, his skin seemed grey-green and not brown. He stared straight @ Irene, which made her step back and shiver with apprehension. 'Then those fucking spheco-freaks fingered us. I got away. I always do. But Heath... I heard his screams.'

Irene wanted to say, 'My son's a sphecoid. They're not all bad,' but she couldn't open her mouth. It was as if Garcia had sniffed her spheco-mum shame out, so his spite would hit home. And they *were* all bad. She looked down @ the ground. 'So, how did you get caught?'

'That androcop raid.' He sighed. 'When you got them apples?'

His wiriness now seemed a weakness, a vulnerability, and not the strength it had been when he'd won their forthcoming meals. He continued to look @ her with an intensity, as though he could see right into her very soul. Irene couldn't fathom whether the venom in his black eyes was directed @ her, sphecoids or both. 'In the Recycling Centre,' she started, 'you... you called...'

After an interminable pause, he said, 'You're thin like me. I'll teach you that manoeuvre. It's really easy. We'll work this place together.'

Irene was aware of her own voice speaking. 'Okay,' it said. She kept avoiding the glare of his eyes. Flint was strongly built, so he'd never squeeze through the wires. This job was best for her.

She thought of George. How she missed him. And Nelson. But what horrified her was a thought, like a naughty child running past her field of vision, a wish that that sphecoid, whoever it was, some poor niceboy born to some equally poor parents, like her and George, had speared both the skinny brothers.

But that would've meant no corn, a treat she'd not had for years.

Garcia stayed close to Irene. 'I'll show you how it's done,' he said. 'It won't take long.'

She nodded, still unwilling to engage him in conversation. She knew what sphecoids did was bad, but she couldn't put Nelson out of her mind. Despite her rejection of him, he was still her baby. So she copied the balletic body bending Garcia was demonstrating, even though she was stiff from the cold.

He made his upper body almost two-dimensional, and she found she could do the same with the right amount of concentration and determination.

'Great,' he said. 'You're almost there. A natural.' He clasped her hand.

Her instinctive reaction was to withdraw it, but there was something warm and strong in his grip, and she allowed him to hold her for a few seconds before pulling away.

He smiled @ her. 'We'll make a great team.'

She looked away from him, her heart racing. She wanted to hit him and yield to him both @ the same time. It confused her. Perhaps he sensed that.

They lay in the grass. Nothing stirred apart from the tall corn stalks swaying in the wind, backlit by the moon.

Irene accompanied Garcia to the fence, her heart in her mouth. He went first, folding himself perfectly like a flat-backed insect, and stepped out onto the fertile eastern soil of the compound. Irene thought carefully through each move. She cleared the first wire, looking down @ the black earth. Next, she raised her leg and slid it over the wire without moving any other part of her locked body.

She could sense Garcia's apprehension and tried to put it out of her mind as she let her upper body follow her leg. She then lifted her other leg and slipped through the gap.

She smiled. It hadn't been too difficult. She'd done it and would do so again. Her skin tingled @ the thought of Garcia's approval.

He was waiting for her. 'Congratulations,' he whispered

close to her ear so the sound waves tickled her. She thought he was going to kiss her. She dreaded that. It was becoming an inevitability.

They penetrated the corn together, stepping gingerly.

Garcia led Irene back towards the fence, but they remained hidden in the tall plants, making their way along what seemed an endless row of empty maize in the hope of finding other cobs.

They only had a few accu-minutes left before the guards returned. There was no more corn.

Suddenly, she saw the arselight's eyes. Gogging down @ her. Blinking. And gob too high to climb up and gag.

A scream escaped her lips. Garcia shushed her. She pointed to the eyes, which clocked Garcia.

The mouth opened. And hissed.

They leapt back. All the floodlights started hissing.

'What did you see?' Androvoices in the distance, shouting, getting louder. Dogs barked. Multiple arselight legs pointed @ the intruders.

'No time,' said Irene.

Garcia scrambled out first and helped her. It was easier now. Her heart clanged against her ribs as she kept her body away from the wires. As soon as she was free, they threw themselves into the grass, and lay still, gulping in air.

'The corn!' They seized a couple of cobs each and left the rest.

The guards shone torches over the field.

Irene felt the ray of light expose her and squeezed her eyes shut. The beam didn't linger. She breathed out and grabbed Garcia's hand. The dogs were whining now. The hissing stopped.

'Halt, or we shoot!'

Gasping for breath, they scooted back on their arses to

where they'd left Flint.
    But Flint had gone.
    Then the first shots rang out.

FIFTEEN

It's dark and chilly over Olympia Heights. Lights glow like blobs of luminous egg-yolk in the mansion windows.

Reza Sharpe's naked apart from his black thigh-huggers. His torso glows with sweat. He has the sort of body I grew up longing for. A tickle in my loins distracts me for a moment, but I manage to control myself. Just.

'You again? Can't you see I'm knackered?' His eyes are hostile blue orbs.

'What did you do after the gig?' I remain standing. Easier to get a stiffy.

'I left with Maxx and came back here.'

'Why didn't you leave with Sauternes?'

'We're not attached @ the hip.'

'You jealous of him?'

He splutters in surprise and shakes his head. 'Where for fuxache does that come from?'

'His beautiful voice. You being the support vocalist.'

He bursts out into an indignant, incredulous laugh. 'No way, man, or should I say...'

The swift appearance of my spheco-cockhead cuts him off. His reaction's clean. Besides, if he killed Sauternes out of jealousy, why would he have got Gobbs as well? I change tack. 'You say goodbye to Sauternes?'

He thinks a bit. 'We came offstage...I went and got changed out of that stupid suit. Fuxache man, the word tight was invented to describe it.' He slaps his taut six-packed gut. 'Uncomfortable, know what I mean? I'm slim, but that was tailored for a stick-insect.'

I smile.

'Maxx came for me. I was ready to leave. Don's door was still closed. Maxx said not to enter without knocking, so I called out, "You coming?" He didn't answer and I was fuckered, so Maxx and I left. He's fucked off without saying goodbye before, according to Maxx, especially if the gig ain't gone too well, and tonight's cop raid was a...setback.'

'What did you talk to Maxx about?'

'Why do you need to know?' His eyes blaze cold fire @ me.

Gotta get to Smacker before the androcops.

'Ain't got time for your questioning me.' My dick shoots further out and quivers an inch from his belly. He leaps back and I advance till he has his back to the gold-papered wall. I'm almost making contact.

'You wouldn't want to seriously piss me off, would you?'

He shakes his head, but is looking round for inspiration to get help and begins to slide sideways away from me. I extend till I hit his appendix scar, without breaking the skin. He grunts, 'Uh.'

'Don't even think about alerting your androguards. I'll've slit you wide open before they arrive.'

He nods.

'And don't breathe a word of this visit to anyone, you hear?'

His eyes are fixed on my cock. 'Loud and clear.'

'Now wash that sweat off or you'll stink tomorrow.'

He twitches his head, as if afraid any untoward movement on his part'll make me change my mind about not running him through there and then.

My next visit is to Smacker, via smashing his loft window. By the time I've calmed him down from his hysteria @ seeing me again, he's in tears.

'Can't you make an appointment? It's expensive having a window repaired.'

'Leave it open in future.'

He isn't in the mood for flippancy. 'Have you any idea how much real glass costs? I'll be claiming for this.'

'D.C. Lagano @ SECOPS'll deal with that,' I improvise.

He resigns himself to being helpful. 'Well, what can I do for you?'

'Just tell me everything you did after the gig.'

His story corroborates Sharpe's. He didn't see Sauternes either.

I'm tired myself and need rest. I leave Smacker in the dark about Sauternes and embark on my flight back to the Eastlands.

I've only gone a few hundred metres when I nearly fall out of the sky. Coming towards me is none other than V157. 'What the fuck you doing here?' Eloquence never deserts me.

'Putting the cock into Cockneytown.' He smiles and circles me. 'No, I got some news.'

As we fly back to our kipcell, he tells me. 'I managed to access some info about Milo Kamara on my eye-screen. His brother's a Freebie, possibly somewhere near our nest. He could be the key.'

SIXTEEN

Gunfire echoed into the night.

Garcia held Irene tight.

Protecting me, or clinging?

They remained where they lay in case the guards were watching for movement. Irene prayed to the powers-that-be.

It started with a buzz, crescendoing to a deafening beating of wings. A cloud descended, and as it came down, divided into millions of identical parts, all raven-sized entomoids.

Giant locusts.

The guards yelled, 'Acridians!'

They blanketed the agrocomplex and surrounding fields, covering Irene and Garcia, pestering them for the corn, crawling over every inch of their bodies before leaping off. Irene squirmed @ the sensation of insect jaws scraping her skin and tickly antennae probing her.

It was hard to bat them away for they kept coming. They devoured three cobs, but Garcia managed to hide the fourth in his trousers.

Eventually, the locusts joined the rest of their swarm. The gunfire stopped.

Irene and Garcia sighed with relief, and got up to make their way home.

Still no sign of Flint.

'We'll have to find him,' said Garcia.

'He might have been scared off by the guards and those

locusts and ran away.'

Garcia shook his head.

Irene's heart missed a beat. 'Or they captured him?'

'Everything's possible. He could be revealing our where-abouts as we speak.'

'You really think he'd betray us?'

'Who can say what anyone'll do under torture. Besides, he's only just joined. How loyal do you expect him to be?'

'Should we go back and warn the others?'

'Is it safe for us to do that? Security could be waiting to round up as many of us as possible.'

'But we can't let those people just get taken. I mean I can't. You run if you want. I'm sure you'll survive. But I can't abandon Samina.'

He looked @ her, and saw her, she felt, for the first time. 'You're right,' he said. 'So we go back and tell them — if they're still there — to be on their guard.'

Irene didn't say anything. She was enjoying her little triumph. This strange man would have happily had her betray her friends, her new family, and all because he was addicted to being on the run. But she'd persuaded him to do the right thing.

Garcia was persuasive too, in his muscular, slim way. She followed him through the woods as his body insinuated itself between the trees and into her life.

Why had he chosen her? She was no beauty any more. Those days were over. Yes, she'd been attractive once, when George was around, but then it all fell away. Perhaps she was wrong and Garcia just saw her as an accomplice. She still hated him, she kept telling herself, for reassurance that the opposite wasn't happening.

They got back. The farmhouse looked bleak, but distant bonfires lit up the landscape. *'Tonguesters.* The peeling whitewashed walls, broken windows and ramshackle sheds presented a picture of gloom.

No sound emanated from within. Irene clutched Garcia's hand, but he shook his head as if to tell her to reserve her worry for real causes for concern.

They crept into the yard. The fire had not long been extinguished; embers were still smouldering and ash flew across the concrete in the wind.

Her heartbeat accelerated as they approached the rear entrance. This could be her last act of freedom, she thought, as she opened the door. It creaked a bit, and she winced, wanting to tell it to be quiet. But wooden doors don't hear.

She slipped inside. He waited outside. *Is he scared?* She dismissed this. *He wasn't afraid to raid the farm.* She took a few steps in the scullery, terrified of breathing lest she be heard, and tiptoed along to the living room.

Then she counted to three and, finally managing to take a deep breath, turned the door handle.

SEVENTEEN

It's another 48 accu-hours before I see Mike again. News of Sauternes's murder on FaceChirp® has rocked the whole of Cockneytown; mass demonstrations of grief have become riots brutally put down by the androcops. Those arrested and not beaten to death are either summarily discontinued and recycled for anti-social actions, or have their PAUL scheme revoked and thus become D-classified.

I give SECOPS two days to process all the extra felon cleansing, and arrange a safe meeting with Mike in his car in a back street @ zero deci/midnight accu. He's off-duty.

'V159,' he says, acknowledging me. 'I assume you've been keeping up with events.'

I nod.

'Ain't looking good.'

I have to agree. 'But I've got some info on Milo Kamara's brother.' I fill him in.

'Great. So, where exactly is he?'

'That I dunno yet. V157's onto it.'

'I see. Not so good. And how come Smacker wants compensation?'

'Uh.' I explain.

'Chizz for that,' he sarks. 'I'll stall him...somehow. Meanwhile, I got some forensics on Sauternes.'

'Yeah?' My Eye-pods hit the inside of the car roof.

'Yeah. Stomach-contents chocolate positive — but the real

stuff, not godshit or chrysochoc. So, Sin-negative. And he was stabbed through his gut. Wound apparently caused by a sharp instrument. But no weapon found @ the scene.'

'Hm. Interesting.'

'And what's even more so is that there were traces of DNA.'

'But that's brilliant.'

His face tells me it isn't. His voice confirms it. 'Spheco DNA. They're working on Eye-D-ing it.'

My heart sinks. I was so careful, made sure I'd not touched the body. But of course...the dressing table, the door handle... I can't keep this to myself. It'll all come out anyway.

'Mike, that was me.'

His head spins round the quickest I've ever seen a humo head spin. 'Care to enlighten me further?'

I tell him what I did and why.

'And you didn't think to let me know?'

'I knew the Aesthetica staff found him and let things take their natural course.'

'This looks bad, V159. They'll trace you. And meanwhile, the real killer's walking about free. How could you be so careless?'

'Sorry. I thought I'd made all the right moves, but I guess I did touch some furniture.'

He clicks his tongue. 'They'll be pursuing that line of enquiry.'

'Can I see the forensic report?'

He dismisses this with a wave of his hand. 'No need. It just says spheco-DNA discovered @ felon scene. More details to come.'

'I remember making a conscious effort not to touch him.'

'This is why we don't like sphecos getting involved with the investigations. You ain't trained for it.'

'But I *was* careful, Mike.'

'Obviously, not enough.'

'Okay. I'm sorry.'

He doesn't answer @ first. Just acknowledges the apology with a slight nod. I can see he's really fucked off with me.

'By the way,' I start in an attempt to make up, 'how was your birthday review the other day?'

He shrugs. 'My head's just above water, but it's tight.' Then he adds, 'Course, I did ask for your help, so...we're okay. Ish.'

I nod.

We check the victim's Britz accounts. Sauternes paid large sums, presumably for his own Sins, but everything seems in order.

'Sauternes might've known who killed Gobbs,' I begin tentatively, 'and had to be silenced. We need to talk to Fraser.'

EIGHTEEN

As Irene entered, Phoebe, Olivier and Samina looked up.

Irene breathed out with relief. 'I'll get Garcia.'

She came in with him and reported Flint's disappearance.

'That's worrying,' said Phoebe.

Olivier nodded. 'We'll have to be extra vigilant now.' His eyes wandered over to Samina, who looked down.

'You alright?' whispered Irene.

Samina smiled. 'Never better.'

Irene couldn't help glancing over @ Olivier. Samina shrugged when she turned back.

Garcia retrieved the corn from his trousers and put it on the floor.

'We had more, but...' Irene recounted everything.

'Told you you'd meet the acridians. Seems they're swarming again.' Phoebe explained. 'Braintown lab experiment. S'posed to be a cheap food source. Agrocomplex security tightened when they escaped. They rampage when hungry. Plus the bonfires'll've disturbed them. We'd better guard our stuff.'

'Important not to overeat after so much hunger,' joked Garcia, rubbing his hands for warmth. 'Especially maize.'

The cob was mouldy in places and had blackened patches, but there were still edible kernels. Irene passed it round before taking a few raw ones.

They sat for a short while. The buzz of casual chat was

interrupted by the sound of footsteps.

They fell silent. Someone was walking through the hall. The conversation with Garcia flashed through Irene's mind. They'd been rumbled.

Androcops coming to discontinue us.

But it wasn't an androcop. In the doorframe was Flint.

'What the fuck happened?' demanded Garcia. 'We were scared they'd got you.'

'I waited for you,' said Flint, smiling, 'but heard the dogs. You didn't come. Thought you'd been caught. I wasn't sure of the way, but finally found the house.' He ran his hands over his scalp and wiped sweat from his brow.

'You must've run here,' said Irene. 'Or you're sickening for something. That shock'll have weakened you.'

'I'm fine. Anyway, as I was trying to retrace my steps, I saw in the distance, by the other side of the agrocomplex, what looked like a couple of large ants.'

Irene gasped. 'Entomoids.' They all looked round. Flint scowled @ the interruption. 'Sorry,' she muttered. He cleared his throat and continued.

'Course it weren't ants. It was Freebies. An andro and gyno. Hiding in the long grass. Watching. Like we was.

'I remembered my group and what that scumbag did. But I also remembered what you'd said, Irene.' He looked over to her.

She raised her eyebrows. *What did I say?*

'About communication,' he explained. 'And I thought, what if this lot are okay and we could help each other?'

'So you followed them?' said Phoebe.

'Yeah, I did,' he said, his confidence taking a slight knock from the force of her voice. 'Why, is that a problem?'

Olivier stirred. 'Dunno yet. Did you make contact?'

Flint looked around the line of long faces. His hesitation

was enough.

'You did, didn't you?' said Phoebe.

He nodded.

'Even after what happened to your group?' Irene detected a glint of pleasure in Olivier's eyes as he spoke. Flint was his rival, the other young man. Garcia was too old. But Flint had ousted him from that top slot the other day. Irene knew that in androland that was unforgivable.

'Okay,' said Flint. 'Perhaps I should've consulted you lot first.'

'Yeah,' snapped Olivier, fixing him now. 'Maybe you should.'

Flint took a deep breath. 'It just seemed like an opportunity we can't afford to miss. I might never have seen them again.'

No one said a word. Phoebe broke the silence. 'Did you learn anything from them, like who they are and where they live?'

Flint scratched his head. He was sweating more now. 'They're a small group. And live quite near here.'

'Did you tell them where we are?'

'Not exactly.'

'What does that mean? Either you did or you didn't.'

Flint tutted. 'No. Look, I just said we were local and hoped we'd make further contact.'

'You're lying,' shouted Olivier. 'You told them where we live, didn't you?'

'No,' protested Flint. 'Course I never.'

'We'll have to move,' said Phoebe. She turned on Flint. 'If you revealed our whereabouts, we might not be safe here.'

'Look, guys, I really dunno what to say. You know what? I'm gonna go out for a bit. I need some fresh air.'

Like you didn't get enough in the fields.

He didn't look so passionate and happy now. He turned on

his heels. They heard him storm down the hall. After a few
moments, Olivier got up and followed him.

NINETEEN

As I approach Orlando Fraser's waterfront villa @ the southernmost edge of Olympia Heights, I'm dazzled by sunlight reflected off its gilded façade and cupola.

From his fourth-floor roof terrace, where I land, I turn to see the grimy top of the Aesthetica Ballroom on the opposite bank, and behind that, steep hills covered with undulating phalanxes of C-class DUBs.

There's a door that opens onto a staircase. I fly in.

The top floor's empty. Just a corridor. I hear no sounds and detect no humo presence, although my Eye-screen alerts me to andros on the floor below.

I crawl down the sloping ceiling, blending in with the red, gold and black design. Androguards, one @ each end of the hallway, wait with guns. I sense no one else.

After an intense sniff of the air, I descend to the second storey.

There's more activity here. Andros are working in what seem to be offices.

Suddenly I hear, 'Don't wanna be disturbed. Understand?' and, 'Yes, Mr Fraser.'

I hold my breath. A guard comes out and doubletakes when I backflip onto the rich-piled carpet.

'Fraser, Orlando?' I ask.

'He's busy.'

My spheco-cock darts out and whips his midriff, making

him grunt.

'So I'll unbusy him.'

The guard staggers back, rubbing his torso. Before he can react, I fling the door open, spring in, close the door and let my spheco-penis do the introductions.

Fraser's eyes flit once to my cock and then to my face.

I motion to him to raise his arms.

'Keep still and don't speak.'

'You'll pay for this,' he growls.

'Threatening a spheco-cop?' The tip of my dick's on his collarbone. 'One false move or word and I'll stab down and bullseye your heart and lungs.'

He shuts up.

I get a better look @ him. Middle-aged, auburn halo-hair grey @ the roots, lined face, incipient paunch.

There's a sharp rap on the door. 'You okay, sir?'

Fraser understands the warning in my spheco-eyes. 'Never better,' he shouts.

Footsteps recede.

'With that army out there,' I say, 'I guess you've no need for the physique you once boasted.'

His brown eyes register the insult.

I chuckle to myself.

He breaks the silence. I've backfooted him. 'What you want?' he whispers. 'Sins? Money?'

I let him sweat a bit.

'This ain't the way I do business, sphecoid. You're making a big mistake.'

I count to ten and clear my elegant spheco-throat. 'How much did Gobbs owe you?'

He frowns. 'Oh, you're conducting an investigation, are you? Well, let me explain. First of all, you need a warrant to question an A-lister, and second, you have to be a proper human androcop. On both counts you fail. Goodbye, spheco-freak.'

I don't budge. He backs off and I let my cock prick his slightly flabby upper tit-flesh.

He yowls.

'That's my warrant, humo.'

He looks down @ the pinprick of blood on his white dun-garette and back up @ me. 'I'll get you discontinued for that, sphreakoid. Boy, am I gonna enjoy complaining about this. I know all about procedure.'

'Don't bluff. You're so dirty you wouldn't dare approach the cops. And you only know how things work cz of your ugly record.'

'You just made a big mistake.'

'Not as big as yours. Now, you tempted Gobbs with Deadly Sins, didn't you?'

'I don't have to say anything. I know my rights.'

'If that's how you want it.' I penetrate another bit. 'I have perfect control over this...limb. How's that?'

He grunts, trying to back off.

'Stay still.' I repeat my question. 'In case you've forgotten.'

'Dunno what you're talking about.'

Another millimetre. Another grunt.

'I'm not here about the Sins. Let the androcops get you for that. I wanna know how much Gobbs owed you.'

He looks down @ my cock impaling his left shoulder. A few more millimetres and he'll be dead. 'A lot.'

'Like, how much?'

'Can't give you exact...but...get that...thing outta me...I'll look it up.'

A millimetre more. His eyes entreat me not to stab further.

'You take me for a fool?' I say. '"A lot" will do for now. You know he was broke?'

He nods.

'Is that why you had him killed?'

He sneers. 'Is that what you think, you stupid, dumb-arse sphreako — sorry, I didn't mean that...'

I twist my dumb-arse *sphreako*-cock without extending it any further. He grimaces in pain. 'Care to rephrase that?'

'I had nothing to do with his death.'

'Or maybe you did, Fraser, scared he'd survive his seventh Sin and break the bank and Sauternes found out so you had to have him murdered too.'

He shakes his head. His hands reach down to grab my dick and pull it from his chest, but he realizes the *nice* implications of touching my penis. The hands stall mid-air. I can't help laughing @ that.

'What's so funny?'

I'm not about to spell it out for him. 'You lost a lot of money. Not like your kind to write off a debt.'

He groans. 'One of the hazards...I wasn't gonna sell Gobbs any more Sins. I wanted my money back...but I didn't kill him...or Sauternes.'

His presumption of immunity from the law cz of his A-list status prompts me to force my cock a tiny bit more into his soft tissue. He gives a repressed cry and screws up his once handsome face.

'Fuxache, remove that monstrosity.'

'Breathe a word of this visit to anyone, I'll be back to finish ...drilling.'

'You got nothing on me,' he gasps.

'You confessed to supplying drugs.'

'You ain't got no evidence.'

One final millimetre, out of sheer spite. 'We'll get you, Fraser, rest assured. But in our own time.'

He screws his eyes shut to cope with the pain and swallows.

'I'm clean.'

'We know where to find you. Don't leave Cockneytown. You're still a suspect.' As I pull my cock out of him, blood pours out. 'Sorry about the dungarettes, humo.'

He clocks his ruined clothes with thunder in his face, but thinks better of wisecracking me. He knows how cheap and worthless his life is to a spheco like me. What he doesn't know is how much I want him to stay alive. If he's indeed the brain behind the killings, I need more evidence.

I fling open a window. 'Get some air in here.' I zoom up and away into the slightly smelly Cockneytown aether, going east, watching the DUBs become B-list houses and finally, flat green fields and tiny forests, my cute spheco-head a-bubbling with ideas and info. I can't entirely believe Fraser's innocent, but we're running out of suspects, apart from Kamara's elusive brother.

A little before I get back, I remember to deactivate my Eye-cam recording device, which I kept on. Just in case...

V157's pleased to see me. This I deduce from his protrusion. I reciprocate, but all we can do for relief is some mutual malicious, having both become experts @ leaping out of the way of each other's — and our own — toxijism shower.

After our spheco-gasms, I bring him up to date. He's happy @ what I say, but seems distracted, almost impatient for me to finish. 'Orgsome, V159. But I got something to tell you, too.'

I raise an I-brow.

He points @ a patch of brown fields to the already darkening east of our copse shelter. 'The other day I saw four Freebies there and from my Eye-screen data, I think Milo Kamara's brother is one of them. If we can talk to him, perhaps he'll help us — and Mike — find the killer.'

I look through the sparse foliage @ where he's pointing and

have a strange sensation that although he's acting on a hunch and a bit of data, he's unwittingly leading me towards my destiny.

TWENTY

From her bed, Irene heard Olivier come back and tell Phoebe that Flint had gone. 'We'll never know what he's done.'

'But you can't stand him. How can I take your word?'

'For fuxache, Phoebz, for once in your life listen to what I'm saying. Flint is bad.'

'We'll talk tomorrow.'

Doors slammed.

All night, Irene tossed and turned. Her worries increased @ every sound — gates and timber in the yard tossed by a gale, doors creaking inside the house. She expected androcops to turn up @ any moment and arrest them when they'd all be sleepy and unable to resist. She reached out for Samina, to touch her hand, but Samina was fast asleep.

Flint didn't come the next day. Or the day after.

It was time for another raid, for anything the acridians had left.

Garcia and Irene managed to get a few potatoes. They returned to the house in higher spirits than when they'd left. When they entered the living room, they found Phoebe on the floor with Flint, holding hands.

'Flint's a wanderer,' she said, letting go of him and rising to greet them. There was no guilt in her gesture. 'He explained. Can't stay in one place long. Has to be on the move, don't you?'

He looked up @ her, nodded and stared @ Irene and

Garcia.

'Spuds,' said Garcia.

They emptied their pockets.

Phoebe was overjoyed. 'That's so fantastic,' she said. 'We won't go hungry tonight.'

'We'll have to scout for other agrocomplexes,' said Garcia. 'Not much left by the perimeter now.'

'Well, if that's what's gotta be done,' said Phoebe.

'I can help.'

They looked @ Flint, who was still squatting. Irene felt he was desperate to win their trust again.

'Yes, why don't you scout for us?' asked Phoebe. 'Especially as you like to be away for days on end.'

Flint stood up, nodding enthusiastically, almost too much, it seemed to Irene. *Has he been waiting for someone to suggest this?*

'Is that such a good idea?' said Olivier. 'You're unreliable and go missing for days. We need the information quickly.'

Flint cleared his throat. 'It might take some time to find a decent agrocomplex. Nearby, low security, suitable crops.'

Olivier put his face close to Flint's. 'If you've betrayed us,' he growled, 'I'll kill you. With my bare hands if necessary.'

Flint clenched his fists.

'Yeah?' Olivier squared up to him.

Garcia stepped between them. 'We all need to cool it.'

Flint unclenched his fists.

With a sneer, Olivier shoulder-butted past him and walked out, leaving Flint open-mouthed.

'Olivier,' shouted Phoebe, 'come back here @ once and apologize.'

No answer.

'I'll sort this,' said Flint, making to follow Olivier, but Garcia pulled him back.

'No,' said Phoebe. 'You stay here. I'll deal with him. He can't talk to you like this.' She went out.

Soon afterwards, Irene was just opening the living room door to go down to bed when she overheard Phoebe's voice.

'Your threatening people weakens us. The atmosphere's poisonous now, thanks to you.'

'Oh, so it's my fault, is it?' Olivier had returned. 'I'm telling you, Phoebz, he's a spy. I don't trust him.'

'Where's your proof?' she screamed. 'You're just thinking with your limp little prick. Just concentrate on finding enough to eat.'

'For fuxache, woman, open your eyes. Thanks to his stupidity, treachery or both, androcops could raid us any day now. We should get rid of him.' Olivier whispered these last words.

Irene heard Phoebe laugh. 'You're jealous. He's better looking and fitter than you. You just want him out cz he's a threat. Don't think I haven't noticed the way you've reacted to him ever since you brought him back.'

'You fancy him.'

'Don't be stupid.'

'It's revenge, isn't it? You want to get your own back on me for Samina. Of course! I've been so blind. You're using that backsliding traitor as a pawn to get @ me.'

'Don't flatter yourself.' Phoebe's voice got louder.

Irene realized she was moving closer and didn't want to be caught eavesdropping. As she backed away from the door, she glimpsed Phoebe flash past, her tattered robe flying about her like a witch's gown, her hair streaming away from her shoulders as if she were airborne.

A hand touched Irene's shoulder. She jumped. It was Samina.

'You gave me such a fright.'

'Sorry. How's everything?'

'Was gonna ask you the same.'

'I'm good.'

'And Olivier?'

Samina tutted. 'Oh, Irene...'

TWENTY-ONE

Mike's parked in the same place as last time.

When I glide down, he lowers his window. 'Fuxache, V159, where you been?' His puffy, bloodshot eyes widen with alarm.

I shake my tired spheco-head. 'Couldn't get through. Too many patrols smashing up demos or burning withertongue victims. Sphecos everywhere. Can't afford to be caught. You need to get some kip.'

He buries his head in his hands. 'If we don't find the killer, I'll be disemployed and...'

'Even Horelka wouldn't do that, surely.'

'Ain't up to him. Ultimatum's come from above.'

'Knox?'

He shrugs.

'Well, anyway, we can rule out Fraser.'

'Fuxache, why?'

'I interviewed...'

'You got an audience with Fraser?' He whistles in surprise and admiration. 'Regular androcops can't get in the same street as him.'

'Let's just say I have a unique calling card.'

'I'm jealous, V159.'

'That wouldn't be penis-envy, by any chance?'

He chuckles.

'He's as good as confessed to tempting Sins, but he ain't our killer.'

He raises his humo eyebrows. *Not a patch on ours.* 'How you figure that?'

'Don't make sense for him to murder Gobbs and Sauternes, unless Sauternes saw him or his agents stab Gobbs. We've no proof either way, but I just got the feeling he was telling the truth about that. Course, I may be wrong. No, I reckon something else is linking the victims. Gobbs, Sauternes...'

'And Smacker.'

'Why do you say that?'

'Had a panic-struck chirrup from Smacker earlier today. He got a threatening call on his Eye-phone. Untraceable. Androcops are with him now, trying to find out more, but it seems the felon uses very sophisticated methods to conceal anything that could link him to the message.'

'Did Smacker speak to the caller?'

'Don't think so.'

'Ring Sharpe.'

'Why?'

'If he's okay, the murderer must be going after the original Satan's Garage members, for one reason or another. If he's being or has been targeted, then our felon wants all the band dead. In the former scenario, it might be something else that links the victims, not the band.'

Mike doesn't respond. Just keys in a number. He speaks softly and hangs up. He gogs @ me. 'An androguard @ Sauternes's villa said Sharpe went out. We don't know if he's okay and he had no idea where he'd gone.'

'We'll have to keep trying. I'll pay Smacker another visit.'

'That'll freak him, for sure.'

'Can't afford to be delicate, Mike.'

'Good luck.' I hardly hear his whisper.

'What's the matter? C'mon. you can tell me.'

'It's nothing.'

'That why you look like you ain't slept for four days...oh, shit, Mike, I forgot. Your mum...How is...?'

'She...she...' He clears his throat. 'She organized a lovely pre-mortem.'

'Oh, Mike, I'm...'

He nods, rather too furiously for a mere agreement. He's trying desperately not to yield to the emotion. 'Yeah, she made such a fantastic send-off speech, said she was only doing what any mum would do in the circumstances. We won't tell Smantha, of course. Everyone came up afterwards and...' He never finishes, cz that's where he breaks down. I fling my spheco-arm round his humo-shoulder. He cries out and flinches.

'Sorry. Forgot.'

'It's okay.' He nurses his shoulder. Forces himself to stop crying. 'No, I'm sorry for blubbing.'

'I understand.'

'We had dancing, food, drink and farewell speeches. I even said a few words myself. About what a brilliant mother she was, selflessly doing this for our family to prosper. That I couldn't believe time had flown so fast and brought us to this pass.' He looks me in the eye. 'I know some folks write poems and songs and make jokes and all that, but I'm no good @ that sort of thing. I just wanted to say what was in my heart.'

I tap his shoulder, extra carefully this time. 'Just wish you were the boss around here, Mike, and things had turned out better, for all of us.'

'Powers-that-be bless you, V159.' He smiles his kind humo-smile. 'Don't be long.'

I sail up into the cold night air.

Fortunately, Smacker's alone in his loft. He's sipping a large neon orange and green cocktail as we speak. He offers me nothing, either because he still considers me an intruder, or an on-duty cop, or maybe he doesn't know how much us sphecos love alcohol, or does, and derives great pleasure from denying me a treat. But I can hardly break in and beg a drink.

As usual, I have to go through the routine of guaranteeing his silence with my spheco-cock. He's so consumed by fear, he'll agree to anything, except perhaps offering me a tipple.

Still holding his real-glass glass, he keeps standing up, sitting down and pacing to and fro. 'Your lot are trying to retrieve the message,' he snaps.

'What did it say?'

'You're next.'

'You recognize the voice?'

'Mechanical. Computer generated.'

'Sit down, Smacker.'

He puts his glass down and sits.

'Who do you think could have it in for Satan's Garage?'

'How long you got?'

'Loads of enemies, huh?'

'Oh,' he wails and buries his head in his hands. 'Not really. Rival bands, I suppose. But it's only play rivalry. All the disco duel bereaved. But we don't do the killings, and why now?' He wrings his hands. 'Doesn't make sense. That's what's unbearable.' He starts crying. Dry sobs @ first, then a few tears roll down his cheeks. 'Don't wanna die yet. I'm young. Just twenty-six. Life's too good to give up. Why must folk be so fuxachingly horrible to one another?'

I don't say a word. Lucky bastard could live a full life if we get the killer. More than can be said for us sphecos. Nice shit doesn't even appreciate how fortunate he is.

'Can you show me the text?'

He dries his eyes, snorts snot back up his nose and shakes

his head. 'Self-deleting message. Why phone and not Face-Chirp®?'

'Did Gobbs and Sauternes get this message?'

He shrugs. 'They never said.'

I'm not going to get much more out of him. I'll have to wait till any results — positive or negative — reach Mike. 'Thanks for your co-operation.'

'Promise me you'll find him. I'm scared.'

'I know you are. We're doing our best.'

'It's not good enough. I want to know I'm safe. Can't sleep. Can't eat.'

'Yeah, I can see. Just drink.'

My comment strikes a nerve. His eyes shoot a flash of outrage @ me. 'It's the only thing keeping me sane.'

I'm about to suggest he gets Sharpe over for company, but something stops me. If Sharpe's still in the frame, that would be unwise.

A counter-breeze has blown up against me, and the Thames River's a choppy bed of black and gold from the late lights still on in the Heights. Fraser's palace's shrouded in darkness.

It's a struggle to wing my way through the wind. Still some time to dawn, and everything's quiet.

Mike's nodded off. My spheco-knuckles tap his window.

He starts. 'Any luck?'

I shake my head. 'He's shitting himself. Androcops haven't traced the source. Could be a hoax. Not much to go on.'

He's staring into the distance, not listening.

'Did you hear me?'

He nods, an automatic reflex, and starts, gogging @ me. 'Sorry, you say something?'

'Chill, Mike. Where you @?'

'V159, I'm so fuxachingly tired. There's no way out. I go

home to get away from everything and to work to escape thinking about my family. Just wanna be disemployed now, discontinued. No more worries and nerves. Just peace.'

'Hey, Mike.' I bang my spheco-fist on the passenger door. 'You gotta quit talking like a loser, giving up on yourself, your folks. On us. You hear? We'll get through this together. We've almost located Kamara's brother. Once I've grilled him, I'll know more.'

'Why Kamara, V159, and not any one of the others who lost kin in Satan's Garage disco duels?' He does a poor job of looking concerned @ my plan.

'Cz the killing started after Milo's death.'

'Might just be coincidence. Someone bereaved from an earlier fight could've taken longer to get their act together.'

I have to try and keep him from dwelling on other problems. 'True, but Kamara Junior's been on the run, and talking to him can't do any harm.'

'Except waste more of our precious time. Kamara's brother'll keep. Horelka's demanding an immediate result.'

'He always wants things yesterday. That's nothing new.'

'I'll be here tomorrow night. Kill if you have to, but fuxache man, make sure you're here. We gotta nail this.'

'Get some rest, Mike. Panicking and giving up won't solve it. We need clear heads.'

He may've wisecracked my sorry spheco-arse for all I know. I don't hang around for his answer.

I get back to V157 in just over five deci-minutes, thrilled stiff to see him. I ignore his grumbling about needing his spheco-kip and tell him exactly what we have to do.

TWENTY-TWO

As the weeks turned into the harsh winter months, they all got cold viruses and their skin became dry and chapped.

The agrocomplex was barren now, and there were rumours withertongue had spread to the agroworkers, but they'd managed to store a decent quantity of apples, potatoes and cabbages, and there were always nettles, dandelions and sowthistles. And thawed snow to drink. Occasionally, Flint brought a rabbit or a pigeon.

He materialized one day with a few dead acridians for roasting when there were withertonguester bonfires so their smoke would be unnoticeable.

'They're edible,' he said. 'Almost palatable. Bit fishy.'

He didn't stay.

It was Irene who first woke to the beating of thousands of wings. She leapt to her feet and ran up to the kitchen. Her cry of horror aroused Garcia, who joined her.

The back door was open. They'd broken in. Acridians.

Swatting wildly, Irene and Garcia shooed the bugs away, helped by the others, who'd now emerged. But too late to save their food. The entomoids had eaten everything.

They scooped out a few acridians that'd drowned in the oil drum.

The next day Flint reappeared, face glowing with passion. Phoebe held her cheek out for him to kiss and summoned the group.

'You bring anything?' she asked him when they'd sat on the floor, and told him about the acridian raid.

He shook his head.

'When you went yesterday,' said Irene, 'did you leave the back door open?'

Flint smacked his forehead. 'Fuxaches! I'm sure I shut it. Oh no, I really hope I didn't...'

'How could you be so fucking careless?' shouted Olivier. 'Now we've got nothing.'

'Look, I'm sorry,' started Flint, 'but hey, you know what? I met that gyno I mentioned after my first raid. Her name's Tania. She's invited us over to see her house. Only a couple of us need to go. Friendly visit.'

Phoebe blew her nose on her robe sleeve. She had catarrh and was sipping a cup of tea. 'It's time we branched out and made contact. We got nothing to lose.' She had tied her hair up high on her head. Irene thought she looked like a goddess, albeit one with a cold. 'And they have a good place?'

'Better than this. They got water. Provisions.'

Phoebe and Irene volunteered to go with Flint.

When Phoebe barred Olivier because of his hostile attitude to anything Flint said or did, he looked like he'd been slapped. His eyes flashed murderous spite and wiped the smirk from Flint's lips.

Excited but apprehensive, they set off the following day.

It was a ten-deci-minute trek north in the opposite direction from the agrocomplex, mostly on the main road. Irene memorized the route as they went.

The farmhouse was a two-storeyed, double-fronted build-ing. The façade was carpeted with ivy, and there were fields all round. The trees were bare but the winter sun added a golden glow to the hard, cracked soil.

Flint ran to the entrance. They followed. 'Tania,' he called.

Tania came out and shook his hand. 'Good to see you again,' she said. Petite and in her twenties, she had cropped black hair and wore a faded grey dress, torn @ the hem.

Tania looked @ Phoebe and Irene. 'These must be...'

'Yeah.' Flint introduced them and they entered.

The hall was clean. Tania led them into a parlour, which had chairs and a table. It was the first time in ages Irene had sat on a chair. All the furniture @ their place had been used as fuel before her arrival.

Tania made them Caffeinola®. 'As you can see, it ain't much,' she said after a few moments' silence, 'but it's home.'

'It's good,' said Irene. Phoebe nodded in agreement.

When they finished their drinks, Tania showed them the kitchen stove, which they could heat with wood. There were latrines outside, real ones, and a bathing area, plus a huge water tank.

'There's also a freshwater stream by that copse,' said Tania. 'So we rarely run short of water.'

Irene remembered having to lick dew off the leaves to slake her thirst.

On the upper floor were six bedrooms with real beds.

It was months since Irene had slept in her bed back in the DUB. She sat on one and sank into the mattress. It was old and worn, and the blankets looked motheaten, but it was above the floor. How she longed to be able to fling her clothes off and wash in the bath and snuggle up. She applied freezing cold water to her body every day. It ticked a box, but she didn't feel clean, not without BestcoeSoap® and the well-being born of cleanliness and hygiene.

'Must be good, in these hard times,' said Tania. She'd come next to Irene and smiled. Irene felt a streak of discomfort, as though she were some poor relation being patronized. She got up and smiled back. 'Where are your lot?'

'Out. There's only three of us. Come down. Got something to ask you.'

TWENTY-THREE

V157's in our copse, very excited about seeing Milo Kamara's brother. 'He's outside, in those fields.' He points to the east. The land's bare, the grass patchy. I'm aware I'm taking a gamble on this, going against Mike's wishes.

He leads me to the clearing. It's a bright cold winter's day.

The sun's risen. Crows caw. Squirrels rustle their way through the dense network of pine branches, which hide us. We wait.

After a few deci-minutes, someone moves. I grip V157's hand. We soar into the sky. Kamara's a dot in a meadow.

I glide down, fifty metres or so. 'Kamara, Olivier?'

He turns, and his eyes and mouth open wide in surprise. 'What the..?'

As he speaks, V157 lands behind him. 'Don't move,' he says. Our cocks spring out, V157's digging into his back, mine against his belly. 'Hands up.'

He obeys.

'Answer our questions, and we won't need to use these.' I prod him a millimetre. He staggers back, but V157's cock blocks his fall.

'Why did you flee Cockneytown?'

A scent emanates off his old, torn coat. My heart stalls.

'You should know. You know everything else about me.' His snarl oozes defiance and primal loathing for us.

I struggle to continue the interrogation. 'Interesting you

become a Freebie just after Jaxxon Gobbs was murdered.'

He shrugs.

It's her *smell.* 'You know who I'm talking about.'

'That muzak singer.'

My Eyelid screen splits into two and my pulse breaks its speed limit. 'He was performing when your brother was killed.'

'Milo.' He sighs and frowns.

'Where were you during and after Milo's flight fight?'

A look of terror races across his cute little andro-face. 'You suspect me? I...I never had nothing to do with it.'

'Gobbs's song rejoiced in his defeat and death. Surely you'd want to teach him a lesson, one he'd take with him to the grave?'

'N-no. It's not like that.'

'So, where were you?'

'I wasn't even in Cockneytown. I was here, a Freebie. Been one for ages.'

'Can anyone verify that?'

'My mother.'

His mum...and what about mine?

V157 telepaths over what he's just accessed on his Eye-screen.

'Okay,' I start, 'since you never passed through Recycling, you still got your Eye-D?'

He shakes his head. 'Are you gonna take me away?'

'Possibly,' I bluff. Let him worry, let them all worry their handsome andro-heads off whenever they see us. I'm past caring about their sensibilities. Fuckers. V157 transceives the signal I telepath, and disengages while I push my cock hard against Kamara's mattressy abdo-flesh. He takes a step back and gasps.

'Don't try anything stupid, like running away. We can always track you down.'

He doesn't say anything. Just gogs @ me and turns his head to check where V157 is. His worn shoes crunch on the stony ground. 'Never killed no-one,' he says.

We don't bid him farewell. The trees afford us an excellent vantage point. Kamara stands a long time staring @ the sky, obviously @ where he thinks we've flown. He then sets off.

We follow him, from field to field, hiding in hedges and bushes, and using our sharp spheco-eyes to keep him under constant surveillance and find out where he'll lead us.

'Is he our man?'

We're crouched behind a hawthorn hedge, peering through gaps in the branches @ his shrinking figure as he makes his way into the next meadow.

I shake my head. 'He's telling the truth.'

'But he could've got in when no one was looking.'

That makes no sense. 'Ain't got the means. Ain't got nothing.'

'So, without the school link, why we still tailing him?'

Why indeed. 'We ain't. That scent... '

'It's the school I'm telling you...shouldn't you...?'

I'm not listening. I telepath V157 to fly close to the ground.

We wait @ the boundary with the next patch of wasteland. In the distance is an old farmhouse.

'Ain't seen that place before,' he whispers.

Kamara dashes into the house.

I peep over the hedge. Movement in the corner of my spheco-eye makes me turn: two Freebies, a gyno and an andro, emerge from the house.

'That's them,' mumbles V157

My heart implodes. I don't see her. I grab V157's hand and squeeze it till he yelps. I shush him and he smacks my arm, gogging @ me bemused.

Cue cardiac drumroll. They're getting closer. Over the light breeze, we hear their Freebie chatter.

I image her gyno-friend and the skinny andro as they throw out garbage, and profile them on my Eyelid-screen Face-Reader. Kamara reappears and all three go inside.

Something about the place links us all.

I tear myself apart.

Decision time.

Dual commitment.

Myself or others?

V157 looks to me for instructions. Now's not the time for a major ditheridoo. I nod once and telepath my choice.

TWENTY-FOUR

They were sitting in the parlour.

Tania got up and stood in front of the hearth. 'I hope you're enjoying your visit. Thing is, I invited you here, cz I think it would be fantastic if both our groups teamed up. You can see what an improvement...sorry, I know that sounds arrogant and insulting...only going by what Flint's told me...but we got good facilities here, more space. Even if we just worked together...'

Before Phoebe could speak, Irene said, 'I've always advocated better communication between groups. Create a network so we can help each other when times are hard, pool our resources, especially in winter, and share intelligence for security.'

'There you go,' said Tania. 'That's exactly what I'm proposing. Couldn't've put it better myself. Strength in numbers. Everyone benefits. There's room for you all here. You could move in right away.'

'We'll have to discuss this with the others first,' said Phoebe.

Tania exchanged a glance with Flint. 'Sure,' she said. 'No problem. Here's what I suggest. Stay tonight, cz it'll soon be dark. Tomorrow you can go back and talk to your group. Tell them what you've seen and what we've got to offer. Return in a couple of days with your answer. Flint'll bring you.'

'Sounds reasonable enough to me,' said Phoebe.

They had potatoes, cabbage and rabbit for dinner and shared

a bottle of red Vinola®, something Irene hadn't enjoyed for ages. The tastes awoke centres of pleasure in her brain and body she'd almost forgotten existed. The sensation of a proper meal in her mouth was like a drunken orgasm.

Where'd they get this from?

'It's a celebration,' said Tania.

Flint winked @ Irene. Phoebe pecked his cheek.

Tania didn't drink much, listened and refilled their cups. Very soon, Irene and Phoebe were tipsy and giggly.

They don't live like this every day.

They were joined later by the other members of the group, Li and Ade.

'We've left the stuff in the kitchen,' said Li, after shaking hands with Irene and Phoebe. They clomped up the stairs. Tania looked @ the ceiling, to where she imagined them to be. 'Very useful to live with. Handy andros.'

'In what way?' asked Irene, yawning.

'Oh, various odd jobs, you know...' She led them up to a room with a view of a rear courtyard and fields beyond, although it was too dark to see very much.

The sound of wings beating against the window alarmed Irene.

'Acridians,' said Tania. 'They know we've got food here and constantly try to get in. You get used to it. We'll talk tomorrow.'

Irene slid into the bed in all her clothes for it was still cold and she wished she'd washed.

Is this too easy?

She wanted to discuss the proposal with Phoebe. But Phoebe was snoring and Irene drifted off almost immediately her head hit the pillow.

Before Tania brought them Caffeinola® in bed, Irene recalled thinking something in the night, but couldn't remember what and it bugged her. They went out to wash, and into the living room for breakfast. Potato and apple.

'We hope you'll get a positive response from your group,' said Tania. 'We'd really like you to live with us. Flint's told me how good you are.'

'Where's Flint?'

'Helping Li and Ade...oh, nearly forgot.' Tania rolled her eyes. 'Always doing that.' She disappeared into the kitchen, rummaged around and emerged holding three potatoes in each hand. 'For you,' she said. 'To show our good will.'

As Irene moved forward to thank her, she saw the bulging sack. 'Wow! How'd you get that?'

'Raiding.' Tania shrugged. 'Giving you some of our bounty gives me such pleasure.'

'We're so grateful,' said Phoebe, smoothing out the creases on her robe. 'Hope one day to return the compliment.'

They were soon on the road home. Irene remembered where to turn off.

They dumped the potatoes in the kitchen and went into the living room.

Waiting for them was Flint.

TWENTY-FIVE

Mike calls me from SECOPS. 'Told you Kamara'd redherring you,' he grumbles. 'And you better sort Smacker out. He's unhappy about something else now. @ least he complained to *me*, didn't take it higher...'

'Why? What've I done now?'

'Best shift your arse and find out.'

'Why did you run away?'

Maxx Smacker's shaking so bad, his real-glass glass is raining drops of alcohol on the cream carpet. He's having a smokestick, and is unable to sit still. Just pacing up and down his private tavern.

I look @ him like he's mad. 'Whaddaya mean? I never ran away.'

'Yes, you did, sphecoid, for fuxache. Yesterday, you appeared there.' He points @ the door. 'And then turned tail. I wanna know why.'

'I wasn't here yesterday.'

'Yes, you were. Don't lie. I saw you. Reza saw you. We couldn't figure out why you fled.'

So who was it? My mind gallops away down various avenues. *If Sharpe's the man, why didn't he finish the job when he had the chance? And is Smacker hallucinating now?* 'Reza Sharpe was here?'

'I just said he was, didn't I?'

'Whoa, whoa! Any more backchat and I'll make sure you get dumped. Understood?' He flinches @ that. Cue spheco-glee. 'Just remember who's watching out for your nice humo arse.'

He thinks about it for a bit, realizes he's gone too far and gives a cursory nod. 'Sorry.' He really doesn't enjoy saying that.

'What was Sharpe doing here?'

'I needed company. Someone to look out for me. Fat lot of use you were. I suppose you saw him and thought it wasn't worth coming to see how I was.'

'Where's Sharpe now?'

'@ home, probably, nursing his hangover. We drank rather a bit too much.'

'You better be careful. Don't wanna escape this killer only to die of cirrhosis.'

He dismisses this with a loud, irritated tut. I snatch the cocktail from his grasp.

A sharp intake of breath scrapes the back of his throat. 'Hey, give that back.' He reaches for it, but I'm too quick for him. It's down the sink before he can say dry martini.

'You're imagining things, Smacker. You saw me last night, but I was nowhere near here.'

He folds his arms and inclines his head to the side in defiance. 'Go ask Reza. He saw you too. We can't both be wrong. I told him who you were. He said he knew, you'd spoken to him. And we couldn't understand why you chose not to hang around...'

'Have you finished?'

He shuts up.

'I'll check this with Sharpe.'

He sneers. 'Good luck getting any sense outta Reza. He was worse than me.'

'Well, I'll just have to detoxify him. And if it turns out

you've been making this up, I'll slap a liquor ban enforcement on you quicker than you can say Beerola®.'

Sharpe's in bed. I dispense with formal entrances and front doors. So much less hassle to use the windows or balconies.

Since Sauternes's murder, Sharpe's in a larger suite with a terrace, which I clock as I circle the mansion.

He's staring up @ the ornate ceiling plasterwork and must've noticed me fly in through the open double doors, but doesn't acknowledge me.

I land @ the foot of his double bed. The sun's rising and already signalling its intention to make this a crisp, cloudless day with no breeze. Hints of the river whiff to come are getting more frequent. Rays of light are reflecting off the gilt patterns on the walls, dazzling me and making Sharpe frown.

He's waiting for me to speak first. I oblige him. Not the time to be bloody minded, yet.

'Last night — where were you?'

He groans, screws up his eyes and squints @ me. 'With Maxx. Why?'

'How much did you have?'

He moans. 'Too much.'

'What happened?'

'I got drunk. He's a bad influence.'

'How you feel now?'

'How you expect, after upchucking non-stop since I woke.' He remembers his nausea and his cheeks distend. He retches, then leans over the side of the bed and vomits copiously into a blue plasticon bucket. The sick splashes noisily and smells sharp and bad. Worse than the Thames. 'Sorry.' He wipes his mouth.

'You recall anything else?'

He shakes his spinning little humo-head.

'I see. Nothing you wanna say to me?'

He doesn't answer. I'll wait till he sobers up, and move towards the terrace.

A small voice stops me in my tracks. 'But why didn't you join us?'

I spin round. 'What was that?'

He repeats his question.

'When?'

'Last night. You showed, and scarpered. S'pose we disgusted you, being so pissed.'

Smacker wasn't imagining it. 'But I wasn't there.'

'Yes, you were.' He smiles, as though this is a fun game, and he's caught me out and is enjoying the thrill of nailing me. 'I saw you.'

'But...' And then the question just falls out of my mouth. It surprises me I haven't asked it before. 'How did you know it was me?'

He sits up in bed, incredulous I can ask such a stupid question. 'Of course it was you. I know what you look like. You're standing there in front of me. It was you. I know a spheco-freak when I see one.'

I march up to the bed and sink my spheco-fist right into the soft spot between his sternum and upper gut. 'The word is spheco, you piece of humo shit.'

He grunts, grimaces with pain, burps and covers his mouth. He waves me away, leans over his bucket and throws up another stinking skinful.

My spheco-brainbeats up their tempo to spasm level. Of course! Dumb, stupid spheco-idiot that I am. We all look the same to these humos. That they saw a spheco the night before is beyond doubt. But if it wasn't me, who was it...and what was that spheco doing there?

My legs are shaking and I can no longer bear the sight of

Sharpe or the stinking contents of his abused stomach, but I'd love to plunge my spheco-dick into that slop bucket and savour the second-hand taste. Still, I've got what I came for, although it isn't what I expected. I was hoping for confirmation that Smacker was seeing things. Now I realize all my and Mike's investigations have been going in the wrong direction.

I leave Sharpe mid-chuck, wince @ the squealy sound as he forces more muck up and @ the sight of the long strands of mucus spooling from his nose and mouth. If only his millions of new gyno fans could see and smell him now, I muse, as I take off from his gorgeous balcony, frantically going over everything in my mind, thinking contrapuntally.

And then it comes to me in a flash. V157's a genius.

The school where the victims went.

I've been blind to the obvious. I now remember where I've seen the name before. My spheco-heart thunders.

Gotta access Mike's computer again. ASAP. I'll just have to risk it.

I soar high above the concrete blocks of SECOPS like a vulture waiting to swoop. My spheco-vision focuses on the orchard. A lone spheco's chewing timberex. On a break.

I fly in closer, hoping it isn't my successor. V146'll have no compunction in raising the alarm if I reappear.

As I approach the tree, I breathe a sigh of relief. V122. I land behind him gentle as a snowflake and release a huge fart-cloud of soli-pherum.

Will it work?

His I-brows flutter.

I'm in. 'Hi.'

He turns, slowly and drowsily. 'Why...?'

I clap my clunking spheco-hand over his loud spheco-gob

and shush him. 'Yes, it's me. I need your help.'

My palm transceives a grunt-type sound issuing from his throat. It seems to be a yes. I stroke his I-brows with mine to employ my charm, and telepath my instructions, praying he'll be able to carry them out before the pheromone wears off, or any of the other sphecos get to him.

'You miss me?'

I get the answer I hoped for. 'Likewise.'

He wants to know if I'm well, and V157.

'No time for that now. Go and do what I told you.'

He leaves, and I fly up and round, away from the Combs and the spheco-quarters. The SECOPS main entrance is busy with androcops coming and going. I land on the steps leading to the swing door and calmly push through. I was right; none of the humos think anything untoward in a spheco-cop mingling in their midst.

Horelka's checking something in reception. My spheco-heart a-throb with nerves, I fuxache and sit on a bench, my back to him.

I smack the side of my stupid spheco-head. Why didn't I ask V122 who was on duty? Horelka's one of the few humos who'd recognize me. Like Mike. If he sees me now... I only hope V122's been able to carry out my orders.

I pretend to busy myself with a non-existent palm screen. From the direction of reception come footsteps.

When they stop, so does my breathing.

TWENTY-SIX

'It's a trap.'

'Calm down, Olivier.' Phoebe flushed with embarrassment. 'I'm sorry, Flint.'

'Don't apologize for me. Can't you see? He's spying on...'

'Just shut up.' Phoebe raised her hand. 'Right now, we're gonna discuss and vote whether to go there tomorrow. You okay with that, or do you just like causing trouble?'

Olivier fuxached.

'You bark a lot,' said Phoebe, blowing her nose on her sleeve. 'That's your problem.'

'I must say,' said Irene to Flint, 'I thought you were with Li and Ade.'

Flint smiled. 'We finished early, so I came here to see if I could help.'

'Oh yeah?' said Olivier, pointing @ him. 'I saw what happened to your last group. We could be sleepwalking to our doom.'

'Why can't you trust him?' asked Phoebe. 'Why must everything be suspicious?'

'Okay. One question. Why give us those spuds?'

Phoebe threw her hands up in despair. 'Are you always looking for an ulterior motive?'

'It's to soften us up.'

'It's a gesture of friendship,' said Irene.

Olivier squatted down and buried his face in his hands.

'Have you all gone mad? We been really careful about who we let in here and what we allow them to know about us. And now it's like you've all forgotten every principle we ever had.'

Samina raised her hand. 'I reckon it's worth the risk. We've all been through hell, and if this house is as good as Phoebe says, then we should go. And we've always got this place if it doesn't work out.'

'But then they'll know where we are,' said Olivier, looking @ her with an intensity, which suggested to Irene that somewhere, deep inside his soul, lurked the still smouldering embers of an unextinguished passion. 'We won't be able to return to this house. Won't be safe. If this group's toxic, we'll have to find a new home...assuming any of us survive.'

'So what's your solution?' Samina looked straight @ him, inviting more than an answer to her question.

Olivier stood up and paced about. 'Dunno,' he said after a few moments. 'Ain't safe here now.'

'But you just don't like Flint,' said Phoebe. 'Whatever he does or suggests is gonna be suspect in your eyes.'

Olivier shrugged. 'Everything about him is suspect. That's why I don't like him. You got it the wrong way round.'

'I'm really torn now,' said Irene. 'It could be wonderful, or...'

'We've no way of knowing unless we try,' said Samina.

'Let's vote,' said Phoebe. 'All those in fav...'

'Why the fuck's Flint...? He ain't one of us.'

Flint marched over to Olivier. 'What's your fucking problem? I been with your lot long enough. You've all eaten the food I bring. I'm part of this group.'

'You're a fuxaching spy.' Olivier pushed Flint out of the room.

Flint raised his fists. 'Come on. What you gonna do about it, eh? Let's see how tough you really are.' He shoved Olivier back.

Olivier's first punch missed. Flint ducked and laughed. 'Crap. Continue outside.'

'No,' said Phoebe.

They ignored her, and jostled each other into the back yard. The others followed.

Flint goaded Olivier, pointing to his chin, guffawing as he blocked very punch. 'You're shit, just like your loser brother.'

Olivier howled. 'How you fucking know about that?'

'Don't be stupid. Word gets around. It was all over Face-Chirp®, how he got kebabbed...served him right for being a useless piece of...'

He didn't finish. Olivier's right hook cracked on Flint's jaw and sent him sprawling. As he lost his footing, the force of his backward fall toppled the oil drum onto its side.

Water gushed out. Everyone screamed, 'No!'

Nursing his jaw, Flint said, 'Oops.'

Garcia managed to lift the drum to minimize the loss, and peered inside. 'Still about a third left.'

'You idiot,' said Phoebe to Olivier. 'Look what you've done. We'll *have* to leave.'

'He...he provoked me.'

Flint shook his head and got to his feet. 'Okay, decision time, but count me out.'

They voted to move, Samina and Phoebe in favour.

Irene abstained, like Garcia.

Olivier was the only no.

'Even without me,' crowed Flint, 'you're outvoted.'

Phoebe looked @ Olivier, eyes filling with tears. 'I'll...we'll miss you. Please reconsider.'

He shook his head. 'I'll start a fire...but won't come with you tomorrow.' He glanced over @ Samina, who looked down.

'What'll you do?' asked Phoebe, putting her hand on his

arm.

'Stay here. Where else can I go?'

Phoebe nodded.

Irene felt Phoebe was probably too choked to speak. She put her arm round her shoulder and gave her a squeeze. 'He'll come round,' she whispered.

'No, he won't,' said Phoebe, the last word louder.

Irene held onto her as she sobbed.

Olivier stormed out.

It was only after Phoebe had stopped crying and dried her eyes on her sleeve, the same one she'd previously wiped her nose on, that Irene noticed Samina had gone.

'You know I have my reservations, Phoebe,' said Irene, 'but I'll be there for you.'

They tucked into the potatoes, although Olivier had his in the kitchen. Samina wasn't with him now. She was with Irene, deep in thought.

'Everything okay?'

Samina shrugged. 'No. I don't want to sacrifice an opportunity like this, but...' She didn't elaborate.

They slept and @ dawn said goodbye to the house and to Olivier.

Olivier and Samina kissed, but said nothing. When they disengaged, Irene saw she was crying, and shook her head. *Two to look after.*

Olivier then approached Flint and once-overed him. 'Remember what I said to you. I mean it.' He turned away, leaving Flint to recall his former threat, and stood face to face with Phoebe for a few accu-seconds before they hugged.

'I'm sorry,' Irene heard him say, his voice choked. 'It's been great, but...I can't do this. Good luck. Pray I'm wrong.'

They kissed. He patted her back and walked slowly towards

the house.

Irene went up to him. It could've been the early morning sunlight promising a mild day, but she fancied there were tears in his eyes.

'Follow us,' she whispered, her hair ruffled by the breeze. She looked over to Samina, hoping he'd understand everything she meant. 'So you know where we are.'

TWENTY-SEVEN

I slowly swivel my spheco-eyes to make out a vague image of his form. He's standing a few paces from me. I need air. I close my eyes tight. My lungs are about to burst, but I know if I give in and breathe, he'll approach me.

So much for superstition. The footsteps get closer and stop. His humo hand touches my shoulder, and his tinny voice speaks.

'You're under arrest, V159. On your feet.'

I could kill him right now, but dunno why I don't, or try to escape. Something deep inside me makes me obey him. I rise slowly and spheco-tears rain from my eyes.

V146 appears.

I fart soli-pherum, but to no effect. V146's immune as I am to him. He nods. Gynocops grab my arms.

'You don't understand,' I say. 'I'm that' — I put my thumb and forefinger almost together — 'close to solving the Satan's Garage murders.'

V146 looks @ me with a sneer in his spheco-eyes. 'Oh yeah? You've been interfering in androcop matters that no longer concern you.'

Horelka raises a hand to hush him. 'And what have you learnt?'

I gog @ him and @ V146. I don't want to share my thoughts with them. Mike and I have our arses too close to the line to give away secrets. 'Just a lead.'

'And what exactly is this "lead"?' The air is thick with Horelka's contempt.

Thinking fast and furious, I hang my head. If I reveal what I suspect, they could act on it and get all the credit, and still have me incarcerated. So I just say, 'Satan's Garage is the target.'

V146 asks, 'What makes you say that?'

I shake my head. 'Dunno.'

'If we find you're hiding information, that'll be another felony you'll have to answer for.'

'That's enough, V146, but I appreciate your zeal.' Horelka has started leading me to the detention cells. The gynocops have me in an armlock.

Shameblood floods my spheco-cheeks as I'm marched past familiar faces, in the undignified position of having my arm twisted behind me. I hear the whispers and exclamations. *Is that really V159...? How did they catch him...?*

There are two staircases down to the cells and I trip a couple of times to add to my disgrace. No one says a word or tries to help me.

We arrive @ a small hexagonal cell and V146 unlocks the door. The gynocops push me in. V146 re-locks it in a trice.

In the barred porthole I see Horelka's face minus his halo-hair. 'I'm disappointed, V159. We expected great things from you. Great things.'

His head vanishes, to be replaced by V146's.

'Abusing your rank of Queen, and arrogant and stupid enough to think you can stroll in here and not face the conse-quences of your crimes. And this ain't the first time you've minced your way back, is it? I've smelt you a couple of times already.' His smile stops distorting his mouthparts and he looks serious again. 'I'm afraid for you, V159. It looks hard, real hard indeed.'

Then Horelka reappears and recites the catalogue of my spheco-crimes — plus a new one. 'The sphecoid DNA on Sauternes made you a suspect, V159. We know you turned out bad. We didn't realize *how* bad.'

'No, you've got it wrong. Okay, I found the body. But I didn't kill him, for fuxache.'

As they leave, I hear V146 ask what'll happen to me and Horelka say, 'What do you think?' and V146 answer, 'Discontinuation?'

I fuxache again and again, banging my spheco-fist on the stone bench and crying out in pain as I don't realize how hard it is.

I'll face vivisexion first...

If I'm still alive after the experiments...discontinuation.

It's no more than I deserve. I've let Mike down. He'll be demoted, or lose his job unless I can communicate this latest lead I have. He'll end up on the scrap heap, eking out a miserable existence as a D-classified before being recycled. All my fault. His family won't last much longer. Wretched PAULies. Not a hope.

And me?

I'll end my spheco-days in pain, disgrace and horror @ leaving poor V157 to rot in the Eastlands.

The cell's floor, ceiling and walls are all whitewashed wood pulp we make ourselves. A single light burns directly above me. Tiny slits high in the walls allow for ventilation but there's nothing remotely resembling a window to look out of. Just a bench to sleep on, not that I'll be able to, the way I feel.

A few pieces of timberex are scattered on the floor for me to chew should I get bored with my own fantasies and terrors. How thoughtful they are, these humos!

Will V122 carry out my instructions?

They haven't mentioned syngastrion and excretorium arrangements. They're probably not planning on custodizing me long enough for it to be worth the bother.

Punishment must be imminent.

Despite my fevered spheco-brain, I must've drifted off because I wake, aching all over on the hard stone floor, to the sight of a pair of black androcop boots and blue uniform dungarettes. I groan. Horelka, no doubt, has come to inform me of my fate.

'Get up, V159.'

Not Horelka's voice. I look up. Mike. I cry out with joy @ seeing him, and stand up to shake his hands.

He shushes me. 'V122's told me everything.'

I close my eyes and telepath V122 my gratitude. 'We gotta act fast, Mike. Have you brought it?'

He points to his pocket computer. 'Where we going with this?'

'Been thinking and it ain't pretty. Gobbs, Sauternes and Smacker @ school together. But not Sharpe. Smacker's twenty-six, the victims twenty. Older, but still @ the same school @ the same time. I need to check this school out again. Something's linking them, and my hunch is that.'

Mike's computer gets me the link. Blueburymead Juniors. I clutch his hands and he winces in pain as I've squeezed him too tight.

'Easy, V159.'

'Sorry. Now, Blueburymead Juniors rang a bell when we first saw that link. I've seen that name before, and it was only today after avoiding being vomited over by Reza Sharpe that I remembered where. It was when I broke into the Institute Database on Olympia Heights. One of my first felonies.

'I'd looked up my and V157's histories, and my entire spheco-swarm's details came up — humo — sorry, human —

names, place and date of birth and the schools they were selected for sphecanthropy from. Too much data to remember, and transfer to my system blocked.

'I can't access that info, but you can.' I direct Mike through my stuff and then the spheco-swarm's.

My heart freezes. The name is there — Blueburymead Juniors. Same dates. Same class, apart from Smacker. Goosepimples erupt on the soft underside of my chitinex plates and my hands tremble.

'Mike,' I whisper. 'I think I know who the killer is.' I point to his miniature screen. 'Look. The link.'

He squints @ the page and whistles.

'It all adds up. Can you get me out of here? Smacker needs protection and I can give him that and apprehend the killer. But I fear the attack is imminent. We've got no time to lose. You gotta let me outta here.'

He chuckles. 'No worries.'

'What about Horelka?'

'Just go. I'll deal with him.'

I stare at him stupefied.

'Well, What are you waiting for?'

I dogshake my spheco-kip off and air breast-stroke my way out of SECOPS.

TWENTY-EIGHT

'We'll play it careful.' Garcia had sneaked up beside Irene and was whispering in her ear. 'Neither of us is a hundred percent sure about this.'

Irene nodded. She always did with Garcia, not being a hundred percent sure about him, either. 'I told Olivier to follow us.'

'Quick thinking.'

'We shouldn't totally bridgeburn.'

'I'll be looking out for you.'

'Likewise.'

Garcia and Samina's wow when they arrived made Flint laugh.

They ran towards the front door.

Li and Ade were standing either side of the porch, arms folded. They didn't smile @ first, just surveyed their future housemates, squinting in the fading sunlight.

Li was shorter than Ade and slimmer. Ade was darker skinned and stockier.

Their stares froze the arrivals into silence. 'Tania mentioned you might be joining us,' said Li, deadpan. He gestured to them to go in. They went inside.

Tania shadow-punched Li's shoulder. Flint highfived him.

The newcomers oohed and aahed @ the living room.

The door closed and they hushed. Tania and Flint came to the hearth in the middle of the wall opposite the door and Ade and Li stood @ each end of the room.

'Welcome to Tey House,' said Tania, and they clapped. 'I hope you'll be very happy here. I know I'm delighted to have you. You must be tired after the walk. Ade and Li will show you to your rooms. Then we'll eat. After dinner, we'll tell you about life @ Tey House.'

Irene was in a bedroom with Samina. As there was only one bed, they put the mattress on the floor. They agreed to swap round and in freezing weather to share the bed.

There was more Vinola® with the potato and cabbage dinner and they soon got drunk and lost their inhibitions.

Tania circulated, trying to make them them feel @ home.

When they finished, Tania asked for volunteers to wash up. Samina's hand was up first and she was whisked into the kitchen, where the others could hear her cries of delight about how good everything was.

After she came back, Ade took them on a quick tour of the house. 'Twilight now,' he said, 'but tomorrow we'll show you what's outside. I understand you have some expert farm raiders.'

Garcia whistled and smiled.

Ade glanced @ him. 'You'll be very useful here,' he said. 'Especially if you've got an accomplice.'

Garcia pointed @ Irene, who felt the blood rush to her cheeks. Not the sort of information she wanted bandied about before people who were still strangers. But it was too late to undo that.

Ade once-overed her with his big dark eyes, and moved on. 'We wake @ daybreak,' he said, 'and retire @ dusk. What you do in your bedtime is up to you. But there is no power, no lighting, except what we get from the sun or the moon. Anyone got a problem with that?'

They shook their heads.

'Good.'

Irene felt he would have benefited from a few tips on charm from Tania.

'@ some stage tomorrow, we'll assign you your duties, which commence the day after, okay?'

They nodded.

'Excellent. And now it's getting dark, what do we do?' He raised his eyebrows like a teacher addressing a class of five-year olds. When there was no answer, he eyed the ceiling, and shook his head @ them.

They went up.

'Missing him?' Irene asked Samina as they undressed.

Samina nodded. 'I wish he'd change his mind.'

Me too.

The dinner, Vinola® and the walk had exhausted them. They were asleep in seconds.

It was past midnight when whispered breath tickled Irene awake.

'Get up. It *is* a trap. Cops are coming.'

TWENTY-NINE

V157 eases himself out of his kip-cell and raises his I-brows when I tell him everything. He whistles with surprise. 'Guess it makes sense. So what now?'

'You're a-coming back with me. You're gonna help me apprehend him.'

We arrive in Olympia Heights @ dusk. Lights are coming on in some of the residences and skyscrapers.

Entering via Smacker's loft window, we land in his bar room.

'My support, and extra protection for you,' I say, introducing V157.

Smacker nods and pours himself a long, green drink.

'Don't make yourself sick.'

Ignoring this, he says, 'Oh, that reminds me. I chirruped Reza to come over. His company reassures me.'

Meaning mine doesn't. I just say, 'You're very brave.'

'I know.' He isn't brave, just caught up in a situation where he can't say no. He's trembling, and downing cocktail after cocktail. But as he wasn't imagining things the day before, and has possibly led me to the killer's Eye-D, I say nothing. *His* liver.

I still have misgivings. Sharpe's presence could make the killer flee again. 'My colleague and I need to hide. Can you suggest anywhere?'

Smacker puts down his glass and points to a door. 'Here,' he says, leading us through to a little anteroom. 'You'll be able to make sure I'm safe, and hear anyone untoward arriving.'

'Okay. What about Sharpe?'

Smacker looks @ me as if I'm crazy. 'He'll be with me.'

'Er...he might ruin the plan. Sit with him for a bit, sure, but when we say so, we want him with us. If what you said is true, the murderer might've run away last night cz he saw you weren't alone. I suspect he prefers to kill without an audience.'

Smacker purses his lips and moves towards his bar room.

I stop him before he disappears through the door. 'First time we met, I asked you if you knew anyone who was selected for the sphecos @ your school. Any fresh memories since then?'

He looks @ me and shakes his head. 'Sorry.' He goes back.

V157 turns to me. 'What was all that about?'

'You'll find out.'

'Can we trust him to play his part?'

I shrug. 'He's too shitting himself to do anything other than what we say. He needs instructing.'

'What are we gonna do after this?'

I look @ him for what could be one of the last times in my life. 'It's so good having you here, V157. I've missed you so much.'

'Likewise, V159.'

We peck lips.

'And now, patience. It's possible he won't come.'

Sharpe arrives. We have the door open enough to observe him and Smacker andro-hugging.

Smacker mixes him a drink and replenishes his own glass.

After a few accu-seconds, we enter their room.

I introduce V157 to Sharpe. 'Can you see the difference in our faces?'

Both Sharpe and Smacker scrutinize us, but after a few moments shake their heads.

'Thought not.'

That seems to irk them, but it proves my point. They really do see us as all the same.

I call Sharpe in. 'Sorry to break up your little soirée, but from now on you stay here with us.'

He remonstrates. 'How dare you order me about! I'm giving up my spare time to help a mate and all you can do is boss people around. You can't stop me being with him.'

He's beginning to seriously piss me off. As soon as he sees what that means, he lets me drag him into our anteroom, sits down on a chair and looks away.

'Now, stay here, do as I say and you won't get hurt.'

He doesn't have the grace to answer. Just keeps showing me his back. I imagine my thoughts about him are worse than his about us.

And so we wait. It gets tedious, tense and there are a few false alarms. V157 and I telepath our reminiscences of good times and bad times.

After about six deci-minutes, boredom has Sharpe nodding off.

When he wakes, it's past midnight. He needs the toilet, but access is via Smacker's bar.

'I'll come straight back, don't worry.'

We hear him mumble to Smacker and Smacker's fraught reply.

He's gone some time before we realize he's disobeyed us. I'm about to steal a quick peep @ Smacker's room when a scent alerts me.

We hear a cry, and run into Smacker.

The killer has struck.

THIRTY

Irene opened her eyes with a start. 'What...?'

Olivier's hand covered her lips. 'Dressed and downstairs as soon as possible.'

She nodded. Olivier woke Samina and went to alert the others.

Irene did not dare speak. She grabbed whatever clothes were to hand and hugged Samina. They tiptoed down the stairs, clinging to the banisters in the dark, shivering in the cold draught breaking in through the slightly open front door.

Snoring upstairs.

Ade and Li.

They hunched over in the nocturnal chill outside. The moonlight revealed Olivier following them out with Garcia and Phoebe, who was scratching her arm.

'Must've been bitten,' she mumbled. 'Bit early for mozzies.'

As Olivier started to lead them away, a barely audible gyno voice froze the blood in their veins. 'What the fuck you doing?'

They turned.

Tania ran out of the house and confronted them. 'You're leaving me, aren't...?'

Something twittered in her pocket.

Her Eye-phone.

'Flint's chirruped me. Yeah, we got FaceChirp®.' She tossed her Eye-D to the ground and stamped her foot on it. 'I'm sick of this fucking greeneye life. Take me with you.

Please.'

Phoebe took Tania's hand and they began walking, silently following Olivier. A distant engine hummed louder and louder.

'You know,' whispered Tania, 'for each Freebie delivered for recycling in the syngastria we get a bottle of Vinola®, a jar of Caffeinola® and a kilo of potatoes. Work it out...can't do this no more...hate this fucking job.'

Without looking back, they sped up a little, across the field and towards a wood. Headlight glare danced in the blackness and the motor whine crescendoed.

'They'll have to come on foot through here.' Olivier spoke @ normal volume. 'Keep going.'

Bushes and brambles slowed their progress. Irene kept close to Samina followed by Garcia with Phoebe and Tania in the rear. She had no idea how much time had elapsed since their departure, or how far from Tey House they'd gone.

'How did you know it was toxic?' she asked Olivier.

'Soon as I saw the façade, I sussed it. Poor attempt @ camouflage. And that lack of vigilance meant I got in easy. Threw a stone @ the door. No one answered. Figured it'd be unlocked. Unguarded. I was right.'

Torchlight spears jousted above and around them. Androvoices, savage, unfamiliar, yelled @ them to halt.

Irene crouched down with Samina, heart pounding, breath stalling.

Shots rang out.

A gyno voice — Tania's — cried, 'Don't shoot me. I'm not a Freebie. I'm one of you.'

'Shh, Tania, don't...' Phoebe tried to coax Tania back into hiding.

Irene sensed bodies scuttling through the undergrowth. More shots sounded. Three, four, she couldn't tell. She heard the gyno screams and rushed over with Samina to Phoebe and

Tania.

Tania was lying on the ground, not moving.

Phoebe crawled towards them. 'I'm so sorry,' she struggled to say. 'It's all my fault.'

Irene hugged her. 'Don't be silly. No one's to blame. We were betrayed.'

'No. I was too trusting. The one time I let my guard down. Should've listened to Olivier.'

Someone grabbed Irene's hand. Garcia. 'We gotta move.'

Samina ran up to Olivier. 'You okay?' she asked.

He nodded and hugged her for a moment. Then he caressed Phoebe, their tearstained faces illuminated by the moonbeams.

'Olivier...Olivier...' Samina tried to get his attention, and walked away, wiping her eyes on her arm.

They stood for a few moments in silence — Irene and Samina in a private hell, Olivier in a nightmare of his own and Phoebe rubbing @ the bite on her arm.

The sudden thud of racing footsteps startled them.

'Olivier,' called Irene, but he wasn't listening.

An andro ran up. 'Going somewhere?'

Flint.

'Hey,' said Olivier. 'Looking forward to all that extra booze, was you? That what you chirruped Tania about...or was you worried she'd deserted you?'

There were shouts in the distance. Torchbeams lasering through the trees. Androcops scouring the area.

From where she was hiding, Irene saw Olivier push Flint's chest. 'Time to fulfil my promise. You should've brought your securicop cronies along for the party. They'll never find us.'

Flint ignored this. 'Knew where you'd be. Crawling your way home to that shithole with your Earth-Mother whore...' He didn't finish cz Olivier jabbed a grief-powered fist deep into his stomach.

Flint jack-knifed, gasping for breath. When he recovered, he made a slashing move across Olivier's torso, but Olivier jumped back and stayed his arm. They wrestled each other to the ground.

Moonlight flashed on the metal in Flint's hand. Irene wanted to drag Olivier away from this stupid fight, save him, but perhaps he craved this duel, the sort of honour thing andros went in for. He might never forgive her if she deprived him of the satisfaction of 'getting' Flint. She knew how their minds worked, or @ least reckoned she did. But she wouldn't forgive herself if she didn't try to protect him and it all turned out bad.

Olivier's voice interrupted her thoughts. He was on top of Flint and pushing with all his might to keep the dagger away. 'So, how much food and drink did you get from betraying your last group?'

'Dunno what you're talking about.'

'That the best you can do? You could've shopped us then, but held out for a bigger haul. You ain't fucking getting away with it again.'

Flint chuckled, but Irene detected a nervous thinness to his laugh.

Over and over they rolled in the leaf-mulch, the knife glistening in Flint's right hand always a millimetre from Olivier's face, and then clouds obscured the moon and in the shadows Irene could only hear grunts of exertion.

When the clouds dispersed, the blade caught the moon-beam as it ploughed deep into Flint's throat.

'I'm a man of my word.' Olivier searched Flint's pockets, removed something Irene couldn't make out, popped it into his trouser pocket and spat. 'Fuxaching greeneye securicop.'

He hates more than he loves.

Jackboots crunched closer and closer. Olivier motioned to the others to run further into the wood. One minute he was following them, the next he was gone.

Irene looked round. Samina was running back, calling for Olivier. There was no reply.

Irene and Phoebe chased after her, dragging her away from her terrible quest.

'They've captured him, haven't they?' Samina burst out crying.

'I'm sure he'll find us.'

Samina shook her head.

They caught up with Garcia and hugged.

They couldn't hear much — just animals scuttling in the undergrowth. Progress was slow.

Then Samina screamed.

Irene thought her heart would explode.

'Why didn't you speak?' Samina yelled. 'You gave me such a fright.'

Olivier suddenly reappeared. 'Didn't wanna make a noise.'

'Thought we'd lost you.'

'You'll never lose me.'

'Powers-that-be,' whispered Irene. 'You okay?'

'I killed Flint,' he muttered.

Phoebe fuxached. 'Shut it. Listen. Footsteps...getting louder.'

An androvoice yelled. 'Give yourselves up now. We're armed.'

THIRTY-ONE

As I suspected, the killer's one of us. The realization that I'll have to bring down one of my former swarm tears me apart.

The scene that confronts me is a balletic tableau. Sharpe stands in front of Smacker, to shield him from the weapon, but has ended up in its way. A spheco-penis has transfixed him right through his lower abdomen, very close to his right side. The lethal tip protruding from Sharpe's back has still managed to scratch Smacker's arm, which Smacker's nursing with his other hand.

The spheco's seen us, but remains perfectly still. The only movement in the room is the slight flutter of the curtain in the breeze by the open window, and Smacker shaking.

I break the silence. 'Retract your spheco-dick now.'

V146 doesn't.

He turns his head to look @ me better, the intense hatred he's been glowering out @ his victims now aimed in my direction. 'You couldn't keep your fuxaching spheco-nose out, could you? This ain't got nothing to do with you, V159, so just get the fuck outta here and take your pervert lover with you.'

V157 and I both get aroused by his aggression. Cocks a-quiver mid-air, we remain in position.

'Oh, but it has everything to do with me. You usurped me, V146. You were the one who abused your position, not me. I want my status back.'

I fart soli-pherum, but it still doesn't work. V146 really was damaged @ metamorphosis.

'Shoulda known it was definitely one of us when they found the real chocolate Sauternes had been guzzling inside him. Double the pleasure, huh?'

'Jealous, huh?'

'Not so much fun now, is it?'

'This idiot,' he says, pointing @ Sharpe, 'got in the way.'

'I said remove your cock from his andro-gut.'

V146 ignores my command. 'Ah, the ex-queen. You ain't so special, V159. Just one tiny little thing I couldn't do on the day meant you got the soli-pherum gland implant and I didn't...but now I have and it's me leading the swarm...'

I let him carry on.

'...and anyway, what do you care about a lousy humo andro for? They're all the same, hate-eros who loathe us and mess up our lives.' He looks over @ Smacker and his voice changes. It becomes deeper and more charged with emotion. 'But some of them are worse than others.'

For the first time since our entry, Smacker addresses V146. 'We didn't mean it. You gotta believe me...it was just fooling about...playing...you know what children are like. How were we supposed to know what was going to happen to you? We were just kids, for fuxache.'

Sharpe's sweating bad and shaking. The shock of the wound is threatening to do for him. We have to get him medical aid quick. V146 hasn't ACEd him, or Smacker.

I telepath V157 to get a doctor to the house ASAP.

Smacker's on his knees now, sobbing and entreating V146. 'When they took you away, we realized what we'd done. I felt terrible...honestly...if I could turn back the clock, I would. You gotta believe me.'

V146 nods slowly. 'Oh, I do. It was bad for you, was it?' He looks @ me and V157. Sharpe doesn't seem to figure for him

@ all except as an obstruction between him and his goal. 'I imagine you two can understand what they did. Gobbs, Sauternes and Smacker. Their little gang. The name calling, the beatings. That was nothing. Only the beginning.

'Then came the knives to the throat, strangling me till I went blue in the face, dunking my head in the river till I almost drowned. And the threats that "today will be your last." I was so frightened and ashamed.

'Gobbs got hold of a gun. I really thought it was loaded and you were going to shoot me, especially when you put the blindfold on. Oh, how you must've laughed @ the little weakling niceboy.

'And thanks to you they took me away and stole my name. My family were discontinued. Did you know that? So upset @ losing me they went to pieces. Lost their shit jobs.'

'Remove your penis from Sharpe. That's an order.'

'He got in the way.'

'And you couldn't wait any longer, even though his presence scared you off the other day.'

'You don't miss a trick, V159. I should've insisted they discontinue you when Horelka arrested you.'

'Your time's up, V146. As a dysfunctional spheco, you'll be the one who's discontinued.'

He puffs up with indignation like a pigeon. 'Dysfunctional, am I?' he roars. 'And which of us is "functional," V159? I'm not dysfunctional, as you put it, just shoulderchipped, like you and V157. I hate "normal" humos the way some PAULies resent those A-listers born to riches and privilege. But @ least I'll've got revenge and justice. Look @ Smacker cowering there. All his A-list Olympia Heights wealth and power, and he's just a frightened little niceboy.

'Yeah, ain't that funny? Smacker, who ring-led the bully-boys, was as nice as me. But making other kids' lives a misery saved him from selection. As for the other two, being normal and popular and famous didn't help them either. My only regret is not being able to enjoy what I did. I mean *really* enjoy. You'll understand that, you two, cz you both went through the same as me.'

I shake my bitter spheco-head. 'You're a fool, V146. Your metamorphosis was obviously damaged, like mine. But you've allowed your hate to consume you instead of sublimating it.'

He laughs. 'I know you sympathize with everything I've said and done. We're exactly the same, you and me. But you can't — won't — admit it. If you could do what I've done to the hate-eros that got you where you are now and get away with it, you would. No hesitation. I'm right, aren't I?'

'If you don't remove your dick from Sharpe, I'll force you to.'

His tone becomes silky. 'Is that a threat? Well, come on. I've done what I wanted and we're all gonna discontinue soon anyway, me, you and your little friend there, so what the fuck do you care?'

He withdraws his penis. Globs of blood spurt from Sharpe's gut, and he collapses backwards into V157's arms.

'It's okay, it's okay,' says V157, laying him on the floor and staunching the bloodflow with the side of his flexicock. 'The doctor'll be here soon.'

A quick glance @ the wound shows me that haemorrhaging is the danger as well as perforation of the intestine. Smacker's just contemplating his carpet.

Stupid move on my part. My attention was diverted from V146. V157 shouts 'Watch out!'

I freeze. The pop-up returns in migraine flashes.

BESTCOE-MENDOZA INSTITUTE OF ENTOMANTHROPY
DEPARTMENT OF SPHECANTHROPY

Training Manual page 451

Squat Manoeuvre 153 — Surprise Back-Jab

When threatened by an attack from the rear, the successful SQUAT candidate and spheco-queen's penis curls up and back over the shoulder to penetrate the assailant through any head orifice to reach the brain.

ACEing may not be necessary as the wound is usually fatal, and to reduce expenses and conserve ACE funded by BestcoeGenetix®, this should only be applied as a last resort if absolutely necessary.

I do not look round. I cannot. I wouldn't be able to see clearly even if I could cz of the tears blurring my vision. I retch @ what I've had to do, and like Smacker, am crying, but for very different reasons.

'The manoeuvre, V146, that you failed. That's why I became queen and you didn't, and all your jealousy and resentment still can't change that.'

I really hope life hasn't left him before I say that. I want my words to be the last he hears.

I rip my dick out and shudder @ the sensation and taste of spheco-brain dripping off it. I register a very light thud as V146 falls to the floor. His words have touched me bad. He was right. I'm no different. Just dysfunctional in another way. I de-soil my cock on the carpet. Smacker stops tutting when he clocks my furious stare.

Androcops bring the doctor up and they stretcher Sharpe away. 'You gonna be okay,' they keep telling him. 'Super comfy stay in the BestcoeMedix® hospital.'

On Olympia Heights, they have hospitals with proper healthcare, sponsored by Bestcoe-Medix®. Not the C-class infirmaries PAULies deal with.

V157 holds my hand. 'What are we gonna do with him?' He kicks @ the kneeling form of Maxx Smacker, who starts.

'Excuse me, I'm also hurt.'

The doctor, who's just left the room behind the androcops, comes back and looks @ the scratch on Smacker's arm. He hendonhaws. 'S'pose you'd better follow them down and get an anti-infection jab. There's always a risk of withertongue, even here on the Heights.'

'Thank you, thank you.' He gets up and makes to leave.

I gog @ V157, my spheco-gob a chasm of shock @ seeing his wondercock is also telescopic as it extends to lasso Smacker round his waist and drag him back.

'It's not an emergency,' I say to the doctor. 'He'll be down soon. He's low priority. Plus, we haven't finished with him yet.' To Smacker I just say, 'Shame on you.'

I nod to V157, who releases him.

Screwing up his face in disgust @ the contact, Smacker says, 'Don't you feel any sympathy for me? After all, I'm the victim here. You're just jealous and bitter, cz you got sphecan-thropized and I didn't, and you can't change that. I'll be complaining about you again, sphecoid.'

'You lied to me, Smacker.'

His frown becomes indignant. 'Huh?'

I set him straight. 'When I asked you if you remembered anyone who got selected for sphecanthropy, you said you didn't.'

He dismisses this with a flick of his wrist. 'I forgot. So what?'

'Obstructing a murder investigation's a serious felony, Smacker, even for A-listers. You still wanna take this up with my boss...?'

He flashes a worried glance @ me and shakes his head. Let him shit himself.

'But I'm already ruined,' he cries, looking @ V157 then @

me for help. 'No band left. Only Sharpe. Satan's Garage is dead.'

I spit, a huge gob of spheco-phlegm in his face. 'That's for me, for V157, but above all for V146, who you and your popstar cronies have forced me to sex-e-q-te. For all of us. And irony of ironies, you turned out nice yourself. A decaff.'

My mucus dripping from his lips and chin, he gets the point and backs off, down his plush staircase and away for treatment and sympathy.

They'll never tell the truth. When the news breaks, he'll be 100% victim. They won't mention V146's motive. I spit again, on their FaceChirp®, and put my arm round V157's waist.

'Chizz for being here with me.'

He squeezes my hand.

'Let's tell Mike all's well.'

Back @ SECOPS, I clock the gynocops, and grab V157's arm. 'I can handle this. Fly back to the copse before the labrats get their grubby humo-hands on you.'

'But I can't leave you.'

'Go.'

'And if you don't...'

'Believe in me.' I kick his skinny spheco-arse. He buzzes off into the air.

The gynocops waste no time armlocking me.

I'm dragged inside. Déja-vu.

Mike's face undergoes a skinquake of embarrassment as he thanks me and begs forgiveness for being unable to help.

Horelka looks me up and down. 'The cells,' he says, deadpan.

THIRTY-TWO

They froze.

There was enough moonlight for the androcops to aim.

The first shots twanged.

No one breathed.

And then it started.

It was just a whisper @ first, but it crescendoed to a roaring stridulation. And as the volume intensified, the night darkened as thousands upon thousands of creatures blanketed everything.

'Acridians,' said Irene.

The cops screamed in terror as the huge locusts covered them from head to toe, the force of numbers knocking them off their feet. In vain, they fired their guns into the swarm.

The fugitives were also carpeted.

'Link arms. Keep moving,' said Olivier. 'They might nip, but they'll stop once they realize you're not food.'

It was hard to progress, but they managed a few steps. Eventually, as the bugs flew off, their arms were free to swat the remainder.

'We left the door open,' said Irene. 'The acridians've been waiting for their big chance, and tonight it came. And with it came ours. Leg it.'

With very few acridians interested in them, they disengaged and ran until they heard a distant engine start. As the van drove off with a screech of brakes, Irene sighed with relief.

They hugged.

'We don't know where we're going,' said Garcia as they disengaged, 'so let's kip here and make our way home in the morning. The old place should be safe. Don't think Li and Ade ever went there. Tania and Flint are both...'

'Good idea,' said Irene, nodding and hating herself for it. She sensed Olivier take Samina aside and heard them mumble, 'See you tomorrow.'

Phoebe followed them.

Shivering now, in the pre-dawn temperature, Irene turned to Garcia. 'So, it's just you and me tonight.'

He didn't speak. They lay down, his coat on top, hers below.

@ first Irene couldn't sleep. Nor could Garcia. They looked up @ the stars freckling the sky and traded pre-D-classification stories.

'We did get caught, eventually, my bro and me...' Garcia swallowed hard. 'Olivier saved me...and then I called out to you in the Recycling Centre. So, that day cemented our fates together. For now...'

She nodded.

'It could be so beautiful,' he said.

She said, 'I'm cold.'

He put his arm on her shoulder. 'It's something.'

She grabbed his hand. 'You're warm.'

His other hand was on her chest. She felt it rise and fall with her breathing. She couldn't see his face clearly in the dark, but knew it was closer to hers than it had been. She let out a little sigh. Was this going to be where it happened? She could think of more comfortable venues for making love. He'd now slipped his arm under her back, pulled her to him and held her tight against his living, warm, taut frame.

Their legs entwined. He massaged her sides slowly @ first,

sensuously, then more quickly. He didn't touch her breasts. Just pressed her shoulders. He was firm, but gentle, his hands now rubbing her thighs.

She uttered a cry of delight. It was one of the most wonderful things that had happened to her. She wondered if she should resist, or @ least make a show of resistance, or whether she should...reciprocate.

She put her hands on his upper arms and held onto him, clinging on to the hope he represented. She'd known all along it would come to this. She'd hated him for that and other things. Still did. And now she loved him too.

He was kneeling, his hands caressing her knees, making circular movements around her shins. Then he flipped her over, and kneaded her back. She groaned, wishing it would never end. But of course, it did.

'Better now?' he whispered into her ear, stroking her hair.

'Mm-mm.'

'Get some sleep. Another tough day tomorrow.'

She lay face down, wanting to scream. Was he going to leave her burning like that? She was indeed warm now, although a thought chilled her blood. Was he like Nelson, but had escaped detection @ seven? Was that why he was so hostile? And she'd fallen for someone who was...*nice.* Her reaction to what had befallen her son. She should've picked it up. She wanted to ask him, but that would be wrong. She said nothing. And took some time to get to sleep.

Did I love George? She fidgeted into a comfortable position. She'd partnered him cz that was the done thing if you wanted to survive and propagate. She'd relied and depended on him, not expecting sex to be much fun. It was a job, another household chore like the ironing. You could do it with the radio on to pass the time. She'd come to see him as a rock, albeit a distant one, but he'd flaked out when Nelson was taken.

And now, was Garcia failing her too?

She woke alone, and started. He'd abandoned her. Remembered he was a niceboy and was horrified @ what he'd done.

But he reappeared with a twinkle in his eyes and a handful of dandelion leaves. 'Breakfast is served. Gotta keep your strength up.' He put his hand on her cheek and ran his finger down it.

She nodded. If only he'd force his finger into her mouth, anywhere...

He squeezed her hand.

He is *nice*. Serves me right. The massage had been bliss, but she hadn't found the courage to hint @ what she desired. Kept telling herself it wasn't her place.

She wanted to kiss him, chizz him for protecting her from whatever enemies lurked in the dark, but he'd let go of her, and mingled with her fear of attack was a mixture of frustration and irritation. *Why hadn't he at least tried?* 'Know the way?' she asked. *Pathetic.*

'Just about.' He described a route, but she wasn't listening.

The first glimmer of daylight smiled in the eastern sky. She took some leaves and looked @ him guiltily. 'Thanks for my massage last night.'

He laughed this off. 'You liked it?'

She closed her eyes. 'Mm.'

'Any time.'

She kept her eyes shut to hide her feelings. And she nodded. Then she got ready, and they went to rouse the others.

'Couldn't you sleep?' asked Samina. 'Heard you wandering about last night. Phoebe said it wasn't her.'

Irene started. 'But we weren't...'

So who was?

THIRTY-THREE

The gynocops lead me down the whitewashed corridor.

Horelka accompanies us. He keeps asking me where V157 is, but I won't tell him. Just smile. Mike's team have got the result. He'll pass his probation and keep his job. His family won't get D-classified.

My thoughts, both spheco and humo, are magnetized to the threat of discontinuation. *How will they do it?* Having survived metamorphosis, I'm @ a loss as to how this can be worse. Apart from the vivisexion.

I'm familiar with the journey down to the cells. My mind's too busy mulling over recent events for me to notice the discomfort of the armlock.

We arrive @ the cell I'm already acquainted with. The gynocops push me in as they did before.

Horelka says, 'That's okay.'

They march off.

I wait for the key to turn in the lock, but the sound never comes. Instead, Horelka remains in the cell with me, closing the door behind him and bidding me to sit on the bench. He shakes his ferrety head and gives me the once over before speaking.

My heart sinks at my prospects: a horrid Horelka lecture on protocol, and then I die. 'Thank you for arresting me, sir,' I start, not without irony, 'I found your murderer for you.'

He inclines his head by way of acknowledgment.

'What's gonna happen to me?'

He looks @ me. 'You disobeyed orders and escaped from custody, not to mention malicious masturbation. What do you think?'

'Was hoping to be re-instated, sir.' Worth a try.

He laughs, a hollow, bitter sound. 'After everything you've done? Last time you were here, yesterday in fact, you were ripe for discontinuation. There are mitigating circumstances, but overall the outlook's not good. Not good @ all. I'm going to lose you.'

'Your dreams will come true, sir.'

'Allow me to finish. I know you dislike me. Let's face it. Everyone does. It's part of my job, to be hated. I can live with that. But don't jump before you're hurt. I haven't come here to gloat @ your demise. I know we haven't always seen eye to eye...'

'Now there's an understatement.'

'Don't interrupt. Hear me out. I want to set the record straight. I know you're an aberration. I was informed about your botched metamorphosis.'

'What?' Anger rises within me, but not of the ACE kind. 'And you never said?'

'Shut up and listen.'

I bite my lip and my mouthparts clamp together.

'You solved the Satan's Garage case. You reckon any androcop would've got half as far as you? Mike's a great guy, but ain't got your mutant genius. He'd never've cracked it. And neither, frankly, would I.'

'You knew...?'

He nods, but refuses to meet my gaze, preferring to find the floor very interesting. 'Of course I did, V159. I'm not Inspector for nothing. But what you don't know, and what I'm telling you now so you'll understand why I've treated you the way I have, is that ever since you've been assigned to us, I've had the Mendoza Institute labrats on my back the whole time.'

I frown. 'What do you mean, sir?' I will him to look @ me. He does.

'They've been monitoring your behaviour. They wanna know what it means to survive what you and V157 went through.' He looks down again. 'Basically,' he resumes, 'they don't want sphecoids being too clever. They're afraid of the implications.'

'Don't understand, sir.'

'Me neither, V159.' He looks up @ me, and his humo expression is honest. 'But I didn't wanna lose you to no B-class labrat shithead, so I kept your achievements under wraps. Otherwise, you'd have been back @ Olympia Heights being meddled with, and vivisexioned, and I'd have been left without a decent spheco swarm to defelonize South East District 13. See what I'm saying? Had to be cruel to be kind...

'...if Knox and his team get any idea you cleaned up the Satan's Garage case, they'll have you discontinued straightaway. I knew you'd sneaked into the investigation. Always knew you would. Pretended not to know. And I was proud of you, V159, even though I couldn't dare say anything. And I'm grateful for your work.'

It feels like fresh sea breezes blowing cobwebs outta my stale spheco-head. 'Dunno what to say, sir.'

'You don't have to say anything, V159. Now it's time I was kind to be kind. You'll understand, believe me. You see, even 'horrid' Horelka has a heart. Goodbye, V159, and thank you.' He turns and walks out of the cell before I can reply.

As the door clicks shut, I call out a feeble 'Bye, sir', but he doesn't acknowledge my words.

How would he be kind? I have no idea what he means, and wish he hadn't been quite so enigmatic. I sit on the bench and consider the white floor.

There's something strange about Horelka's departure I can't quite pin down. My gaze follows him out and stops in the direction he's gone.

He's left a clue, but my overwrought spheco-head's too thick to get it. Until I realize it isn't what he's done so much as what he *hasn't*. Of course! The door — it's not locked. The crafty weasel's granting me my freedom.

I don't have much time, just enough for a couple of things.

Mike's in his new office, arranging his furniture. His pinched face melts into a big smile when he sees me standing outside.

I fly over his desk.

He stretches out his arms and embraces me. 'V159, I love you like a brother. Words don't suffice to thank you for what you've done for me and my family.'

'Likewise, Mike. You helped me when I was all alone, and you let me escape.'

He laughs. 'Actually, you can thank Horelka for that.'

I look @ him, not as surprised as I would've been yesterday.

'He told me to keep it under wraps for a day or two, but on no account were we to allow you to fall into their hands. He didn't elaborate whose.'

I know, though.

'I'd gone to remonstrate with him, to plea for your release. Imagine my shock when he agreed with everything I said. Oh, I'm gonna miss you.'

'Likewise. No chance of me coming back.' It's a statement, but deep in my boyish spheco-heart it's a question, a plea. But I know the answer.

He shakes his head. 'The next queen'll soon arrive. Your swarm are starting to discontinue naturally. There'll be a whole lot of new spheco-faces around here come the spring.'

I nod. The inevitable. Come early. I put on a brave smile. 'Well, congratulations, Mike, you're through your probation.'

He pats his gleaming new badge and beams @ me. 'All thanks to you, though. How did you work out the killer's Eye-D?'

'Remember the traces of spheco DNA on Sauternes's body? I know I didn't touch him. I made a conscious effort not to come into contact with him. And both Smacker and Sharpe thought they'd seen me, when it was V146.'

He wide-eyes me.

'We'd been looking in all the wrong places.'

V157 and I weren't the only dysfunctional sphecos.

'And what about you, V159? What are you gonna do now?'

His smile fades, but I keep mine. 'Gonna find V157 and we'll take it from there.'

A couple of old scores to settle, too.

'Watch your back. Knox's after you. Good luck.'

'Powers-that-be bless you, Mike. Oh, I almost forgot. A little farewell present. Something for your database.'

He looks puzzled as he activates it. I transfer a file.

'What is it?'

'Incriminating. That's what. All the evidence you need to arrest Fraser. Even though most of Olympia Heights thinks they've got immunity, they ain't. So, go get him. Hardtime him.'

He kisses me. For the first time in my spheco-life a humo puts his soft lips on my chitinex face.

As I pass Horelka's office on my way out, I hear him on his Eye-phone. My spheco-ears prick up. '...he got away. I did everything I could...whaddaya mean it's not enough? The resources I have, it was always gonna be tough...slippery character...I'm sorry, Professor, but I've got other priorities right now...like quelling the withertongue quarantine riots and nailing the number one Sin Tempter in Cockneytown.' He flips it shut.

I can't help smiling. A friend I never knew I had. A guardian angel disguised as a rat.

Beneath me spread the northeastern districts of Cockneytown. Black withertongue flags on numerous DUBs now. Unburied corpses in the streets. I check my Eye-screen for plague updates and almost stall mid-air @ the grimmery I read.

Thousands dead. Is it all falling apart?

Part Three
Withertongue

ONE

V157's waiting for me like the best friend he is. He's built a cosy kip-cell from wood paper. 'Been so bored,' he says, like it's my fault. 'Could've made a whole comb.'

I palpate it with my I-brows and sniff. 'I'm impressed. And with that wondercock you could've been a queen...if you'd bothered to do your homework.'

He laughs and whips my back with his I-brow.

I retaliate. He yelps. We roll over on top of each other in the spiky grass and I break the news to him. 'We're moving. Knox wants to recall us.'

'Eh?' He runs his spheco-fingers along the smooth surface of his comb. 'And what about this?'

'It's beautiful. You're a natural. But time to make another one — and not here.'

I can see the riverbed pebbles through the shallow, dancing water. We kneel to drink from the crystal stream, lapping and sipping the cool liquid. It's good. There's early blossom we can suck for nectar, but shelter, not food, is our priority.

We can swim, but sphecos don't like getting wet. Holding hands to save energy and opening just one wing each, we fly across. It's been a long search and now we're almost there.

We fold our wings and hug. There's a small forest nearby. The late afternoon sunlight's reflected on the underside of the first deciduous leaves. A breeze tickles the foliage, making it flutter and giggle in a thousand different ways.

'We'll hide in there, V157.'

As we enter the dense treedom, dark brown bark and rays of gold camouflage us.

I scan the large stretch of waste ground, with a farmhouse in the middle. *That* farmhouse. I've retraced the scent Kamara radiated. I'll find her again, though I fear what she'll say.

We dart from tree to tree and bush to bush so as not to be seen, and, lying on the bare soil, wait @ least ten deci-minutes. The sun moves down the sky towards its melting place on the horizon.

'Why are we doing this?' asks V157.

'I told you. I just want to speak to her. Get her to acknowledge me. Then we go. Wherever you want.'

'What choice do we have? We're outlawed...'

Suddenly aware of movement, I touch his arm. 'You see that, approaching the house? Couple of...looks like andro Freebies lurking about... They the ones you saw before?'

V157 scratches his shiny spheco-head. 'Not sure.'

The andros glance furtively left and right and enter the house.

'What next?'

'We go in,' I say, flying towards the entrance, heart in my spheco-gob. 'Make sure you're transceptive.'

The moon's a nail-clipping in the now dark sky. Fresh gathering clouds hide the stars.

My spheco-wings unfold and vibrate me up from the prickly grass, beating so many thousands of times per accu-minute. I soar, blinking as the air rush makes me cry. In a trice I'm in the backyard.

We fly through the door they left open into a dismal room. We're in.

My spheco-heart hammers away. I take one step forward,

breathing heavy, then use my wings to float.

The room we've entered is some sort of kitchen. Horizontal now, we glide into a dark hallway.

Will she be here?

The rumble of androvoices from below distracts me. I gog @ V157 and fingerhush him. Like dragonflies we hover.

V157 calms me and kisses my cheek. *Patience.*

He dares not speak, but I transceive his sentiment and uncertainty about the Eye-dentity of these andros. Then he flits down the narrow stairwell to investigate the cellar.

Hardly able to breathe, I follow, dreading the truth, my spheco-heart overpumping.

'Bedding's cold.' We hear them clearly now. One of them appears, looking back to address someone else. He is Freebie-clad, but FaceReader reveals it doesn't smell right.

'When is a Freebie not a Freebie?' I telepath.

The andro reaches the first stair and walks straight into V157's erection, gasping as it tears into his shoulder.

'One sound and you're ACEd,' says V157. 'Eye-D?'

The andro is shaking, from pain, fear and shock. I dunno how deep V157 has stabbed him but he manages to surrender a greeneye.

When is a Freebie not a Freebie?

'Pretending to be a Freebie?' I ask as his mate arrives. 'Company. How sweet!'

Smell lures me downstairs to the cellar.

There's a room with blankets. I grab one and press the material to my spheco-face and drink in the gynoscent.

V157 gogs @ me incredulous and points to the doorway. 'What are we gonna do about them?'

They must not contaminate her *home.* We lug the paralysed andros up the stairs.

'Dump them in the yard,' I say as we reach the landing.

But before V157 can answer, we hear footsteps crunching in that very same yard. Time to go.

'Fuxaches! We left the door open.' Her voice pierces my heart.

We stare @ each other for what seems an eternity, V157 looking to me for guidance, but my brain shuts down. I shake my scared spheco-head. I cannot do it, not now. Not ready for that. *What am I gonna say? To come this far and be lost for words. It can't be worse than last time...or can it?*

V157 squeezes my hand and we stroke I-brows. He understands. We leave the bodies at the top of the cellar stairs. He points ceilingwards, dragging me after him, higher and higher up ruined staircases. In a daze, I fly behind him into an attic. Broken mirror shards litter the floorboards, but there's a paneless window we can squeeze through and launch ourselves from.

It's so difficult to leave, now I've found that house, that trace, but I wrench myself away, and swallowing hard, level with V157 in the air, and stroke his arm.

'This is the place,' I say.

He smiles.

And then we hear the cry.

TWO

Irene turned to the others and pointed @ what, in the dimness of the hall, looked like piles of clothes lying by the cellar staircase. 'Someone's been here.'

Their eyes widened, but they remained silent. Irene tiptoed towards the piles, cringing @ every creak of the floorboards. Then she stopped still and put her hand over her mouth.

They crowded round the stiff bodies.

'Who are they?' asked Olivier.

Phoebe explained, slowly as if she was so exhausted, speaking was an effort, and went down to her bed.

'That must be who I heard last night,' said Samina. 'They'll've followed us.'

'But how would they have got here first?' Irene's mind was about to detonate with worry. 'Unless they knew about us, all along. From Tanya.'

'And Flint.' Olivier spat.

As they hauled Li and Ade out to the yard, they noticed the wounds. Garcia whistled. 'Stabbed right through.'

Olivier nodded. 'Could be...sphecoids.'

Stony silence.

Garcia screwed up his thin, swarthy face in a mixture of disbelief and disgust and fuxached. 'Sphecoids? Burn'em all, I say, together with the withertonguesters. But they don't come out here.' His turn to spit.

Olivier nodded his approval @ this sentiment and high-fived

Garcia. 'They do now.' He told them about his previous encounter.

'But...why?' asked Irene, more to herself than the others.

Olivier shrugged. '@ least they got the right guys for once.'

Irene had gone very quiet. She knew what was coming. She looked down @ the floor to hide her embarrassment. Perhaps, Olivier too had had a bad experience with sphecoids. She couldn't take that away from him, had no right to. But Nelson...spheco-mum...she couldn't tell them, say those terrible words. And how she wanted to, shout them out so that the world would know what her son was and how she'd lost him, *she*, who could never talk about her child.

'Wonder what they were doing here?' she mumbled.

Recent rainfall meant the oildrum brimmed. Light from local withertonguester incinerations made it safe to cook. And the flames deterred the acridians.

Garcia lit a fire. As they prepared their meagre supper of steamed leaves, they kept returning to *that* topic. 'We should arm ourselves as best we can,' said Garcia.

Samina caught Irene's eye, as if she understood what this meant for her. 'But we don't know what they're after. Maybe, we should wait and see if they reappear,' she said. 'And ask them.'

Garcia scoffed. 'You don't approach a sphecoid,' he said, 'or ask questions. We all know what they wanna do.'

Samina changed the subject to grumbling about the food, and sat with Olivier, who was improvising on his guitar.

Irene breathed a sigh of relief. Once again she buried Nelson somewhere in the remotest part of her mind, aware that was crucial if she was to survive.

Outside, the sky morphed from creamy to blood, then inky.

As they got ready for bed, Irene touched Samina's arm. 'Thank you.'

Samina looked nonplussed.

'For coming to my rescue when they were discussing sphecoids.'

The look of realization lit up Samina's face. 'Oh, I guessed you weren't enjoying that conversation.'

'You're right. I wasn't.'

'My offer still stands. If you wanna talk about it, I'm happy to listen.'

'Not a good time. You don't have to...'

Samina looked @ her. 'How long've we known each other? What've we been through together? Do you honestly think I'd betray you? Never, Irene. Friends stick together. We're solid.'

Irene started to cry, and rested her head on Samina's shoulder. 'That's the sweetest thing anyone's ever said to me. I love you, Samina. You're a true friend. I only hope I'm as good a friend to you.'

'But you are. You've saved me so many times.'

'Can hardly keep my eyes open,' said Irene as she hugged her friend goodnight. She felt a wave of euphoria well up inside her.

Rain lashed against the walls. Irene imagined vans driving by and jackboots marching up the path and was unable to erase the image of Nelson's face as a little boy from her mind.

It was dark when Irene woke in a panic, trying to catch her breath. Instinctively, she reached out for Samina sleeping nearby, and was comforted by the familiar feel of her soft arm.

She wasn't sure if she'd been dreaming, but when she woke, it was to the sensation that someone...or something was breathing in her face.

But when she groped with her hands in the air before her, there was nothing.

She called, softly @ first, so as not to wake the others, surprised the name that left her lips was not Samina's, Garcia's, or even Olivier's. It was another. She said it a second time, louder.

'Nelson.'

There was no answer.

THREE

The next day would, perhaps, bring fresh hope.

The land looked golden in the morning sunlight and the earth black and juicy, full of promise. No longer winter, but not yet spring, the limbo period when the weather gives trailers of the warmth to come.

'We need provisions,' said Garcia. He looked @ Irene, who nodded.

'The old agrocomplex?' she asked.

He chuckled. 'Let's try something else.'

Leaving an underweathery Phoebe in bed, they all set off with apples and water, and headed south into a milder, but drizzly morning. After a ten-kilometre struggle through paths overgrown with dead brambles and anthill-clumped meadows, they came upon a ghost village. Everything that could have crumbled to dust or rusted had done so.

There was a single terrace of cottages. All the windows had blown out and fire had blackened the brickwork.

They moved out of the main street onto what was once a trunk road. Dotted along the way were a number of farm-houses, and behind those, an agrocomplex.

It was now afternoon. Birds chirruped. A breeze swayed the branches of the trees bordering the fields.

'Eureka,' said Garcia.

On the long trudge home with heavy potatoes and cabbages,

their skins glistened with sweat.

Sudden movement in the distance made them stop.

Garcia stiffened. 'In the trees,' he said. 'Too big for acridians. Means only one thing. Fucking sphecoids. Hide.'

Irene's insides churned up. *It can't be.*

But it was.

'Have they seen us?' panted Samina. 'They could be the ones you met.'

'Dunno,' said Olivier. 'Should be safe in that wood, though.'

The sphecocops were too far for the humans to make out where their sightlines were aimed, but there was no point being an obvious target.

'Perhaps they're using them now as scouts to locate Freebie groups before raiding.' Irene spoke with little conviction.

They ran to some dense shrubbery and paused to get their breath back.

Irene peered out from the bushes. The light had almost gone now, but she could still make out shapes in the air. 'They're closing in,' she said.

The dark forms glided from branch to branch, scanning their faces.

'Nothing for you here, spheco-freaks,' yelled Garcia. 'So fuck off.'

The sphecos continued scrutinizing. One gasped, flew down to the ground and stared @ Irene.

Samina clasped her arm.

Irene backed away, shaking with fear. 'What do you want from me?'

'Mum.'

Spheco-mum. 'No,' screamed Irene.

'It is you. I knew it. I've found you, Mum.'

'You're making a mistake.'

'It's me, Nelson.'

She swallowed hard and looked into his spheco-eyes. 'I don't know no Nelson.'

Garcia pushed forward. 'Hey, sphecoid, leave her alone.'

'I'm not talking to you, humo.'

Garcia shut up.

The spheco stood still, Eye-brows waving and vibrating in the cool air, concentrating on Irene. 'I've come back, Mum.'

Irene shook her head. 'No, no.'

'Aren't you happy?'

She squeezed her eyes shut as if that way she could squeeze the reality of *him* out of her life. The others would tear her to pieces if she admitted the truth. She yelled @ him again, the sheer desperation and power of her voice a physical force pushing him back and preventing him from running up and flinging his arms around her. 'I'm not your mother. You're not my son.'

'What the fuck did you just say?' Garcia looked @ her and Samina, and beyond the gulf dividing them from the spheco.

Samina grasped Garcia's hand to calm him.

Irene was still shaking her head. 'I never gave birth to no fucking insect.' She spoke quietly, to the ground.

'It's Nelson, Mum.'

Her hands were over her ears. She couldn't take this. *No, not Nelson. Is this what they did to you?* She was weeping now, knowing that her tiny, dreadful world was coming apart.

Garcia backed away from her in horror.

Now the truth's out, will Samina be so sympathetic?

Irene felt the stigma burning holes in her body, her face pumping with the bloodrush of shame.

The spheco was standing in front of her. 'Please listen to me. I'm sorry I was taken away. I'm sorry for everything. I love you, Mum.'

He stepped closer.

Irene sensed Garcia move beside her, hatred buzzing off his skin. She shook her head and looked down, away, anywhere else but @ that hideous countenance.

'What do you want from me?'

'To...to...' He shifted on his great spheco-feet. 'Just...you're my Mum. I love you.' He gazed into her face, hope boiling in his eyes.

Irene reached out, as though in encouragement, and he came a pace nearer, but then she nudged him away like before, a tiny movement, but it said all the words she was unable to find.

She's pushed me as far as I can go. Now the only way is back @ her.

'And me?' I shout.

She turns to confront me. 'What?'

'What about me? How do you think I feel?'

'I don't fucking care,' she shrieks, her eyes stealing a nervous glance at the others. 'I don't know who you are. This ain't about you.'

'It *is* about me...*and* you. You're still my mother, however I've turned out. I've never fingerlifted against you, and this is how you treat me. Aren't you glad I've found you again after all these years. You think this is a game I'm playing?'

'I...' She looks round again.

'Look what they did to me...and all you're bothered about is what your friends'll think. Well, if that's more important, I've got nothing more to say.'

I dunno how I manage to fly away while trembling so much.

'I...' Her voice falters.

Go back. Sort it now.

Instincts rage @ me, tears forcing my eyes shut.

What have I done?

There is an incline in the field with a hedge @ the top. When Mum and the humos disappear over the brow of the little hill I land and sink to my knees.

I'm only vaguely aware of V157 standing behind me, massaging my shoulders as they earthquake through my sobs.

I reach up and clutch one of his hands. 'It's all my fault.'

'Give her time. Didn't you see the conflict in her eyes? She wanted to accept you, but was afraid. And there were the other humos.'

'No. She hates me. I revolt her. That's what I saw. Disgust.'

He kisses my shoulder blades, and runs his spheco-fingers over my glossy spheco-head.

We lie in the grass a long time, just staring up @ the violet clouds flooding the sky and imagining what, if anything, the shapes signify.

'You found her.'

I don't reply @ first. He's trying to console me, soothe the pain. But I'm not ready for that. Eventually I say, 'I did what I could.'

'No. You still have to win her round. Don't give up.'

We doze, hugging each other for warmth and comfort.

Irene led the others away without speaking.

'What the fuck was that about?' Garcia turned to her, horror infecting his bulging eyes. 'Your boy's one of them sphecoid killers?'

She shook her head. 'I don't have a son.'

'But he called you Mum.'

She didn't look @ him. 'He made a mistake. Took me for somebody else.'

'Spheco-freaks don't make mistakes like that.'

'I told you he's not my son. Why won't you believe me?'

'Cz he called you Mum.'

'Look, he got me mixed up with his real mother. I must look like her.'

'So you don't know him?'

She turned on him and screamed. 'Course I don't fucking know him. What do you think — I spawned a monster? You saying I'm a spheco-mum?'

He shook his head. He had no words to counter her rage. He just mumbled, 'Fucking sphecoid shit. I'd fucking burn the whole fucking lot of them.'

She said nothing, but surged ahead like a tidal wave towards some point in the distance she alone could see. Rumours would start now. She tried to leave him trailing behind, but he ran up to her. 'Irene, I can understand why you might be ashamed if your boy turned out nice and they made him a sphecoid, but we have a right to the truth. If he's your son, and he's stalking you, he could become a danger if he thinks we're obstructing him. We'd have to use force against him...'

'So use force. I doubt he'll be back. He'll have realized his error by now.' She couldn't look him in the eye.

Samina caught up with them. 'If she says he's not her son, he's not her son.'

Irene smiled @ her. Temporary reprieve, but she knew Samina didn't believe her for one moment. Loyalty, pure and simple. She was just sticking up for her. The real interrogation would come later.

She dreaded that moment; she'd not be able to hold out against Samina. Eventually, she'd break and blab the truth.

And that moment wasn't long in coming. Samina linked arms with her and led her away a little.

She repeated what she'd said in the Recycling Centre. 'You wanna talk about it?'

'Talk about what?'

'You know...what that spheco said?'

'What's there to talk about? He got me confused with someone else. Easily done, if you've been...'

'So you ain't his Mum then.'

Thunderbolts shot out from Irene's eyes. 'Don't you believe me either?'

'Yes...of course...but I just wondered if it would help if we talked.'

'Well it won't cz there's nothing to help.'

'Okay, but the offer's there.'

'Why?'

'Maybe this ain't the right time...'

'Fucking right it ain't.' She blazed her way through the fields. The sun was low in the western sky and the temperature was falling. They walked quickly to keep warm. No one said a word now.

Irene broke the silence, pointing to rising smoke plumes. 'Looks like they're burning more withertonguesters. There's some trees there. That's where we'll camp.'

They didn't respond. In silence, they started a fire and set up their sleeping arrangements. Once everything was in place, and they sat around munching their apples, Irene said, 'We can't go on ignoring this forever, so for fuxache, tell me what's on your mind. Like I can't guess.'

Garcia cleared his throat. 'Why didn't you say?'

If Irene's eyes'd had voltage, they'd've electrocuted him, but the softness of his tone slew her resistance. Her voice was barely audible when she finally responded. 'And say what? Hi, I'm Irene. My son's one of the monsters you hate so much?'

'I would've understood.'

'No, you wouldn't. You made your feelings clear from the outset.'

'And you should've done the same.'

'Well, I didn't. Okay?'

'That's what hurts.'

'Oh, so this is just about me not saying. Is that supposed to make me feel any better?'

'It's not about how you feel, Irene. It's about you not trusting me enough to tell me the whole story.'

She blustered. 'But, why should I have to tell you everything, for fuxache? Who the fuck are you anyway? Have you told me everything about your sordid little past?'

'Everything that mattered, yes.'

She clicked her tongue in exasperation and turned from him.

'Who am I?' he went on. 'I'm just one of the best friends you've got right now. @ least I considered myself so, until today.'

She started, but no words came out.

He continued. 'And I look out for you.'

She turned on him. 'But he *is* my son, for fuxache. Don't you get it? He's my flesh and blood and you'd wanna kill him. You hate him and his ilk. How am I supposed to deal with that?' She stopped, and covered her eyes with her hands. She'd said too much, given away her feelings. He'd read into those comments, understand her dilemma too well.

'So you disowned him, your son.'

'Course I did. What else could I do?'

'But you just said he was your son.'

'How dare you moralize to me!' she roared. 'Have you had children?'

He shook his head and realized the balance of the argument had shifted in her favour. 'What's that got to do with anything?'

Samina came to the rescue. 'It means you don't understand how hard this is for her.'

Irene nodded slowly. Samina put her arm round her and

they both started crying.

'I knew, I knew, didn't I, all along I knew,' Samina kept saying. 'Ever since that day outside the Recycling Centre. What you said then. But why reject him?'

'Oh, I don't know now,' wailed Irene.

'So.' Garcia spoke very slowly and loud, to re-establish his voice in the argument. 'You upset your son and me, both @ the same time, without wanting to hurt either of us. Well done, Irene. Congratulations.'

Samina looked over @ him. 'Garcia, just shut up.'

'He's right. I've just done a terrible thing.'

'You can undo it.'

'No. I had my chance. I ruined it.'

'He'll come again.'

'He won't. He was looking for me, and I... It's all my fault. I'll never see him again.'

'You will. Have faith. He found you, didn't he? Well, you'll find him.'

'Oh, Samina, you're so sweet. But I'll never forgive myself. I've been so stupid. Just one word. That's all it'll take.'

They lay close to each other, on the other side of the fire from Garcia, who'd remained silent throughout their conversation, and looked out over the darkening fields. Perhaps he was coming to terms with what he'd discovered about her. Irene wasn't sure. It was hard to sleep. Another time, without Samina there, she'd have the thrill of Garcia's warm body next to hers, even though he'd never... She revisited her earlier suspicions of his niceness. *Maybe that's why he hates sphecos so much. They remind him of what he is.* No, she dismissed that. *Heathcote.*

She got up. The fire was still smouldering. Treading carefully so as not to wake Samina, she tiptoed out of their copse and stood @ the edge of the field. The stars twinkled in the inky sky and she wished she knew their names.

The earth was damp and she shivered in the cold night air. Nothing stirred. She thought she could see him flying overhead, searching for her, but it was nothing. She recalled everything that had happened, how she'd ended up where she was, and she remembered too not only who he was, but what he was, and how he made his living. And she started to understand her reaction better, even justify it till a throat cleared next to her.

'Garcia...I...'

'I still hate them, but you did wrong.' He was staring straight ahead. Also unable to sleep.

'I've lost you as well.'

He didn't answer that, which made her stomach lurch.

'He wouldn't have killed your brother.'

'How do you know that?'

'I don't.' She started crying, but tears weren't working on him. 'I'm sorry I never told you before and you had to find out like this.'

Again no response. She said his name into a void. She began to feel he'd punished her enough. 'Actually, Garcia, I dunno exactly what I'm apologizing for.'

'I'll never accept him. Or his friend. Sphecoids and us don't mix. You did right. But you did it the wrong way. I thought you'd be able to handle that. I thought I knew you better. Well, I found out a whole lot about you today.'

'What are you saying?' She turned to him with a desperate look in her eyes.

'No more than those words.' He went back to the dying embers. She heard him sigh and lie down. He'd left her, like a soldier leaves the body of someone he's just killed. She stood still, rooted to the earth, unable to remove her gaze from the now almost invisible horizon, lest her whole universe disintegrate, and stared at the black clouds resembling evil mountains beyond the flat terrain. The tears just kept flowing, but she made no sound. It was her way.

She remembered other times she'd been left, abandoned like that, and they intertwined and got mixed up till nothing was clear in her mind any more. Then she collapsed.

FOUR

'Don't give up now,' shouts V157. 'She'll come round. You'll see.'

Weakened by grief, I heed his words and let him lead me. We tail them back home.

They examine the flyblown corpses they abandoned outside their house. They keep turning their heads and coughing from the stench. Kamara gesticulates @ the bodies and speaks, but I can make nothing out from where we lurk.

The wiry andro she calls Garcia races inside and returns with shovels. Kamara embraces him. They dig away. It takes them @ least ten deci-minutes to finish the grave and cover the dead securicops.

We keep ourselves apart, unseen. There is no time to construct a kip-cell, so we rest in the boughs of a great oak.

I monitor her closely. She's a creature of habit.

On V157's advice, I get her early in the morning. She's up first as usual, taking in the buttery sunrise. Her eyes are swollen and red. Not wishing to startle her, I let myself down, gently buzzing 'Mum.'

She looks up and stops dead.

I slowly approach. She glances @ the house. Stillness. Then back @ me. Something flickers in her eyes.

Hope?

'You've come back.'

'Never left.'

'I'm...I'm...'

'I'm also...'

She backs off, still wary, her face hard again.

'Don't be afraid. I won't hurt you.'

'You already have.'

'Not intentionally,' I whisper.

She says nothing.

'Come. Talk to me...please?'

I turn and take a few steps. When I swivel my spheco-eyes round, she is the same distance behind me. My heart soars. I walk on.

Mum and I sit in the woods, V157 a little way off. She's agreed to speak, but I'm not expecting much now.

'They all hate you back there. Do you not realize that?'

I nod. What else can I do, or say?

'They're frightened. Of you. Your friend. And me now. You've tainted me too.'

'We don't want to hurt anyone.'

She sits up as if she's going to end the audience and leave. I stand.

'Mum...'

'Don't call me that.'

'But...'

'But what? You think you can just waltz back into my life?'

I sink to my knees. 'You've no idea...what I've done to find you again. Everywhere...I've looked...*everywhere*...even been to your farmhouse.'

Her face a rainbow of emotions, she gogs @ me. 'You tear my life apart and then stalk me?'

'You blaming *me*? I didn't ask to be taken away. Just want to say sorry for never saying goodbye. Dunno what I've done to make you hate me — your son — so much.'

'My s...? You telling me I gave birth to an insect?'

'I had no control over what they did.'

'We all know what you do, what it means to be a sphecoid. They'll never accept you. Or me, now. How many you killed so far?'

I can't answer. Don't know myself any more. The first few you notch up, but soon it becomes part of the daily routine. You lose count. I hang my head. 'I just wanted to talk to you. See you were okay.'

'If I'm okay?' she screams, her features screwed up in disgust. 'Course I'm okay. Look how fucking okay I am. And here I am and we've talked. So what else do you want from me?'

I pluck up courage from somewhere deep within, knowing if she totally rejects me now, it'll be the end.

''Spose love would be asking too much...'

She scoffs.

'...but recognition of who I am. Just having this conversation with you, even though it ain't going how I want, is a miracle.'

She stares @ the damp ground, gets up and wanders over to V157.

'What do you reckon, Spheco?'

V157 shakes his head.

'Don't involve him.'

She ignores me. 'You think I should talk to this...this...?'

'He's all right. Don't bridgeburn him. Give him a chance.'

She touches his shoulder and wipes her palm on her thigh. 'You love him?'

V157 shoots a glance over @ me and smiles. 'That's...we're not supposed to...but...' He lowers his gaze. 'I do.'

She looks @ us both and pecks his cheek. He grins. She comes back.

'And Dad?'

'Fat lot you care. All that money we saved up for you, to give you a decent start, to buy your first few years in life. It cost 7,143 Britz per child per annum in those days. We were hoping to scrape together the money for the ten-year package. Didn't know how we'd manage. But it didn't matter. You were gonna be our future. We were lucky to be able to afford a kid.

'BestcoeLifeInsure® offered us a deal. "We can see you're hard-working, loving parents," the andro said. "So we're offering a special tariff — ten years for fifty thousand. Save over two and a half grand."

'It meant a struggle, but we didn't mind. You were an investment. But then you go and turn out nice.'

Silence.

'They took you away. All the money was lost. You don't get nothing back. If the kid dies or gets taken, there's no refund. Just count your losses and put on a brave face.

'Fifty thousand Britz down the fucking drain, and we lost you anyway. All that going without. For a niceboy. "Waste of a shag," your Dad said.

'He looked back @ everything we'd sacrificed, and forward to the shame of being a spheco-dad. Couldn't hack it.

'Me, I'm strong. Hard as fuck. Shrug my shoulders and move on. Don't for a minute think it was easy cz it weren't. I had to manage on my own. Just the one wage. But I coped. Could only buy each year separately. Never had enough for the three-year or five-year deals. Always made sure I had those 9,887 Britz for the next twelve months safe for my annual birthday review, though. But it went wrong. I got disemployed. And now you see me here, a D-classified Freebie. Thanks to you. I'd call you Nelson but you ain't what I gave birth to no more.'

The contempt in her eyes drives me back. I know I have to say something.

'But Mum.' My voice is choked up. 'You gotta understand. I was only seven for fuxache. I love you. Never stop thinking about you. I'm still your son. Don't you feel nothing for me?'

Something changes in her face, as I churn out what's been fermenting inside me all these years. But it isn't what I hoped for.

'Just take a look in the mirror and you'll understand.'

'Gimme a chance, M...'

'Don't call me that.'

I turn my back on her, quivering with rage. 'If all you're worried about is that fucking fifty grand, you ain't my Mum.' I spit the words out. 'A real mother wouldn't put a price on her son.'

'You think...' she starts.

I face her again, but her eyes blowtorch mine.

'...this is about the money, you stupid fucking idiot?' she yells.

I step back.

'Alright. You asked for it. Wanna know what you really cost me? Remember your gran's funeral?'

Images of a big party flash before me. I was six.

'I flew there,' I say, 'to Soxbury Ness, before I found you.'

'You went back?'

I nod. 'It's my...I had to see it.'

She gogs @ me. 'Dunno how I'd feel there...Noxbury Cess we used to call it.' Her smile doesn't last. 'Anyway, you wanna know why my mum had *her* funeral?'

She can't bear to look @ me now. Like I've slapped her round the face.

FIVE

Grace Hassan had just turned 72 when she chirruped Irene. They hadn't been re-housed in Dagtown yet.

In area. Dropping in 2 c-u cz made decision.

What she said left Irene winded from shock. 'Please, Mum, I can't...not @ the cost of you...

'...taking voluntary...' Grace said more, but Irene was too upset to take it in. Once she'd stopped screaming, she said, 'But you're my Mum...'

'And you're my little girl. Your family's my family. I love you all, but you'll do as I say. My mind's made up. It's booked. Week tomorrow. They'll come for me @ 75 deci. Can't be changed. You know what the bureaucracy's like. The funds'll be in your Eye-account the following day. Don't cry. It's all for the best.' She hugged Irene close.

To stay sane, Irene made sure she saw her every day for the next week.

Nelson had been such a good boy. He'd helped Irene put out all the food and the cake — that creamy thing everyone called Tyranny Sue — and never picked any before the guests came. Irene was so proud of him, and beginning to think it was all worth the sacrifice they were making.

Someone from BestcoeDisinfex® came to make sure everything went smoothly. Saleem. He was tall and thin and had a musty smell, like he'd been mothballed in a drawer for years. Irene laughed @ the recollection.

Grace wore her best blue dress, and real glass necklace. She looked stunning, @ least 10 years younger.

Irene's aunts and uncles were the first to arrive. They sat with Grace and reminisced over the good times. They laughed, drank Beerola® and picked @ the sandwiches.

Irene'd so wanted to show Grace how much she was gonna miss her, but was run off her feet making sure all the relatives and friends were being properly looked after. And Nelson needed feeding.

Next Saleem got up and made a speech. 'Ladies and gentlemen, relatives and friends, we are gathered here today to celebrate the life of Grace Hassan, and to thank BestcoeDisinfex® for making it possible to honour her in this civilized way. In the old days, only the mourners were able to do this. We @ BestcoeDisinfex® recognize the need for the discontinuees themselves to mark the occasion. I now call upon Franco Smemley to say a few words.'

Everyone clapped as Irene's uncle stood up and cleared his throat, beaming @ everyone. 'Being three years older than Grace meant I had to look after her when our mum discontinued. And she took a lot of looking after.'

Laughter.

'I'm not saying she was naughty, but if it hadn't been for her, gynocops wouldn't have been invented.'

More laughter.

'But whatever I did for her way back then, she's more than paid back over the years, nursing my Vera through her illness...' His voice caught, and he ran a finger across his eye, taking a deep breath before he was able to carry on. 'Course, I was fuxached when she told me what she was planning, but that's our Grace. Always was a bit of a girl, bit of a shocker. Powers-that-be bless you.'

Applause.

'I'll miss you, Gracie.' He hugged her and kissed her cheek, and sat down, frowning, as if that would stop him crying.

Irene suddenly found herself standing, sandwiched between George and Nelson. 'Mum,' she began.

Tears flooded out. 'Mum,' she shrieked, desperate to say how much she loved her and didn't want this to be happening, how not all the Britz in the world could make up for losing her mother, how, although they'd all be grateful for what she was doing, she was breaking their hearts — everyone in that poky little front room was devastated underneath the jokes and banter and false cheer of this pre-mortem funeral brought to them courtesy of BestcoeDisinfex®. But she couldn't utter a word as her sobbing had become too powerful, and in the end George said what a fabbo mother-in-law Grace had been and everybody agreed and drank toast after toast and Grace even asked Saleem if it was okay to mix alcohol with the anaesthetic.

'Of course,' he said, getting to his feet. 'Grace Hassan was an exemplary employee of BestcoeDisinfex® for 56 years, never once late or insubordinate, qualities she instilled in her daughter, who also has an excellent punctuality record.

'Grace's sense of humour and friendliness over the years made BestcoeDisinfex® a brighter place to work. As her immediate boss, I was always satisfied with her output. I understand in her spare time she was a considerable seamstress, kitting Irene's family out over the years. She'll also be remembered for the wonderful apple pies she used to bring in every so often and...'

A knock on the door stopped him. He nodded to George, who went to open it and came back with a startled look, closely followed by two huge andros in blue dungarette uniforms.

'Grace Hassan?' asked one.

Grace stood up. 'That's me.'

'Would you like to come with us?'

'Wait a moment.' Irene found her voice. 'It's only 69 deci. You're not due till 75. It's on FaceChirp®'

'And you are?'

'This is outrageous.' Irene's eyes opened wide in disbelief. 'George!'

George cleared his throat. 'Er, can't you come back in about 5 deci-minutes. We haven't finished...'

'Sorry, mate. We have to take her now. So, if you don't mind...'

'It's okay.' Grace's voice rang out over the general babble. 'It's my time, folks. Life's been a lovely journey, with its ups and downs, but now I just want to say thank you and goodbye to everyone I've met on the way.' She blew a kiss round the room and went up to Irene and Nelson, whom she pecked on the cheek. Then she walked over to one of the andros, who kept tutting and looking @ his watch, and was gone in an instant.

Saleem went out last. 'Thank you all for attending Grace Hassan's pre-mortem voluntary discontinuation funeral sponsored by BestcoeDisinfex®. Enjoy your day.'

The door closed behind them. In the silence that followed, they hugged and wept. The guests got up and left. They all knew why she'd done what she had.

Irene collared Saleem @ work the next day. 'How dare those thugs ruin my mum's voluntary discontinuation!'

'It's usual practice in case the subject changes their mind,' he said. 'Happens quite often, and BestcoeDisinfex® loses out on enforcement costs.'

@ first, Irene wanted nothing to do with the money, but George told her not to be nice. So that's how they got Nelson on the tariff when he was just six. And the following year, he turned out...and they took him away.

V159 had his hands over his ears.

'And we lost everything.' Irene wasn't looking @ him. 'Mum and the money. All for you. Plus, they lied about the anaesthetic.'

He raised his head, startled. 'Please...no...don't let this be true.'

'It paid for what they did to you. BestcoeDisinfex® credited us 417 Britz towards the funeral costs — party, anaesthetic and discontinuation fee. Me and your father had to find another 400, although that wasn't so difficult then, especially as we knew we'd be getting a few thousand from Mum, cz they only take 5% tax if it's voluntary.'

'And...Dad?'

'It broke him. He got depressed. Lost his job. Became D-classified, like me, and disappeared. I used to think, to hope, recycling meant being moved to another town to start up again. Till I ended up in one of them centres.

'Mum and me often talked about the bad old days, the stories handed down through the generations. How her grandma wouldn't have had the freedom to choose when she discontinued, with dignity. It was all untidy and messy back then.'

She paused to take a breath and wipe her eyes. 'She was beautiful, your grandma Grace, on the outside and the inside, and she gave it all up for...'

Shouting interrupts her. Her three friends appear, maintaining a safe distance.

'Harm her, sphecoids, and you'll pay.' Garcia's hand's in his pocket.

A gun?

SIX

He'd had two ambitions in life. When had the first one started? Was it the night his mother had got through a bottle of Scotcheze® and shouted and swore @ them, and the neighbours heard her every word all through the DUB and probably as far away as South East District 6 and Garcia and his brother Simon cried without knowing why and she threw the empty bottle @ Garcia's father and missed and the bottle smashed on the paper-thin wall and she collapsed on the floor and they all had to carry her to bed?

They'd been fuxaching @ the robbers. If they hadn't coshed Dad, he'd still've been fit and strong and fucking BestcoeCarz® wouldn't have disemployed him for not coping with the long hours, shifts and heavy labour any more, his eyesight not being what it was. And he wouldn't have lost his sense of taste and smell from the blow and been left prone to depression and anxiety.

The PAUL team review board decreed that his mother's pay from the shop, just over eleven grand a year, was enough for her and one child.

'Last in, first out,' the reviewer said. 'Simon won't know what's happening.'

Garcia thought Dad and Simon were being relocated. Everybody did. Thinking otherwise was the first step on the road to madness.

Or was it three months later, when Dad's D-classification

expired and andros in white coats came and gave Simon the injection, which meant Garcia never got to say goodbye to him, although @ the time, that didn't matter cz he was sure they'd catch up later, and Mum screamed and bawled her head off, but then she always overreacted to everything?

Dad had taken him aside and hugged him. Garcia remembered the tears. First time his father had cried.

'Go before I lose my mind,' his mother shrieked and slammed the door shut.

Dad waited @ the DUB entrance cradling Simon in his arms in the freezing February wind and rain. Garcia watched from their unit window on the second floor till the van arrived. His mother howled the rest of that day. Garcia had to lock her in the kitchenette so she wouldn't see them taken away.

'That's your job,' Dad had said. 'It'll make you grow up.'

Their own little conspiracy. Garcia liked that. Helping Mum.

Only after weeks of nagging her when she came out of the infirmary and was in a fit state to talk and make sense, did Garcia begin to realize what had happened.

She carried on working, sullen and bitter, @ the B-class silvereye supermarket with really good food and clothes, but out of their price range.

She wasn't allowed anything, but she'd tell him about all the wonderful stuff there. 'Mushrooms, bananas, real coffee and chocolate, salmon, wine — although you're not old enough,' she'd say, listing the things from memory according to their place in the aisles. 'One day, if I get a rise, I'll get a new Eye-D,' but by then, he knew she wouldn't.

They had her down as unstable. Their Eye-Ds would only ever get them through PAULie shop turnstiles

One could only dream about A-list produce — reserved for celebrities and the super-wealthy. Folk on Olympia Heights.

Everybody knew about the Heights. They could see it from their DUB. A-listers never got reviewed. Had a life they could call their own. Did whatever they liked. The androcops didn't bully them. Luxury surrounded them. They were where Garcia wanted to be, knowing he'd made it as a chav-not.

That was his first ambition. How he'd achieve it, he didn't exactly know.

His second was born the evening she ranted @ a handsome young andro on the telly. 'That's the fucking bastard that ruined us.' She'd never minced her words.

The ex-con was on a chat show. He'd just won Amnesty, the programme where felons arrested and convicted in the winter when there were no sphecoids about for summary sex-e-q-tions, were released from prisons and tried to elude the androcops hunting them. As each one was caught, he was sent back into detention to be discontinued and recycled, depending on a public vote, which usually condemned them all, even those with winning personalities. 'Freedom or your life' was the catchphrase.

The last one to be captured won celebrity status, a new FaceChirp® dashtag and a home on the Heights.

'How did you do it?' gushed the interviewer.

'Let's just say friends in high places.' The ex-con laughed. He still had all his teeth.

His mother's sobbing sounded like laughter. Garcia made her a strong cup of Tanninola® to save enough milk for breakfast and gave her a pill. She didn't want any time off cz depression no longer merited sick pay and she couldn't afford to lose a day's money.

He was thirteen now. Old enough to understand. His mother pulled herself together and told him about that andro. That's when he knew what his other ambition in life was.

He'd be out of school soon. PAULie kids weren't encouraged to stay on after fourteen, and then only if they displayed academic genius. And he didn't.

'Garcia,' he said to himself, 'your time has come.'

SEVEN

Mum clears her throat.

'He's no danger,' she shouts. 'If you harm him, you'll have to come through me first.'

'Walk away slowly before something bad happens.'

'Nothing's gonna happen, Garcia.'

V157 and I take off to show we mean no ill, but still he persists.

'If that monster's done...'

V157's flexicock telescopes out and coils round Garcia's throat. 'Just shut up, for fuxache. Can't you see how upset she is?'

Garcia gags. V157 releases him.

'Okay,' I say. 'I know what we are in your eyes, but...'

Mum says nothing @ first. Just nods. But she's still with me. I take some comfort in that. She speaks quietly. 'He's...he's not a monster.' The others mumble. Then a scream, a gyno scream, rings out and silences everyone.

'He's my...*son*.'

Without looking @ me or Garcia, she hurls the word son around. Again and again she shrieks that phrase 'my son' until she's hoarse and seems hundreds of kilos lighter and floats up to glide with me through the air. There are tears in her eyes.

Shocked silence follows the echo of her voice's final utterance. She looks up @ me from the ground just once and says, 'My Nelson.'

It is the first time she's called me by my humo name since I was seven. I blink and try to swallow.

She looks down as if she needs to recover from what she just said.

Samina walks over to her and points @ me. 'He's come back to you. You must be very proud. And very lucky. So many are lost. You're special.'

They embrace, gyno-backs shaking with emotion. I'm part of that hug, perhaps, but I need to be invited.

'We ain't no threat,' I say. 'We can help if you want.'

'How?' asks Mum. 'We're starving here.'

'We can get stuff. We're immune.'

They look puzzled.

'Withertongue's spread further,' I say, recalling my Eye-screen info and pointing to the fires blazing on the horizon. 'It's come from the north. The new syngastria in Brumtown and Scousetown incubated the virus from recycled matter. Bestcoe-Disinfex® is ineffective. Tens of thousands dead now.'

Blood drains from Samina's face. 'Oh, please no,' she mutters. 'The plague...'

'Fraid so. Withertongue's bullseyed Cockneytown. Mass graves. Panic-buying. Riots. Looting. PAULies shot for curfew-breach.'

Samina cries out. 'Mum, Dad...'

I gog @ her. 'I'm sorry.'

Samina takes a few steps to gather her thoughts. 'It was my job once to find a cure.' She's weeping.

Irene puts her arm round her shoulder. 'Maybe one day you...'

'If we'd been allowed to continue our research, I might've been able to save them, and thousands more, but our funding got cut.'

'Let's hope we're safe from contagion here,' says Irene.

'Best wait and see what transpires in Cockneytown.'

'Anyone seen Phoebz?' asks Kamara. 'She told me to fuck off earlier...'

'She must still be unwell,' said Irene.

They have potatoes, and are surprised sphecos don't consume solids. We enjoy their Tanninola® and Kamara's guitar-strumming.

It's cold and dark. The fire deters acridians, but does little to banish the damp from the air or the worries about wither-tongue.

We sleep apart from the Freebies cz by being traceable, we constitute a threat to their security. Besides, the andros still can't bring themselves to look us in our spheco-eyes. Mum both avoids me and gazes wistfully @ me. Can't suss that.

It's late @ night. We're squeezed into a new duplex kip-cell V157's made.

'I love you so much,' I buzz into his spheco-ear.

He smiles drowsily.

We doze off.

The noise wakes me. I hear the vans before I see them in the dawn glow, and freeze.

Knox? Who's he sent?

EIGHT

A black van rounds the corner. After a screech of brakes, doors open and out spew four androcops, guns ready.

Wrath cooks in my groin, and my cock darts out @ the sight of sleek male opponents in black torsohuggers. V157 reappears, copying me.

The androcops stall, staring @ our protrusions. Their leader looks quickly around, never taking his humo-eyes off our e-rections.

Mum and her friends rush out of the house.

'Reinforcements will deal with the sphecoids,' he barks, his last word stiffening our resolve. 'Concentrate on the Freebie scum.'

'I heard that,' yells a thick voice.

No one's noticed this gyno holding back from the others. Emaciated, skin sweat-glossed, hair matted, eyes bloodshot. Limping.

Tongue dark-blue and swollen...

'Phoebe...' cries Kamara. 'What the fuck....?'

'Oh, no, Phoebe,' wails Samina. 'You poor...you got...withertongue.'

Phoebe hobbles towards the cops. 'Wanna arrest me?'

Her laughter, crazed and altered, becomes a cough. She swallows her phlegm.

'Back away now,' yells an androcop.

Phoebe sways on the spot. 'Make me.'

A single shot rings out. Impossible to see who fired it.

Phoebe collapses like a demolished DUB, her robe ruffling in the breeze.

Everyone screams. Kamara shrieks and runs @ the cops.

They turn to him, one of the last moves they'll ever make.

V157 dispatches two with neat eviscerating slashes. The remaining pair go for me, one behind the other. Bad planning.

I land in front of them and bullseye both. Double skewer. But nothing worth savouring, just C-class syngastrion muck.

As I withdraw, Mum surveys the carnage. Her eyes have a different expression that I hope is acceptance. She nods and says, 'Thank you, Nelson.'

But before I can reply, the second van arrives.

Heartsink pink. Four gynocops tumble out. Advantage Bestcoe.

I telepath V157 to fly away, like me, but they're too quick and surround him. He struggles, spheco-flexidick now useless.

I swoop down and grab his arm, but in the tug-of-war their superior strength wrenches him away and prevents him taking off. We cry in despair.

'Fight,' I yell as they bundle him into the back of the van and secure the door. I kick the side, the windscreen and yank @ the doors, but they drive off, apparently satisfied with one of us.

I am still aroused, soiled from running through androguts, but unmilked. I banish my anguish @ V157's capture to the far corners of my mind and concentrate on the imminent challenge.

'Sorry, Mum. I must go.' I levitate, swivelling my spheco-eyes back to catch a glimpse of her watching me soar and reaching out to say something.

I want to turn round and land next to her, but I carry on, with only the lump in my spheco-throat telling me that darting through the chilled air is not the reason my spheco-eyes are streaming.

It's a long journey over meadows and forests. Here and there I see acridian clouds and earthbound humos, Freebies or agro-toilers. As I fight fatigue, I transceive V157's distress and telepath back my own.

I catch up with the pink van @ the entrance of the Institute of Entomanthropy's Department of Sphecanthropy Database just as a phalanx of obknoxian mantoids marches out. Like us... his creatures.

The gynocops hand over V157 and melt away.

Two obknoxians flank V157. His arms suddenly belong to his captors. Their grip is steel, but he doesn't scream. I observe from a windowsill.

'You're-un-der-ar-rest-for-de-ser-tion...' says a third obknoxian facing him. The list of his crimes continues.

'Yeah, yeah, etcetera.'

I swell with spheco-pride as V157 mockingly echoes the words of the obknoxian, who gets flustered and keeps clicking his tongue.

V157 is taken away.

I follow them deep into the Database bowels. They fling V157 into a high-ceilinged cell. He cries as he lands with a thud. The obknoxians hurry out.

The door gives as I push. I should be more suspicious, but all I can think of is V157. He gogs @ me. I think I'm going to die of longing. I can bear it no more. But as we rush to each other, arms outstretched, the cell door clicks shut.

NINE

Irene was split by a welling-up of pride and misery. Phoebe was dead and Nelson had left her again.

The field was cold and patches of frost adorned the grassy clumps. A few dandelions bore flowers. The leaves would sustain them.

Now there were four androcop corpses to dispose of. And Phoebe.

They dared not touch her.

'That mosquito bite,' said Samina. 'They're carriers. This we knew. If their season's starting, we'll need protection. Nets...'

'There'll be something in the house,' said Irene.

Olivier struggled to dig a shallow grave beyond the olive trees, away from the house. He and Garcia used a rotten plank to roll her body into the pit before tossing the plank in. Olivier howled as they shovelled earth back onto her.

They stared in silence @ the grave. Eventually Irene spoke. 'Couldn't find any netting.'

'Hopefully, that mosquito was in Tey House,' said Samina, 'and there aren't any here. Yet. No stagnant water. Almost warm enough, though. Better quarantine her room @ least a month. Then burn her stuff.'

The house had a real-wood name panel, but the letters had worn off. They decided to call it Phoebe's House in her memory.

Later, Garcia joined Irene by a hedge and pointed to the abandoned van, androcop ignition key-Eye-Ds and guns. 'So, your spheco-freak son was of use after all.'

That's when she turned on him, her eyes blazing. 'You know, Garcia, you're one fucking shoulderchipped niceboy, aren't you?'

He took a step back. His mouth opened, but no words came out, just a spluttering of vowels. 'I...I...'

'That's why you hate sphecos so much, why you...you didn't...'

'I didn't what?'

She walked away. She'd finally said what had been burning her up all this time.

He repeated his question louder, and followed her, made her face him and complete her accusation.

'...do anything.'

'When?'

Is he doing this deliberately?

She hesitated. 'When...you massaged...'

He closed his eyes and thought hard. When he opened them, he saw she was stronger than ever, as if she could see right into his very soul. It was time. He nodded.

Her eyes left him for an instant. His spell over her was broken.

'Why didn't you say?' She didn't return his smile.

'It didn't seem important. It *isn't* important, is it?'

She turned away from him. 'You fucking hypocrite.' She walked off.

He ran after her. 'Irene, I'm sorry.'

She didn't answer him.

She was right, of course. In his heart he knew that. He'd done a stupid thing, a terrible thing, to someone he loved and respected. And for the first time in his life, he didn't know how to get out of this hellhole of his own making.

She would not speak to him. All day she avoided him.

It had been the night he first realized cheese could be so good. Garcia didn't know what type it was, but it was soft and creamy and had a crust like warm snow. Rich flavour, runny consistency, almost liquid near the edge and firm in the centre with a sharper taste.

It took him a whole deci-minute to savour that morsel, which barely covered his thumbnail and lick his fingers clean.

First meal for 300 deci. There was nothing to drink, so he put the lid back on the bin and made his way to the public water fountain.

His throat was beginning to crack from the lack of moisture, but he hesitated. So many horror stories about untreated urine.

It hadn't always been like this. He'd had a job in a silvereye store, like his Mum, but got disemployed and the three-month grace had expired.

They'd impounded him in the South East District 6 D-classified enclosure, but he hid the night the androcops and sphecoids came to take him to the Recycling Centre. So slim, they missed him. Didn't think to rip up the rotting floorboards. He owed it to Dad, Simon and Mum to survive.

South East District 8. Safe in the crowds milling in the broadway. He wanted to get across the Thames, steal into the Heights, live his wild dreams, but his heart pounded and his skin felt as if it had been torn off and put back, but not entirely right. He could hardly swallow from his dryness and his voice was hoarse.

Androcops decided for him. The fountain was cordoned off. Withertongue.

Without a valid Eye-D, he was in mortal danger. He

stepped into a side street and hurried towards South East District 14.

It was quieter there by the disused railway station. A charity stall was distributing cups of milky Tanninola® and broken biscuits, but only for those with an unexpired Eye-D.

Many D-classifieds slept rough on the old platforms and tracks. Garcia had himself once or twice, but the area was now turnstiled.

'Erected last week,' moaned another hopeful, pointing @ new railings.

Garcia ran his grubby hands down the damp tiles of the station façade and licked the moisture off his palms. It tasted of oil, dirt and cheese, but the sensation of cool liquid on his furry tongue was bliss, a lifesaver.

It was getting chilly and had started to rain.

The main boulevard to South East District 1 would get him closer to the other side. He knew how to spot the androcop patrols a kilometre off, but it was a different matter in the unlit back streets. There, vigilantes didn't waste time checking Eye-Ds. Couldn't afford to get burgled...or infected.

He was tempted to ask for shelter, or even just a cup of water, from people still living in the condemned tenements, but they'd sooner knife someone than listen.

Thinking about reaching the Heights kept him going. Two packed autobuses chugged past on their way to South East District 13 and beyond, splashing his torn coat, but he saw none going in the opposite direction. No need for PAULies to go into town.

He put his hands in his pockets to stave off the cold. The coat reeked, but he had to wear it. He'd look suspicious without protective clothing in such weather. That's why he'd nicked it. Well, not really. He was sure the tramp was dead. He'd tripped over him in a doorway and he didn't move. No one was paying any attention, so he removed the coat, gagging @ the stench of the stale body infusing it and checking for withertongue lesions before putting it on.

Garcia was sure they'd got rid of all the down-and-outs and homeless. The tramp could've been part of a new D-classified wave. Like he was.

Sirens and lights again. Androcops had closed off the road. People crowded round what looked like a pile of bodies and scattered in panic. Withertonguesters?

Garcia held his breath and braved his way into the back streets, ignoring the hostile faces @ the transplasticon DUB window squares and the twitching curtains, eyes fixed on the middle distance ahead.

'Walk fast and purposeful,' his Dad used to say in the good old days. 'Look like you know where you're going.'

Then his heart somersaulted and stopped. Three andros walking towards him. Behind them his destination. Another main road. Free of cops. Safe.

Sweat poured off his brow mixed with the rain dripping down his cheeks. Water squelched in his leaky shoes.

The andros stopped.

This is it. Let them speak first.

'Bad night to be out.' The one who spoke had a knife.

'Yeah, terrible.' Garcia swallowed, desperate to hide his terror, but they'd see through that. 'Gave up on the autobus.'

They moved closer, cutting off all escape routes. The one with the knife breathed Beerola® fumes into Garcia's face. 'Reckon you missed the last one.' They laughed.

'Looks like it.'

'This ain't your district.' The knife-guy tested the tip on his finger and whistled.

'N-no.'

'You a 'tonguester?'

Garcia shook his head.

'So what are you fucking doing here?' He thrust the point into Garcia's throat, not hard enough to cut the skin but sufficient to press against his Adam's apple and make him cry out.

He squawked some rubbish yarn about seeing a mate. If they found out he was Eye-D-less and didn't legally exist, they could discontinue him with impunity.

Knife-guy used the force of the blade to manoeuvre Garcia round 180 degrees so he had to walk backwards. The other two got behind him to stop him running away, and pushed him, the weapon still on his throat, a kilometre to the main road.

Still hidden in the shadows, Knife-guy pretended to slit his throat with a dramatic sideways swipe and kicked him in the testicles.

Garcia made a sucking noise and slowly crumpled to the wet pavement, the pain ebbing and flowing in tidal waves.

'Now cut him!'

'No, don't, please...'

Garcia tried in vain to dodge the downward thrust of the blade that would rip his flesh as it tore through his coat. His heartbeats exploded like bombs.

'Androcops!'

First time in his life, Garcia reacted to that word with gratitude, aware terror would follow.

'Count yourself lucky, cunt.' Knife-guy's cronies kicked him in the ribs.

'Show your fucking ugly face in our manor again...' Knife-guy bent over Garcia and slashed his cheek open. 'Souvenir from South East District 16.' Without a second glance, they disappeared into the gloom.

Garcia wanted to scream. He lay soaked and bleeding, but forced himself to his feet cz he dared not be found like that.

He'd been lucky to escape with his life.

He wiped the blood with his sleeve, hoping it wouldn't get infected, and staggered into the miserable orange glow of the main road. Nearby was the disused bridge with the open halves like the raised palms of authority barring entry. The next bridge would be curfewed.

He went by the riverside with the expensive B-class eateries, but androcops were rounding people up and checking Eye-Ds, so he turned back to the passage with bijou gift shops towards the second bridge.

He'd been right about the curfew and was stuck on the South side with nowhere to go. Well, almost nowhere. There was still one possibility, which he didn't relish the prospect of, but it was the only option. His partner.

The area by the bridge was festive in contrast to the depressed swathes of South East Cockneytown he'd left.

Pubs were open and revellers, obviously B-class silvereyes, spilled out onto the sodden pavements, oblivious to the weather. Garcia wandered round the historic courtyards, where old taverns still thrived, and entered one.

The bar was so packed no one would notice he'd not bought a drink. Everywhere he looked were empties and almost empties. The Beerola® was glorious, but concerned about dehydration, he downed some soft drink and left.

There was a small square between the second and third bridges, where he used to live with her. His manor. Well, almost. Had been once. A couple of andros eyed him up and down as he climbed to the third floor of the DUB.

Jean was out.

He didn't fancy waiting. The andros had never seen him before. Things could get nasty, so he walked away, aware they were tailing him.

He'd go back in the morning. The worst trouble was after

dark and there was still one last resort. The PAULie infirmary by the bridge.

Relieved there were no staff about, he had a drink of water from the toilet sink and sat on the crowded waiting area floor all night, dozing off intermittently.

A metal prod tapping his cheek startled him awake. It was getting light. The rain had stopped.

'Oy, you need anything for that cut?' asked a bleary-eyed gyno-nurse.

He shook his head. 'It's okay, chizz. I'm with someone.'

Too late.

She'd pressed a button.

Out of nowhere appeared two huge andros wearing protective suits and masks.

'There he is!' screeched the nurse, pointing the prod @ Garcia. 'Careful. He could have symptoms.'

As they hurtled towards him, he ran towards the entrance, yelling, 'I'm clean! I'm clean!' but still they came.

The infirmary doors started sliding shut. They were locking him in. With one desperate dash, he threw himself into the ever-decreasing gap, thanking the powers-that-be for his slimness, and raced into the dawn, each footstep pummelling his heart and lungs as it pounded the pavement.

Access over the Thames was still blocked, so he turned on his heels and made for Jean's.

The street was quiet with the sun appearing over the roof of her DUB, radiating a halo of intense light.

He banged on the door.

'Open up!'

After about an accu-minute, he pushed open the letter-slot and yelled, 'Jean, it's urgent.'

A few accu-seconds later, he heard slippers shuffling on the worn carpet and saw the lower half of her faded pink dressing gown amble to the door.

It opened on the chain and her worn-out face snarled @ him. 'You've got a fucking nerve coming here.'

'Please, Jean, let me in.'

She clicked her tongue and opened the door. He went in.

She backed away, terror stretching her face. 'You ain't got...?'

'No, don't worry.'

'One deci-minute and you go.'

He collapsed on the floor.

'What are you after?'

Garcia'd just come round. His deci-minute was well up. 'I need help.'

'You need a wash.' She shook her head with exasperation and cleansed his cheek wound. He yelled when she applied the BestcoeDisinfex®. She ignored him and ran a bath. 'One day you'll pay me back. As if.'

When he was clean and dry, and wearing some of his old clothes she hadn't got round to throwing out or bartering, she gave him some bread and caffeinola.

'I wanna get over the water,' he said when he'd finished.

'And what do you expect me to do about it?'

'Nothing.' He explained everything. 'And that's how I ended up here.'

'You've ended up the way you deserve.'

'I'm sorry for everything, Jean, but what's happened's happened.' He cringed @ his banality.

She snatched the plate and mug from him. 'I've gotta go to work. You'll leave with me.'

'Chizz.'

It hadn't worked out. She'd chucked him out and he'd been allocated a poky room in the suburbs.

'I didn't know anything back then, Jean. Didn't understand those things.'

'No, you fucking didn't.' Her face was granite. She left him looking out of the window to get changed and then reappeared in her uniform. 'Wanna cross the Thames? Use the old tunnel. Nothing for you here now.'

He said not a word. She let him go first and locked the door. When they reached the foot of the stairs, she pecked his cheek. 'This is it. If you still had FaceChirp®, I'd transfer some Britz to help you out. You know I would, but...' She stalled. 'Good luck, Garcia.'

'Chizz, Jean.' He kissed her back, knowing they'd never meet again.

Garcia didn't cry. He blocked the world out and told himself once again what a fool he'd been. Then he got up and searched for her.

She was in a field, gathering leaves by the hedgerows, her back to him. Dandelion and nettle. Their supper. She must've seen him approach, somehow felt his presence, but carried on picking greens and tossing them into her torn plasticon bag.

He cleared his throat. Irene didn't turn round. That's how he understood she knew he was there.

'Irene, I...'

'What?'

'Can we talk?'

'And say what? Sorry for the fiftieth time? We've been through all that. I know you are. I am too. My sorry's not an apology. It's a regret.'

'I've treated you terribly. I admit that. I wanna make it up to you.'

She turned to face him. 'So, make it up to me.'

'How?'

'You have to ask? I'm sure you'll find a way, clever boy like you.'

'Irene, if I could wind time back and start all over again, I'd tell you everything. It was just never the right moment.'

'And this is?' She returned to her picking.

'I'm...I'm...' He left her, tentative @ first, looking round a couple of times to see her busy with her leaves. She'd written him off. He went back. 'You're my best friend,' he started, more confident now. 'Let's not destroy what we had.'

She looked him in the eye again. 'So, it's all my fault? I'm the one destroying our so-called friendship? And what exactly did we have — you call it friendship — when neither of us could be open and honest with each other? Is that what you wanna return to?'

'No, of course we mustn't go back there,' he said quietly. 'You're right, but now we know, we can be friends again.'

Silence. He carried on. 'We both been forced to reveal ourselves. Remember the good times.'

'The good times?' She threw her bag onto the ground. 'You mean the starvation, cold and fear times? The times I thought you...' She stopped. Enough.

'The times I what?'

'Oh, forget it. Figure it out for yourself.'

He didn't have to. He knew. Had done since they first started raiding the agrocomplexes together. Hadn't said anything cz he thought it'd go away, cz he was scared, cz deep down he enjoyed the frisson of knowing. It gave him power over her, and he relished every accu-second of the little game he was playing with her. Now it didn't seem so good. He'd used her, but couldn't admit it. She'd *know* all that anyway, as gynos always do.

She'd seen his feet of clay and stamped on his toes in revenge.

TEN

I see no escape. V157 and I entwine Eye-pods and hold hands.

'Whatever happens, I'll always love you.'

A smile on his lips. He says nothing.

I draw him close and hug him, my mouthparts looking for his, our kiss multiplied ad infinitum by mirrors on opposite walls.

Shaking my sad spheco-head I stroke his arm and back with all the longing in my spheco-soul. I want to cry.

The door opens. Light dazzles us.

We shield our eyes with our forearms. The torch is gradually lowered and a thunderous voice booms, 'Pro-fess-or-Knox-is-ex-pect-ing-you. V-one-five-sev-en-was-per-fect-bait.'

Two massive obknoxians swivel their heads round and confront us.

I acknowledge the bodyguards. Knox doesn't trust us. That makes me mad. I try to control my anger so it won't show and provoke them, but this is hard. I flick my slit, and think of Mum and Dad, and V157's parents, who died of broken hearts, but still the ire inside me mounts.

Excited by the prospect of carnage, the obknoxians clock my distemper and reveal their disapproval, pointing their spiked forearms @ us.

Their superior smiles do it. My cock shoots out like a spear and quivers in the air. @ the sight of this, V157 backs me up with his.

'Not so fast,' I say, keeping an eye on the obknoxians. Dunno how this'll pan out. Never been up against obknoxians before. My spheco-arse releases clouds of soli-pherum, but the hostile spikes remain *en garde*.

'Let's go.' V157 comes and stands by me.

I remember the metallic flash of chitinex as V157's penis zigzags lightning-fast sideways into the nearest obknoxian's leg. His face trembles and swells with enmity. Then he sighs and discharges his load into the mantoid thigh.

As the obknoxian falls off the blade and collapses, his colleague embraces V157, latticing his thorax.

I close my eyes and scream no. So does V157.

The obknoxian removes his arms from V157, who staggers back and falls.

I shriek again and strike out blindly with my sting, desperate to slay him before he starts eating V157.

He ducks, but I take off and spheco-dodge his mantis arms opening and snapping shut to hook me, all the ire within me guiding my sphecocock into his spindly obknoxian neck. ACE delethalizes his now drooping arms. The blade works itself clear and spills his head blood on the floor tiles. Red on white.

He falls, looking @ me with fury in his eyes as he stumbles forward, his forehead smashing against the wall.

Grieve now | Grieve later | Cancel pops up on my eyelid-screen.

I select the middle item and wipe the obknoxian tissue off with my spheco-palm. Grief now suspended, I bend down and caress V157's shiny spheco-head.

He's still breathing, but the air is rasping. His eyes are fixed on me, and his mouthparts attempt a smile.

I kiss him and stroke his flopping I-brows with mine.

'I'm sorry,' he says as though discontinuing is his fault.

'No, *I'm* sorry. Sorry it's got to end like this. I love you,

V157, more than anyone else in the whole Bestcoe-World.'

He squeezes my hand, I think, to say the words he can't articulate. He's crying now.

And so am I, but I have to stay strong, for both of us. 'You're my best friend. My everything. I remember every accu-minute I've spent with you, every accu-second you've been part of my life. I just wish...we could go on...together...'

He hasn't heard my last few words. The breathy sound has stopped and his thorax is still. Grief is about to drown me in its deluge, but I have no time for that now. The grey box with the three links pops up again before my spheco-eyes:

Grieve now | Grieve later | Cancel

I blink on the second one. Gotta stay alive. Grieve I shall, but when I can do so properly.

Leaving his body on the floor where he fell cuts my spheco-heart in twain. My I-brows are inflamed with feelings of loss and regret, but also what must be love. I don't care what Knox says about us. I know I love V157 and he loved me.

Fearless now, I get to my feet. I have nothing more to lose. I lay V157 on his back and close his spheco-eyes and straighten his beautiful I-brow antennae. I kiss him for the last time on his still-warm lips and clasp his spheco-hands tight. Filling my mind with his image, I walk away.

I've lost him, forever.

I only manage a few metres when it hits me bad. I howl and scream. Sinking to my knees, I pound the lino with my spheco-fists.

I turn once, hoping he'll revive and fly by my side, but there are just broken bodies on the floor. Loss sears my eye-sockets, and tears flowing down my cheeks try to quench the fire of grief. My chest spasms and jerks as I catch my breath and my nose fills with snot. Cascading tears blur my vision.

He gave me love, mutilated, but still love, and Knox and his obknoxians have taken it away. I fly down endless corridors, trying to shut out of my mind what I've lost.

Vespine emotions are a mere simplex of links. Sphecos shouldn't cry.

But my sobs come ever stronger. I can do nothing to stop them, or worry about the obknoxian I see coming towards me.

I don't clock the gynocops till they grab me from behind.

ELEVEN

Spring shoots were punching up out of the earth, but it was freezing in the field as the north wind tore at their skin. With rags wrapped round their hands, they picked the sprouting nettles.

Irene consoled herself with the realization that she'd managed to stay alive thus far and was being granted another chance. But how many more would she be given?

She thought about Nelson. The others hadn't mentioned him, although Samina squeezed her hand and whispered, 'He'll come back. You'll see.'

'Oh, I don't know what to think or hope for any more.' She looked @ Garcia. 'I read you wrong,' she said. 'Heathcote was more than a brother.'

He nodded and hung his head.

Sometimes the foot tunnel in South East District 10 was guarded and sometimes you could sneak through. Lots of kids did it; it was a rite of passage that Garcia had longed to have the courage to perform. If you got past the androcop patrol and slipped inside the railings, you still had to get through the pitch-black darkness to the other side of the Thames with rats and worse. The rule was no torches or matches, and it had to be a return journey. Your mates would see you when you emerged on the opposite bank and wait for you to get back safe.

Not everyone did.

There were no kids about when Garcia arrived @ the tunnel, but a fair number of androcops. He thought about the disused road tunnels, but they were a long way off and were just as bad. Besides, he'd walked enough. His cheek was still smarting, although it was getting better.

He caught the eye of a young andro in a light blue torsohugger watching him, and was afraid he was a securicop. He stood back, taking in his surroundings. The ancient ship was there, mounted on the pavement and people were admiring it and touching the sides, some of them screwing up their noses @ the stench emanating from the river, on the other side of which loomed his goal. The Heights.

He wandered over to the ship and sat on the raised steps. Pigeons and seagulls flocked in the air, fighting over discarded food, and the DUBs rose high on the hills further inland.

The young andro was now sitting next to him. He had a pleasant face, dark Caffeinola® woolly hair and was slim. 'I see you gogging @ the tunnel,' he said, without looking @ Garcia.

Garcia turned away from him. 'What's it to you?'

'I see you gogging @ a lot of stuff.'

'You see too much.'

'You wanna cross?'

'What makes you think that?'

'You scared? I can help.'

'Ain't scared and don't need your help.' Garcia wanted to walk away, give up now. He was certain this was a trap and the andro'd be asking for his Eye-D. He got up, but the andro told him to sit.

'We can help each other,' he said.

'How?'

'Look, mister. Too much androcop round here. We go west. I wanna go over too. Can you swim?'

'Are you serious?'

'River's narrower and shallower in the west. And cleaner. I been there. Follow me.' He stood, stretched and walked back into the built-up zone.

Head buzzing with conflicting ideas of what he should or shouldn't do, but relieved he wouldn't have to do the tunnel, Garcia followed him behind a parade of boarded-up shops and into an old DUB.

The andro opened a door on the street level and invited him in.

Half wishing he'd walked away, and half-intrigued by the promise of the unknown, Garcia looked round to make sure they hadn't been tailed and it wasn't an ambush, and went in, certain this was the most stupid thing he had ever done in his entire life, even more stupid than partnering Jean all those years before, but there was something about this andro he couldn't say no to. He was expecting any accu-minute to be rushed and attacked, but his host just said, 'Caffeinola®?'

Garcia said yes and introduced himself as he sat on a threadbare purple sofa, the only furniture he could see.

'Heathcote.' He plonked a steaming plasticon mug in front of him.

'Nice place.'

'Not mine. A mate's.'

'Why do you wanna go across?'

'Cz you do.'

'What's that supposed to mean?'

'It means if I help you, you can pay me.'

'Oh, no. I knew it. If you weren't with the greeneyes, you'd be on the make. Fuck you.' He rose to leave, but Heathcote pushed him back down again, surprisingly strong for someone of such slight build.

'Not so fast, mister. You owe me.'

'I don't owe you nothing.'

'I told you where the crossing is. I've given you a drink.'

'Ain't yours to give. Your mate's, remember?'

'Fuck you.'

Garcia hit Heathcote, straight left to the face. Heathcote swore again and sat on the sofa, cradling his nose. 'That fucking hurt.'

Garcia had pulled his punch. It was just a warning. Heathcote lashed out @ Garcia's ear and Garcia found himself on top of Heathcote on the bare floorboards, face to face, pummelling his head and chest.

Heathcote begged him to stop. 'I ain't done nothing to you.'

Garcia left off, fist in mid-air, loving the thrill of this moment, of the conquering, the possession. He thought of Jean and how they'd split up and why, and the answer was all here, right beneath him.

He lowered his fist, caressed Heathcote's lamb-thick hair and snogged him, taking his head in both his hands and sucking the life out of his mouth.

They were writhing on the floor now, breathing heavily, hands exploring each other.

'When's your mate coming back?' Garcia panted.

'We got time. Don't worry.'

They got dressed and Heathcote made more caffeinola. 'No food,' he said.

They had another fuck and set out west.

'So, why *do* you wanna go over the river?'

'Same reason as you, Garcia.'

'Which is?'

'You got no Eye-D or FaceChirp®, innit?'

'How could you tell?'

'Bloodied cheek, clothes not right. You just look wrong.'

'Chizz, Heathcote. You sure know how to flatter.'

Heathcote chuckled. 'I quit my job. Couldn't stand it. BestcoeCond® vinegar factory up the road. The stink every day. Couldn't wash it out. Hair, clothes everything. So, I'm outta Britz.'

'Me too. Who's your mate?'

'Someone. Feeds me. Bed for the night.'

'Bet that costs you.'

A look of affront flashed across Heathcote's eyes. 'It's okay.'

'So, you escaped @ seven?'

'Mm-mm. Got sick. Infantile Meltz, but bad. Off school months and months. Was so ill they were thinking of discontinuing me, but I suddenly recovered. As I was well over seven, they said it was too late for selection. So I stayed on @ school, everyone knew I was nice, called me a decaff, made life hell, but I survived and ran away. Worst thing is, no one came looking for me.

'So I turned my back on my privileged silvereye background. My parents had enough Britz for two kids, so I guess they never missed me. Probably relieved to be rid of the burden I was becoming.

'Some Bestcoe big cheese decaff picked me up. He introduced me to his entourage. I must have something in my face that says, "Mother me," cz they were constantly fighting over whose turn it was to have me. The owner of this flat took me in, but I've always been on the move. Besides, I can't take his temper no more. Surprised a fit andro-mandro like you ain't been snapped up.'

People are such shitz. Even I hit him.

Garcia handed Heathcote a half-smoked cigarette. 'Partnered a gyno. Thought that's what you did. Never really sussed it. Course, it didn't work out and here I am.'

'You dodged it too? A toughie, eh?'

'Better get going.' He laughed.

They kept to the main streets of South West Cockneytown. Garcia explained where he wanted to go and why.

'Don't you wanna join the Freebies?'

Garcia shook his head. 'Not unless I have to.'

'Freebies are orgsome. I'll get to them one day.'

'I'm sure you will. You know something, Heathcote, you're a really orgsome andro. Sorry I punched you before.'

Heathcote dismissed this. 'Oh, I'm used to that.

His 'mate'. 'Well, you got me to protect you now. You're the younger bro they stole from me. We'll make a good team.'

'That's nothing to be ashamed of,' said Irene.

'Not ashamed. Just remembering what they did to him. I'm sorry.'

'Yes.' Irene attempted a smile. 'I heard you the first time.'

He swallowed hard. 'Wouldn't listen to me, didn't trust me enough. "Stay close," I told him during the raid, "I'll protect you. They'll never find us," but he panicked. Never seen such fear. Eyes gogging, breath panting, body shaking. He ran. I called to him to come back, but he was deaf to me. Perhaps he was tired of me too, like his other mates and it was time to move on again. Or he'd had enough of life. Whatever, some sphecoid darted down outta nowhere, speared his neck clean through and carried on flying low with Heathcote dangling on its dick and that was the last I saw of him.'

She managed to smile.

Garcia felt so much happier, he didn't notice the nettle-stings, but he knew it wasn't enough, and that to really quench the thirst raging in his soul, he would have to return to Cockneytown and fulfil his life's remaining ambition.

TWELVE

Knox clears his throat. 'You've only brought one impaired sphecoid back, you fuxaching idiot.' He slaps the obknoxian's face hard. 'I said I wanted them both alive.'

The obknoxian bows his head in submission, but growls.

Knox smacks his other cheek to silence him.

I'm armlocked by gynocops. Six obknoxians guard either side of the Dominic Knox Lecture Theatre entrance, their raised arms an arched gauntlet.

Knox has a specimen spheco crouched in a vitreola cube and is extolling 'its' virtues to a bunch of labrats. 'We discovered how to manipulate the sexual psyche.'

Er...not completely.

The psychosexual world-view of each individual is unique, there being an infinite number of variations on common themes. Human sexuality requires a logic, which may or may not conform to one's social world-view.

'In some cases, this psychosexual world-view is murderous. The logic of arousal demands the death of the object of desire. We found that with niceboys @ the infantile stage this symptom undergoes the process of formation; being the victim of bullying facilitates it, provoking a desire for revenge to become sexualised as bullying is usually same-sex and conceals a message of gender identification. The birth of this desire is sublimated into homosexual attraction, erotic romantic or erotic sado-masochistic. The former is of no use to us. The latter can be further divided, our interest being solely in androlads with underlying erotic-sadistic urges, which naturally are suppressed or otherly expressed, but which we can, and do, nurture during training, blackboxing and metamorphosis into fully functioning sphecanthropes, in whose makeup the distinction between the social and psychosexual world views is blurred.

'Satisfying the psychosexual urge is an addiction, which demands vindication for each spheco-gasm. No sooner has one climaxed than all is negated, and the individual must start again from nothing to re-establish their psychosexual reality.

'We pass no judgement on the nature of their psychosexual world-view as long as it serves our goal of genetically cleansing BestcoeBritain®.'

As if any judgement of yours could be valid.

'Former niceboys lose the ability to love...'

Yeah, right...

'...but, driven by sexual hate, contribute to BestcoeBritain® in a pleasurable manner that benefits all save andro felons...'

Sipping water, he drones on. 'Brainscans reveal the lust trigger is a negative attraction based on hatred and a desire to avenge the early-years marginalization.

'It was all proved scientifically in experiments to howls of protest. Electro-magnetic treatment reinforces the association of the object of desire in the patient's mind with intense anger and hate, and a need to inject with sperm, a variation on both *Vespula vulgaris*, the common wasp's urgency to sting prey, and the male *Anterhyncium gibbifrons* mason wasp's instinctive use of its spiked penis in self-defence against predators, the lethal member in all cases a modified genital organ.

'BestcoeGenetix® exploits this propensity for andro-on-andro violent sex to fight crime. And sphecocops are the best. Flying, stinging death machines, impervious to emotion, efficient felonbusters loved by law-abiding folk everywhere.

They enjoy their work. The best integration of homosexuality into society any civilization has ever conceived.'

Really? Ask V146...

'Entomanthropy is the way forward for *Homo sapiens*. We take the best from each suitable species. Ultimately we will create a super-race of beings that combine the abilities of all extant animal life with omnipotent AI − the evolutionary dream. And sphecoids are the first step down that glorious road to perfection.'

'And you, Professor O. B. Knox,' I yell to gasps, 'you are the last one on mine.'

Knox gogs @ me, eyes full of loathing. 'The lab,' he shouts.

THIRTEEN

When Garcia stole away, it was the cold, tarmac-dark dead of night, but he remembered the way to the van.

He'd spirit himself out of their lives and do what he had to even if it killed him, which was a possibility. Would they miss him? After the last few days, he doubted it.

Each time a twig snapped underfoot he cringed, lest they heard it even as far away as the house. He fingered the andro-cop Eye-D in his pocket for comfort.

Van useless without it.

He reached the clearing and walked hesitantly, arms stretched out before him towards where they'd parked it. Presently, his hands came into contact with freezing metal and he breathed a sigh of relief. Still there.

He was groping round the side of the van when something was clamped round his neck. Terrified he was about to be discontinued, he tried to scream, but couldn't get the sound out.

'Who the fuck are you and what are you looking for?'

The voice was familiar. Garcia struggled to say, 'let me go,' but the andro maintained the headlock.

A sharp jab in the kidneys made him cry and lose the security of his feet on the ground. As he started to slide down, he was pushed hard and banged his face on the van.

He lay where he fell for what seemed a long time. The next thing he knew, he was sitting in the van with Olivier in the driving seat. It was getting light.

'What were you thinking of — doing a runner?'

Garcia shook his head. 'You wouldn't understand. Something I gotta do.'

'And you never thought to tell us?'

'It's nothing to do with any of you. The problem's about me and me alone.'

'Sure...problem, is it? And say you didn't sort it?'

'Fuxaches, Olivier, I'm sorry. But I just gotta do this one thing.'

'Which is..?'

'It's kinda personal.'

'Not telling makes it harder to forgive.'

Garcia bristled. 'And what the fuck were *you* doing out here? Also "running away"?'

Olivier tutted and shook his head. 'Heard footsteps. Came to investigate and hey...'

'I...I desperately need to get to Cockneytown.'

Olivier whistled and smiled. 'Even with the withertongue outbreak?'

Garcia nodded.

Olivier looked @ him. 'I'll drive you if you tell me what's going on.'

Garcia thought for a bit and then shook his head. 'Can't burden you with this. Wouldn't be right.'

Olivier breathed deep. 'Okay,' he started and opened the door. 'Walk.'

'Oh, c'mon, Olivier...I just need it for one trip. Anyway, ain't your van.'

'Ain't yours either, and you might not come back.'

'And you might not either.'

'Why not? For fuxache, Garcia, stop bushbeating and tell me the truth.'

'Okay.' Garcia explained everything. When he finished, Olivier lit one of the cigarettes 'inherited' from the androcops and swiped the Eye-D. The engine purred into life.

'You sure about this?'

'Mm-mm. You need a mate.'

'Thank you, Olivier.' They shook hands. 'We got enough faeco-fuel?'

'Should do.' Olivier tutted. 'I know *what you are*, Garcia. Just for the record, it don't bother me.'

Garcia nodded. 'Orgsome. We both been through it.'

Olivier turned to him. 'How many guns we got?'

Garcia wide-eyed him. 'Fuck. Forgot about that.'

Olivier switched the engine off. 'That's why you need me. Run back and get two.'

Garcia hurried to the house, slowing down as he approached. Day had dawned and Irene was an early riser. He really didn't want to have to explain himself to her, or lie to her again.

He tiptoed in. The house was silent. He shut his eyes and exhaled in relief.

The guns were where they'd left them. Everything was still quiet when he stepped out of the door into the cold morning.

Birds were singing although he couldn't spot any in the trees. The sun was hiding behind the white cloudy sky. He shivered and rushed to the van.

Olivier acknowledged him with a nod. 'Sorry about before.'

'No worries.'

'Can't let you do this alone. Besides, it makes me feel alive again.'

Garcia chizzed him.

Once again the van started and they drove out of the clearing towards the highway to Cockneytown.

FOURTEEN

After ten flights you lose count. My frogmarched descent comes to an end and a dingy little corridor leads to silver swing doors.

I look through the round windows. This was once part of a hospital. Surgery was performed on me here. My I-brows tell me.

Labrats in white torso'n'thigh-hugging uniforms fuss by workbenches, where liquids of different primary colours bubble and boil in real glass flasks. Steam billows everywhere.

Looking puzzled and reproachful, Knox nods @ the gyno-cops, who release me. 'I don't get why you aren't grateful. I plucked you up from the jaws of victimhood. Gave you a sense of worth and corporate pride. And you spit it back in my face.'

'You took away my life. It may have been miserable, but it was mine. You wrenched me apart from my family and home. You destroyed my identity in return for a few months of pre-programmed violence. And when I find love, you snuff it out. You expect me to thank you for that?'

'Imbecile,' he screams @ me. 'Do you understand nothing? I saved you. Do you know what would have become of you if I'd left you festering?'

I shrug my surliest spheco-shrug.

'You'd have been lucky to see your eighth birthday. If those boys @ school hadn't beaten you to death by then, the fear, stress and misery would've caused you such psychological problems, with major psychosomatic side-effects, you'd've been discontinued. Sphecanthropy's kept you alive. Given you a second chance.' He headshakes.

'BestcoeGenetix® are the first, indeed the only social engineers in the history of humankind to be humane, putting the quality back into e-quality. We only discontinue those too old to be of any use.'

When he sees me open my spheco-gob to disagree, he cuts in quick. 'Sphecoids, myrmecoid formicans, blattoids and others. Even the rogue acridians. My dream. My lasting gift to humanity.

'Our raw materials are chavspawn, whose lives PAULie or D-classified parents can't afford. Before adolescence, we can mould them any way we like. BestcoeGenetix® only works with pre-pubescent livestock. Entomanthropy @ its most effective.

'The programme is vast; I will show you our plans for future entomoid slaves...' Here he pauses. '...assistants is a better word, yes, *assistants* serving BestcoeBritain®'s superhumans-to-be.

He walks me through the lab, past benches with gurgling flasks. He's sprightly and strong-voiced. 'There will always be humans. Your entomoid role is to ensure we survive and prosper. You've encountered the myrmecoids and the blattoids. Yes, I've done my homework.' He seems very pleased with himself. 'And you sworded my obknoxians.'

I raise an I-brow. 'So you'll know about the murder of V157.'

'Killed in self defence.'

'No,' I shout, aware that my anger level is rising close to e-rection alert. 'I was there. Obknoxians stabbed him in cold blood.'

'He constituted a threat. Threats have to be neutralized.' He stands back a little and looks me up and down. 'Don't they?' His voice falls on 'they'. *I need to be neutralized too.* His demeanour thaws again.

'Our latest experiment is to get blattoids to reproduce. Yes, the genitalia are entomanthropized — and I am very proud to announce the discovery of the first blattoid eggs.'

He points to a case on the floor. Inside, tiny brown prostrate creatures with recognizably humo heads and knee-length I-brows crawl over each other in an attempt to escape the glare of his torch.

'Voila — the first blattoid nymphs.'

I stare, dumbstruck. A thousand implications clamour for attention in my spheco-brain, but he continues.

'Cockroach-people with the strength of humans and the brains and instincts of insects. Like the myrmecoid formicans, selected for BestcoeWaste®. And they communicate. Basic language as well as telepathy and transception. The advantage of allowing these docile creatures to self-perpetuate, is that we can concentrate our energies on creating new species to serve BestcoeBritain®. And as long as the more wretched strata of PAULies overbreed and contribute to the population surplus, we will have the wherewithal to fuel our projects.'

As I take this in, he leads me into another lab.

'And look here.' In a darkened vitreola chamber are ento-moids, brown apart from their green-glowing abdomen tips.

'Colophotians, sphecoid. Means arselights.' He sniggers like a naughty schoolboy, perhaps the one I might have been allowed to become if they hadn't taken me... 'Human glow-worms. Light givers, already being employed in our agro-complexes. Imagine, unprepaid chavspawn providing Bestcoe-Energy® with our lighting needs. At no cost.'

'@ great cost to them.'

'They won't know, without consciousness.'

Fury notches my cock up to an even harder state. 'But I'm an entomoid and I still have my consciousness.'

'You were a mistake,' he spits. 'You and that V157 chum of yours. We won't let that happen again.'

I recoil from the contempt in his voice, which heavyhearts me. Deep down a tiny sliver of me still craves his approval.

'You were just an experiment.'

My rage almost bursts forth from my groin, but I keep it under control. A lesser spheco would have gored Knox by now. But I want him to blab on.

'And who will be these superhumos of the future?'

His eyes gleam. 'Leaders. A-listers. Andros and gynos who rise to the top. The best sportsmen, the outstanding brains — academics, scientists, thinkers. Famous, acclaimed artists. We'll streamline the human gene pool, weed out the defective, recessive elements, cancel the population surplus. They had derogatory names for that in the past, but it's the only way forward. A small, elite human population of genetically enhanced supermen, served by docile entomoid underlings bred specifically for their purpose in life.'

'We entomanthropoids'll outlive you. You're sowing the seeds of humankind's destruction by creating your successor.'

Knox's smile departs his face, and his eyes bore into mine.

'And what will you know of it? Time's running out for you. You started over a year ago. You've stopped a lot of felons. Very proud I am. But it'll soon be time to say...goodbye.' He snaps his fingers.

Six obknoxians surround me.

I pump out soli-pherum in great clouds, waving my I-brows to brush theirs, but they're canny and hang theirs low.

Muscular hands seize mine, and I'm marched back to the lab, my cock pistoning impotently now as Knox is out of range. *Why didn't I spear him when I had the chance?*

Whining to each other in their unintelligible mantoid tele-lingo, the obknoxians entwine my vibrating I-brows in theirs — entomoid cuffs — and secure me in a seat, my head and wrists electroded, my ankles strapped to the legs. The headboard and armrests dwarf me. I recall metamorphosis, a vision of spino-cerebral modification, and shake with fear.

Knox is over in a flash.

'M...more experiments?'

'Essential. For your type's benefit.'

'Fuxaches, stop exceiving us this way.'

'But you're only niceboys. It's your...tax.' He points to a black door. 'Next year's sphecoids. Incubating. Getting over metamorphosis.'

I shudder. That was me not so long before.

He continues. 'Your batch will have discontinued now. That's why I don't understand the drama over V157. He was gonna decease soon anyway.'

'You want me to answer that?'

He waves this aside. 'There's a mysterious little black box we haven't been able to crack open so far. It constitutes our human consciousness. We can only destroy it or leave it alone. We can't create it yet, or use it. But you provide the perfect specimen. Yours is still intact, thanks to that stupid accident that's been thornsiding me ever since.

'I'm attempting something I've never dared before. It may complete your sphecanthropization or even kill you. It'll certainly hurt, like no pain you've ever experienced. Think of it as your contribution to the future of humanity.

'I'm going to try to examine your blackbox. I've wanted to do this for ages, but we only had you and V157 who this process would work on. Please bear with me. It might be a bit sore.' He chuckles and stands behind me, way out of reach of my cock.

Metal clasps further imprison my wrists and ankles. He

takes hold of my I-brows, gingerly @ first, but lets go cz of the electro-shock they give him and smacks my pate.

'Fuck you, spheco-freak.'

'Is this necessary?' I ask, kicking myself for betraying anxiety.

'Oh, yes.' He grabs my I-brows more firmly this time so the static won't jerk him and coils them round something metallic on the headboard. 'It is now.'

I remember who's left and what I must do. 'They need me,' I say, strawclutching.

Knox flies into a rage. 'No one needs you,' he roars, his voice stinging my ears before it becomes a whisper directed @ the back of my sorry goose-pimpled spheco-head. 'We give you a chance and you fuck it up cz you're a snivelling, mutant invert.'

I cringe as his breath tickles my pate.

He flicks a switch.

A red hot guillotine slices through my skull, cleaving it in twain, accompanied by a shrill, motorized alarm. My I-brows burn like a lit fuse. My screams smash flasks in the lab. A sponge, wedged in my mouthparts, gags me. Sweat breaks out like war on my spheco-brow. Nausea makes me lurch from side to side and up and down although I'm securely seated. Discontinuation must be nigh, I think. I wish. My hands and feet clench as I fall countless fathoms and my head spins @ centrifugal speed, the force almost popping my eyes out. My innards sizzle and dissolve.

Knox is shouting, but I can't hear his words. I want to vomit.

Images of my life pass before me, but I can't focus, such is my vertigo. The lab spins, but still those visions torture me. I'm a little boy crying in the playground, crying as they drive me away, interfere with me and change me, crying cz of Mum and cz the power-cut leaves me raw with yearning, cz I know my fate, and Knox knows, and hates and despises me, but crying most of all for V157.

The jangling, grinding noise whines to a halt and I sag in my seat, smoke pluming from my spheco-feet. All that remains is a throbbing echo of my excruciation, being turned inside out, blowtorched and reassembled badly, my marrow scraped out with a stiletto.

He checks his control panel, sniffs and shakes his head. 'Hasn't worked.' He fuxaches. 'Still alive, sphecoid?'

I don't answer. Let him work it out for himself.

He yells @ the obknoxians, who prick me with their fore-arms. Nerves in my limbs tingle.

'Couple of accu-minutes, then we go again.' He raises one of his pointless humo-eyebrows and considers me, scorn radiating from his stare.

The jabbing ceases. Obknoxians check I'm strapped in. Knox tuts and goes into a small side-room. I hear him fussing about with papers and books. I exercise my eyes till I can see the back of the seat and flex my fingers.

My feelings for him are intact.

FIFTEEN

Maidstone Tower. South East District 9. They'd dodged the checkpoints by going the long way round via the south west.

'A chance to check up. Milo I know about. Won't be long.' Olivier was right. It only took a few accu-seconds to spot the black flag draped over the DUB roof, just like over Jean's.

They stayed in the van. Olivier cupped his face in his hands and bawled. 'Oh, Mum. I never meant...'

Garcia patted his back. It's what one did. 'I'll take over.'

'The last time I came back,' started Olivier, 'I never made it either.' He sniffled. 'That was the day I saved you lot. There were four of us. We were gonna get some Bestcoe stuff and I thought I'd say hi to Mum. But androcops stopped us outside the Recycling Centre cz of that quarantine riot. That's when we went in, thinking we'd set you all free. You were lucky. I couldn't see Phoebe. Thought they'd got her too...' He paused, his voice struggling to continue over his sobs. '...so we stormed the gyno centre, but she was hiding in the van all the time, and thanks to you, I found Irene and Samina.'

Garcia was a more cautious driver, which was good as he had to contend with fires and gangs appearing out of nowhere. His reflexes were swift enough to enable him to swerve and dodge debris in the road and andros rushing wildly @ them.

He saw the piles of withertonguesters being burnt in side streets and told Olivier to look straight ahead. Groups of huge cockroachlike blattoids picked @ charred body-parts. Acridian-clouds searched for anything edible.

The quickest route, through South East District 12, was cordoned off, so they had to make a detour.

Somewhere in South East District 13, rocks and missiles smashed into the rear of the van, and Garcia found himself zigzagging through narrow turnings he remembered vividly from his youth, until he lost their pursuers.

And then the faeco-fuel ran out and the van juddered to a halt. They got out.

'Thought you said we had enough.'

Olivier shrugged.

'Probably for the best,' continued Garcia. 'We'd never get this over the water. Androcop patrols everywhere.'

Olivier shook his head. 'It'll have to be the tunnel.'

Garcia's insides lurched @ the prospect. Deep down, he always knew one day he'd have to brave it. He even craved the chance to make up for chickshitting out all those years before.

They backed up on themselves, running from DUB to DUB, constantly looking over their shoulders. They could hear explosions and shouting in the distance, but not in the direction they were heading. The Thames.

The towpath in South East District 8 seemed deserted. DUBs overlooking the water had the familiar signs of withertongue festooned from their flat roofs. Even a friendly face round there was dangerous.

They crept on, close to the walls, towards South East District 10. On the opposite bank they could see their destination gleaming in the midday sunshine, looming over them like a divine statue out of the muck and grime where they were trapped.

People were running on the Heights, but they couldn't make out more than that, and then it was still again.

They arrived @ the entrance to the tunnel mid-afternoon.

The other tunnel would've taken them too far west. This one led directly to the Heights.

The railings were buckled in places, and being very slim andros, they squeezed through.

An ancient gyno in grey rags sat on the ground watching them, cackling and haranguing them with nonsense. They ignored her.

Inside was pitch black.

'I...I dunno if I can do this,' said Olivier. 'Couldn't when I was a kid.'

'Hey, me neither.' Garcia chuckled. 'But we gotta get across and there's no other way. What'll be down here? Rats? Withertonguesters? Just hold my hand, okay, and don't let go.'

Olivier's hand was warm and strong in his grip and Garcia felt a twinge of arousal stir in his loins. Despite the danger surrounding them and the uncertainty plus the colossal nature of his own personal mission, this was a special moment, his first chance for ages to be so close to another andro, a strong, young, handsome andro, whom he found attractive. But this was not the time or the place for that, or Olivier the andro to initiate anything with. The feeling wasn't mutual, Garcia knew that well enough, but he clung onto that hand as they gingerly descended the spiral steps one @ a time, feeling with their feet and kicking a little in front to ascertain what lay ahead.

Eventually, there were no more stairs, just a cold stone floor.

'Why the fuck didn't we bring a torch?' whispered Garcia, aware that the slightest sound would echo and be picked up by any hostile ears lurking down there.

'There's one in the van.'

'Ssh!'

'Sorry. Wanna go b...'

'For fuxache, Olivier, if you can't say anything sensible, shut up.'

They heard rats — it must've been rats — scurrying about and squeaking. Progress was interminably slow as they probed with their feet before advancing. Water dripped on them. Above, the Thames stagnated.

'When this is over, they'll have to restore the tides,' thought Garcia as he gagged @ the sewer stink of the river. 'If it ever *does* get over.'

Olivier's hand was clammy now and slippery, and Garcia feared losing contact with him, but he was still there, probably thinking about his mother.

A sudden flicker of light stopped them in their tracks. It was coming from a bend to the left. They looked @ each other, now able to see for the first time down there, and their breaths came heavy.

Withertonguesters? Androcops? Toxic urban Freebies?

Garcia tiptoed to the corner and peered round, Olivier right behind him.

The crackle of flames. Garcia's heart stopped. *We gonna burn?* He squinted hard, his eyes adjusting to the new light.

An andro and gyno were sat by a fire with a boy, watching the flames and mumbling prayers. A bundle of rags was piled nearby.

Garcia pulled Olivier round so he could see too. 'Make ourselves known?' he whispered.

Olivier nodded.

They counted to three and cleared the bend.

The andro gasped and stood, pointing a gun @ them. 'Hands up!'

They obeyed.

'You 'tonguesters?'

Garcia cleared his throat. 'Bless them powers-that-be, we're clear.'

'So what the fuck you doing down here?'

'Could ask you the same question,' said Garcia.

'It's okay, honey.' The gyno spoke up. ' We're living out...'

'Shut it.' The andro swiped her cheek. 'What she means is...'

'We don't want no trouble,' said Olivier. 'Just trying to get across.'

The gyno pointed towards the end of the tunnel. As if there were any other way.

Garcia was about to say goodbye when movement in the corner of his eye made him look down.

The bundle of rags twitched.

It was alive.

Groaning and rasping for air.

In the flickering flamelight, Garcia realized it was an old andro, whose lips were a slimy pool of pus, from which dangled an ulcerated bluish lump of tongue. He was trying to kick filthy bandages off the grossly misshapen mass of his feet.

'Too late,' said the gyno, her tone menacing now. 'Didn't know Dad was infected.' She moved closer. 'Long as you don't...'

Garcia and Olivier began skirting round them. Then Garcia noticed a bloody sore on the andro's chin.

The andro clocked him. 'That's how it starts,' he sniggered. 'We'll all be bonfire fuel soon. You too if we...only needs one touch...wanna play 'tonguester tag?'

With a yell, the three of them surrounded Olivier.

'What the...?' Before he'd finished speaking, they'd got hold of Olivier's coat sleeves and were dragging him towards the dying old andro.

'Let him go,' yelled Garcia as Olivier struggled to free himself from their grip.

'You really want him...now he's a 'tonguester?' crowed the

andro.

His cackle was cut dead by a gunshot.

In the dimness, Garcia saw the wet crimson patch growing on the andro's forehead as he fell sideways onto the fire, sending sparks flying.

The andro's gun disappeared into the gloom with a clatter.

The gyno screamed and yanked the andro out of the flames, fuxaching @ him and Garcia, who was suddenly aware of the pistol in his hand and realized what he'd done.

With a cry of relief, Olivier ran to Garcia and hugged him.

'Why'd you do that?' shrieked the gyno. Arms outstretched, she and the boy flew @ Olivier and Garcia, who aimed their guns @ them, making them back off.

Bending their heads close into their chests for protection, Garcia and Olivier ran into the dark, every so often turning and kicking blindly.

The 'tonguesters came after them. Garcia felt something tap his back. He spun round and pulled the trigger. The shot reverberated like a thunderclap.

Silence.

The 'tonguesters gave up the chase, their cusswords echoing through the blackness.

Garcia and Olivier fumbled for each other's hand.

'You okay?' asked Olivier. 'They touched my coat.'

Garcia grunted. 'And mine. We'll have to ditch them. To be absolutely sure.'

They shrugged them off and left them on the dank tunnel floor, running to stay warm.

'I...I...killed that andro...' started Garcia.

'You saved my life.'

Every drip, every echo of their footsteps made them dread whatever could be waiting for them in the blackness. Garcia thought he heard voices and quickened his pace.

'We being followed?' whispered Olivier.

'Ssh.'

Drops of icy water landed on Garcia's head. He cried out. Olivier squeezed his hand to hush him.

When they reached the foot of the steps leading up to street level, Garcia felt something touch his back. He wanted to scream. But nothing happened.

His foot hit a wall — the old elevator. They inched their way to the staircase.

The fading daylight still dazzled them as they emerged from the railings and took in their new surroundings.

A few derelict cottages, an overgrown, cordoned off park and in the distance, the gateway to the Heights.

Standing beneath that mound only made it seem taller and steeper.

'You sure he's gonna be there?'

Garcia nodded.

'And we ain't wasting our time?'

'Been tracking him for ages. Don't think he'll have left yet.'

'So, you only *think* we'll find him.'

'I warned you I had to do this on my own, but you insisted.'

'The good news is that I can't smell any androcops.' Olivier sniffed exaggeratedly. 'But the bad news is that the PAULies have probably broken in and contaminated the place with withertongue.'

'That's a risk we have to take. Anyway, we could've been bitten by mozzies in the tunnel...'

'Don't remind me. You know which house is his?'

'Think so.'

Olivier rolled his eyes to the summit of the artificial mountain. 'Fuxaches, Garcia, ever heard of planning?'

They arrived @ one of the gateways, usually a patrolled checkpoint, but the booths on either side of the road were empty.

'Saves a bullet,' said Garcia.

They entered and immediately were faced with a steep ascent. Being nearly twice Olivier's age meant Garcia was soon out of breath.

'Steady, granddad.'

'Shut it.'

'We being followed?'

'Probably.'

'How much further?'

'Not much.'

They skirted the main area of the Heights, keeping close to the river.

Garcia stopped dead, having got his breath back, and stared straight ahead. 'There.' He pointed @ a marble palace with a gilt roof.

Olivier whistled in admiration. 'Not bad for a gaff. Nearly as swanky as Phoebe's House.'

'There's a way round the back.'

'Been here before?'

'Oh yes,' said Garcia, his eyes misting over and his voice starting to tremble. 'Once when I was young. Dodged through the roadblocks. I watched this place and made my escape. Knew I'd be back. And today's the day.'

He clicked the safety catch on his gun and Olivier followed suit.

SIXTEEN

Knox smiles. 'Shall I attempt this once more?' His hand hovers over a lever. 'The procedure will be extremely painful again. Should you wish me to reconsider, however, I would be absolutely thrilled to explain the alternative.'

Sweat drips off my smooth spheco-pate. The gag stops me from speaking and the head-clamp prevents all movement. I make a noise in my throat not unlike the growl of a dog.

'What's that?' he says, feigning concern. 'Oh, I am sorry. Forgot about all this apparatus. Was that a yes?'

I repeat the sound and he removes the gag with a brusque pull that burns the sides of my mouthparts.

He apologizes again. 'Is that better?'

'Yes.'

'Orgsome, as you would say. Now I have your attention, listen carefully. A little trip is in order. There's a scourge abroad that requires lancing, a felon, who's yet to answer for his multiple crimes. He's murdered, robbed and controls the drugs corrupting our youth. You're acquainted.'

I think, but not for long. 'Fraser?'

'You penetrated his defences once. Now it's time to repeat that performance and obey your instinct to the full.' He flicks his finger on my dickslit.

I cry out @ the sudden pain and explain how I passed his recorded confession to Mike. He dismisses this.

'Useless. His legal team will devour the androcops — if it

ever gets to court. Fair try, V159, but with the Frasers of this world one needs to be more cunning.'

'Why Fraser? What's he done to you?'

He looks away. 'It's personal. My...'

'Your what?'

'My son.' His eyes shut tight and he covers his face with his hands.

'He tempted your son?'

He opens his eyes briefly and stares @ me. 'I know what it means to lose a child.' He's quietly weeping. 'We doted on him, my partner Deniece and I. She...we split up. It was awful. I never stopped loving her. Losing Dominic finished her. I was with her @ the end.' He wipes his eyes. 'Do this for me and I'll make sure you live out the rest of your days in comfort.'

I nod and phew when he releases the manacles and straps and stands back out of reach as I rise from the chair, unsteady on my feet. He doesn't trust me enough to not fear me, but he's letting me go free.

My relief doesn't last long. He summons the obknoxians, who armlock me while he continues. 'Fraser won't be far cz of the quarantine. Don't ask any questions. Just ACE him. Think of all his offences. Report back with news I wanna hear. Come. You're still useful.' He sips from a glass of something pink. Rosé champagne?

The obknoxians prod me. I follow Knox out of the lab. I think about taking those zombie guards out, but it isn't in my interest yet. I want to know where we're going, and I'm sure he wants to tell me something significant. The jabs from the obknoxians' spikes are beginning to seriously irritate me, tiny needles pricking the back of my thighs.

'Stop that,' I shout @ them, and they all say, 'So-rry.' I'm beginning to assert control over them, a development which does not escape Knox's attention, for he looks round sharply

@ this point. I fart a big, fat, silent cloud of soli-pherum as he does this; it could work on his obknoxians, although any effect it might be having is invisible.

Pangs of hunger gnaw @ me. I haven't fed for many accu-hours, and doubt I will soon. Knox will hardly be leading me to a syngastrion.

We enter a large plasticon elevator, which hums fast and shakes as we ascend. No one says a word, but the obknoxians keep their armspikes on my chitin-hard skin without breaking it as a warning to behave myself.

The machine pings and the door opens like a barrier lifting, and we walk out onto a windswept roof, Knox in front, me goaded by my escorts.

Around us in the twilight are the illuminated skyscrapers and palaces of Olympia Heights, homes of the celebs, the A class, the famous, rich and powerful, stacked up the sides of the artificial pyramidal mound, shielded by wealth and privilege from the ravages of withertongue.

Below the Heights, the river and the rest of the city. The ordinary humos. Bs, Cs and any Ds still around.

Cries and shouts reach my ears. My I-brows scan the land-scape on the other side of the building to take in vast swathes of urban devastation scorched by fires and smoke plumes, and then scrubland.

Taking off from the skyscraper roof, I orient myself. My nav-sys has me high above the Heights. I turn in the air and head south. The palace by the Thames seems so small from this altitude. I describe an arc, descending with Fraser's place behind me, and wing my way homeward.

Many of the southeast Cockneytown DUBs I pass sport black flags.

SECOPS has a similar banner flapping in the grimy air; I am not deterred as withertongue hasn't jumped to sphecos. We have other afflictions.

The streets are deserted. In the distance, there are shouts, screams and gunshots. And an explosion. My Eyelid-screen locates the disturbances due west of my current position.

I circle the area and make for the pillar of smoke. A syngastrion. Humo voices yell and rapid footsteps echo. I return to SECOPS and glide unchallenged through the main entrance.

I call hello. No answer. I telepath but no sphecos transceive my greeting. The reception desk is unstaffed although the computer is still functioning. I tap the screen. Mike is logged in, but there's no trace of his last action or the time.

I dash through the corridors to the Combs, heartstopped by the first andro and gynocop corpses littering the floor. I toeflip their heads to identify them, but recognize none.

A gasp escapes my tight gob when I chance upon the sphecos. Some are face down on the floor, others are supine or seated, heads slumped forward. V103...V108...V122... Tears flow. Their time was up. Too soon. A silent farewell.

The bodies should have been sent for recycling, but there is no one left to authorize that.

The Combs present a similar tableau of fallen sphecos. All my swarm, hostages to the brief vespine life-cycle, plus newer ones I don't recognize.

More sphecos have fallen where they squatted in the excretorium, or as they struggled to mount the ladders to the syngastrion vat, which is only one third full of cold congealed slop. It smells rotten. I guess it has been putrefying for days.

The timberyard alone is as I remember it.

Whimpering alerts me. I follow my spheco-ears back inside the sepulchral SECOPS to a closed door and knock.

Silence.

I knock again. 'Who's in there?' I ask.

No answer.

I take a deep breath and turn the handle. The crying starts up once more. As light from the corridor fills the little room, I see a small gynokid cowering in a corner, her eyes moist from tears.

'It's okay,' I say. Her eyes are now wide open with terror @ the sight of me. I think she's going to scream. 'Ssh! I'm a friend. I won't hurt you.'

She shrinks back into a heap.

'What's your name?' I smile, hoping my stretched spheco-gob won't frighten her more.

A tiny voice says, 'Smantha.'

I recognize that name and my heart leaps. 'Where's your Daddy?'

She shakes her head.

'What's your Daddy's name, Smantha?'

'Mike.'

Oh, Mike, what's happened to you? 'And please, Smantha, think very hard. Where is he?'

'He's not well.'

My heart misses a beat.

She's still trembling, but opens up. 'Mummy got poorly and Daddy brought me here. I don't like it.'

'Can you take me to your Daddy?'

She shakes her head again. 'He said I mustn't see him or I'll get ill too.'

'Of course. How silly of me.' I hold out my spheco-hand. 'I'm V159, Smantha. I'm a friend of your Daddy's. It's very nice to meet you.'

She takes my hand in hers and runs her fingers over the smooth, shiny chitinex surface.

'That tickles,' I say and she giggles. I squat down. 'Smantha, listen carefully. I want you to do what your Daddy says and stay here. I'm going to look for him and promise I'll come back for you. Don't let anyone else in. Okay?'

'Yes.'

'Good.' I close the door. He'll not be far. I hope I'm not too late.

All the offices on the ground and upper levels have been abandoned. A few more cadavers scattered here and there and a smell of death.

There is one final room on the top floor. The door is closed. I try it. Locked. I bang. 'Open up!'

A groan.

'Mike? Is that you?'

Another humo sound resembling the first. Improvizing, I discover another use for my spheco-dick. The lock gives. I'm in, wincing @ the taste of furniture oil.

He's on the floor, resting against a desk, gaunt and haggard. His hair is thinner and unkempt and his eyes have heavy rings round them. He attempts a smile. 'V159? Is it really you?' His voice is thick and altered.

We embrace. I make sure I'm gentle. 'Oh, Mike.'

He keeps his smile. 'Database?'

'Fraid so.'

He exhales a single laugh, which becomes a heavy cough. I tap his back. He clings onto my arm as I kneel beside him.

'Smantha's okay,' I say.

'Lin got it. Fucking mozzie-bite.' He pauses to control his breathing and suppress his tears. 'I brought Smantha here. Figured your Combs would be disease-free.'

'You figured right. I gotta get her outta Cockneytown. Freebies'll take her in. It'll be some time before it's safe to come back.'

'I know. I...'

'It's okay. You don't have to tell me. Just rest.'

'I can't walk any more, otherwise I'd be with her...I was okay, so I left her...been here two days and it's just started, so she's never been exposed to wet symptoms... Look after her...is all I ask.'

I smile my hugest spheco-smile. 'My number one priority from now on.'

He closes his eyes. 'I was hoping I'd stay well so I could go back to her...if not maybe someone would find her.'

'What were you thinking? Say I hadn't come...'

'Dunno,' he drawled. 'It must malaffect the brain. Forgot everything, her toys...' He was starting to ramble. I changed the subject.

'Hey, Mike, this is Horelka's office.'

'Poor Tony.'

'He got the bug too?'

'Knox had him discontinued.'

I frown. 'Why...?'

'Tony protected you. Remember? He set you free.'

I click my tongue. 'Not a good enough reason.'

'They never needed much of an excuse.'

'True.' *Perhaps Horelka had something on Knox.* 'While I'm here, Mike, I'm gonna check a few things.'

'Wouldn't be the same if you didn't.' He manages a chuckle.

'Take it easy.' Making light of what's tearing me up inside, I steal a swift glance @ him struggling for every accu-second of humo-life and fight back my own tears. I take a deep breath and thank whatever powers watch over us that Tony Horelka's system is still on.

I key in Knox and wait for the profile to come up. *If he can have Horelka obliviated, why does he need me to finish off Fraser?*

I recall my misgivings when he asked me. Now I'm glad I

came to SECOPS first.

Standard info about Knox pops up — his full name, which makes me smile, but no mention of a son.

'That's odd.' I explain everything to Mike, who's beginning to drift into a fever. He signals his understanding by slowly blinking. 'Easy now.'

I turn away abruptly. Don't want him to see how choked I am. I type in some BestcoePol passwords Mike taught me during the Satan's Garage case. The info I want hits the screen and my I-brows hit the ceiling. 'Wow.'

Mike comes to. 'What is it, V159?'

'A lot of money's been changing hands.'

'Yeah?'

'Knox's been paying out huge sums. Plus there's something weird about his database entry.' I tell him everything I know and say goodbye, promising to come back, but in my heart of hearts I fear this will be our last coherent conversation.

'Can I see Daddy?'

I shake my head. Poor Smantha. I have to decide what is best to tell her. The truth, but when? 'He says not yet.'

Her face crumples.

I caress her.

@ first she tries to shrug me off, but then gives in. I wait for her crying to subside and then get some water from our sphecowell. It won't be contaminated.

She drinks a whole cupful. 'I'm hungry.'

'Sure you are. But there's nothing.' Humo food will not be safe. 'Wait here. I'm sorry. I have to go and do something.'

She tugs @ my spheco-thigh. 'He's got sick too, hasn't he?'

I look @ her. Time for the truth. 'You're a very clever little girl. Yes, your Daddy's not well, which is why...' It's hard to go on, but I try. '...which is why you have to stay here cz he doesn't want you to catch it.'

'What about you?'

I smile. 'People like me don't get this bug.'

People. I say people and she doesn't correct me. 'So, you're safe with me. Just wait for me in this room.' I bring her more water and force myself to be deaf to her crying. 'You gonna be a brave girl like your Daddy says?'

She nods. I squeeze her hand.

SEVENTEEN

The Heights seem virus-free thanks to the double quarantine. The flight is a short one. The sky is bleak and grey and the Thames already pungent.

I block out thoughts of Mike and Smantha and dive towards the marble and gold villa, where I hope to surprise my quarry.

The air is mine alone; some birds flock here and there, but I see no spheco-swarms patrolling East Cockneytown. Next season's batch will still be incubating.

There are more fires in the city now. The sound of sirens means not all law and order has been destroyed, but gunshots close to my spheco-ears alert me to new dangers.

If the rebels have breached the Olympia Heights defences, withertongue will spread there too. I beat my arm-wings faster and swoop down to the main entrance. The guards I remember from my first visit have gone.

The door is open. I fly in, land on chessboard tiles and continue on foot. Familiar scents waft up my spheco-nostrils. One is Fraser's.

'Fraser?' I have no fear now. What Horelka had on Knox is that Fraser had something on him too. But Horelka never found out. It's what I've come here to learn.

'Fraser!' Let him worry his humo-balls off. He's not going to reveal himself, but he can't hide forever.

Like all denizens of the Heights, Fraser has a first-floor balcony with gold banisters sweeping round the slick of walkway and continuing down the curved staircase.

'dashtagFrasercommaOrlando!'

Has he too succumbed, like his staff? The guards may've defected or joined the rebellion. It doesn't matter now. They aren't here to intercept me.

'Knew you'd be back.'

The C-class voice I was expecting. A thrill shoots up my dickslit. I look up.

He's on the balcony, partly hidden behind a huge chandelier. 'They always return to the scene of the crime. That's what they say, innit spheco-freak?' He knows that winds me up.

I don't rise to it. I am concentrating on the pistol he's aiming down @ me.

'I see I have your attention.'

'Knox sent me.'

'You present an easy target.' He laughs and fires.

I've already switched to entomoid-reflex mode and clocked where the bullet is aimed. I see it start its downward trajectory, leap and swerve. It pings on his expensive hall tiles.

'Fuck you, sphecoid. What did the good Prof want?'

'Your humo arse.'

He laughs and shoots again. I dodge out of the way.

'Neat reflexes, but I'm ready for you, sphecoid.'

The insult gets to me every time. 'Why's he paying you so much money, Fraser? You tempting him?'

'That what you think?'

'I think a lot of things.'

'Well, there you go.'

'How many has he committed? Payments indicate more than seven. Didn't know that was possible.'

He laughs again. 'He ain't on Sins. He owes me.'

'Oh, and there's me thinking it's the other way round.'

'Meaning?'

'You tell me.'

Silence.

'By the way, Fraser, where are your guards? You must be missing them.'

'Still got a few hanging around. Don't worry, sphecoid. We saw you coming. I knew who it was.'

'Thought you humos couldn't tell us apart.'

'You've got the stink of a sphecoid cunt that'd film evidence and hand it over.'

My turn to laugh. 'Chizz for the compliment, humo.'

He fires again. And misses. And fuxaches. 'Didn't stick though, freako. My lawyers...'

Plural. Knox was right.

'Yeah, yeah, Fraser. Knox said.'

'Knox says a lotta things.'

'Sure. Like how you killed his son.'

He whistles. 'Wow! He told you about that, did he?'

'How many Sins did it take, humo?'

He looks surprised. 'Fuxaches, is that what he said?'

'I inferred it.'

He laughs, a long drawn out guffaw which ends with him firing @ the chandelier. I sense it falling and sidestep. He leans over the banister and tuts @ the wreckage. Four square metres of shattered glass and broken metal. 'You inferred wrong.'

'Oh, yeah?'

'So that's why he sent you.' He speaks as if reasoning it out for himself. 'Cz of Dominic.'

I don't respond. It's hard keeping my spheco-dick under control. Not time yet.

'Why's he giving you tens of thousands of Britz?'

He paces back and forth and then fixes me. 'In the old days they had them bombs. Terrible bombs. Deterrents, they called them. Well, me and Knox, we both got bombs, if you know what I'm saying.'

I raise my I-brows to show my interest. He buys it.

'He knows what I done, and I know what he done. But I got escape routes.'

'How did you kill Dominic?'

He clears his throat. 'You know how easy it is to smother a sleeping kid? You just press down with the pillow till they stop struggling.' He laughs with pride.

A kid? 'Why, humo?'

'Ask Knox. His call. And don't forget the mother.'

A horrible thought blights my spheco-mind. 'How old was Dominic?'

'Six. Nearly seven.'

'So why the hush money?'

'He's got more to lose. Plus, I'm more slippery than him.'

'So, what about the mother?' I ask, but andro voices from deep below interrupt us. Fraser's guards have been hiding in his cellar.

Shouting and gunshots alarm him. He crouches down and aims his gun, not @ me but @ the hall below.

Rapid footsteps and cries precede the entrance of two of Fraser's guards. A shot rings out and the first one crashes to the floor, a bloody mess on his forehead. A second shot drops the second guard with a hole in his neck.

Two andros rush up in pursuit. I take to the air. I know their scent.

Kamara and Garcia.

Garcia yells Fraser's name and shoots up @ the gallery. Fraser rolls over and fires back.

Kamara makes a sound and sits on the floor. Garcia calls to him and gogs up @ me. 'What you doing here, spheco-freak?'

'Same as you, it seems.'

'Keep outta my way, sphecoid.'

Kamara sighs. Garcia leans over. 'It's okay,' he whispers. 'You're gonna be alright.'

Kamara's in a bad way. Blood on his chest. He's catching his breath now. Sounds like he's saying Ma...Ma... Mum and Milo? Then he whispers Fee, Samina, Irene...

Garcia strokes his shoulder.

Fraser takes aim. Almost as quick as a spheco, Garcia shoots.

Dropping his gun, Fraser crashes down and clutches his knee.

'Fuxaches! That fucking hurts.' He's writhing on the floor, screaming. As he reaches for his gun, I dart down and snatch it away from his grasp.

'Fuck you to hell, sphecoid.'

Garcia clocks that and scales the stairs. 'Look after Olivier,' he says.

I obey. *Let someone else do Knox's dirty work.*

'Been waiting years for this moment.' Garcia stands back from Fraser, who kicks out with his good leg. Another shot, another fuxache, more howling and Fraser's clutching his other knee.

'Who the fuck are you?'

'Course you don't know me, Mr Fraser.' Garcia speaks clearly, but his voice trembles. 'I was only a little'un when you coshed my Dad. Oh dear, memory failing us, is it? Well, let me remind you. The PAULie second-hand carstore in South East District 13. All coming back now? The money you got was pathetic, but out of sheer spite you made sure my father, the first salesman you found, who never fingerlifted against you, would never work again. You know what that means, don't you?'

Fraser stares. 'Oh, I get you now. That fucking shop.'

'Under all this glitz, you're no different from me. Both from the same shitty manor. And you know what happened next, while you were on the run and starring in Amnesty? Dad got discontinued, surprise surprise, and Mum couldn't afford my kid brother, so they took him as well. I was twelve. It was all downhill for her. She didn't last more than a year. So I did a lot of growing up very fast. But before she went, she recognized you. On the telly.

'When you won Amnesty, they said your resourcefulness and initiative showed your genetic qualities far outweighed the defects. And they made you a celeb. An Olympian god, with your own temple up here on the Heights. And you know what I did when she screamed out, "That's the bastard that killed your Dad"? I said to myself one day I'll get him and that day has finally come.'

He shoots again. Fraser's groin. The shriek would have done for the real glass of the chandelier if it hadn't already been broken.

Kamara's closed his eyes, his breaths shallow.

'There, there.'

A tear flows down his cheek, leaving a long wet strip, like the adhesive bands on the envelopes I once saw @ the BestcoeRetro® Museum.

'You boasted about how deprived you were, how hard your kidhood was.' Garcia's still berating Fraser, who's stopped screaming and is lying still.

'Don't you dare die on me before I've finished. Deprived, were you? And that gave you the right to dump your deprivation on us? We never fucked up your life, or deprived you. We never done nothing to you. But you know what? From that robbery, you deprived me of my father, brother and mother. So, *I'm* the deprived one now, you shoulderchipped me, and you can fucking die.'

His voice is steady. I hear the click and the subsequent bang. The report reverberates through the hall. 'I could kill you too,' he says to me, but I know he won't. I stay by Kamara, who's looking up @ the hole in the ceiling, where the chandelier was.

'How is he?'

I shake my head.

He runs down to us and puts his ear on Kamara's chest. Then he closes Kamara's eyes. 'Why'd you grab Fraser's gun?'

'You still don't trust me, do you?'

Crying now, he thinks for a bit. 'You saved me.'

I say nothing @ first. 'There's something I want you to do for me in return.'

He narrows his eyes. 'If it's about your...'

'Yes, that too. But first, there's something really urgent.'

He raises his eyebrows.

'Wait here. It's safe. I think they were his last guards.'

'They were. We got the rest.'

I smile. 'I'll be back. I promise. You got transport?'

'Nope. Van's a write-off.'

'Take one of Fraser's. Tank should be full.'

I grab Kamara's gun. I've never used one, although I know how to, but fear I'll need it now.

EIGHTEEN

A mob has surrounded SECOPS and is forcing their way in. When they see me in the air, they hurl missiles @ me, but miss.

'Go back to your homes,' I shout. 'It's not safe here. The virus has struck.'

They pay me no heed. They want to hit out @ any authority figures and symbols. I gotta act fast. I descend into the timberyard and race to the entrance to our Combs. I lock the door to give myself some time and check on Smantha.

She starts when I open the door.

'Don't worry. Everything's gonna be fine.'

'I'm thirsty.'

'Get you some water soon.'

'Where's Daddy?'

'I'm going to find him. You've been a very good girl. I want you to be even better and wait a little bit more.'

'Why are they shouting, those people?'

'They're angry. But not with you.' I close the door and fly up the back way to Horelka's office.

I nearly scream.

Mike's flat out on his back, stringy foamy saliva bubbling out of his mouth. His tongue is @ the swollen stage, an ulcerated blue lump I can see under the dribble and drool. The gums are swollen and red round his teeth and his septum is eaten away. His eyes are rolled back so only the whites are showing and he is struggling to breathe with heavy gasps. He can't see me. He can't see.

He's taken his shoes and socks off. His feet are double their size and oozing bloody pus from large blisters by the toenails, which have come away from the flesh and appear to be adrift in a crimson mush. If he survives this stage, his tongue will shrink back down his throat and asphyxiate him.

I cannot bring myself to use my penis on him. The best humo I ever met and this is what I have to do. I take one of Horelka's cushions, thanking the Inspector for liking his comfort and hoping his end was easy.

The cushion isn't bad as a silencer. My aim is true. A sob heaves me. Every day there are more to remember. But no time.

Shouts and cries. I fly out and back down to Smantha.

'I'm scared.'

'That makes two of us.'

They've broken in. We can hear them rampaging.

'Lock the door.'

'They'll start a fire.'

Which is what they do. I smell it and put my spheco-finger on Smantha's mouth to hush her. 'We're going on a trip,' I whisper. 'It's important you keep quiet and hold onto me as tight as you can.'

I bend forward and get her to climb onto my back. 'Put your arms round my neck. That's a good girl.'

When I'm happy she's secure, I open my arm wings. She wows; I hush her as I take off.

She's light and easy to bear. We soar above the heads of ragged PAULies and D-classifieds smashing everything in sight. I ignore them and exit into a cool day.

'Don't let go.'

I mount higher, and as the roofs of DUBs recede from view, I turn my head and say, 'You can talk now. We're safe.'

She yells. I hope it's with delight.

In no time we are landing by Fraser's place. 'Did you enjoy that?'

She nods.

'Sorry it was only a short ride. Now I have to tell you something and you've got to promise me you're going to be grown up, okay?'

'Is it about Daddy?'

I bend down and take her hands in mine. 'Yes. Daddy got very sick and died.'

She cries and I cradle her head in my arms. 'I'm very sorry, Smantha. Your Daddy was a good andro. One of the best.'

'Has he...he gone to be with Mummy?'

'Yes. They'll be together now.'

She looks down in silence. I put my arm round her shoulder and feel her sob-breaths rocking her. After a few moments, she looks up. 'Where's this?'

'A house. I'm going to take you to meet someone, alright?'

I lead her by the hand just inside. 'Wait here. Understand?'

Garcia's shrouding Kamara in a net curtain.

I fly over. 'Chizz for waiting,' I say. 'Don't let that girl see the bodies.' I explain who she is. 'Get her out of here. Take your pick of Fraser's fleet. Look after her. Bring her up a Freebie.'

He nods. 'Where?'

'Wherever you can. And...Mum?'

'Knew you'd ask me that.'

My heart stalls and when it restarts, I have to fight back tears. 'How...?'

'She's good. Calls for you in her sleep. Keeps saying your name, your human name, and she wants you to forgive her. "I'm so sorry, Nelson," she says.' He looks @ Kamara. 'Now it's just your mother, her friend and myself.'

I shake my spheco-head and close my eyes. Not too late. I open them and fix him. 'You love her?'

'Like a sister.' He gogs @ me, intense. 'And you now, like a brother.' He puts his hand on my arm. 'Don't wanna burn your type any more.'

I smile @ him. 'Get the girl back to Mum and her friend. They'll know what to do.'

'Come with us.'

'Later. I've got unfinished business of my own here.'

Smantha has joined us, and is looking nervously @ Garcia.

'Don't be afraid,' I whisper. 'Be the brave little girl I know you are.'

I introduce them and give her a peck on her tear-stained cheek.

She chizzes me and clings to my spheco-arm.

I stroke her hand and let her go.

The sight of Garcia, my new brother, heaving Kamara's corpse into the back of a FraserVan and driving away out of my life heavyhearts me, like millstones crushing my spirit. But I am not yet done.

NINETEEN

He's busy with his apparatus. I clear my spheco-throat to get his attention.

He looks round sharply. 'Well?'

'Professor...Opportunity Bertram Knox?'

He splutters. 'How the fuck did you find...?'

I wave this away. 'They're all dead and gone now. Fraser too. You can relax. Pity you didn't inherit your parents' sense of humour.'

He half smiles.

'One tiny thing's bugging me, though. Your partner, Deniece... '

'Oh yes?'

'I found no record of her.'

He blusters. 'Database gets it wrong sometimes.'

Face-reader tells me he's lying. But I know that anyway. 'Not basic personal info.'

'We never registered.'

'Why not?'

'Must've slipped our minds.'

'That would be okay if it was up to you. But people don't log partnerships. The database does it automatically.'

He looks down @ the ground. 'Done your homework, you sly little sphecoid,' he says very quietly.

'You always had faith in me. So tell me about Dominic.'

He smiles, paces up and down, as if gathering his thoughts,

wondering how he's gonna spin this. 'You ain't got long...' he starts.

'Yeah, rub it in.'

'So it doesn't matter any more. I erased them both. Officially, neither existed.'

A throb of excitement pulses through my fluids-only spheco-gut. Let him hang himself. 'But why delete your past? Tampering with public info...we're talking redcardable felony.'

He gogs @ me. 'I thought I knew how without leaving a trace. Only you and that creep Horelka were smart enough to realize.'

'Don't understand.' But the humo in me does.

He continues. 'The shame of Professor Knox being a spheco-dad was unthinkable. I'd have been a jokebutt.'

My spheco-blood simmers. 'So you've sacrificed all our lives on your family's funeral pyre and underneath the veneer of all that science and erudition you're just another narrow-minded hate-ero.'

For the first time, there's a bolt of naked terror in his eyes. 'It's not like that. I've used my genius for your benefit. Can't you appreciate that...get it into your stupid, arrogant sphecoid head, for fuxache?'

'I'm so, so sorry,' I say, shaking that stupid, but cute spheco-head. 'I might be young and arrogant, but you, you've had all these years and still haven't acquired the wisdom to see why gratitude isn't the main feeling I have for you right now. Your old age has been wasted on you.'

'I don't expect a sphecoid to understand.'

'Oh, but I do, Professor. I just don't sympathize.'

'I don't want your sympathy,' he snaps @ me.

'And we don't want yours,' I snap back. 'How did Deniece die?'

'I don't know.' He isn't looking @ me, just playing with

some controls. 'We separated. I found out later she was dead.'

'She discontinued pretty soon afterwards, if my memory serves me.'

'I never mentioned any dates.'

'No, Professor. This is what I discovered on the database.'

He gives an incredulous little laugh. 'But I wiped it.'

I return his laugh. 'You forget I'm a spheco-cop. We can retrieve some pretty surprising stuff.'

He stops tinkering with his knobs and buttons. 'And?'

'I checked your finances @ the time. As one does. Seems you made several payment transfers of 10,000. Who were they to?'

He frowns and scowls. 'How can you expect me to remember transactions from that long ago?'

'If your memory's fading, let me remind you. It was all handed over to Fraser.'

'We had some agreement.'

'10,000 is a lot of Britz. Left you quite broke for a time. That's not an agreement, Professor. It's blackmail.'

Blood rushes to his face and he roars, 'What are you insinuating, sphecoid?'

'Calm down. @ your age you don't wanna get overexcited. You killed them, didn't you?'

'I don't know what you're talking about.' He's shaking now. He replaces some instrument down on his console and puts his hand on his forehead, breathing in deeply. 'I remember her playing with her alcofizz cocktail, all made up, blonde hair. The way she danced. I still wanted her. She was the only one for me.'

'Liar. And you can still sleep @ night?'

'How dare you moralize to me, sphecoid!' he growls. 'Yes, I've got blood on my hands, but the numbers you've despatched...you're no better than the insect I made you. A jumped-up rehabilitated niceboy.' He spits on his marble floor.

'I'm programmed to kill,' I say. 'I can't help it. Whereas you, you elected to.'

'Regrettably, right now I don't have time to debate the finer points of ethics with a sphecoid.' He isn't addressing me directly, just looking for something on his control panel and speaking almost absent-mindedly. I hear an 'Aha' and he's fiddling with a tool, completely absorbed with some data on his computer. He's letting me know I'm no more than a bug, unworthy of his philosophizing.

My spheco-blood boils @ this slight. My spheco-dick lashes out and up and lands a nanometre off his left eyeball.

He squeals. That's gotta smart some. His humo eyelids spasm a hundred times an accu-second to close round the tip. My perfect poise prevents the point from touching the jelly surface.

'Why did you do it?'

'Take that thing off my eye, for fuxache,' he screams.

'Ah, the move you taught me. I'm skilled enough to be able to extend it through your brain to the back of your skull. It's how I dealt with another murderer. That would be most painful, I imagine. Should you wish me to retract it, however, I would be more than happy to oblige. Shall we discuss your options?'

He doesn't surrender that easily. 'And Fraser? How did you sex-e-q-te him?'

I chuckle. 'Whaddaya know? Someone else beat me to it. Good old-fashioned bullets. Would you believe it — he had more than one enemy! Your call, he said, and I should ask you about Deniece.'

'Fuck you, sphecoid.' He winces with pain. 'Should've aborted the three of you after that power cut.'

'But you didn't.' I press a micro bit more with my penis.

He howls. His hands grasp the shaft, but the movement causes my cock to scratch his eyeball and slice his fingers. He shrieks again and lets go.

'Easy does it.'

'What do you want, sphecoid?' he gasps.

'The truth. About Dominic, Deniece and you and Fraser.'

He swallows hard. 'Okay.' He's struggling to stand statue-still and keep his bleeding hands off me. 'I couldn't bear the prospect of Dominic ending up like you. Sorry. He was better off dead. But I couldn't do it myself. Not my own boy, my only kid. Fraser was introduced through a contact. He came up with the scenario. The quickest, cleanest method. Very resourceful was Fraser.

'I was going to have him silenced, but he got arrested for some other stupid petty felony, a failed C-class shop robbery. It was winter. Not enough sphecoids to have him discontinued, so he went to gaol. In those days PAULies could still be tried in courts. I lost access. Then the bastard not only went on Amnesty, but fucking won it and you wanna know the worst of it? I helped him.

'He came to me, eyes wild, desperate, arms flailing. It was midnight. I'd got a small villa here on the Heights. After Dominic...

'"You gotta help me." Fraser was screaming the words in my face. @ first, I thought it was a plea for help, but quickly realized it was a command, a threat. He meant I had no choice. He'd blab. I'd go down, and have a harder fall than him.

'"Okay," I said. "In the cellar." Last place they'd look is the Heights. Felons only rob here, if they get access that is.

'I had to watch that fuxachingly tedious show twice a day and update him on who'd been caught. Seven ghastly weeks later, there were just two of them still on the loose. The other andro had been located. Androcops and securicops moved in.

It was only a matter of time. @ this point it actually got quite exciting. The inevitable happened and they issued a call for Fraser to reveal himself.

'Being pretty smart, he kept it on the boil a few days. "Shall I tell them where I am?" he taunted me. "Please, Orlando." He'd laugh and lightly smack my cheek. I couldn't sleep. Didn't know what he was gonna do.

'He stole out one day and made his media appearance in a West Cockneytown cop station. Before he left, he said, "My silence has a tariff, you know. Keep in touch." Sick joke. Like I'm gonna disappear off his radar. We've been neighbours ever since.

'Had the cheek to demand hush money. I said, "No way. I paid." He said, "Not enough. I got immunity now. I'm A-list just like you. A celeb on the Heights. An Olympian god. They can't retry me, whereas you..." That was his opening gambit. Said he'd tell Deniece if I didn't cough up.

'I called his bluff. He told her everything. She confronted me, with him there to back her up. We had a fight. She fell. Split her head open. Died in my arms. I loved her, sphecoid, and even though you'll never understand what that really means whatever you say, it's the truth. She was the best, but she got in the way and that cunt put her there. Had to delete her from the Database as well.

'Fraser found out about that too and that's when the real blackmail started. I told him I had enough on him to send him back to prison or the Recycling Centre, but he said he'd never get caught again, and he had more on me, but as he was a big-hearted sort of andro-mandro, he'd accommodate my moderate wealth and arrange a small sum to be transferred to him on a regular basis.

'I'm getting on now. Don't wanna be paying out to a common felon for the rest of my life. Silence is indeed golden.

Especially his.'

'And you were happy to get me to do your dirty work just like you used him in the beginning.'

'You're a professional.'

'And Horelka?'

He sighs. 'Poor Tony. Too zealous. Threatened to go after Fraser. Course, I knew he'd never succeed, but just in case something stuck...couldn't afford to not have Fraser sweet. By then it was out of all our hands, but Fraser's brief came good anyway.'

'You know, I used to look up to you as the father-figure I needed. You taught me everything. Too much. I now see what sort of dad you really are.'

'What are you gonna do?'

'Terrified, aren't you? There's no future for you now, no place to hide. You're gonna do some things for me.'

'Whatever you ask. Just take that prick out of my eye.'

'Soon. Not yet.'

'Make it quick, I beg you.'

I laugh. 'You begging me for mercy? Wow, that's rich.' I get serious. 'First, I want you to reallocate the BestcoeGenetix® entomanthropy programme funds to BestcoeMedix® withertongue research.'

'Are you mad?'

'Nope. Do it.'

'Okay.' He begrudges saying that. 'But I can't do anything with a cock in my eye.'

'Use your other one.' I slowly reverse him to his computer.

He clicks his tongue and types in some words and numbers, hissing at the pain of hitting his injured fingers on the keys. 'Done.'

'Also, while we're @ it, I want an apology for V157, cz what I really want you're unable to give me.'

He hesitates.

'What's the problem? Disaggrieve me and the millions like me, whose lives you've ruined.'

He clears his throat. 'I'm sorry about V157...'

'V157's murder.'

He repeats that and adds the rest.

'There is a scientist with the Freebies, who could help find a vaccine and cure for withertongue. She must be re-employed.'

He dares not nod, so he whispers, 'Alright.'

I tell him her name and he types some more. 'Sorted.'

'Thank you.' I remove my penis.

He sighs with relief.

'There's been too much killing,' I say. 'Better get that eye seen to. Must be rather sore.'

'I thought...I thought...'

'You thought wrong.'

'What'll become of me?'

'Most likely arrest, and as a lucky A-lister, you'll be entitled to a BestcoeJust® fair trial. But you know what? I don't really care.' I just spit and walk away, loving the tap-tap of my spheco-feet on the polished tiles in the silence, which isn't silence but the marvellous sound of Professor Opportunity Bertram Knox, the architect of Nelson Fialka's sphecanthropization and killer of his own family, finally rendered speechless.

TWENTY

Samina punched Garcia in the chest when he told her, just like he'd seen gynos do in old films.

'Olivier discontinued for *you*?' she kept bellowing between sobs.

'He insisted on coming,' he repeated, like a mantra to calm both of them. He'd been dreading this moment all the way back. 'I wanted to go alone.'

She stopped hitting him and collapsed onto him, her long greasy hair tickling his face. He held her and comforted her, gently squeezing her shoulders. She was right. Olivier had sacrificed his life for him.

'He said your name @ the end, before he...'

Samina nodded.

'And who's this?' Irene bent down to welcome the little girl standing hesitant and bewildered.

Smantha introduced herself the way she'd learnt @ school: surname first, Lagano...

'What a pretty name for such a pretty girl! And I'm Irene.'

'The wasp man said I could live here.'

Something happened to Irene's face. It was hard to tell whether she was going to laugh or cry. 'Which wasp man, Smantha?'

'His brother.' She pointed @ Garcia.

'She means Nelson.'

Irene gogged @ him. 'Your what?'

He looked sheepish. 'She must've overheard me...I...I kinda changed my mind about them sphecos.'

She kissed him.

He explained everything that had happened and why he'd stolen away. 'He asked for you,' he said. 'I told him to come back with us, but he needed to sort something first.'

Irene covered him with a searching look. 'So, is he coming?' She realized she was clinging onto his arm, and let go.

'That's what I understood.'

'When?'

He shrugged.

'Why are you crying?' Smantha was tugging @ Samina's skirt. Everyone looked @ her.

'Her friend discontinued,' said Irene.

Smantha nodded and turned to Garcia. 'That andro I weren't supposed to see when I first met you?'

'Yes, that's right.'

Samina crumpled to the floor. 'He'll never know now,' she howled. 'I was gonna tell him. Too late.'

'Tell him what?' asked Garcia.

Samina looked @ him. More tears flooded her eyes. 'I think...I think... ' Then she blurted it out. 'He was gonna be a dad.' She buried her face in her hands and shook.

'Oh, Samina... ' All the blood drained from Garcia's face. 'I'm so, so sorry.'

Irene knelt beside her. 'Samina, what are you saying?'

'My p...maybe it's just malnutrition shrivelling me up. I was sick again this morning. It's what I want most in the world and it's terrifying.'

Irene hugged her. 'We're all here for you.'

Samina nodded as Irene helped her to her feet, and glared @ Garcia, bloodshot with grief and rage. 'Where is he? I wanna see him.'

Garcia pointed to the FraserVan.

Samina ran out and banged on the side of the vehicle, all the time wailing. They rushed after her. Garcia opened the back and she clambered in, her words mingling incomprehensibly with sobs. When she emerged, Garcia held out his hand to help her down.

She screamed, 'No,' leapt out and smacked his face.

He closed his eyes and let her. 'He'll have a decent funeral, I promise,' he said. 'A proper send-off.'

She turned from him and clung to Irene, who said, 'That curtain'll make good mosquito nets, which we'll need when it's warmer.'

A little voice rang out. 'Are you pregnacious?'

They looked @ Smantha, whose eyes were wide open with wonder. Their laughter was tempered by grief.

Samina wiped her eyes on her sleeve and held Smantha's little hand. 'That's right. I'm preg...nant.' She swallowed. 'He was a very good friend, the daddy. Now it's just us four.' She ran her fingers through Smantha's hair. 'Thick and black just like mine.'

'Will you show me how to tie it up like yours?'

'Of course.'

While Samina was doing Smantha's hair, the girl asked, 'What you gonna call the baby?'

Samina stopped. 'You know, I haven't thought about that. I suppose now you ask, Olivier if it's a boy and Olivia if it's a girl.'

'Was that the daddy's name?'

'More or less.'

When Garcia was alone with Irene, he said, 'We should stay here for the time being. It's safe. There's nothing in Cockney-town.'

She thought hard. *Yes, @ least he'll know where to find me.*

'Folk are going crazy there. Thousands more disemployed and no-one to D-classify them...you've no idea. Burning, looting, shooting withertonguesters to put them out of their misery. Even acridians... Bestcoe leaders have fled — fucknose where — but I bet they'll be planning a comeback. When Smantha and I left, people were rampaging through the Heights shocked by what they found. Couldn't believe what they'd been missing, I reckon. No, Irene, for now this is our home.'

'Thank you. And I mean that.' She smiled and hugged him. 'We'll be okay. We're a team, remember?'

TWENTY-ONE

My glee doesn't last long. I've only gone a few steps when I hear him.

'Let me explain, Nelson.' Knox is running after me.

I take in the full picture. His left hand is holding a handkerchief to his bloodied eye and his right hand is pointing a gun @ me, but is lowered by the green arms of his obknoxian guards, who frogmarch him back to the lab.

He screams once and is silent.

Something heavy falls to the floor.

Mantoid justice returning the compliment, Prof: reduction of life-expectancy.

I hope the goodbye hug was from the one he slapped.

The obknoxians re-emerge, wiping their armspikes.

And march towards me.

Farting out vast clouds of soli-pherum, I tweak their I-brow antennae. Vain hopes. These have been deeply programmed and don't respond to my pheromone.

But they don't attack me either. They just stand, impassive, probably confused. Their leader is dead and they slew him.

I envy them their lack of consciousness. They'll live out the rest of their paltry lifespans and drop from exhaustion, never once questioning the point of it all.

'We must programme the new sphecoids correctly,' I say. 'Professor Knox changed his mind about his babies. He realized we have been imperfect.'

The obknoxian mantoids stare @ me without reacting.

I gamble further. 'He was gonna re-process them and start again, but now he's discontinued, we must perform the operation.'

There's still no reaction as if they've all gone deaf.

'Watch me,' I command with the authority of the Queen bestowed on me by the deceased. 'Do as I do.'

I go into a chamber. Fifty sphecoids-to-be under 'hairdryers' awaiting the final metamorphosis.

My finger hovers over the machine keys and strokes them lightly. I turn away for an accu-minute.

Bridgeburn time.

Is this what we want? To go back? We've broken through now, acquired the knowledge, earned our expulsion from another of the Edens we're gradually discovering we're Russian-dolled in.

I can put a stop to it with one jab of my spheco-index finger. But only temporarily. Short-term respite. I can thwart the labrats now, but others may succeed after I've discontinued.

I dither. There's still time. Sweat condenses on my exo-skeleton, each droplet making my back twitch as it trickles down to my comely spheco-arsecrack. Is it my destiny to start the next chapter of history, although I won't survive to see how it ends?

Through the window, hundreds of lights twinkle under the blue-beige sky fading over Olympia Heights. No sphecos patrol the south eastern sectors, like I once did, like they may do again one day if Knox was right. I go with my instinct.

Punching the control buttons without knowing what I'm doing, I spark off flashing red lights and an alarm.

I can't turn the clock back. I hope their agonies will not be great, no more than I suffered. I pray they'll quietly cease to register the pain, and drift off, but they scream, the intensity in their voices rebuking me and me alone. Why should they be grateful for being metamorphosed? Their humo consciousness is aware and bitter. But I have saved them.

My hand shaking from the electric fear and excitement @ what I'm doing, I switch the machine off mid-programme. It's what happened to me.

The 'hairdryers' are raised and the new sphecos slump forwards, collapse and expire.

I am sobbing from guilt when one of them gets to his feet, dazed and wobbly, but palpating his imbricated chitinex torso plates with his new spheco-fingers and humming. He has no Queen as yet; I assume that role and fart a cubic litre of solipherum, which bonds him to me, and he hums his transception of my telepathed message to live for himself and feel nothing but enmity for BestcoeBritain®.

He is high-fiving his I-brows now, whining and testing his arm-wings. I lead him to a still-functioning syngastrion, where he feeds and regurgitates with me.

I stroke his I-brows, delighting in the realization that his humo past has not been obliviated, and that he is of the retroceptive ilk. V187.

He extends his I-brows in anticipation, and I transceive the pain in his soul as he reciprocates.

He will be the last spheco.

TWENTY-TWO

They buried Olivier next to Phoebe by the olive trees. Garcia dug the grave, his way of saying sorry to Samina.

They kept his guitar in the house.

Smantha held Samina's hand throughout as they stood around and said their goodbyes to the friend, thanks to whom they were still alive.

They all kissed, and as Samina chizzed Garcia, Irene put her arms round both of them and they cried out the end of Olivier's funeral.

Irene gazed up @ the sky every day, but he didn't come. Had he forgotten her? Written her off? Had she overhardtimed him? Had Garcia lied?

She would've driven herself insane had Smantha not been there to look after.

Irene had caught her crying once. She'd tried to console her, talk to her, but Smantha'd only opened up to Samina @ first.

However, when Irene mentioned the wasp man, her face lit up.

'Will I see him again?' She was helping Irene make mosquito nets.

Irene laughed, and then felt a pang of remorse. 'I don't know. Would you like to?

Smantha nodded. 'He was kind...and a friend of Daddy's.'

Her smile vanished.

Irene took her hands in her own and looked her in the eye. 'Smantha...' she started. It was a battle for her to continue. 'I want to see him again, too.'

'Why?'

'I...I'm his Mum.'

Smantha's eyes widened with surprise. 'Oh.'

Irene hugged her and Smantha kissed her cheek.

As for Samina, she hadn't cried — that Irene was aware of — since the funeral. *She's toughening up @ last.*

They were all bereft one way or another, but Irene felt they were stronger than ever and they'd manage. It was still necessary to disguise Phoebe's House to conceal signs of habitation, but not from securicops any more. Just toxic Freebies. And acridians.

The agrocomplexes had shut down one by one. Perhaps they'd re-open them once withertongue had declined and it was safe to move people about, but no one knew who would be making decisions like that. @ least they could forage what remained with impunity.

Irene fantasized about working officially on re-planting the local farms, even managing an agrocomplex to get food production going again and finding ways of controlling the acridians.

In an ideal world, Smantha would've had another kid to play with, toys and a junior dashtag. Irene marvelled @ how well the girl was adapting.

It was the dream that did it. Incoherent, disturbing, dyspeptic images. Irene woke in the middle of the night drenched in sweat. She couldn't recall any details, but she knew then what she had to do.

She couldn't get back to sleep after that.

In the morning, she took Garcia aside. 'I want you to do me a special favour.'

TWENTY-THREE

I could have put V187 out of his misery, scotched him @ his sphecanthropization, but there's been too much slaughter.

Another chamber beyond. I fly in, aware V187 is behind me with the now curious obknoxians, who fetch water to extinguish the little fires that have started on the consoles before leaving.

As I abort myrmecoid formicans, colophotians and blattoids-to-be forming in their metamorphosis booths, I hear a cry, and turn.

'Hands up!'

A labrat's standing behind V187, his gun trained on the back of his head.

V187 smiles @ me. The erection erupts from his dickslit and curls back between his legs, skewering the shrieking labrat. His I-brows quiver with ecstasy as his ACE pulses out. Accu-seconds later, the mucky spheco-cock slides home.

Clutching his bloodied belly, the paralysed labrat topples to the floor.

'You must leave Cockneytown,' I say, gratified V187's so ilky. 'It ain't safe. There are many here who hate you and want to discontinue you. Even after all the other troubles, they still consider you their worst enemy. You'll be in constant danger if you remain.

'There's a place you can go, where the humos will accept you, although you mustn't abide too close. They'll seem hostile

@ first, but I'll help you overcome their initial enmity.'

I visualize all the places where Mum could be. V187's transception is acute.

'Speak to them. Tell them not to fear you. Take them my humo name for they don't know my spheco number.'

Images of Mum, Samina, Garcia and Smantha flash in my head as I telepath them so V187 knows who to look for and what to tell each one of them. Visions of V157 and what became of him pop up. He must convey that too.

'You may not survive the journey. Many humos will attack you, but you know how to defend yourself. Hopefully, you will make it and get through.

'I have a message for each of them. For Mum, I love her and wish her happiness. We'll meet again one day, perhaps. It's what I hope, but I'm getting weaker by the accu-hour.

'I have set the wheels in motion for Samina to return to working on finding an antiviral treatment and vaccine for withertongue. They'll come for her.

'Garcia I chizz for hailing me as his brother. Smantha is the bravest, cleverest girl ever and will grow into a wonderful gyno.

'When you find these Freebies, tell them Nelson sent you with love. Protect them when they are under attack or in danger. Bond with them and let them know you are the last of the ilk and that you must be the last. Warn them of the labrats, who will try to create more entomoids in the future, so they and their children will have to be constantly on guard to prevent that from happening again. Ever. They will have many choices about what new world to create. They may look back to the old times for inspiration, but not all was good then. I hope they will make wise decisions.

'Remember your humo name and go.'

I dismiss him.

Now I am spent. If I could make one more long flight, I'd

go there. She'd understand why. I'd meet her for the last time to say goodbye, but I can scarcely shift my weight. Only lying down on the floor is possible.

Grieve now | grieve later | cancel pops up again. I wink on the left one and my breath stalls. Not all the tears in the universe will ever quench my grief.

Last night, I dreamt in the flash of an accu-second I was there again and everything was beautiful and safe.

When I wake, I am back in my old bedroom. I have made it. My final voyage. All I need do is wait.

TWENTY-FOUR

Garcia switched the engine off, to save faeco-fuel and their noses, and tapped his hands on the steering wheel. '@ least we're safe from withertongue here,' he joked. 'And there's just enough juice to get us home.'

Irene lit a cigarette for both of them and passed Garcia his. He murmured chizz and took a drag. The van filled with the heady smell of tobacco smoke. He wound the window down.

She put her hand on his knee. He flinched and then relaxed.

'Thanks for doing this.'

He nodded. He'd taken over the nodding role, she reflected, as they sat in the drizzly gloom.

'I owe you one, Irene.'

'You owe me more than one.'

He looked round. She smiled and he smiled back. 'We've both come a long way,' he said.

'I don't know if he'll show. I dreamt...'

'What?'

'It's just a premonition. Something he said once.'

He shrugged.

They sat in silence for a bit. Then she said, 'Wonder how Samina's getting on with the girl.'

'Take her mind off you-know-who.'

'She won't get over that in a hurry. Those things take time.'

'Rain's stopped. Shall we stretch our legs?'

'Thought you'd never ask.' Irene undid her seat belt and stepped onto the crumbling tarmac.

She took a deep breath, savouring the sea air. It'd been years, decades. She was surprised how calm she felt. She'd expected to be overwhelmed by memories and ghosts and was dreading her return, but all she wanted to do was look @ the sea. She led Garcia by the hand through the ruined back streets, pulled as if by her own secret current to the water. Did that only affect people born of the sea? She didn't know.

She stopped still @ the sound of the swishing of the waves and let go of his hand and ran, ran for all her life's worth to what remained of the old esplanade.

The seawall was broken in places and the little shelter she used to sit in with George on wet days like this was a pile of wood and real glass. Her breath stuck in her throat as she remembered the struggles of those first years partnered to him and the sacrifices they made for Nelson.

Nelson. Would her premonition come true? She'd had such a powerful urge to come here, the last thing they had in common.

Several times she caught glimpses of specks in the grey-white sky, but they were gulls, terns, their shrieks mocking her hopes and prayers.

Garcia said little. He too was deep in reminiscences of his own childhood and everything that had occurred since. His heart stalled when he recalled the happiness he'd known with Heathcote and how that had been wrenched out of his being and left him disfigured. He realized he loved Irene and would do anything for her and he would think of Nelson as his brother. But this town meant little to him. He appreciated how important it had to be for her, and tried to re-create the South East District 13 of his own childhood, but all he could imagine

was the destruction of his family. The geography didn't figure.
And he'd chosen to leave; Irene'd been rehoused.

It was getting dark and cold. She snuggled up to him and
this time he yielded to her physical warmth, and put his arm
round her shoulder. 'We've soulmated again,' he said shyly
like an awkward teenager, and she squeezed his waist.

'Do you reckon he'll come?'

He shrugged. 'Who can say?'

'You don't mind doing this, do you? I mean, we can go back
whenever you get fed up.'

He tutted. 'Nonsense. We'll stay here till you decide you've
had enough.'

She chizzed him and they sauntered back to the van.

They got in, locked the doors and had an apple before
curling up on the seat to sleep.

The direct rays of the sun through the windscreen woke them.
In the clear light of day, Irene gasped when she saw the
devastation wrought on her birthplace.

The image she had was smashed. The buildings on the sea
front had fallen into ruin, roofs caved in, windowpanes broken
or missing and several houses demolished. Piles of rubble
littered the townscape and many of the façades still standing
were pocked with bullet holes. She didn't recall any shooting.
That must've been after she and George had been rehoused,
and the stragglers and protesters must've put up enough of a
fight to merit a violent solution, but no one heard about it in
the Dagtown DUB and all contact had been severed.

She led Garcia through what remained of the main
thoroughfare, the old shopping centre. It all came back to her
— which stores were on which foundations.

He listened to her fluent reminiscences, never once interrupting. They found themselves in a residential area, where the

little red-brick terraced houses still standing were overgrown with ivy. She was pulling him along, almost running, but not talking now. And then she stopped and he heard an animal sound that came from deep within her, not exactly a scream, nor a cry, but a primal noise that said far more than mere words.

She was facing a dilapidated cottage, which was little more than a shell. Half the front had collapsed in a pile of red bricks reclaimed by weeds, mould and lichen. 'Here,' she managed to say finally. 'This was my home.'

He hugged her close to him and kept hold of her while she shook uncontrollably from sobbing. After a few accu-minutes, she pecked his cheek and he twitched @ the sensation of her wet eyelashes on his skin, and she led him inside.

They had to tread carefully cz of the rubble on the floor, but she managed to get them both indoors. She stood silently in that poky living room and then in the kitchen.

There was more rubbish in the back yard and several steps were missing.

'It's dangerous,' he said. 'Don't go upstairs. I won't let you. What will you find there? Broken memories and furniture.'

She remained @ the foot of the stairs for a long time, staring up @ the space, calling to Nelson, but there was no answer.

'Do you think he's here?' she asked him. 'He could fly up there.' She started to climb, carefully @ first, then more boldly. The stairs creaked and broke under her feet.

Garcia rushed up to her when he heard her cry. Her leg had gone through the rotten wood. He helped her pull it out. The skin was grazed, but not bleeding.

'Nelson, Nelson!' she shrieked. 'I'm sorry. I love you. Nelson...are you there?' Her words became more and more unclear as the tears flowed down her cheeks and her voice cracked. 'I've come for you,' she wailed. Nothing happened.

Garcia shrugged. 'Perhaps he's somewhere in the town. But surely he'd come home. If he was here, he'd have heard us and come down.'

She nodded, looking up one last time, and clung onto Garcia. There was still the old school, but she couldn't bring herself to see it again. She didn't need that memory, of that day. So much had been truncated and dislocated in her head. The reality she now confronted had shifted from the one in her imagination.

They spent another 100 deci-minutes in the town, sitting huddled up in their patched coats on the beach, one eye constantly on the van.

'It's a long walk back,' he said. The wind blew wisps of his black hair over his forehead and Irene realized he was still very attractive.

'You need a partner,' she said.

'We all do.'

'Another Heathcote.'

'One day, maybe.' He tossed a pebble into the gentle waves breaking a few metres before them and watched it spin. 'And what about you?'

'One day, maybe.'

They chuckled.

'We oughtta be heading back,' she said. 'Mosquitoes'll be active soon. Plus Samina'll be worrying about us. And she's all alone with Smantha.'

'You sure?'

She nodded, for the first time in ages and it made her laugh again. 'Perhaps he lost his way.'

'He knows Phoebe's House.' Garcia got up and brushed the sand off him. He then helped Irene to her feet, and arm-in-arm like an old couple, they wandered back to the van.

It was still light, but cold inside. They warmed up once the engine started. Then he drove her away from Soxbury forever.

TWENTY-FIVE

There is light, there is always light and hope. I close my eyes and let the warmth of the sun bathe my spheco-eyelids, and drink the rays filtering through the fleshy chitinex patina.

When I open my eyes, the sun is radiating a gentle heat, once again our friend. The water tickles my feet as I lie on my back, gouging fistfuls of soft sand and relishing the whisper of the breeze and the rhythmic hush of the breaking waves.

'Go in and paddle. It's clean. Safe.'

Dad. He's behind me.

'Not falling for any of your jokes this time.'

He laughs and mumbles to Mum.

'What's that?'

'Nothing.'

I kick my feet up in the water and splash them.

'Hey!' They're not angry. Mum puts her hand on my shoulder. 'It *is* safe. He's not kidding.'

The sea is calm and warm. Briny sharpness clears my head. I giggle as swirling strands of seaweed caress my legs.

'Tide's coming in.'

Mum. Always worrying. I stay where I am. The water reaches my knees.

He's there, V157, on the sandbank, a little way out, waiting for me, like I always knew he would, his arms outstretched. He's seen me and is calling to me to come and join him.

It isn't far. Mum and Dad relax their grip on my shoulders

and I slide into the sea and start swimming.

They're still behind me. Mike's joined them, I think, and Mum's friends.

V157 has dived in now. The water's glass-clear. I can see the rocks and shells on the bed and the fish and the marine plants.

'The view's better underwater.' Mum's right. The colours are brighter and the smell purer. V157 is smiling. Like I am.

He's opened his arms wide to embrace me.

I mirror him.

He loves me.

And he's so proud of me.

THE END

ACKNOWLEDGEMENTS

I would like to thank Kathryn Bell and Ross Burgess for all their assistance and practical help in preparing this book for publication. Heartfelt thanks are also due to everyone at Gay Authors Workshop and Paradise Press for constant guidance and encouragement. In addition, I am hugely grateful to Lucy Whitman and Gary McGhee for their invaluable feedback. I'd also like to express my eternal gratitude to my family for their loving support. And above all, I owe a special thank you to Farilla B, without whose patience, editorial skills and persistent urging to 'get it into print', this novel would still be a pile of A4 paper on my desk.